DRAMA COMES TO
PRIOR'S FORD

}

}   013
      13

      14
         2014

      09 15

2 9

Also by Eve Houston

Secrets in Prior's Ford

DRAMA COMES TO PRIOR'S FORD

Eve Houston

SPHERE

First published in Great Britain as a paperback original in 2009
by Sphere

A CIP catalogue record for this book
is available from the British Library.

ISBN 978-0-7515-3962-2

Typeset in Bembo by Palimpsest Book Production Limited,
Grangemouth, Stirlingshire
Printed and bound in Great Britain by Clays Ltd, St Ives plc

Papers used by Sphere are natural, renewable and recyclable
products made from wood grown in sustainable forests and certified
in accordance with the rules of the Forest Stewardship Council.

Mixed Sources
Product group from well-managed
forests and other controlled sources
www.fsc.org Cert no. SGS-COC-004081
© 1996 Forest Stewardship Council

FSC

Sphere

Acknowledgements and Dedication

It takes quite a bit of courage to say to experts, 'I'm writing a novel and I need to find out about quarries and rare birds in your area. Can you please help – and by the way, I will probably ask some really daft questions.'

To my relief, both Alastair Clark, Scottish Natural Heritage's Area Officer based in East Galloway, and Graham Platt, Economic & Community Development Worker for Dalbeattie Community Initiative, responded promptly, and didn't even laugh at me, bless 'em.

My thanks to Alastair for his help in researching peregrine falcons, and for putting me in touch with Graham, who gave up valuable time to show me round local granite quarries, and also shared his knowledge of peregrine falcons.

Not being, alas, an accomplished traveller, I owe a deep debt of gratitude to my dear friends Janet and Duncan Beaton, who have visited many parts of the globe, for agreeing to undertake the itinerary of Clarissa's travels for this book, and also give me descriptions of various places. Bless you both!

This book is dedicated to you, Alastair and Graham, because thanks to you, no peregrine falcons were, or will be, harmed in the writing of the Prior's Ford series; and to you, Janet and Duncan, for having had the foresight to love travelling.

It is also dedicated to Scottish Natural Heritage, which does sterling work in promoting and protecting Scotland's wildlife, habitats and landscapes.

Eve Houston

Main Characters

Meredith Whitelaw – A professional actress 'resting' in Prior's Ford for a year

Genevieve (Ginny) Whitelaw – Meredith's daughter

Kevin and Elinor Pearce – Live in Daisy Cottage, beside the Gift Horse gift shop. Kevin is a retired journalist and the leading light of the local drama club. Elinor makes the club's costumes

Joe and Gracie Fisher – The new landlord and landlady of the Neurotic Cuckoo. They live on the premises with their widowed daughter **Alison Greenlees** and her young son **Jamie**

Ingrid and Peter MacKenzie – Ingrid owns the local craft shop, the Gift Horse. She and Peter, a college lecturer, have two daughters, **Freya** and **Ella**

Jenny and Andrew Forsyth – Jenny helps in the Gift Horse. She and Andrew, an architect, have a son, **Calum**

Maggie Cameron – Jenny Forsyth's teenage stepdaughter

Helen and Duncan Campbell – Helen records the village news for a local newspaper. Duncan is the gardener at Linn Hall, the 'big house'. They have four children, **Gregor, Gemma, Lachlan** and **Irene**

Clarissa Ramsay – A retired teacher and a comparative newcomer to Prior's Ford. Recently bereaved, she is travelling the world before settling down in Willow Cottage

Sam Brennan – Lives in Rowan Cottage and runs the local Village Store. Pining for his partner, **Marcy Copleton**, who left the village after they fell out

The Reverend Naomi Hennessey – The local Church of Scotland minister. Lives in the manse with her godson, **Ethan Baptiste**

Bert and Jess McNair – own Tarbethill Farm and work it with their two sons, **Victor** and **Ewan**

Fliss and Hector Ralston-Kerr – live with their son **Lewis** in ramshackle Linn Hall

Alastair Marshall – An artist, lives in a small farm cottage on the outskirts of the village

Jinty McDonald – Wife to **Tom McDonald**, mother to a large brood, and willing helper in Linn Hall

DRAMA COMES TO PRIOR'S FORD

1

The red Post Office van provided a welcome splash of colour in the grey December landscape as it drove down the lane from Tarbethill Farm and turned left towards the village of Prior's Ford. Entering the village, it passed the primary school, its playground swarming with rosy-cheeked children bundled in duffel coats and anoraks burning off their early-morning energy. Several came running to the railings, reaching through the bars to wave to the driver, who tooted his horn at them.

An hour or so later, having delivered post in the neat little village and to the cottages and farms further afield, the van headed back towards its depot, leaving behind a paper trail of letters bearing good tidings for some, bad tidings for others, and a heartfelt plea that was to change one family's comfortable existence for ever.

In the village store-cum-Post Office, Sam Brennan turned his back on the shoppers browsing along shelves and pulled off the elastic band holding the day's post together. He skimmed swiftly through the bundle, finding only bills and junk mail, but no envelope with his name written on it in a familiar hand.

Almost three months had passed since Marcy Copleton had walked out on him and still there was no word of where she was, how she was, when she was coming back – *if* she was coming back.

He went through the post again, hoping against hope that the letter he sought might have got caught up in something else and been bypassed. But again, the search was fruitless.

'Morning, Sam!' a cheerful voice called, and he tried to pin a smile on his face as he turned back to where a customer waited, a full wire basket slung over her arm.

Perhaps tomorrow, he thought as he unpacked the basket and pressed keys on the till. Until then, he was faced with another day of waiting.

Another twenty-four hours.

In his isolated farm cottage, Alastair Marshall abandoned the half-finished painting on the easel as soon as the single letter came through the letter box. Wiping paint from his hands he opened the envelope and began to read.

Dear Alastair, Clarissa Ramsay had written. *Here I am, in Honolulu on the first lap of my year's adventure. It has been wonderful so far – the cruise from San Francisco was perfect and everyone on board ship so friendly. Next stop West Samoa. It is hard to believe that if I was still in Prior's Ford I would be enduring winter weather . . .*

A photograph slipped from between the pages and fell to the floor. Alastair picked it up and looked down at the smiling middle-aged woman, wearing a blue summer dress, and standing before a mass of flowering bushes.

The young artist ran the tip of a finger over the happy face. The first time he had laid eyes on this woman, almost

2

exactly a year before, she had been grey and haggard, steeped in despair and unhappiness. Now, her eyes sparkled and her skin glowed; now she was beautiful, and she didn't look much older than his own thirty-four years.

He laid the photograph and letter down and reached for the sketchbook never far from his hand. Normally he painted landscapes to be sold, if he was lucky, to summer tourists, but now he began to sketch the woman in the photograph.

At Tarbethill Farm, Jess McNair had poured her morning mug of tea and was filling three more mugs, larger than hers, when her husband Bert and their two sons arrived, the dogs hot on their heels and eager to get to the Aga's warmth.

'Idle buggers,' their master growled at them, and both collies, mother and son, flattened their ears and slid apologetic glances at him from the corners of narrowed eyes before subsiding gratefully on to the old rug that had covered the flagged floor for as long as anyone could remember. Jess's mother-in-law had made the rug when she was a young bride; it had had a pattern then, but nobody remembered now what it had looked like.

As the farm dogs nosed in beside him, Old Saul struggled to his feet slowly and painfully in order to give his master's reddened lumpy hand a swift lick. He had been born on the farm when Bert was a comparatively young man; now, they were both slow-moving and rheumaticky. Old Saul had the best of it – he was retired and spent most of his days by the Aga while Bert struggled on with help from Jess and their sons, Victor and Ewan.

'Somethin' smells good, Ma,' Ewan said now, rubbing chilled hands together and sniffing the warm air.

'Pancakes.' It was generally agreed by the women of Prior's Ford that nobody could make pancakes like Jess McNair.

'Mind an' put plenty butter on 'em.'

'Don't you read the papers, Dad?' Ewan asked, winking at his older brother as Jess began to lather butter on the still-warm pancakes. 'Butter's bad for you. Gives you cholesterol and all sorts.'

'Get away with ye – I've eaten it all my life an' I'll eat it till the day I die.' Bert tugged his old cap, put on every morning when he got dressed and kept on until he undressed again at bedtime, more securely over his thinning grey hair. He pulled out one of the chairs set round the scrubbed kitchen table and dropped into it, picking up his mug, to which Jess had already added milk and sugar, just as he liked it.

'Post's in.'

'Haven't you opened it yet?'

'I opened a letter from our Alice; she's doin' fine, but the rest's for you.'

'I thought women were supposed to be nosy.'

'If you got hand-written letters smellin' of perfume, Bert McNair, I'd open them, but I'm not bothered with the other sort. They're on the dresser, d'you want them over?'

'I do not, for it'll only be beggin' letters and bad news. It can wait.'

Even in wintertime there are things to be done on a farm, and as soon as they had downed their tea and had three pancakes apiece, Victor and Ewan went back to work while Bert picked up the post and began to rip envelopes open with a yellowing thumbnail.

'Bills, bills an' bloody bills,' he said gruffly.

'Is the cheque for the milk not due today?' Jess asked. Like her husband, she was weathered from an outdoor life, and her hair, too, was grey and beginning to thin. 'It's usually in by this time.'

4

'Aye, it's here.' Bert took it from its envelope. 'But for all there is, it might as well not be. Puttin' that into the bank's like throwin' a pebble in the river. I'd like to hear what the bloody supermarket owners'd say if it cost *them* more to provide their produce than they were paid for it.' He wrenched at his cap, pulling it down almost to the bridge of his nose. 'We can't go on like this, Jess.'

'We'll weather the winter. We always have.'

'Aye, but it gets harder every year. Brussels an' our own governments an' the supermarkets between em's dug a mass grave for farmers. I reckon they've just about tipped us into it now. We're goin' to have to talk things over with the lads before the soil starts bein' shovelled in on top of us.'

Bert stamped to the outer door, opened it and roared, 'Out!' with such ferocity that the dogs leapt to their feet and bolted past him and into the yard. Even Old Saul woke from his doze with a start, his head and legs flailing in a vain try at jumping to attention before he gave up and dropped back to the rug.

When Bert had gone, slamming the sturdy wooden door behind him, Jess watched from the window as he strode off across the yard. His eyes were on the ground and his head almost lost between shoulders that had once been straight and broad, but were now bowed.

Once he had rounded the byre and disappeared from sight she went to the table and picked up the envelopes, going through them one by one. Bert was right – the bills outweighed the single cheque; it was happening too often. They couldn't go on like this.

Old Saul whimpered slightly and she went to him, bending to run a hand over his side. 'Settle yourself, lad, you've done your bit,' she said, and his tail flopped against the rug in gratitude.

Jess went back to the window and looked out at the farmyard. The sky was low and heavy and the cold wind fluttered the feathers of the few hens pecking among the cobbles.

She suddenly shivered, as if the wind had managed to find its way inside and was blowing through her snug, safe kitchen.

Jenny Forsyth and Helen Campbell got off the afternoon bus in Main Street, each loaded down with Christmas shopping. As they turned down River Lane, Helen talked about her plans for the latest chapter in her novel. Helen's big ambition was to become a writer, and for more than a year she had been taking a postal writers' course. She had recently sold her first short story to a woman's magazine, but her plans for fiction writing had been put on hold when the abandoned granite quarry near to the village was almost reopened.

Against her will, Helen had become the secretary of the local protest committee, a job that led to a meeting with one of the reporters on the *Dumfries News*, a weekly local newspaper.

When plans for the quarry were dropped she had been asked to write a weekly column on the happenings in Prior's Ford. The good thing was that it brought in some much-needed money. The drawback was that it got in the way of the novel writing.

'Come in for a cup of tea,' Jenny offered as they came to the parting of the ways.

'The children'll be home from school in half an hour,' Helen said doubtfully; then, succumbing to temptation, 'but I'll just pop home and hide these things while you put the kettle on.'

Helen hurried off to the left, into Slaemuir council estate, while Jenny turned right into the more affluent Mill Walk estate. Once Jenny had put her own shopping away and switched the kettle on she collected the post from the doormat. Two letters addressed to her husband Andrew were placed on the telephone table while she opened the single letter addressed to her personally.

When Helen arrived a few moments later, a radiant Jenny whisked her into the house. 'You'll never guess what's happened!'

'You've won the Lottery?'

'Better than that!'

'There is nothing better than that,' said Helen, who had four children to feed and a husband on a low wage.

'There is!' Jenny waved a letter at her friend. 'Maggie's coming to live with us!'

'Maggie? Are you talking about your wee step-daughter?'

Jenny nodded, her eyes suddenly filling with tears of joy. Her first husband had been a bully, and the only happiness Jenny had known during their brief marriage came from Neil's small daughter from his first marriage. She had finally run away from Neil, but had never stopped missing Maggie. A few months earlier, Neil's brother Malcolm had discovered where she lived, and Jenny had heard from him that Neil was dead, and Maggie living with his parents.

'Malcolm's written to say that his father's ill and his mother can't look after Maggie as well as him, so they want us to take her. Oh, Helen – I'm getting Maggie back – for good this time!' Then, suddenly remembering why Helen was there, 'Come into the kitchen, it won't take a minute to make the tea.'

'Jenny—' Helen followed her into the spacious kitchen, 'Maggie's not the wee girl you knew. She's about twelve now, isn't she?'

'Fourteen. It'll be great to have a daughter! We can go shopping together, and— Oh, it'll be lovely!'

'You'll have to talk this over with Andrew.'

Jenny spooned loose tealeaves into the teapot and added boiling water. 'He'll be thrilled.'

'Are you sure?'

'Of course I am – he knows how bad I felt at having to leave her. She was such a sweet little girl.'

'She's not a little girl any more.'

Jenny was setting mugs out on the kitchen counter. 'We're the only people who can take Maggie. Malcolm's wife has multiple sclerosis, and without us to take her she might have had to go into care.'

'What about Calum? You have to think of him as well.'

'But it'll be so good for him. We were never happy about him being an only child, but we just didn't get lucky again.' She poured tea into the mugs. 'Now, he's going to have a sister!'

'Who's going to have a sister?' Calum asked from the kitchen doorway, and both women jumped.

'That's not the school out already, is it?' Helen asked.

'Yes, that's why I'm home,' nine-year-old Calum explained patiently. 'Mum, who's—?'

'That means the children are home and I'm not there. Jenny, I have to rush.'

'Your tea!'

'Must go – talk to Andrew,' Helen said, and fled.

As Helen crossed River Lane and ran towards her own house the school bus bringing the older Prior's Ford children home from Kirkcudbright Academy stopped outside the village store. Its uniformed passengers flowed off, some of them lingering on the pavement.

'Wow!' Jimmy McDonald said, and they all turned to look at the long, sleek car coming along Main Street. A young

8

woman was at the wheel with an older woman, beautifully dressed and immaculately groomed, in the passenger
seat.

As the car passed the teenagers Steph McDonald stepped
forward, beaming, and stooped down to wave in at the
passenger window. The older woman turned, smiled at her,
and lifted a gloved hand in an elegant salute.

'Who's that, Steph?' Freya MacKenzie asked.

'Oh, its Mrs . . . it's . . . you know her!'

'No I don't.'

'Did you see the way she waved? Just like the Queen.'
Jimmy sniggered.

Steph was knitting her brows, trying to think of the woman's
name. 'She's— Oh, we've all seen her around the village!'

'Not in that car,' Jimmy said, while Ethan Baptiste, the
Jamaican godson of local minister Naomi Hennessey, herself
part-Jamaican, added, 'I'd know if I'd ever seen that car
around here. Right, Jimmy?'

'Right on, Ethan.'

They began to straggle off to their homes, Steph still
racking her brains, while the car turned into Adams Crescent
and stopped at the first house, a pretty two-storey detached
villa set in a neat garden.

The driver, a dark-haired girl, got out and went round
to open her passenger's door. The woman who had caught
Steph's attention emerged gracefully from the car, smoothing
down her pearl grey, fur-collared coat, and surveyed the
house carefully.

'Willow Cottage,' she said in the husky voice known to
millions of avid television soap fans. 'A pretty name, don't
you think, Genevieve?'

'It's as good as any.'

'I just hope that this Mrs Ramsay has got taste. I couldn't

9

bear to live in a house that has no taste, even though it's only for a short while.'

'You saw the photographs, Mother. It's fine.'

Meredith Whitelaw shot her daughter a pained look. 'Genevieve, how often do I have to tell you to call me Meredith?'

'And how often do I have to ask you to call me Ginny?'

'You're too old to call anyone "Mother"!'

'I hate Genevieve. Do I look like a Genevieve?'

Meredith eyed her daughter's cropped hair, only just framing a square face with not a spot of make-up on it.

'You were a beautiful baby – how was I to know that you were going to take after your father?' Then as a blood-curdling yowl came from the back seat she opened the rear door and brought out a cat basket.

'Gielgud, my poor darling! Poor liddle pussums. Did Mummy forget you, den?'

A pair of furious blue eyes glared at her through a space in the basket and the Siamese began a steady low grumble.

'Just one more minute, sweetie, and you'll be out of that nasty nasty basket – promise!'

As Ginny hauled cases and bags from the car's roomy boot, Meredith turned to survey the village green and, beyond it, the sleepy Main Street. Above the shop roofs, rounded hills could be glimpsed, their tops wreathed in cloud.

'Sweetie,' she said to the cat rather than to her daughter. 'I rather believe that we're going to enjoy living in this pretty little backwater. Though methinks that we just might have to spice things up a little . . .'

2

'Who's going to have a sister?' Calum Forsyth asked his mother again as the front door closed behind Helen.

'You are – isn't it exciting?'

'Oh no!' He dropped his schoolbag on the kitchen floor and glared at Jenny. 'Fred Stacey in my class has had a terrible time – his mum and dad promised him a new brother to play with and he had to wait for ages before it happened. And it's still not big enough to play with. Fred says that it was a right swizz!'

'I'm not talking about a baby, I'm talking about a big sister. Her name's Maggie, and she's fourteen.'

Calum gave his mother a long, level look, then went to the refrigerator to fetch the jug of orange juice. 'If she's that old, where has she been until now?' he asked, still suspicious. 'Why hasn't she been here, with us?'

Jenny brought a glass from the dresser and put it on the table, then sat down and picked up her tea.

'Well, she's not exactly your sister, just a sort of sister. I looked after her when she was a little girl, before you were born, and I really liked her. Then I met Dad and we came here, and you came along, and I didn't see Maggie again.'

Calum filled his glass carefully, and then carried the jug back to the refrigerator before asking, 'So who's been looking after her while you've been here with us?'

'Her grandparents, because her mother had died and her father had to work far away. But now her grandparents aren't well, so Maggie's coming to stay with us instead. As your big sister.'

'She's a girl.'

'Girls are all right. Look at Ella – you play with her all the time, don't you?' Ella MacKenzie, the younger daughter of Jenny's close friend Ingrid, was a tomboy, and mad about football.

'Ella's OK. D'you think that this Maggie might be like her?'

'Probably.' Jenny put aside her own dreams of a girl to go shopping with, and concentrated on painting a picture of the sort of sister her son would accept.

'Well, that would be all right,' he acknowledged, and took a huge gulp of juice. Then, picking up a biscuit from the plate she had put out for herself and Helen, said, 'When's she coming?'

'I don't know, but soon. I'll have to get the spare room made up for her.' Jenny's excitement began to build again. Ever since meeting Andrew and bringing Calum into the world her life had been perfect, but there had always been a dark shadow in the corner of her mind. She felt like a jigsaw that was finished apart from one piece – Maggie. Once they were reunited, her life would really be complete. She longed to phone Andrew, but she knew that he was having a busy day, so she would have to wait for him to get home.

When at last he came in the front door, it was Calum who reached him first. He had either had time to get used to the idea of having an older sibling, or he may simply have been influenced by his mother's excitement; whatever the reason, he rushed along the hall and threw himself at his father, yelling, 'I'm going to get a sister!'

'What?' Andrew Forsyth had had a hectic day and, between busy traffic and road works, a frustratingly slow drive home. All he was thinking of as he let himself into the house was a drink, dinner and a lazy evening in front of the television set. Now he hurried towards the kitchen, meeting his wife on her way to the hall.

'What?' he said again, and then, delight dawning in his eyes, 'Jenny, does this mean that you're—'

'Calum, could you get the flowery salad bowl from the dining-room sideboard?' Jenny asked, and then hurriedly, as Calum scampered off, 'No, it's not that, it's Maggie. She's coming to live with us.'

'What?' It struck Andrew Forsyth, even as the word exploded for the third time from his lips, that he was going to have to stop repeating himself.

'Leave it until we're on our own. I'll explain everything later,' Jenny hissed at him as Calum returned with the salad bowl.

'I think I'll just go upstairs and wash my hands,' Andrew said, and took refuge in the bathroom.

The McDonald family lived in a three-bedroomed house on the Slaemuir council estate behind Prior's Ford primary school. As their brood grew in number, Jinty and Tom McDonald had moved into the smallest bedroom, not much more than a box room, while the girls, sixteen-year-old Steph, Merle, aged twelve, Heather, ten, and Faith, the youngest at six years old, shared one room and the boys – Steph's twin Grant, fourteen-year-old Jimmy and Norrie, aged eight, shared the other. When the entire family was at home the square living room could scarcely hold all of them.

Tonight, Tom, who had been persuaded to take on the job of stage manager for the Prior's Ford Drama Group, had gone to the village hall to work on scenery for the annual pantomime, Grant was out with his mates, and Jimmy, a keen gardener, had bagged his absent father's armchair and was studying a gardening catalogue that had come through the letter box that morning. Merle, Heather, Faith and Norrie were doing their homework at the table while Steph, who was supposed to be supervising them, mouthed silently over the script spread out before her. She loved acting and had won the part of the principal boy in the pantomime.

For once, the house was peaceful and Jinty took advantage of the lull to relax in an armchair, teacup in hand as she watched a soap opera on television. She was addicted to soaps; she felt as though she knew all the characters, and it cheered and comforted her to see that their lives could be just as hard as hers. Jinty loved her large brood and adored her still-handsome husband Tom, a joiner by trade. Since Tom spent a lot of his free time in the Neurotic Cuckoo and was an unsuccessful gambler, Jinty was frequently the family's main wage earner. In the summer she worked at Linn Hall, the largest house in the village, and she was also a cleaner at the pub, the village hall, the primary school and the church, as well as charring for one or two of the career women living in the Mill Walk housing estate.

There were those who thought that Jinty, born and

raised in Prior's Ford, and a much-liked member of the community, deserved a better husband, but she wouldn't have exchanged him for the richest man in the world. Tom's waistline, like hers, had spread and his thick auburn hair was well seeded with silver, but even so he still had more than a passing resemblance to the handsome young man who had swept her off her feet almost twenty years earlier, the man she still saw every time she looked at him.

Now, without taking her eyes from the television screen, she held out her cup. 'Pour us some more tea, will you, Heather?' she asked, and Heather laid down her pen and left her seat, glad of the chance to take a break.

She splashed tea into her mother's cup, added some milk, then leaned on the back of Jinty's chair to watch the drama unfolding itself on the flickering screen. 'Why's that man crying?'

'His mother's just been badly hurt in an accident.' Jinty took a sip of tea. 'They don't think she's going to survive. Surely they're not going to let her die – I can't imagine *Bridlington Close* going on without Imogen Goldberg. She's the leader of the pack, that one. See, there she is.'

The scene had changed to a bedroom, the camera zooming in on a woman lying in bed, propped up on a pile of pillows. Her short white hair was immaculate, her face perfectly made up, but her voice, as she spoke to the people clustered about the bed, was weak.

'I think she's going. Oh, poor Imogen,' Jinty mourned as Steph, suddenly realising that one of her charges was missing, turned round.

'Heather, you're supposed to be doing your homework!'
'I'm coming – just let me see what happens first.'
Steph cast an irritated glance at the television screen, and

15

then her eyes widened and she screamed out, 'Oh my God, it's her!'

The whole room was suddenly thrown into confusion. Merle, Faith and Norrie all stopped work and stared at their elder sister, mouths falling open. Heather, still leaning against the back of her mother's chair, gave a startled leap, then lost her balance and almost fell as her elbow skidded off the old chair's slippery leather. Jinty, about to take another sip of tea, also jumped, and hot tea slopped over the rim of the cup on to her hand.

'Steph! For God's-goodness' sake, what's got into you?'

'It's her!' Steph, oblivious to the chaos she had caused, pointed a trembling hand at the screen, where Imogen Goldberg was gracefully taking her final breath. 'I thought I knew her because she lived here, but it was because I've seen her on the telly! That woman – she's the one who drove into Prior's Ford this afternoon when we were all getting off the school bus!'

During dinner, and for the hour he was allowed before going to bed, Calum Forsyth chatted happily about getting a big sister, while his parents both, for separate reasons, longed for the hands of the clock to reach eight.

Around the time when Steph McDonald was discovering that a real live television star had come to sleepy Prior's Ford, Calum headed upstairs to bed and Andrew, closing the living-room door to make sure that they couldn't be overheard, was finally free to ask, 'Jenny, what the hell is going on?'

'This came today – from Malcolm.' She took a letter from her skirt pocket.

'Your late husband's brother Malcolm?' Then, when she nodded, 'I thought that that part of your life was over and done with.'

16

'Something's happened, listen,' she said, unfolding the letter when Andrew would have taken it from her.

'Dear Jenny, you were probably hoping that you would not hear from me again, but I have a big favour to ask of you. My father's had a serious heart attack, and although he's making a slow recovery and we hope that he'll be coming home from hospital soon, it means that my mother is going to have to nurse him. It will be a full-time job and Mum can't be expected to look after Maggie as well. We can't take her because of Liz's poor health and you are the only other person we can turn to for help. Could you and your husband give Maggie a home for the time being? It looks as though it could be quite a long-term arrangement, so I know that you will both have to think about this. I hope that your answer will be yes. Maggie is a nice kid and if you can't help, then the only alternative is to have her taken into care. It would mean so much to us to know that she's with someone who, in our eyes, is still family.

Please let me know your decision soon as arrangements will have to be made one way or the other. Sincerely, Malcolm.

'Isn't it wonderful, Andrew? I'm going to see Maggie again! I'm going to be able to make it up to her for deserting her when I left her father.'

'I could do with a drink.' Andrew went over to the sideboard. 'Want one?'

'I do believe that I'll have a gin and tonic to celebrate the good news.' Jenny dropped into a fireside chair. 'We'll have to redecorate the spare room – make it nice for her. That shouldn't take long. And we'll have to replace some of the furniture. I'll see to all that – I'll ask Helen and Ingrid to come shopping with me to save you any hassle. I'll do the decorating too, during the day. I know that you're busy at the office. Thanks, love.' She took the proffered glass. 'Freya Mackenzie's round about Maggie's age, she can help

17

Maggie to settle in here, and at the academy, and they'll become great chums.' Then, as Andrew turned from the sideboard, a generous tumblerful of whisky in his hand, she raised her own glass. 'To Maggie, and to families!'

'I wish to God that you hadn't told Calum about this before you told me. It's made things more – complicated.'

'I'm sorry about that. I was so excited when I read the letter, then Helen came in for a cup of tea and I was telling her when Calum arrived from school. We didn't realise that he was in the house until it was too late.'

'What does Helen think about this . . . this situation?' Andrew asked, only just managing in time to substitute another word for 'bombshell'.

'We didn't get a chance to talk about it, she had to dash home to see to her brood. About the bedroom, I thought that something in pastel shades would be nice—'

'Jenny, you're going too fast with all this talk about re-decorating and buying furniture and finding friends for Maggie.'

'But you heard what Malcolm said, there's not much time. Her grandfather could be home soon.'

'How old is she, exactly?'

'Fourteen. Her birthday's on the 23rd of March.' That date had always been a difficult day for Jenny, but now . . . 'We'll be able to organise a party for her next birthday!'

'Hang on a minute, Jenny. You're talking about a girl we don't know and who doesn't know us.'

'*I* know her – and it wouldn't be good for her to have to live in a house with a sick grandfather. It wouldn't be good for them, either. How could her grandmother find time to look after her as well as an invalid?'

Andrew took a mouthful of whisky, for once swallowing it straight down instead of taking time to savour its bouquet. 'She's in her teens. That's a difficult time for kids – and parents.'

'All the more reason to give her a stable background. Kirkcudbright Academy's very good, and she'll have friends here in the village to support her from the word go.'

'Your brother-in-law's right, we do have to think about this.'

'You can't mean that you would let that little girl – a little girl I love and miss – go into care, sent to live with people she doesn't know?'

'She doesn't know us.'

'She knows me – knew me. I'm sure she remembers me. Andrew, we can't refuse to take her!' Jenny's voice began to rise. 'Are you saying that you want me to turn my back on her, and on Neil's parents? They're lovely people and it wasn't their fault that he was a bully. I want to help them as well as Maggie.'

'I'm just saying that we need to think about this, and talk about it. Perhaps we should leave it for twenty-four hours,' Andrew suggested. 'Give ourselves time to mull it over and then talk about it again tomorrow evening.'

'I don't need to mull anything over. I want Maggie to live with us and as far as I'm concerned there's nothing else to think about!'

Andrew massaged his forehead with the fingers of one hand. 'Jenny, I've just come home from a difficult day at work and walked straight into this bombshell. I need time to think!'

Jenny stared at him for a moment, and then finished her drink before rising and facing him defiantly.

'Andrew, I've deserted Maggie once and I'm not going to do it again. This is my chance to make it up to her and I'm taking it, whether you like it or not. I know that we aren't blood kin, but in my heart she's always been my daughter. And now I've been given the opportunity to be a proper mother to her. I won't let that chance go by.'

19

She carried the empty glass to the kitchen while Andrew finished off his own drink and then muttered, 'Oh hell!'

Something told him that life would never be the same again.

3

The three Ralston-Kerrs – Hector, his wife Fliss and their son Lewis – had been away from home all day on a very important mission.

Hector's family had been the landed gentry of Prior's Ford for generations; his great-great-grandfather had owned the local granite quarry, a lucrative site in its day, and had built Linn Hall, an imposing mansion surrounded by acres of handsome gardens, fields and woodland on the hill above the village. But the quarry had long since closed and the family fortunes dwindled; now Linn Hall was beginning to crumble quite seriously and Hector and his wife and son were locked in a constant battle to keep it, and the grounds, going. The fields had long since been sold or let to local farmers, the woodlands left to nature, the Hall roof leaked like a sieve and the current family rooms consisted of the large kitchen, the butler's pantry, which made a passable living room and also acted as Hector's study, and two bedrooms on the first floor.

Just when they began to fear that the house might start

to fall about their ears through lack of finance, things began to take a turn for the better. There was talk of the quarry being reopened, which meant that Hector would benefit from renting out the area to the company interested in extracting the granite still there. As he agonised whether or not he could afford to take the much-needed rent and risk antagonising villagers opposed to seeing the quarry opened up again, an anonymous source had offered to donate two hundred thousand pounds in return for Hector rejecting the application to rent the quarry.

Poor Hector, a peaceful man who hated to upset anyone, didn't know which way to turn, but was saved when the quarry company unexpectedly changed their minds. Glen Mason, the landlord of the Neurotic Cuckoo, had been vehemently against the idea of the quarry being reopened, and when he was revealed to be a multi-million-pound Lottery winner who, with his wife Libby, had moved to Prior's Ford in search of a peaceful haven, they left hurriedly to seek peace elsewhere. It turned out that Glen was behind the bribe to the Ralston-Kerrs, and he had offered it again, together with a generous cheque for the installation of a children's playground on the quarry site, as an apology for the chaos he had caused.

Hector, Fliss and Lewis had started the day in the penny-pinching way they had had to become used to. After travelling to Kirkcudbright in Lewis's rattly old car and partaking of a soup-and-sandwich lunch in the café they always frequented when in town, they visited their bank manager and were stunned by their reception. Mr Whistler had never been more welcoming or hospitable, and it was only after speaking to him that the three Ralston-Kerrs fully realised that, for the first time in their lives, they actually had money to spend.

They had celebrated by enjoying a superb dinner in a highly popular restaurant, and arrived back in Prior's Ford in high spirits.

'I can't believe that we're actually going to get the roof fixed,' Hector said rapturously. 'No more leaks when it rains!'

'And it will be so good to get the place properly heated again,' Fliss chimed in, while Lewis, at the wheel of his small car, made happy plans to turn part of the old stable block into a shop where they could sell garden produce – once they had spruced up the gardens and were able to open them to the public. The bank was drawing up a business plan aimed at spending two thirds of the windfall on the house, and the remaining third on the grounds.

He turned the car into the long, overgrown driveway leading to Linn Hall, and said, when they arrived at the kitchen door, 'I think I'll go down to the pub for a pint. Tom'll probably be there and I want to find out how he's been getting on with the scenery for the pantomime.'

The Ralston-Kerrs never used the imposing front entrance, nor did they lock the kitchen door because, as Fliss always said, all the local people were trustworthy, and in any case, they had absolutely nothing worth stealing, though she would appreciate it if someone broke in now and again to donate something useful.

The morning post had arrived after they left for Kirkcudbright, and as usual, the postman had opened the door and tossed the letters and junk mail onto a chair. Fliss paused to pick it up as she followed her husband in.

'Junk mail, plastic, something for the occupier, junk mail, bill, something for Lewis, bill.' She ripped open one of the envelopes and after scanning the single sheet of paper it contained, said, 'Look at me, Hector!'

He turned to see her beaming at him, holding the paper aloft in imitation of the Statue of Liberty.

'What am I supposed to be looking at, dear?'

'Me – holding a bill and *smiling* because for once, we can actually pay it, thanks to Glen Mason!'

'Oh yes. Mind you,' cautioned Hector, who would never be able to shake off a lifetime of financial worry, 'even two hundred thousand can melt away quickly. It's not a lot, given how much needs doing.'

'I know, darling, but it's a wonderful feeling, knowing that we can pay this bill, and the others. Let me enjoy it while I can.'

He gave her a loving smile and, to her surprise, took her free hand and kissed it. 'Enjoy it, Fliss – you deserve that after all the years you've struggled and done without and never complained. You've blessed my life, and I take you for granted.'

The words, and the sincerity in his eyes, were so unlike Hector, a natural daydreamer, that Fliss was taken aback. She blushed, giggled like a schoolgirl, then pulled herself together and said briskly, 'A cup of hot chocolate, I think, before bed.'

She tossed the plastic-wrapped brochures and the enve-lope seeking the attention of the occupier into the bucket that served as a waste-paper bin and carried the bills into the pantry, to be dealt with at a later date. The single letter addressed to Lewis in a round, almost childish hand was left on the chair, where he found it when he returned from the Neurotic Cuckoo an hour later.

His parents had gone to bed and he turned the lights off and went out of the kitchen, along the passageway, once used only by servants, and leading to the large, dark entrance hall. Lewis knew his way so well that he didn't need any lighting as he went up the wide staircase to the first floor, where he and his parents occupied two of the smaller bedrooms.

Once in his room he switched on the light, sat down on the edge of his four-poster bed, and opened his letter. And then his life changed, never to be quite the same again.

Lewis needed little sleep, and so Fliss and Hector were used to finding him up and about when they came downstairs in the morning, either out in the grounds, which were his special domain, or halfway through breakfast in the pantry. But this morning they were surprised to see that instead of his usual jeans and jersey he wore his best clothes.

'I have to go,' he said as soon as they went in.

'Go where?'

'Inverness. To see Molly.'

'Who the hell is Molly?' Hector was thoroughly confused.

Fliss had gone, as she always did, to the cupboard to fetch the cereal, and then to the refrigerator. Now she set a bowl before her husband and started shaking cornflakes into it. 'That nice red-headed girl who worked here last summer,' she explained, and then, to her son, 'the letter that arrived for you yesterday was from Molly? Is she all right?'

'Yes – well, no – I suppose it depends on the way you look at it. She's pregnant.'

Looking back on the conversation, Fliss, usually quick to grasp things, could only think that her brain must have gone into instant shock – or denial, because the first words from her mouth were, 'But what has that got to do with you?'

'Girls can't get pregnant on their own, Fliss,' Hector said. 'It takes two to tango, as they say.'

'Good God!' Her arm jerked wildly and cornflakes sprayed over the table. 'You mean that Lewis is—?'

25

'Yes I am, and I have to go to Inverness to see Molly and her parents.' Lewis was pulling on his coat.

'Now?'

'Yes, Mum, right now. I phoned her this morning so they're expecting me. I shouldn't be long – a few days, just. The garden's dormant at the moment anyway so that doesn't matter. But I was supposed to work on the scenery tonight for the pantomime. Give Tom my apologies, will you, Dad?'

'But Lewis, this baby – it might not be yours.'

'It is, Mum.' He picked up a bag, already packed. 'Sorry, but I've got to make sure that she's all right. And face her parents.'

He gave his mother a quick peck on the cheek, nodded at his father, and left.

'Lewis!'

'Fliss, sit down and pour yourself a cup of tea,' urged Hector, busily scooping up scattered cornflakes. 'If this girl's having a baby and Lewis is the father, it stands to reason that he must go and speak to her, make sure she's all right, and so on.' Then, glancing at his wife's ashen face, 'What is it? I thought you'd enjoy being a grandmother.'

'Well yes, I suppose I would.' Fliss sank down on to her usual chair. 'It's just, well, I'd expected to have an engagement and a wedding first. This is so sudden!' Then, groping for the handle of the big battered teapot, 'Hector, how can we be sure that this is Lewis's child?'

'Isn't Molly the girl he was friendly with during the summer? The bonny lass with the red hair? Here, let me,' he added as her hand continued to flail about in the vicinity of the teapot. He dumped the cornflakes collection into his bowl and picked up the teapot.

'Yes, but, she was only here for a few months, and now it's what? December?'

'You probably know more about that sort of thing than

26

I do, but I suppose it could be possible. Lewis certainly seems to think so.' Hector, who had suddenly and for the first time become the practical member of their partnership, poured out a mug of strong tea, splashed in milk and then added two spoonfuls of sugar.

'I don't take sugar!'

'It's good for shock. Brandy would be even better but we don't have any.'

'Hector, has Lewis been writing to this girl?'

'He might have been. How would I know?'

'I just wondered,' Fliss said slowly. She sipped at her tea, trying not to screw her face up against the horrible sweetness of it, and wondering if Lewis had written to tell Molly about the money Glen and Libby had donated towards the restoration of Linn Hall. But she knew that if she said such a thing aloud, Hector would be shocked. An honest, gentle soul, he always saw the best in people.

'We should get some brandy, now that we can afford it,' he was saying now, cheerfully. 'Just a half bottle. I expect I could buy it in the village store, or the Neurotic Cuckoo.'

Fliss said nothing. She was too busy counting up months in her head. Molly had come to Linn Hall round about last May, as far as she could recall, and left again in September.

When, Fliss wondered, was this baby due?

4

Ingrid, Jenny and Helen met for coffee every week, taking turns to play hostess. Today they were making Christmas gifts at Ingrid's, one of the largest houses in the Mill Walk estate. Jenny loved the spacious living room, opening onto a handsome conservatory which, in turn, overlooked an immaculate back garden. Ingrid, a former fashion model, was Norwegian, and her choice of furnishings ran to comfortable cream leather chairs and sofas massed with multi-coloured cushions, wooden flooring with beige and black rugs here and there, elegant occasional tables and modern art studies on the walls.

Helen, who lived with her husband Duncan, the gardener at Linn Hall, and their four children in a council house on the Slaemuir estate, also loved going to Ingrid's house for coffee, but in her case it was because it was so clean and neat and free of children and noise.

Jenny and Ingrid, owner of the local gift shop The Gift Horse, were both skilled at making toys and cards, while Helen, who was making new jerseys for each of her four children and her husband for Christmas, was joining them with her knitting. The glass doors to the conservatory were firmly closed and the fireplace gave out welcome warmth. The room was untidy for once, covered with the makings of Christmas cards and toys; Ingrid, tall and blonde and as perfect as her home in black trousers and a cream-coloured polo-necked sweater with crimson flowers appliquéd here and there, created Christmas cards at the table while Jenny, stitching busily at tiny clothes for a hedgehog family she was making for one of Helen's daughters, told her about Andrew's reaction to Maggie's potential arrival.

'I just can't believe that he's being so pig-headed about this! He knows how much I loved Maggie and how much I've missed her, and yet now that I've finally got the chance to be a proper mother to her he's holding back!'

Ingrid eyed her friend thoughtfully for a moment, then said in her almost-perfect English, 'Perhaps Andrew is thinking that the Maggie you're talking about now is not the Maggie you've been yearning for. Your Maggie was a baby; today she is standing on the threshold of womanhood.'

'She's only fourteen.'

'Believe me, girls grow up very quickly nowadays. You are going into the unknown, Jenny – and I think that Andrew is feeling a little frightened.'

'Frightened? That's—'The doorbell's two melodious chimes sounded and Ingrid set down the card she was working on and got to her feet in one smooth sinuous movement.

'Our future novelist has finally arrived,' she said. 'Excuse me, Jenny,' and she walked elegantly from the room, just as she had once walked along catwalks, modelling appallingly expensive clothes for appallingly rich women. Today her corn-coloured hair was in one long braid bouncing gently against her straight spine as she moved.

' – balderdash!' Jenny finished when she was alone. She heard the front door open and seconds later Helen erupted into the room, rosy cheeked and unwinding a woollen scarf from around her head.

'Sorry I'm late, but you'll never guess what I just heard!' She handed the scarf to Ingrid, took off her woollen gloves and pushed them into her coat pocket, then ran her hands through her almost-shoulder-length straight brown hair. 'Oh heck, my glasses have steamed up!' She whipped them off and rubbed them on the skirt of her coat, then popped them back in place.

'That's better, though I bet my nose is like a cherry.' She unbuttoned the coat and handed it to Ingrid, who laid it and the scarf neatly across an upright chair.

'Where's your knitting bag, Helen?'

'I knew I'd forgotten something! I'll go back for it—'

'No, we'll have coffee now you're here. It's all ready. Be careful, you could get chilblains doing that,' Ingrid chided the newcomer, who was holding her hands out to the fire's heat.

'I don't care – those gloves don't do much to keep the cold out. It's bitter, isn't it? You'll never guess what's happened!' Helen said again as Ingrid went to the kitchen.

'You've finally finished your first chapter?' Jenny asked, realising that her own news would have to be put on the back burner for the moment.

'No, it's . . . actually no, I still can't work out a proper cliffhanger of an ending. You need to end each chapter in such a way that the reader wants to know what happens next.'

'Well if it's not your writing, what is it?' Jenny was beginning to get exasperated.

'I met Jinty McDonald in the village store just now and she says that we've got a celebrity in the village.'

'Really?' Ingrid had returned, pushing a neatly laid hostess trolley. 'What sort of celebrity?'

'A television actress — Meredith Whitelaw.'

'I have never heard of her.' Ingrid's charm bracelet chimed like tiny bells as she poured coffee.

'I have,' Jenny said, intrigued. 'She's in that soap, *Bridlington Close*. She plays Imogen Goldberg, the bossy mother who runs the family business.'

'She did. She died last night.'

'Meredith Whitelaw died? Here, in the village?'

'No, in last night's episode. Didn't you see it?' Jenny and Helen were both keen on soaps and enjoyed discussing them.

'I missed it. What happened?'

'A tractor toppled onto her car when she went to that farm to sort out the boy that got her granddaughter pregnant.'

'But how can the programme go on without Imogen Goldberg? She was the kingpin of the family. Or should that be queenpin?'

'Do you two have any idea what you sound like?' Ingrid enquired, fixing first Helen and then Jenny with her vivid blue gaze as she served their coffee. 'You are discussing soap operas about imaginary people, and you talk about them as if they are real.'

'They are real, to us,' Helen defended herself.

'Real life is real, Helen. Real people are real. All the rest is make-believe. Have a biscuit.'

'What about Meredith Whitelaw?' Jenny wanted to know.

'Jinty says that her Steph saw a fancy car go by when she got off the school bus yesterday afternoon, and she waved to the woman passenger, recognising her and thinking that she must be someone local, the way you do when you see a familiar face. And the woman waved back. It was only when Jinty was watching *Bridlington Close* last night that Steph realised where she'd seen the woman before. It turns out that she and her daughter have rented Willow Cottage for the year while Mrs Ramsay's away. She must be what they call "resting" at the moment. Between performances.'

'That was quick, wasn't it? Turning up in the village yesterday afternoon when she was going to die on screen that very night.'

'They film these programmes weeks in advance. The thing is – do you think she would mind if I asked for an interview for the *Dumfries News*? It would do me a lot of good with the editor.' Helen wound a strand of hair around her forefinger, as she often did when she was uncertain.

'She would love it,' Ingrid said firmly. 'Actors like to be in the public eye, especially when they've just been killed off on the screen.'

'I'd give her a day or two to settle in, though,' Jenny added.

'Now that that's decided, Jenny wants our advice on a very important situation. One that's real, not from a script.'

'Oh, Jenny, I'm so sorry, gushing on about Meredith Whitelaw when you were waiting to talk about something more important,' Helen said five minutes later. 'But I must say that I'm surprised to hear what Andrew thinks. I've always thought that he'd do anything to make you happy.'

There were times when Helen secretly envied her friends' nice houses and well-paid husbands. Duncan, a rather dour man, didn't earn much as the gardener at Linn Hall, while Ingrid's husband Peter, a lecturer, and Jenny's Andrew, an architect, enjoyed nine-to-five, weekend-free, well-paid careers.

'Not this time.' Jenny's voice was grim. 'You'd have

32

thought that he'd be pleased to give Maggie a decent life here, in nice surroundings, with friends like your children.'

'Before you arrived, Helen, I pointed out to Jenny that this girl is no longer a little toddler to be kissed better when she falls and tucked up in bed in the early evening. Andrew may feel that you both need to take time to consider all the options before making any decisions.'

'Couldn't you go and visit her several times – all three of you? That way you could get to know her and let her get to know you.'

'There isn't much time, Helen. Neil's father's very ill, and his mother must be frantic with worry. Liz and Malcolm can't do anything to help because Liz needs care too, and Malcolm has a full-time job. I have to turn the spare bedroom into a nice bed-sitting room for her, and I was hoping that you two would go into Kirkcudbright with me in a day or two to look at furniture and curtains and things like that.'

'Of course we will,' Helen said at once. 'Won't we, Ingrid?'

'What else are friends for?'

'There's another thing – you're the only people who know about me being married to Neil, but that's going to change when I tell everyone my stepdaughter's coming to stay with us. If anyone asks questions, could you both say that you've known about me and Neil all along, and leave it at that?'

'Of course,' Ingrid spoke for them both. 'If your mind is set on bringing Maggie into your family, then Helen and I are with you every step of the way, but I hope that this won't have to be done against Andrew's wishes. You need his support – and so does Maggie, not to mention Calum.'

'I know,' Jenny said glumly. And then, drawing herself upright and pushing her shoulders back, 'And I'll make sure that I get it!'

*　　*　　*

When Jenny returned home she began to sort through the bits and pieces that had been left in the spare bedroom until more permanent homes could be found for them, then tried to think of a colour scheme that Maggie might like. The green curtains were too dull for a start, she thought, bouncing on the bed to test the mattress. They would have to be replaced by something cheerful, and the mattress was too soft. Come to think of it, the bedstead was a bit dreary too; there were probably more modern styles in the shops now.

She began to imagine the room as it could be, fresh and pretty, with a homework desk in the corner and perhaps some fluffy toys on the new bed. Floral curtains fluttered at the open window – in her mind's eye, winter had been replaced by summer – and there was enough space to hold two small but comfortable easy chairs where Maggie could sit chatting to a friend, probably Ingrid's Freya, or perhaps one of the McDonald girls.

Or, perhaps, to Jenny herself. They would be able to have lovely mother-and-daughter sessions once Maggie had settled in. Jenny heaved a happy sigh as she went back downstairs. She adored Calum, but already he was beginning to prefer the company of his pals to his mother. It would be lovely to have a daughter.

Andrew would come round. He would have to, for Jenny's mind was made up. Maggie was coming to live with them, as soon as it could be arranged.

Despite the cold weather she had hung out a wash before going to Ingrid's house; when she went to the back garden that afternoon she found that, as expected, the clothes hanging from the whirligig were still very damp. But at least they held the fresh outdoors smell that could never quite be captured by detergents or conditioners, no matter what the manufacturers claimed.

As she unpegged the laundry she could hear the river that cupped the village of Prior's Ford in a protective semi-circle gurgle over its stony bed on the other side of the garden wall.

She dropped the last item, Calum's football shorts, into her basket and returned to the snug warmth of the kitchen, where she filled the tumble drier before going to her bedroom to rummage in a spare handbag for her old address book. She didn't really need it, for her former parents-in-law's phone number was still lodged in her memory, and always would be. But she checked it anyway before picking up the bedroom phone and dialling the number.

'Anne?' she said, heart thumping, when the receiver at the other end of the line was lifted and a familiar voice gave the number. 'Anne, it's Jenny – Janet.'

There was a pause, long enough for her to wonder if the call was going to be accepted or not, then Anne Cameron said softly, 'Oh, Janet, pet, it's so good to hear your voice!'

'And yours,' Jenny said through a throat thickened by tears. She had always liked her parents-in-law, and their younger son, Malcolm. She could never understand why Neil, raised by such lovely people, had turned out to be a bully. 'How are you, and John? I know he's not been well.'

'John's . . . he's been very ill, but he's coming on now. I'm hoping to get him home soon.'

'Did Malcolm tell you that he'd seen me?'

'Aye, he did, but just last week. I wish we'd known sooner. We've wondered where you were – and hoped that you were happy.'

'Oh, I am, very happy. Andrew's a good man.'

'I can't tell you how pleased I am to know that. We've often talked about you, Janet. I don't believe in speaking ill of the dead, but I know that Neil wasn't an easy man to live with. I don't know why . . . he had the same upbringing as Malcolm, but the two of them were as different as chalk and cheese.'

'I've worried too, about what you thought of me for running away without a word to you. I thought you must be blaming me for being a coward.'

'We never once blamed you, pet!'

'I'm so glad, Anne. I've got a son now, Calum – he's nine years old. And I'm hoping—' Jenny hesitated, then said, 'Malcolm said that it was going to be difficult for you to look after Maggie as well as John, when you get him home from the hospital.'

'John's going to need a lot of attention, and Malcolm's right when he says that living with an invalid wouldn't be fair on Maggie, not at her age. I've been worried sick about what's to be done for her,' Anne confessed.

'We'll take her. I've missed her every day, Anne, and I'd love to have her here.'

'Are you sure? What does your husband say?'

'Andrew agrees with me,' Jenny said firmly. He would agree when he realised that it was the only way – he would! 'And Calum's excited at the thought of having a big sister. When . . . when do you think she might come here?'

'John won't be out of the hospital for a while yet, and I'd like to have one more Christmas and New Year with the lassie. The end of January, maybe?'

'That would give me time to get her room ready,' Jenny said happily.

'And it'll give me time to get Maggie used to the idea. Nobody's said anything to her yet. I'd not want her to think that we don't want her any more,' Anne said anxiously.

'Of course not. Maybe you could tell her that Malcolm and I met each other, then we could come to see you – and her – and get her used to the idea. I'm longing to have her with me again,' Jenny confessed.

'Give me your phone number, pet,' Anne Cameron said, and then, a tremor in her voice, 'you've no idea what a weight's off my mind, knowing that she'll be looked after, and by family, not strangers!'

5

As the time approached for Andrew's return home, Jenny began to wonder if she had done the right thing in phoning her former mother-in-law. Perhaps she should have had a word with him first.

She made one of his favourite meals, and decided to wait until Calum was in bed and the two of them alone in the living room before mentioning, as though in passing, the phone call. But as it happened, Andrew was the one to bring up the subject.

'I suppose we're going to have to talk about this business of adding a teenager to our family.'

'It's not just a teenager, Andrew, it's Maggie – my step-daughter.'

'A stepdaughter you haven't seen since she was a baby. She's going to be as much of a stranger to you as she is to me and Calum.'

'Not for long. You're not going to refuse to let her stay with us, are you? You couldn't be so cruel!'

He had been sitting in his usual armchair; now he got

up and began to pace the room, running a hand through his hair. 'Jen, I don't want to be difficult, but I can't help feeling that you're looking at this business through rose-coloured spectacles.'

'I am not!'

'Just give me a minute,' Andrew said patiently. 'Let's look at the facts. I know that you've never forgotten her, and never forgiven yourself for deserting her – not that you had any choice in the matter. But it all happened a long time ago and people change, especially children. We're being asked to make a big decision here, and we have to think it through carefully. Don't you agree?'

'Yes, but—'

'Thank goodness for that,' he said on a long sigh of relief. 'Now we can start to talk things through properly. I'm not saying that I don't want this girl to come to us, I just need to know that whether she does or not, it's as the result of a joint decision. Agreed?'

He smiled at her, and Jenny stared back, suddenly beginning to realise that she had dug herself into a deep hole, and there was no way out of it other than telling the truth.

'Now then,' Andrew went on briskly, 'the first point we have to consider is this letter from Malcolm. It sounds to me as though he's making decisions for his parents, possibly without their agreement. They might not want to hand her over to us.'

'Andrew, they do.' She ran a tongue over her dry lips. 'I spoke to Malcolm's mother this afternoon, on the phone.'

There was a brief silence, during which Andrew studied his wife, while Jenny gazed at a spot beyond one of his shoulders, guilty heat rising to her face. Then he asked, quietly, 'Who phoned who?'

'I called her. I wanted to hear her side of the story.'

'Which is—?'

'She's at her wit's end. John should be home late in January and he really is going to need her full attention. She's been worried sick about Maggie, and it would be such a relief to know that she can come to us.'

She stopped, searching his face and finding it closed to her.

'So,' Andrew said at last, 'it's been decided between the two of you, without any need for input from me.'

'What else could I do but put her mind at rest?'

'You could have left that phone call until we'd had a chance to talk, as we agreed. As I *thought* we had agreed.'

'You don't want Maggie here, do you?'

'I didn't say that. I just want to point out the pitfalls before we take the next step. Maggie's no longer the little girl you remember. You're living in a fantasy world, Jenny.'

'And you're jealous.' The accusation was out before Jenny knew it.

'Jealous of a slip of a girl?' His voice was incredulous.

'Jealous because she's Neil's daughter. She was part of my life before you came into it, and you're scared that she's going to take my attention away from you, and from Calum. That's childish, Andrew!'

For a moment he stared at her as though she had just slapped him, then he said quietly, 'I think I'll go out for some fresh air.'

'Do you realise,' he added, turning back from the door, 'that this is first time ever that we haven't talked something through together?'

Then he was gone, leaving Jenny alone with her guilt.

As Andrew Forsyth walked out into the dark night Bert McNair was saying in the kitchen at Tarbethill Farm, 'We're goin' tae have tae rent out the big field.'

'Come on, Dad, we've rented out two of our best fields already,' protested Ewan, the younger of his sons. 'There's scarce enough ground left for our own herd as it is.'

Bert's big hand rasped over the wiry grey stubble on his chin. 'Aye, I know that, but what's the sense in havin' land if ye cannae afford tae run beasts on it? And that's the stage we're gettin' tae.'

'But surely we can hang on for another year!' Ewan had been born with his father's, grandfather's and great-grandfather's passion for the family farm burning in his veins. All he had ever wanted was to inherit his share when the time came, and run the farm alongside Victor, his older brother.

'We said that last year,' Victor pointed out. 'And what's happened? The price of the milk we sell's gone down again, and the cost of keepin' the beasts has gone up.'

'There's the EU grants—'

'They're not enough tae cover our losses – when we finally get our hands on them.' Bert spat his disgust at the coal fire and for once, Jess, who normally chastised him for such behaviour, held her tongue. She sat at the table, hands lying idly in her lap, watching her husband with a worried frown. She knew as well as he did that time was running out for them. 'If it wasnae for your mother growin' her own vegetables and able tae make a meal out o' next tae nothin',' Bert rumbled on, 'we'd go tae our beds with empty bellies as often as not. And the bank's not goin' tae keep quiet about that overdraft for much longer.'

'Have ye not thought of selling off the big field to a developer?' Victor suggested. 'Ye'd make enough money out of that one field tae pay off the overdraft and put somethin' by for the future, and help me and Ewan into the bargain.' Then, as his parents and brother turned on him, he added sulkily, 'There's others doin' it.'

'Aye, there are – an' hell mend them for it!' Bert barked. 'How anyone can bear to see good farmin' land disappear for ever under rows of boxy wee houses beats me! At least the land'll be used if we rent it out, same as the other fields that have gone. And the rent could just make the difference between stayin' on here or havin' tae move out.'

'It's as bad as that, Dad?' Ewan's grey eyes were troubled.

'Aye, son, it is. It's almost as if the government wants tae see dairy farmers goin' tae the wall. My faither'd turn in his grave if he knew what's been happenin'. We're at the stage where the beasts cost more tae keep than their milk brings in – you know that.'

Victor had been glancing at his watch and now he got up from his chair. 'I'm supposed tae be on my way tae see Janette and if I don't go now I'll be late.'

'On ye go. I just wanted tae let the two of ye know the situation. If ye can think of anythin' that might help I'd like tae hear it. But I think it's too late for that,' Bert said.

'You can drop me off at the end of the lane,' Ewan told his brother. 'I'm goin' out for a pint. Comin', Dad?'

Bert had picked up his newspaper; he shook his head and then asked his wife, when their sons had gone, 'D'ye think they've grasped the truth of it?'

'I think so.' She moved to her usual fireside chair and lifted her sewing basket onto her ample lap. 'It's a pity that Alice's man isn't farmin' in this area. We might have been able to link up the two farms and pull together.'

'She's best where she is. Her Jack's doin' all right and it's good tae know that at least one of our bairns is well settled. The lads arenae goin' tae get much of an inheritance, are they? Other than debts!'

42

'Ewan'll be hard hit, poor soul. He's only ever wanted tae work Tarbethill. Victor's not goin' tae mind much,' Jess said sadly. She, like Bert, came from farming stock, but Victor's interest lay more in engines than in livestock. He had always been the one to look after the farm machinery while Ewan helped his father with the cows.

'And Janette hasnae the makin's of a farmer's wife,' Jess went on. For the past year Victor had been courting a girl who lived in Kirkcudbright. Her father had his own iron-mongery business and on the few occasions Janette visited the farm she had screwed up her nose at the country smells and squeaked every time one of Jess's hens ventured near her.

'If ye ask me, that's just as well since there's not goin' tae be a farm for her tae come tae if they wed.' Bert grunted, and buried his head in the paper, rustling the pages briskly to indicate that the discussion was over for the time being.

'I wish we could think of some way of bringin' in more money,' Ewan was saying as Victor guided his car down the long farm lane. Even in the dark he knew where every rut and hole lay, and he constantly twitched the steering wheel from side to side in order to avoid the worst of them.

'There is no way, not now. Dad's been too slow in his thinkin' – and granddad, and his father afore him. They should've bought up smaller farms and added to their stock instead of stickin' tae dairy farmin' and a small herd. Then we'd've inherited a farm each.'

'I doubt if you'd have wanted your own farm,' Ewan pointed out.

'If it was doin' well I could put in a manager, or have somethin' to sell. As it is' – Victor gave the wheel a sudden wrench and his brother was thrown against the passenger door as the car veered sharply to one side – 'you and me could be left with nothin'. Mebbe it's time for us tae think of our own futu— dammit!' he exploded as the car juddered into a new pothole.

At the lane end they parted company, Victor driving off to meet his beloved while Ewan headed for the village. As he trudged along he tried in vain to think of new ways to help his parents to hold onto Tarbethill Farm. Unlike Victor, he had never wanted to be anything other than a farmer and he loved every brick, every animal and every blade of grass on Tarbethill land.

He reached the Neurotic Cuckoo without coming up with a single idea. For several years now he had been hiring himself out to other local farmers during their busiest times, when they were ploughing, dipping sheep or cutting and drying grass for winter feed. The extra money had been like a drop in the ocean, he thought bitterly, then his spirits began to rise as he pushed open the pub door and went into the bar.

His first, carefully casual glance showed that only two people – Joe Fisher and his wife Gracie – were serving. Ewan's heart sank, then lifted again as he spotted Alison Greenlees setting out drinks at a crowded corner table. Beaming, he marched up to the bar and ordered a pint.

'Nippy tonight,' Gracie observed as she served him.

'Goin' tae be worse in the early mornin', when we're milkin' the cows.'

'Rather you than me, then.'

'Och, it's not all that bad,' Ewan said swiftly. 'At least they're indoors this time of year so we don't have tae go out tae the fields tae fetch 'em.' To be honest, he loved the morning milking in winter, when the byre was warm from the cows' body heat. He enjoyed working with them, washing their udders before fitting on the milking machines,

44

listening to the chug of the machinery and watching the milk surge and foam into its containers.

All four family members were required for the morning milking, then his mother went off to the kitchen while he and his father and brother gave the milking shed a thorough cleaning. Once the milk was safely in the huge cans and awaiting collection came the best bit of all – the short walk back to the farm kitchen for the huge breakfast his mother had prepared.

He was so caught up in his thoughts that he didn't even notice Alison's return to the bar until her soft voice said, 'Evening, Ewan.'

He choked on the mouthful of beer he had just taken, set the glass down hurriedly and dashed the back of his hand across his mouth before spluttering, 'Evening, Alison.'

'You were a million miles away there.' She smiled at him, the smile that always caught at his heartstrings because although her brown eyes tried hard, they could never quite rid themselves of their deep sorrow.

'Only one mile. I was thinkin' about the farm.'

She opened her mouth to say something, then froze, her straight brown hair swinging to one side as she cocked her head. 'Did I hear Jamie then . . . ?'

Gracie glanced over at the baby monitor propped behind the bar. 'I don't think so, dear. I looked in on him ten minutes ago and he was sleeping soundly.'

'I'd best make sure,' Alison said, and disappeared through the door leading to the living quarters. Ewan watched her go, then picked up his pint and went to join friends at one of the tables.

'I wish she would notice him,' Gracie said to her husband. 'He's such a nice laddie.'

'Ach, you women are all the same – hungry for romance.'

'He likes her,' Gracie insisted. 'More than likes her. Mebbe if he was a bit more forthcoming . . .'

'If he was, our Alison might run like a hare. She's still mournin', and it's too soon for her to think of movin' on and takin' another husband.'

'Not too soon for Jamie, though. A bairn needs a father.'

'He's got me!'

'A bairn needs a grandfather too,' Gracie pointed out.

'So I'll be both, for as long as Alison wants.'

'Aye, I know you will. I just wish . . .' Gracie said, but just then the door opened to let in more thirsty customers and the bar suddenly got busy, leaving her unspoken wish to hang in the air until, like a twist of smoke, it disappeared.

6

'Lewis, get up!'

'I'm asking you to marry me and I'm down on one knee because that's the right way to do it. It's romantic.'

'It's daft,' Molly Ewing giggled. 'Get up!'

'OK.' Lewis got to his feet. 'I can do it just as well standing. Molly, will you marry me?'

'I don't think so, Lewis,' she said; and then, as he gaped at her, 'I'm not ready to marry and settle down yet.'

'But you're having our baby. We've got to get married!'

'Being pregnant doesn't mean having to get married. I'm not ready for marriage,' Molly repeated. 'I shouldn't even have written to you so soon, but I'd just found out, and I panicked. Then after I had posted the letter I told Mum and Dad and they sat me down and told me to take my time before deciding what to do for the best.'

'They know that I'm here, don't they? And how do they feel about that?' Lewis asked when she nodded.

'They're cool. You'll like them,' Molly assured him, 'Don't

worry, Dad's not about to get his shotgun out and insist on a wedding.'

'Molly, I want to marry you, I've wanted to since I first set eyes on you.'

'Oh, Lewis, you are so sweet.' Molly, as slender as ever, kissed him. 'You're my prince! Imagine driving all the way here as soon as you got my letter.'

'Doesn't that show how much I want you? You and our child. You're not' – Lewis was suddenly struck by a terrible thought – 'thinking of having an abortion, are you?'

'I don't know what to do yet. Probably not, because Mum's desperate to be a granny. Take your coat off and sit down and I'll make you a cup of tea,' Molly ordered. 'You've come a long way.'

Stella Ewing arrived home from school while they were drinking their tea. She came into the small living room, dropped an extremely large satchel in a corner, stuck her hands in her blazer pockets and ran cool hazel eyes over her sister's visitor.

'So you're Lewis.'

'This,' Molly said with a marked lack of enthusiasm, 'is my kid sister, Stella. The clever one.'

'Not all that much of a kid. But clever, yes. I'm in sixth year at school.' Stella stuck a hand out for Lewis to shake. 'How long are you staying?'

'Mind your own business!' Molly snapped.

'It is my business. I had to move into her room so that you could have mine,' Stella told Lewis. 'I've got exams coming up after the holiday so I need space and peace to study. That's why I'm asking.'

'Only for the one night. I have to get back, there's a lot to do at home.'

'That's OK then. Any tea in the pot?'

Molly picked up the teapot and shook it. 'What a shame, we've finished it. But if you're making more for yourself, I wouldn't mind another cup. And while you're waiting for the kettle to boil,' she added as her sister took the teapot and headed for the kitchen, 'you could put the casserole in the oven and start peeling the potatoes.'

'What did your last slave die of?' Lewis heard Stella mutter as she flounced out of the room, her long auburn ponytail swinging from side to side.

'Seems a nice kid,' he said, and Molly snorted.

'It's well seen that you don't have any kid sisters. She's a pain. Pay no attention to her.'

Molly's mother was small and plump, with hair a milder shade of red than her daughter's, cut short and curling round a pretty face. Like Molly, she had green eyes and a wide smile. Her husband, at first glance, was quite intimidating; tall and burly, with a thick head of hair that had once been dark, but was now mostly grey. His moustache, also thick, was grey and his eyes hazel. As soon as he came into the house he discarded his jacket to reveal a short-sleeved shirt open at the neck. Both arms and what could be seen of his chest were heavily tattooed and his handshake was bone crushing.

'Been looking forward to meeting you, mate. We've heard a lot about you from our Molly here.'

'All good, though.' His wife took Lewis's hand in both of hers. 'It was very nice of you to drive all the way up here to see us.'

'It was the least I could do under the circumstances, Mrs Ewing, Mr Ewing.'

'Oh, for goodness' sake – it's Val and Tony. We don't stand on ceremony in this house, though I did ask Molly when

49

I heard you were coming if I should curtsey, with you being a laird's son. But she said, "Don't be silly, Mum, he's just like the rest of us," didn't you, Pusscat? And so you are.'

'I'm off for a shower.' Tony Ewing held out his large hands, turning them over to display black fingernails. 'I'm a garage mechanic, Lewis, and no matter how much I scrub my hands when I finish work they never get properly clean until I get into my own bathroom.'

'Yes, off you go, Tony, and I'm going to get washed and changed too.' Val had taken her coat off to reveal an overall with the pocket bearing the logo of a famous supermarket. 'I'm on the checkout all day and the money doesn't half make your skin feel dirty.' She raised her voice so that it could be heard in the kitchen. 'When's the dinner going to be ready, Stella pet?'

'Twenty minutes.' Stella carried a tray from the kitchen and began to set the table.

'Lovely. Time for a glass of sherry first, if we're quick.'

'Your parents didn't have to go to so much bother just for me,' Lewis protested to Molly, noticing that her sister was putting out wine glasses as well as cutlery.

'They're not,' Stella tossed the words over her shoulder. 'They always have wine with their dinner, and Mum likes a drop of sherry first.'

'There now, babes, that wasn't too hard, was it?' Molly twined her arms round Lewis's neck and reached up to kiss him. 'They like you.'

'They might not like me so much when they hear that you don't want to get married in spite of—' He stopped, glancing at Stella.

'In spite of her having a bun in the oven?'

'Stella, don't be so coarse!'

'They'll be all right about it. What Molly wants,' Stella

50

told him cryptically, ignoring her sister, 'Molly gets. Know what I mean? I'm sure you do.'

'Little cow!' Molly snapped at her, and when Stella had returned to the kitchen she ordered Lewis, 'Pay no attention to her; she's always been a troublemaker. Too clever for her own good, that's what's wrong with her!'

After dinner Stella went upstairs to do her homework and Lewis got the chance to broach the reason for his hurried visit.

'About Molly and me and the baby—'

'He went down on one knee and proposed to me, Mum,' Molly said proudly. She had steered him over to the sofa after dinner, and was now curled up beside him, nestling against him in a way that made Lewis feel embarrassed, given that her parents were in the room. Not that they seemed to be at all bothered.

'Oh, isn't that romantic, Tony? You never went down on one knee to me, did you?'

'I'd have felt like a prat. We were in the fairground where I worked,' her husband pointed out, 'with people all round us. They'd have fallen over me if I'd knelt down.'

'The thing is, Molly says she doesn't want to get married.'

'Not yet, I said, Lewis. I didn't mean not ever.'

'You don't need to worry, love,' Val said easily. 'We've already had a good long talk about it, haven't we, Tony? And we think Molly should wait until she's ready to marry.'

'But the baby—'

'Don't you worry your head about that, she'll go on living here and we'll help with the baby. It'll be nice to have a little one about the house.'

'You don't mind us not marrying?'

'Bless you, no! What's a signature on a piece of paper? Look at me and Tony.' Val held out her left hand, wiggling her fingers to show off a sparkling engagement ring and an eternity ring, one on either side of a broad gold band. 'We never got married and it's not bothered us, has it, babes? I'll admit that I'd have quite liked a wedding at the time, with Molly on the way, but Tony already had a wife. So that was that.'

Lewis swallowed hard. He had never met a family like this before. 'I'll pay maintenance, of course.'

'That would be useful,' Molly's father said, reaching for the remote control. 'Now then, it's time for *Who Wants to be a Millionaire.*'

It seemed strange, Lewis thought ruefully, that a couple so liberated and relaxed about their daughter's decision to become an unmarried mother should expect her child's father to sleep in a separate room when he visited.

He turned over in the single bed, wondering why, with its firm mattress and soft pillows, he couldn't get to sleep, then realised that it was because his body missed the sagging mattress and flat pillow of his four-poster at home.

He reached out from under the duvet and pressed his hand against the wall. Molly was on the other side of that wall, only inches away from him. So near, and yet so far. He could hear the murmur of voices, hers and her sister's. It must be nice to have someone to speak to in bed, Lewis thought as sleep finally began to steal over him. One day, he and Molly would be able to do that . . .

'For goodness' sake, Stella, will you stop tossing and turning!' Molly was complaining in the adjoining room.

'I can't get comfortable in a bed with a pink flowery duvet and fluffy toys along the bottom.'

'Just think yourself lucky I've got a double bed. If it'd been a single you'd have had to sleep on the floor.'

'I think I'd prefer that.'

'Oh, shut up and go to sleep!'

'Charming. Does your Lewis know what he's letting himself in for?'

Molly didn't answer, and for several minutes there was silence, before Stella said into the darkness, 'Actually, he's a really nice bloke – nicer than your usual boyfriends. Why won't you marry him and go and live in his big house and be the lady of the manor? I thought that would be right up your street.'

'I didn't say that I wouldn't marry him, but you ought to see that big house. It's falling apart, and it's cold, and most of the rooms are locked up and they live in the kitchen. But someone's given them a fortune to do it up. Once that's done,' Molly said, 'I'll probably marry him and live there. But not until they've got the place decent.'

'Mmmmm. Does he know about you having an abortion two years ago?'

Molly shot upright in bed. 'I don't know what you're talking about!'

'Yes you do. I heard you and Mum and Dad muttering to each other after you came back from Canada. Before you went into hospital to have the *endoscopy*. I take it that Lewis doesn't know about the – endoscopy.'

'One more word—'

'Keep your hair on,' Stella said. 'My lips are sealed – fortunately for you.'

'They'd better be!' Molly fell back on to her pillows and Stella, smiling to herself, turned over in bed so that her back was to her sister and she was facing the wall. She reached out and touched it longingly. Her lovely single bed

53

was on the other side, only inches away. So near, and yet so far . . .

'Willow Cottage.'

'Good morning, I wonder if I could speak to Meredith Whitelaw?'

'Who's calling?'

'You don't know me,' Helen's heart was thumping, 'but my name is Helen Campbell and I live in the village – in Prior's Ford, I mean – and I write about village life for the *Dumfries News*. And I was wondering if Ms Whitelaw would be willing to give me an interview.'

'Ah,' the voice on the other end of the line said. 'Just hold on a moment while I go and ask her.'

'Thank you.' Helen took advantage of the lull to pull her handkerchief from the sleeve of her sweater and give the slippery receiver a good rub. In Willow Cottage Ginny Whitelaw clamped her hand over the phone. 'It's someone called Helen Campbell. She lives here and she writes for one of the local newspapers. Do you want to give her an interview.'

'Of course I do!'

'I thought you might want to be incognito for a while.'

'Don't be silly, darling, I'm an actress, I don't do incognito! Who did you say?'

'Helen something.'

Meredith plucked the phone from her daughter's hand. 'Helen, how very kind of you to call me. I would love to talk to you, my dear,' Ginny heard her say as she went into the kitchen. 'Now then, when can we find a time convenient to both of us?'

7

On her way to Willow Cottage that afternoon, Helen met Jenny.

'Guess what? I'm going to interview Meredith Whitelaw for the *Dumfries News*.'

'I thought you were going to give her time to settle in?'

'I meant to, but the more I thought about it the more anxious I got, so I finally decided that I was going to have to go for it now or have a nervous breakdown tomorrow. So I phoned her, and she was really nice about it, and agreed on this afternoon. Then I phoned Bob to tell him, and he's tickled to bits. He says I've landed a real scoop!'

'That's wonderful, Helen. I'm pleased for you.'

'I've told the children to go to your house if I'm not back home by the time the school comes out. That's all right, isn't it?'

'Yes, of course.'

'Jenny, what's up?' Helen suddenly noticed that Jenny's normally sunny smile was missing, and there were faint smudges beneath her dark blue eyes, indicating that she hadn't slept well the night before.

Jenny opened her mouth to deny that there was anything wrong, then realised that she wouldn't be able to fool her best friend. 'It's Andrew, we had words last night, and I don't think he's going to agree to Maggie coming to live with us.'

'Oh, Jenny!' Helen gave her friend's arm a comforting rub. 'Are you sure? Perhaps you're trying to push him into it too quickly.'

'That's exactly what I have done. I phoned Anne – my mother-in-law – yesterday and more or less said that we would be happy to take Maggie in. She's desperate, Helen; she really isn't going to be able to cope with an invalid husband and a schoolgirl.'

'You phoned her without talking to Andrew first? Oh heck, why did you have to do that? You must have known that he'd feel hurt when he found out.'

'I just didn't think. I was clearing the spare room and thinking about getting it nice for Maggie, and before I knew it I was speaking to Anne on the phone.' Tears filled Jenny's eyes. 'Have you time for a coffee? I need someone to talk to and Ingrid would probably say she told me so. I need someone comforting, like you!'

'I'm due at Willow Cottage. But I tell you what,' Helen said hurriedly, 'we'll make time to talk after my interview.'

Walking along Main Street towards Willow Cottage at one end of the half-moon shaped village green, she agonised over Jenny's problem. Andrew would surely come round – but there was no denying that Jenny had been too impetuous. Much as she loved her friend, Helen felt just as sorry for Andrew, faced with a situation he had been thrown into without the opportunity to say his piece.

Then, as she walked up the path and rang the doorbell, nerves and excitement swept everything else from her mind. This was her first big story, and she absolutely had to get it right!

The young woman who opened the door was sturdily built with short, spiky dark hair and a square face devoid of make-up. Her smile was quick, and friendly. 'Hello, you must be here to interview my mother. I'm Ginny Whitelaw.' Her handshake was firm and brisk. 'Come in, she's ready for you.'

Coming face to face with someone she had seen so often on her television screen but had never actually met in person was quite eerie, Helen told Jenny later. 'I felt as though I knew her so well, but at the same time, she was a stranger. For one thing, Imogen Goldberg in *Bridlington Close* was from Yorkshire, but Meredith Whitelaw doesn't really have an accent at all.'

As she was ushered into the living room Meredith Whitelaw swept across the room towards her, both hands outstretched. 'Helen, my dear, how lovely to meet you!' Her grip, as she took Helen's hands in hers, was firm and to her surprise, Helen realised that the woman she had always thought of as tall was slightly smaller than herself.

'You've met my daughter, Genevieve.'

'She has, and it's Ginny.'

'She is so naughty,' Meredith told Helen with a mother's martyred sigh. 'I gave her a beautiful name and she insists on shortening it. So vulgar!'

'I look more like a Ginny than a Genevieve.' Ginny indicated her blue jeans and checked wool shirt. 'Tea, or coffee?'

'Er — tea, please.'

'I'll see to it,' Ginny said, and left the room.

'Do sit down. Over here, I think.' Meredith indicated a

seat by the window and Helen, turning towards it, realised that a handsome Siamese cat already occupied it.

'Em—'

'Gielgud, naughty puss-tat!' Meredith swept past her to lift the animal into her arms. 'You're supposed to be having your nap in the kitchen, aren't you? He always knows when people are coming to the house – he has a sixth sense. I sometimes think that I should have called him Merlin. Cats are so inquisitive, aren't they? He wants to meet you. Gielgud, this is Helen, and she's come to interview me, not you.'

The cat studied Helen with slanted blue eyes, yawned widely, revealing a pink mouth and wickedly sharp white teeth, then leapt from his mistress's arms to stalk out of the door, head and tail held high.

'He's so adorable – my baby! I realise that Genevieve should be my baby, but for some reason known only to her, she never was. Do sit down, my dear.' Meredith, wearing a loose, silky top in a pattern of blues and greens over tight black trousers, settled herself in a deep armchair facing Helen, who realised that her hostess had placed herself so that the light from the window fell full on her face. Although she was probably in her early fifties, and her stylishly cut short hair was snowy white, her face and neck were flawless and unlined. She had the good bone structure and high cheekbones that kept a woman beautiful no matter how long she might live.

'So – what would you like to know?'

Helen scrabbled in her bag for the notebook and pen she had bought from the village store that morning. Over a quick sandwich lunch she had phoned Bob at the newspaper office and noted down the questions he suggested.

'The most obvious question, Ms – er – Mrs Whitelaw, is—'

'It would be Ms, but do call me Meredith. After all, we're neighbours.'

'Meredith. The most obvious question is, what are you doing here in Prior's Ford?'

'Resting, dear. Taking a break from a frantically hectic schedule. You have no idea how much work goes into starring in a television soap. If one isn't studying one's lines, one's rehearsing, filming, in make-up or wardrobe. Scarcely time to draw breath. I badly needed to recharge my batteries, and where better to do that than a nice quiet village in a beautiful part of our lovely country?'

'And of course, you're free to enjoy a break, having been killed off— I mean, having left *Bridlington Close*,' Helen altered the sentence hurriedly as a sudden frown creased the creamy skin between Meredith Whitelaw's beautifully shaped eyebrows.

'Yes, quite.' Her voice was suddenly cool.

'Did it come as a surprise?'

'It certainly did to my character. Poor Imogen, crushed under a tractor after giving years of faithful service to the programme! As for myself, I was surprised,' Meredith said carefully. 'After all, Imogen is – was a very popular character. I received sackfuls of mail from viewers who loved her. I believe that there will be quite an outcry over the decision to kill her off.'

'Can I say that it will leave you free to explore other avenues?' Helen suggested tactfully, and was rewarded with a dazzling smile.

'My dear, I was about to say that very thing myself. I've decided to take a year out to recharge my batteries and consider my options. When one has been a household name for seven years, one has to be very careful as to the parts one chooses to take on.'

'What about the stage?' Helen asked as Ginny came in carrying a large tray. Gielgud followed her and curled up by his mistress's feet, watching Helen's every movement.

'Ah yes, the stage. Since you mention it, I would quite like to tread the boards again.'

'And there are a lot of good plays about at the moment, aren't there, Mother?' Ginny put a small table by Helen's elbow and poured tea.

'Indeed there are.'

'We have an amateur company here in Prior's Ford,' Helen ventured, and then, as Meredith raised an eyebrow at her, 'Not that I'm suggesting that you would want to join them. You're a professional, after all. I just meant that they're very popular, and they put on good shows. They're rehearsing a pantomime at the moment. Thank you.' She chose a small piece of cake from the plate Ginny was offering. 'Last year they did *Blithe Spirit*.'

'A wonderful play. I was Elvira once, many years ago. Before television claimed me. We must go and see this pantomime, Genevieve. I want to become involved in village life while I'm here,' Meredith told Helen, who put her teacup down and reached for her notebook. 'I feel the need to live the simple life for a while, away from the glare of publicity.'

'Prior's Ford is a very nice village – friendly, but not intrusive. I'm sure that you'll find it an excellent place to recharge your batteries.'

'Perhaps' – Meredith said, feeding a morsel of cake to Gielgud – 'I should hold a party so that Genevieve and I can introduce ourselves to our new neighbours. You must come, of course, Helen, and your husband – or is it your partner? One never knows these days.'

'My husband, Duncan, and I would be delighted. Duncan's

60

head gardener – well, the only gardener, really – at Linn Hall. That's where the local laird lives with his family.'

'You have a laird? How wonderful!' Meredith pointed at the notebook. 'You must write down the names of the people we should invite. I'm looking forward to the party already! What about that man who lives next door? I've seen him come and go but he always seems to be on his own. Rather dark and brooding. The Heathcliff type.'

'That's Sam Brennan. He runs the village store, and he did have a partner, Marcy Copleton, but she's . . . away at the moment,' Helen said, and then changed the subject swiftly. 'I'm sure that our readers would love to hear something about your career. Weren't you a stage actress before television claimed you?'

For the next half hour her pen darted down the pages as Meredith's voice flowed on. Ginny cleared away the tea things and then reappeared just as the interview was coming to an end and her mother was telling Helen, 'Don't forget to write down the list of people we should invite to our party.'

'Of course.' Although her hand was aching, Helen jotted down several names before tearing out the page and handing it over. 'Oh goodness, is that the time? I must go; the schools are out and my friend Jenny's looking after my children.'

'You really are the most awful fraud,' Ginny said when she returned to the living room after showing Helen out.

'I don't know what you mean. Gielgud, darling, come to mother. There's my good little puss–tat,' Meredith crooned as the cat leapt onto her knee and held his head up so that she could stroke his throat.

'I keep thinking that Sir John would hate to know that his namesake's pet name is puss–tat. So undignified for a man of his stature.'

'Sadly, I never met him, but for all we know, he might have loved to be given a pet name. We all have our little foibles. Why do you think of me as a fraud?'

'Telling that nice young woman how interested you are in the local drama club. "We must go to see the pantomime, Genevieve."' She imitated her mother's voice to perfection. 'You've always sneered at amateurs.'

'Of course, but that was when we lived in London. Now that we're sampling village life, we must do as the Romans do. And besides,' Meredith dropped a kiss on the cat's head and then gave her daughter a smile of pure mischief, 'Think of the fun I could have with an amateur drama club!'

8

The children were all playing a noisy game of football in Jenny's back garden when Helen arrived, and the kettle was already on.

'Well? How did your interview go?'

'All right, I think.' Helen was still pink-cheeked with excitement. 'She's very friendly, and very glamorous. She's named her cat after Sir John Gielgud, and her daughter's called Genevieve, though she hates it and calls herself Ginny. She's not in the least like her mother. I've got loads of information, and she's going to have a party. She asked me to draw up a list of people to invite and I put you and Ingrid on it – and Peter and Andrew too, of course.'

'Good for you. Will instant do?' Jenny spooned coffee grains into mugs and added hot water. 'We'll have it in here so that we can hear the children if they come in.'

'Fine. So what's happening with Andrew?' Helen asked when they were both settled at the table.

'I've made a terrible mess of things. He's furious because I've more or less promised my ex-mother-in-law that we'll take Maggie. Then one thing led to another and I ended up accusing him of being jealous of my time with Neil and Maggie.'

'Jenny, what's the matter with you? Have you got a death wish or something?'

'I know.' Jenny's eyes flooded and she dashed the tears away with an impatient hand. 'I don't know what I was thinking of. I just felt that Andrew didn't want Maggie because she's Neil's daughter.'

'I doubt that.'

'So do I. That's the way Neil would behave, but never Andrew. I don't know if I'm on my head or my heels, Helen!'

'Why don't you take a deep breath and talk it through with him this evening? Try not to rush things, just listen to what he has to say and take it all seriously. If he's really against Maggie coming to live with you, then it's not going to work, love, and losing your temper with him isn't going to change things.'

'But what will happen to Maggie then?'

'When all's said and done,' Helen said gently, 'she isn't really your problem. You have to put your marriage and Calum first. If Andrew's really determined not to take her in, then we'll try to help you to think of something else for Maggie – I'm talking about me and Ingrid. But let's cross that bridge when we come to it.'

'You're so rational, Helen. How do you manage it?'

'I have a younger sister who's always on the phone looking for answers to her problems. She makes me feel like an agony aunt,' Helen said wryly, and then, as the children's voices grew louder, 'They're coming in – nip upstairs and splash some cold water on your eyes.'

'I'll use the cloakroom,' Jenny said, and hurried out, while

Helen wished that her house had a downstairs cloakroom instead of one upstairs bathroom to serve all six of them. The back door flew open and her four poured into the kitchen after Calum, who was in his element at having so many playmates.

Perhaps, Helen thought as she crossed River Lane on her way to her own house ten minutes later, the children running ahead of her, it would be good for Calum to have an older sister.

To Jenny's relief, Andrew was more like his usual self when he got home that evening. He helped Calum with his homework after dinner, and once their son had gone to bed and the two of them were on their own, he said bluntly, 'You still feel that you want Maggie to come and live with us?'

'Yes, I do. I'm sorry about going about things the wrong way, but I don't see that we have any option. I know we're not blood kin but I'm the nearest she's got to family other than the grandparents who can't care for her now. Malcolm and Liz would have taken her like a shot, but that's impossible. There's only me, now.'

'I know. I suppose,' he said slowly, 'that I just wanted to make sure that you understood just what you were taking on.'

'I do. But it's not just me, I realise that. It's you, and Calum. Everything's going to change, but it could be for the better, Andrew,' Jenny said eagerly. 'We'd have a daughter, and Calum would have a sister. And Maggie would have a proper family. She deserves that, surely.'

'Yes she does, and if it means that much to you, there's nothing more to say. When's she coming?'

'In January. Her grandmother wants her to have one

more Christmas with them. You really mean it, Andrew?' Jenny couldn't believe that the arguing was over.

'If it's what you want – and it would probably be good for Calum to have a big sister to look out for him. But there's just one thing,' Andrew added as his wife threw herself at him, 'I'm not jealous of your past. Never have been, never will be.'

'I know, and it was a horrible, stupid thing to say. Oh, Andrew,' Jenny said against his shoulder, 'I do love you!'

Lewis didn't say much to his parents when he got back from Inverness, other than confirming that Molly was indeed pregnant, and that the baby was his.

'Are you absolutely sure, dear?' Fliss ventured, and he gave her a stony look that was totally unlike Lewis, and said shortly, 'Of course I'm sure.'

He didn't look very happy about impending fatherhood – but then, Fliss wasn't too happy about the thought of becoming a grandmother. It was something she had looked forward to, but it was happening too fast, as though life had become a runaway train rushing down a hill to its ruin. She was uneasy, and she wondered if Lewis was, too.

'How's Molly?'

'Very well. Looking marvellous, in fact.'

'She's going to have the baby, then?'

'As far as I know.'

'When is it due?' Fliss asked casually.

'May.'

'Oh.' It tied in with her calculations.

'So,' Hector said encouragingly, 'Is she coming to live here?'

'This place isn't really the right environment for a baby, is it? Not the way it is at the moment. She wants to stay with her parents until the baby's born, and they're happy with that. They've been marvellous about it, by the way,' Lewis said. 'I'll be supporting her, of course, sending money every month.'

'It's fortunate that we got that windfall from Glen Mason.'

'It's got nothing to do with that money, Dad, this is something that I have to do myself.'

'What about— Are you thinking of getting married?' Fliss asked tentatively.

'Not at the moment. We're going to take things one step at a time. I reckon we've got enough on our plates for the time being in any case, getting this place back on its feet. I've been thinking,' Lewis suddenly reverted back to his old self, 'that if we work hard this coming summer Duncan and I could get the grounds into decent order. Then the following year, we'll open them to the public for a small entrance fee. I've been making plans during the drive home. I'm going to grow more plants and vegetables, and sell the surplus in our own shop – it'll be in the stable block. What do you think?'

'I don't see why not. The essential thing,' Hector said earnestly, 'is to make the house and the estate capable of bringing in revenue in the future. We need to open up the house to visitors too – let some of the rooms out for holidays, perhaps. But the first thing we have to do is to get an architect to advise us.'

Father and son settled down to business and the subject of Molly and her pregnancy was dropped, as far as they were concerned.

When Fliss tried to talk to Hector once Lewis had gone to the garden to start making plans for the sweeping changes he envisaged, her husband was evasive.

'My darling Fliss, it's Lewis's business, not ours.'

'It's our business if the baby isn't his.'

'You think this girl might be lying to him?'

'She could be. After all, his children will inherit this place.'

'And you see that as an attractive proposition?' Hector was amused. 'What modern young woman would want to saddle her offspring with Linn Hall and its upkeep?'

'Things have changed now, Hector. We've been given the opportunity to restore the place and if it all works out the way we hope, this estate could be worth inheriting. Do you think we could find a way to suggest one of those DNA tests once the baby's born, to make sure that it really is Lewis's responsibility?'

'I don't know about Lewis, but I personally find that idea pretty cold-blooded. I still say that we have to keep our noses out of his business. We've got enough to think of as it is. Let's just wait and see how everything works out,' Hector said, and Fliss had no option but to let the subject drop.

9

Almost from birth Kevin Pearce had assumed that he would become successful in whatever profession he honoured with his presence. On leaving school, where he had been an average pupil, he had started work as a cub reporter on his local paper, planning to move to the editor's desk in a few years. Once he had outgrown that position he would move to Fleet Street and then, possibly, end up with a career in television as a political pundit or a chat show presenter.

Unfortunately for Kevin, his prowess as a reporter had been much the same as his prowess in every other aspect of his life. He tolerated rather than enjoyed a comparatively unremarkable career spent at the same desk, writing about people with more interesting and fulfilling lives than his, and watching editors come and go but never achieving the editorial chair himself.

When he retired, his wife Elinor insisted on a move to Dumfries and Galloway, where she had been born and still had family. Kevin agreed, believing that in a small puddle like Prior's Ford, he might finally manage to become a fairly large fish.

Kevin had been quite good-looking in his younger days; with long fair hair and rather attractive blue eyes, and had favoured floral shirts, cravats and carefully stylish clothes.

By the time he retired his eyes had faded and become rather watery, and his hair had dulled, edging a balding dome, though what remained still fell to his shoulders – and sometimes fell *on* his shoulders. He still favoured colourful clothes, fondly regarding them as Bohemian.

Kevin's main hobby throughout his adult life had been amateur drama – again, without any outstanding success – but once settled in Prior's Ford, he discovered that the local drama group was failing for lack of a director, and had promptly taken over the position.

Now, he sat in the centre of the hall, clipboard on knee and pencil in hand, watching his chorus bounce energetically through the opening song of this year's pantomime *There Was An Old Woman*. The show was fast approaching its production date and at last the chorus was moving about the stage confidently, managing to interweave without bumping into each other. At one side of the hall a large tarpaulin had been spread to safeguard the floor, and Alastair Marshall, Lewis Ralston-Kerr and Tom McDonald, with the assistance of some teenagers, were busy creating scenery. In the lesser hall, not much larger than a good-sized room, Kevin's wife Elinor was making costumes.

'Keep smiling!' Kevin scribbled on his clipboard, one foot tapping to the piano music. This, he decided as the chorus moved into place for the final chorus, was going to be a particularly good show.

As the song came to an end and the chorus held their positions he put the clipboard and pencil on the folding table by his side and got to his feet, clapping energetically. Then he spun round as someone at the back of the hall joined in the applause and a woman's voice rang out. 'Bravo! Bravo!'

If there was one thing that Kevin would not allow, it was people dropping in during rehearsals. He opened his mouth to ask, politely, if the interloper would mind leaving, then it remained open as he saw who it was. He had heard from an excited Steph McDonald that Meredith Whitelaw, the well-known television actress, had moved to their village, and had been wondering how he could wangle an introduction to the woman. But now, it seemed, she had come to him.

Kevin couldn't believe it. His mouth was still hanging open when she came towards him, seized his hand in both of hers and said, in her rich, rounded voice, 'Please forgive me for gatecrashing, but I heard that the local drama club were rehearsing and I couldn't resist popping in to watch. How do you do? I am—'

'Meredith Whitelaw!' Kevin squeaked.

'How sweet – you recognised me. And you are?'

'K-Kevin. Kevin Pearce.'

'The di-*rec*-tor!' Meredith gave dramatic emphasis to the second syllable. 'How wonderful. And what a talented group you have here in Prior's Ford!' Gemstones flashed as she waved a hand at the chorus, huddled in a goggling group at the front of the stage. 'Good evening, everybody! Please don't allow me to interrupt your work, Mr Pearce. I do hope that you will allow me to stay for a little while, though, to watch.'

'Of course. It's time for our break in any case.' Kevin gathered his scattered wits together and waved at his cast. 'Ten minutes, everyone. Would you like some coffee, Miss Whitelaw?'

'How kind. Please do call me Meredith,' she said sweetly, laying a hand on his arm. Kevin's cup of joy filled to the brim and began to splash over.

At last – at last! – fame had sought out Kevin Pearce.

'I thought Mr Pearce was going to wet himself,' Steph said when she got back from the rehearsal that night and told her mother the news.

'Steph! Don't be vulgar in front of your sister!' The two youngest were in bed and Jinty was brushing ten-year-old Heather's long red hair, her crowning glory.

'It's not vulgar if it's true, and I honestly thought he was going to, when he recognised Ms Whitelaw. Anyway, she hears worse in the playground, don't you, Heather?'

'Uh-huh. But he didn't really, did he?'

'Heather McDonald!' Jinty reversed the brush smartly and rapped her daughter's skull with it.

'Ouch, Mum! So what's she like, Steph?'

'Beautiful! So glamorous!'

Heather wrinkled her snub nose. 'She doesn't look glamorous in *Bridlington Close*.'

'That was because she played the grandmother. Meredith Whitelaw doesn't look anything like Imogen Goldberg. Her hair's perfect, and you should see her make-up, Mum, it's flawless! And she was wearing a blue trouser suit and a long silvery scarf. She looked so sophisticated!'

'You wouldn't get much rehearsal with her there, surely.'

'We'd a very long break,' Steph admitted. 'Mr Pearce gave her coffee, and then took her round to introduce her to everyone. She shook hands with me – and with Dad.'

'He'll be all excited about that,' Jinty said dryly. At that very moment, she knew, Tom would be in the Neurotic Cuckoo, bragging to all and sundry about his meeting with a television personality.

In Daisy Cottage, beside Ingrid's gift and craft shop, Kevin Pearce was gloating, 'Imagine us meeting Meredith Whitelaw! Who'd have thought it?'

'Who indeed,' Elinor agreed placidly. 'I'll heat up the milk, will I, for our cocoa?'

'Mmm.' Kevin, drawing the blinds against the December night, paused and peered through the window. 'Her lights are on.'

'That's probably because she doesn't like to sit in the dark,' Elinor said on her way into the kitchen. She was pouring milk into a saucepan when her husband arrived.

'Did I say that she's going to have a party, and we've been invited?'

'I was there when she invited us, dear.' She lit the gas stove and set the pan on the ring.

'Oh yes, of course. Just think of all the times we've watched her in *Bridlington Close* and never dreamed that one day she'd be inviting us to a party! God, I wish I was still in the editorial department! The rest of them would go green with envy if I walked in and told them that we're on first name terms with Meredith Whitelaw!'

'If you'd still been in the editorial department you wouldn't have met her here, or been invited to her party.' Elinor set out two mugs and then fetched the sugar bowl from the cupboard.

'I suppose you're right. Anything I can do?'

'You could take the tray in to the living room.'

'Right you are!' Kevin, still in a happy daze, seized the

tray and hurried out, leaving Elinor, who had been about to put the mugs on the tray, standing in the kitchen, a mug in each hand.

She sighed, smiled and shook her head. An ambitious woman, she had believed Kevin when he assured her that the local newspaper he worked on was only a stepping-stone to greater things. Realising, eventually, that it was never going to happen, she turned her ambitions in her own direction. A talented seamstress, she set up a dress-making business from home, then became so successful that she was able to rent a small shop and hire three women, one to do counter duty and the other two to work with her in the roomy back shop, making clothes from patterns.

It was the money raised from the sale of her thriving business, together with the proceeds from their flat in Manchester, that had made it possible for the Pearces to buy Daisy Cottage and settle down to a comfortable and pleasant retirement. Kevin pottered in the garden and was soon running the drama club, while Elinor took over the duties of wardrobe mistress, and taught needlework to the children in the village's primary school.

Once, on a visit to the school, Naomi Hennessey sat in on a lesson, and told Elinor afterwards that it was a pity that she had never had children of her own.

'You've got such patience with the little ones,' Naomi said warmly, 'and it's clear that they all adore you. You would have been a wonderful mother.'

'Perhaps,' Elinor had said, and then added, smiling at the minister, 'But I never felt that I needed children. I have Kevin.'

10

Now that she had Andrew's blessing, Jenny plunged into the task of decorating the spare room, already known as Maggie's bedroom. Helen and Ingrid accompanied her on shopping trips to choose wallpaper, tins of paint, rugs and patterns for curtains and cushions, which Ingrid helped to make.

Every spare minute was devoted to getting the room ready in time, and she would even have put it before Meredith Whitelaw's cocktail party if her two friends hadn't insisted that she go with them.

'I feel strange out of jeans and a painty sweater; and very underdressed too,' she murmured as the three of them sipped cocktails in Willow Cottage's living room.

'You look more dressed than I do.' Helen glanced down at her own floral blouse and pleated yellow skirt, envying Jenny's bronze silk skirt and blouse and Ingrid's long black, figure-hugging gown with its thin shoulder straps. In Helen's eyes, Jenny had even looked stylish that afternoon in her decorating clothes, with a lock of fair hair falling over her flushed face.

'I think that you all look fabulous,' Ingrid's husband Peter said firmly.

'Thank you, darling, I agree,' his wife chipped in. 'We have to face it – nobody could outshine the famous Meredith Whitelaw, and even if you could, imagine how upset she would be. We can't upset our hostess!'

'I suppose not.' Jenny glanced over at Meredith, who looked fabulous in a floor-length chiffon gown patterned in dramatic black geometric shapes against a vivid orange background. Glass in hand, she was telling Fliss, wearing her well-known 'I now declare this function open', frock, and Hector, in a somewhat dated suit that hung loosely on his thin body, 'But I do have hopes of returning to *Bridlington Close* in the not-too-distant future. Several of the cast members – such darlings, every one of them – have written to beg me to come back.'

'And so say all of us,' broke in Kevin Pearce, who had scarcely left her side since his arrival.

'I'm afraid I rarely see television programmes because our old set is very temperamental, but when Jinty McDonald comes to help me out in the kitchen she keeps me up to date with all the soaps,' Fliss said apologetically. 'But am I wrong in thinking that your character was crushed to death by a tractor?'

'Yes, poor Imogen. After giving years of good service to the programme, one would have thought that the writers might have given her a more graceful exit. Although the death bed scene was well done, I thought.'

'Extremely moving,' Kevin agreed.

'How does someone who's been crushed to death come back to life?' Hector wanted to know.

'Oh, Imogen's dead and gone for ever, poor woman, but there are ways. A twin sister, perhaps.'

76

'Does the character *have* a twin sister?' Fliss asked.

'That's the point – I've checked back and nothing's been mentioned as to her family. So she could quite easily have an identical twin. In fact, Kevin, I intend to discuss the idea with you some time. As a writer—'

'A journalist, actually.'

'Writing is writing,' Meredith told him briskly. 'We must have that talk, and soon. For now, would you be a darling and freshen up my drink?'

Alastair Marshall was wishing that he hadn't accepted the surprise invitation to the party. His main reason for being there was that he had promised Clarissa that he would keep an eye on her home while it was being rented out, and short of marching up to the door and demanding entry in order to inspect the place, this was his only opportunity.

Everything seemed to be in order, he thought, easing his way slowly to the hall and from there to the dining room. Apart from a cluster of framed photographs on Clarissa's sideboard, every one of them featuring Meredith Whitelaw accepting bouquets, opening supermarkets, signing autographs, or posing cheek-to-cheek with celebrities, this room, too, was much as he remembered it. Two of his paintings, bought by Clarissa and hung on the wall to surprise him on the night she announced that she was going off to see the world for a year, were still in place.

Alastair gazed up at them, wishing that there was some way of making time whiz by like lightning, and that Clarissa was back in Prior's Ford, where she belonged.

Ginny had resisted all her mother's attempts to buy her 'something really nice' to wear for the party.

'I'm going to be looking after your guests,' she argued. 'I don't need to look pretty.'

'But you're my daughter!'

'No, I'm me, and you're the famous one, the one they all want to meet,' Ginny said, and would not be moved. Dressed in her favourite blue cotton shirt over black jeans, she moved from guest to guest, freshening up drinks and passing round trays of canapés.

On one of her trips to the kitchen she found a man slumped against the sink unit, glass in hand, scowling at the floor. He jumped when she walked in, and liquid slopped from his glass to the floor.

'Oh, sorry!' He hurriedly put the glass on the draining board and took a handkerchief from his pocket.

'Don't do that,' Ginny said swiftly as he dropped to his knees. 'Let me.' She grabbed the mop and whisked it over the floor. 'There, all cleared up.'

'Thanks.' He scrambled to his feet and gave her an embarrassed grin. 'I probably shouldn't be in here. Sorry.'

'Don't be silly, it's open house tonight.' Ginny started to refill the empty serving plates she had brought from the living room. 'I take it that you're like me – not a party animal.'

'No. Can I help?'

'You could fetch some more glasses from that cupboard, top shelf, and put them on the flowery tray.' She cast sidelong glances at him as he arranged the glasses. Average height, dark brown hair with a slight curl, a straight nose and good profile.

'There,' he said when he had finished, and then, 'By the way, I'm Lewis Ralston-Kerr.'

'I should have known – you have a look of the nobility about you,' she said, and then flushed as he laughed. 'Sorry, that sounded silly.'

'I'm not laughing at you, I'm laughing at myself.' He indicated his well-worn jacket with its leather elbow patches and his jeans, dark like hers. 'I wouldn't describe myself as looking like nobility.'

'I meant your profile. Your family owns the big house, don't they? I've heard that you're hoping to open up the gardens to the public.'

'If I can. The grounds are my area and we recently got a . . . a sort of grant to do up the place. I'm hoping to put my share of it to good use.'

'I don't suppose I could have a look round, could I? I like gardens,' Ginny added as his eyebrows, well shaped and set above steady grey eyes, lifted slightly.

'Of course you can. Come up tomorrow afternoon, if you're free.'

'Thanks, I will. I'm Ginny Whitelaw, by the way.'

'Tomorrow afternoon, then.' He picked up the tray and headed towards the door. Ginny followed, all at once feeling more optimistic about her stay in Prior's Ford.

Sam Brennan hadn't accepted the invitation to his new neighbour's party, but although Rowan Cottage and its neighbour, Willow Cottage, were separate from each other, he couldn't ignore the festivities. Seated in his living room, trying to involve himself in a televised football match, he could hear, and sometimes see, people passing the house on their way to the party. Later, for some reason, he found himself edgily aware of the difference between the living room next door, crowded with people talking and laughing and enjoying themselves, and the room where he sat on his own. Finally, just as the game moved into extra time, he switched the set off and went out of the house and into the dark night, grabbing a thick, fleece-lined anorak from the stand in the hall as he went.

Every window in Clarissa Ramsay's house – or, rather, Meredith Whitelaw's house for the time being – blazed with light and as he stamped down his own garden path he could hear voices and music. He was glad when the sounds faded behind him as he went out on to Main Street, turning to the left and stepping out until he was almost speed walking.

Once clear of the village with its street lighting he was plunged into total darkness, but that didn't bother Sam. He crossed the bridge over the river and walked on, hedges and trees beginning to show up as faint shapes as his eyes became accustomed to the night.

It was cold, and he thrust gloveless hands into his anorak's deep pockets. His left hand encountered something soft, and as he drew it out he caught a faint trace of the perfume Marcy always used. The last time he had worn that anorak – almost a year ago now – he and Marcy had gone for a long Sunday walk in the country. The silky scarf wound round her neck had loosened and almost been whipped away by the wind, and she had given it to him for safe-keeping. He hadn't worn that anorak since.

Now, he stopped and as he buried his face in the scarf's folds, breathing in the smell of her, the ache that hadn't left him for a moment since the day a taxi had taken her from the village, and out of his life, sharpened until it became an almost unbearable pain lancing not just through his heart, but through the very core of his soul.

He groaned into the material, holding it tightly to his mouth to muffle the primeval howl of loss and despair that wanted to escape into the star-dusted sky. He had been such a fool!

When the village heard that the old granite quarry on its outskirts might be reopened, Sam had welcomed the prospect, believing that it might bring more custom to his village store, and more money to the till. Marcy, on the other hand, was bitterly opposed to the idea because she loved the tranquillity of village life. And she had every right to try to cling to a peaceful life, Sam thought as he strode on, the scarf held against his cheek now. Before they met she had had a troubled existence, and he should have remembered that instead of squabbling like a stupid child and becoming angry when she went on to the committee fighting the quarry reopening.

By the time the proposal was dropped, a terrifying gulf had opened between them, but even so it had come as a shock to Sam when Marcy decided that she couldn't live with him any more. Now, a woman from the village had taken Marcy's place behind the shop counter, and he slept alone in the bed they had once shared. He hadn't heard from Marcy for months, and had no idea where she was. He suspected that Ingrid, Jenny and Helen, her close friends, were still in contact with her, but he couldn't bring himself to ask for her address, knowing that she had almost certainly sworn them to secrecy.

Stupid, stupid idiot, to lose the most important person in his life because he hadn't the sense to look her in the eye and tell her that she mattered more to him than the extra money the quarrymen might have brought to the shop! Sam was so angry with himself that he stumbled off the road in the dark and lurched against a tree. He punched its cold rough bark with all his strength, but only succeeded in hurting his hand.

He was standing there, sucking scraped knuckles, when the night's silence was ripped open by a torrent of barks and two dogs rushed from the darkness to circle him, making threatening lunges at his legs.

'What've you got there? Get back here, ye daft dugs!' a voice rasped from further along the road.

'Bert?' Sam had already recognised the dogs as Bert McNair's collies; they always accompanied him on his trips to the Neurotic Cuckoo, waiting patently outside while their master downed his pint of beer and caught up on the local gossip. 'It's Sam Brennan.'

He stuffed the scarf back into his pocket as Bert loomed out of the night, walking stick in hand and his old cap pulled down over grey eyebrows.

'It's you, Sam. Come by!' the farmer ordered the dogs. Trained to herd animals, they immediately stopped their clamour and dropped to the ground. 'What're you doin' out on a night like this, Sam?'

'I just felt like stretching my legs.'

'I've not seen ye in the pub for a while. Have ye taken the pledge, man?'

'I've not been in the mood lately.'

'If ye've been doin' yer drinkin' in the house, on yer own, be careful. A man needs company when he's takin' a drink. It helps tae keep it social, ye ken.'

'I've not even been doing that. No taste for it at all.'

'I wish I could say the same; even a couple of pints once or twice a week costs more than I can afford, but tae tell the truth, sometimes it's the only thing that keeps me goin'.'

'Are things that bad?'

'Aye, they are. We're almost at the end of the year, Sam. I used tae hope for better things in the new year, but now − well, it stopped bein' better a while back.' Sam couldn't see Bert's face, but the old man's voice was bleak. 'I inherited a good farm from my faither, but now—' Bert's voice shook slightly and he stopped and took a deep breath before going on. 'Now, what with all the regulations and

82

the interference and that damned foot and mouth that took our herd a few years back – there's no pleasure in farmin' nowadays, Sam. My faither worked hard till the day he died tae leave me a good inheritance, but with all the will in the world, I cannae see me doin' the same for my own lads.'

'I'm sorry, Bert.'

'Aye, so am I.' Bert McNair wasn't a man to reveal his true feelings to anyone, even to his wife, but in the dark, with two pints of beer under his belt, his tongue seemed to be running away with itself. 'Best be on our way,' he said, 'for there's no comfort in bein' out on a cold night like this.'

He brought the dogs to their feet with a muttered word, and then added gruffly, 'What I said the now – between ourselves, right?'

'Of course, Bert.'

'Good night tae ye,' the old farmer said, and struck out across the road to the mouth of the lane leading to his farm.

At least, Sam thought as he walked slowly back to the village, Bert had a wife waiting for him, while he himself had nothing to go home for. And all because of his own stupidity!

11

Ginny walked up the drive at Linn Hall on the following afternoon to find Lewis waiting for her at the top.

'I was working around this area to make sure that I didn't miss you.'

"Wow!' Ginny eyed the big house. 'Quite a stately pile you have there.'

'More pile than stately — it's crumbling from the roof down, but now that my parents can afford to get some work done on it, we might be able to save it. D'you want to go in for a coffee or some tea first?' he asked, and when she shook her head, 'then let's start the tour. I'm glad to see that you're dressed for the occasion.'

Ginny grinned at him. On this cold and windy day she wore thick corduroy trousers, sturdy boots and a warm anorak over a polo-necked sweater. Strands of short black hair peeped out from beneath a bright red knitted hat, and her hands were encased in matching red woollen gloves.

'I'm used to the outdoors. Lead on, if you will.'

She insisted on seeing everything, and the next two hours

flew past for both of them. Lewis was appalled when he looked at his watch.

'Look at the time! You must be desperate for some tea.'

'It would be nice,' his guest agreed amiably, then, 'What's along that path? I don't think we've been there yet.'

'It used to lead to a stone grotto and a lake − more of a pond, really − but it's all overgrown now, and the water's more of a puddle.'

'Can we have a quick look?' Ginny begged.

'You're a glutton for punishment, aren't you? Just as well you're wearing trousers and boots, because the path's over-grown and there are nettles in there.' Lewis led the way, holding back tree branches to prevent them from whipping into her face. After struggling forward for about five minutes they came on the lake, a large soggy expanse of tangled weeds with, at one end, a small round summer-house built from chunks of natural stone.

'This must have been beautiful in its time,' Ginny said, awed.

'It was. We've got pictures in the house showing it with people in old-fashioned clothes sitting outside the grotto − that's what I've always called it. It was built with stone from the quarry. My pals and I used to play in it, and we collected frogspawn from the lake so that we could watch the tadpoles turning into frogs. Poor old thing,' Lewis added, looking across at the small building, its flat roof covered in weeds, 'it probably looked good in its time, but now it's like a dumpy little old lady with an elaborate green hat balanced on her head.'

'Was the lake man-made?'

'No, it's natural. It was fed from a linn − a Scottish word for a waterfall,' he explained to his English guest, 'in the hill behind the house. I believe that that's where Linn Hall's name came from. But the linn must have dried up a long time ago.'

'Nothing dries up in a rainy country like Scotland; the more likely answer is a blockage. You should have a look at it some time,' Ginny suggested.

'One day, when I've got the time. Come on, I'm hungry. You seem to know quite a lot about gardens,' Lewis said when they had fought their way back through the undergrowth and were crossing the lawn towards the Hall.

'I love them. I visit every stately home I can during the season. When I left school my mother wanted me to go into the theatre – not as an actress, I'm hopeless at that sort of thing – but to learn stage directing or something like that. Not my scene at all, so I went off to stay with an aunt in Leeds and got a job in a flower shop. I got so interested in the pot plants we sold that I applied for a job in a garden centre, and I learned enough there to become a gardener with the local council.'

'Are you still with them?'

'No. I loved the work,' Ginny said as the two of them reached the terrace and began to walk round the house. 'But then my mother was axed from *Bridlington Close* and it hit her harder than she lets on. When she decided to take a year out, I decided that it was time I became a better daughter, so I gave up the job and offered to spend the year with her. At least Willow Cottage has a garden I can potter in, though I won't be able to make any changes since it's not ours.'

'How would you feel,' Lewis said cautiously, 'about a part-time job while you're living here, helping Duncan and me to get this place in order?'

'You mean it?' Ginny stopped and faced him, her blue eyes blazing with pleasure. All at once the year that had been stretching drearily ahead of her began to look interesting.

'I do, but we might not be able to pay much. You could take on responsibility for the kitchen garden if you want.' During the tour Ginny had shown particular interest in the large walled kitchen garden, almost completely overgrown.

'Can I start tomorrow? I hate having nothing to do! And the money isn't important right now. I've always been good at saving, and I'm living off my mother at the moment in any case.' Ginny hauled her right glove off and pretended to spit on the palm of her hand before they shook hands on the deal, grinning at each other.

Fliss, always ready for tea, made a fresh pot and joined them at the large table, where she and Lewis outlined some of their hopes for Linn Hall's future. Ginny listened, fascinated, putting in an occasional comment or suggestion.

'It's such a beautiful old place,' she said warmly, nodding as Fliss lifted the big teapot enquiringly. 'I'm beginning to get a picture in my mind of what it looked like when it was first built. And the kitchen garden's huge!'

'It had to be, because there were servants to feed as well as the family and their guests,' Lewis told her. 'If we could get it back to the way it was, it would keep us going all year round, and supply vegetables and fruit and herbs for the village store as well as the shop I want to set up in the stable block. And the chance to see round a proper old-fashioned kitchen garden would help to draw in the visitors we're hoping to get. Ginny's interested in working with Duncan and me while she's living in the village, Mum. She's going to have a crack at putting the kitchen garden to rights.'

Ginny nodded her dark head enthusiastically. 'It would be great if I could get it back to the way it once was.'

'That's too big a job for one person,' Fliss objected.

'I could get Jimmy McDonald in to help. He's one of the village lads, and he's mad on gardening,' Lewis told Ginny. 'He looks after several gardens – including Willow Cottage, so you'll see him come the spring. He works here in the summer holidays, but we might be able to get him in on Saturdays just now, while things are quiet.'

'Sounds good,' Ginny said happily.

'One day I'll bring out the albums and show you the photographs,' Fliss promised, pouring more tea all round. 'The house parties looked very grand. I feel sorry for the place now – so neglected! But with any luck, things are going to change, at least a little.'

'What a nice young woman!' she enthused when their guest had gone. 'Much more approachable than her mother. That woman intimidated me last night, and your poor father was so afraid of her that he stuck to me like a limpet.'

Meredith Whitelaw became a regular visitor to the pantomime rehearsals. Kevin took to placing a comfortable chair for her in the centre of the hall each evening, where she sat watching the stage closely and making notes which she discussed with him during the halfway break.

Each discussion was preceded by, 'You don't mind a tiny little comment, do you, darling?' to which Kevin, by that time lulled into something close to a trance by the nearness of such a great personage, not to mention the fragrance of her perfume, would reply, 'Not at all, Meredith, you know how much I value your opinion,' then scribble down her thoughts on his clipboard and follow them to the letter, while giving his cast to understand that they were his ideas.

Jenny, enlisted by Elinor Pearce to help out with the costumes as time for the show drew nearer, watched Kevin fall further under Meredith's spell. 'Doesn't it bother you?' she asked Elinor as the two of them stitched busily while Casey and Agnes, the pantomime's comedy duo, were being chased about the stage by Steph McDonald's twin Grant, playing the part of a large bedbug.

'Goodness no,' Elinor said. 'She's an actress – flirting's second nature to her. There's no harm in it – and truth to tell, it's given my Kev a new lease of life. Every little cloud has its silver lining, dear.'

Freya MacKenzie was the pantomime's principal girl and Steph McDonald the principal boy. It didn't take Meredith long to recognise that Steph had acting talents that went well beyond the village pantomime, and when she happened to meet the girl in the street one day she invited her to Willow Cottage for coffee.

'Have you ever thought of studying drama, dear?' she asked when the two of them were settled in the sitting room.

'Oh yes, it's what I'm going to do when I leave school, if I can get a place. I like acting, I've been in all the school plays since I was old enough. It's fun, isn't it?' Steph was a true McDonald in that she totally lacked any sense of class and therefore felt quite at home anywhere, be it the smallest house in the village, or Linn Hall. 'I love dressing up and going on stage in front of an audience. I specially like being someone completely different to the ordinary me.'

'It's hard work too, if you want to do it properly.'

'You don't think that I'm doing the pantomime the right way?' Steph was concerned. 'Mr Pearce seems to be all right with it, but mind you, I don't think he knows much about drama. He does his best, though.'

'Oh no, you're very good, my dear. Too good for Prior's Ford.'

Steph took a gulp of coffee and smiled at her hostess. 'It would be brilliant to be a real actress like Helen Mirren and Judi Dench.'

'Indeed.' Meredith's tone was just a little cool at the mention of actresses other than herself. 'So you're going to apply for RADA, then?' And when Steph nodded, 'Perhaps I could help you – give you some acting lessons while I'm living in the village.'

'How much would they cost?' Steph asked cautiously.

'Nothing at all. That's the thing about actors,' Meredith rolled the final word off her tongue. 'We professionals consider it our duty to reach out and help others struggling up the ladder. I shall help you – on Saturday mornings.'

'Could we make it Saturday afternoons?' Steph asked. 'I help out in the village store in the mornings.'

Watching from the window as the girl walked down the garden path and then paused to shut the gate behind her, Meredith frowned slightly over the way young people nowadays took things for granted. She herself would have been breathless with excitement and gratitude had a famous professional actress offered to help her to set her foot on the first rung of the ladder.

On the other hand, there was something about Steph McDonald that hinted of a glowing career to come, and if that were to happen it would be nice to be able to say that she, Meredith Whitelaw, had been the girl's mentor, and first to recognise her talent.

Although shops all over the country had fallen into the unattractive habit of anticipating Christmas months rather than weeks before the event, thus making sure that everyone was fed up with the festive season by the time it actually arrived, Prior's Ford insisted on clinging to sanity. This meant that not a trace of Christmas could be seen in the village until the middle of December. As the Forsyths set out on a dark, cold morning to visit Maggie and her grand-mother they passed a council lorry, its flat bed filled with greenery, going in the opposite direction.

'On their way to set up the Christmas tree on the village green,' Andrew said cheerfully. 'It'll be all lit up by the time we get home again, Calum. That'll signal that Christmas has really started.'

A grunt came from the back seat, where Calum, never at his best first thing in the morning, was huddled among rugs and pillows, grieving at having been made to get up at what seemed to him to be a ridiculously early hour on a non-school day.

Twenty minutes later he was asleep. 'So much the better,' Andrew said as the car ate up the miles. 'He won't be asking every two minutes when we're going to get there.'

Jenny put a hand on his arm. 'Thanks, Andrew, for agreeing to this.'

'If we're going to do it we have to do it properly. Maggie needs to meet us and we need to meet her. Why don't you try to get some sleep? You were tossing and turning during the night.'

'I was too excited to sleep.' She still was. The boot was filled with wrapped gifts for her in-laws and for Maggie, and she couldn't wait to get there. At last, she had been given the chance to make up for all the years since walking – or, rather, fleeing – from Maggie's life.

Anne Cameron must have been watching for them; as soon as the car stopped outside the garden gate the front door opened, and as Jenny got out, a thin grey-haired woman hurried down the garden path, her arms wide.

'Janet – oh, Janet, pet!' Anne hugged the younger woman tightly. Andrew, getting out of the car, saw over his wife's shoulder that her mother-in-law's eyes were squeezed shut, as though she struggled to hold back tears.

'You've no idea how much we've wanted to see you again!' Anne said when she finally drew back. 'How are you? You look bonny! And happy!'

'I am – and so glad to see you, too. Andrew. Calum.' Jenny turned and held her hand out to the two of them. Calum had climbed out of the back seat and was standing on the pavement, blinking uncertainly at the stranger who was making such a fuss of his mother.

'Come on, old son, it's OK.' Andrew held out his hand and was glad when Calum gripped it, for he, too, was feeling uncomfortable at being drawn – or perhaps the word should be 'dragged' – into Jenny's previous life.

Anne Cameron gave them both a warm welcome, drawing them into her welcoming living room.

'Where's Maggie?'

'Upstairs, she'll be down in a minute. I gave her a call when I saw the car stopping. She's a bit nervous.'

'So am I,' Jenny admitted.

'It's only natural. It's been a while, but she's a lovely lassie, never a bit of bother to John and me. You'll like her – you all will – and I can't tell you how grateful we are to you for taking her into your home.'

Anne addressed the final remark directly to Andrew, who despite the misgivings that still gnawed at him, had no option but to smile and assure her that they were all looking forward to having Maggie with them.

'How's John? I'm just sorry that we can't visit him this

afternoon but it's quite a long drive home and we don't want to be out too late.'

'Of course. He's coming along fine, but it's going to take a long time to get him back to the way he was – or as close to it as we can get. So this is Calum?' Anne held out her hand, and after only a second's pause, Calum shook it. 'It's very nice to meet you, Calum. You've a look of your mother about you. You'll all be ready for your lunch, eh?'

'Yes, we are!' Calum said at once.

'Calum, where's your—' Jenny began but the word 'manners' died on her lips as she glanced towards the door. Following her gaze, Andrew saw a girl who looked, to his mind, a little younger than he had expected. She still had a childish plumpness about her round face and sturdy body.

Jenny stepped forward impulsively, holding out her hands as the girl came into the room. 'Hello, Maggie,' she said softly. 'I'm Jenny. I used to look after you. D'you remember me?'

Maggie Cameron's dark brown eyes studied her for a long moment, and then she smiled, and nodded her dark, curly head. 'Yes, I remember you. I have photographs.'

'So do I. It's lovely to see you again, Maggie. I've missed you very much.'

'I missed you, too,' Maggie said. And then, with a sudden smile that revealed to Andrew the promise of a very lovely young woman behind the childish features, 'I was so glad when Gran said that you want me to live with you until Granddad gets stronger.'

12

The visit was all too short, and when they left, Jenny, twisting round to wave to the two figures by the gate until they were out of sight, relaxed back into her seat with a long-drawn-out sigh of relief and pleasure.

'Isn't she a lovely girl? Anne's brought her up very well.'

'She certainly seems to be easy to get on with.'

'What d'you think about your new big sister, Calum?'

'She's OK. Better than a baby one.' Maggie had taken Calum up to her room to play computer games which, he was glad to hear, she was bringing with her to Prior's Ford. She had remembered to buy him a Christmas present, which now resided, still wrapped and looking interesting, in the boot of the car. He was looking forward to bragging about her in the school playground. He would be the only boy in the school to have a ready-made big sister. It made him feel special.

'Why did Mrs Cameron keep calling you Janet, Mum?' he asked. 'It's Jenny.'

'Yes, but my full name's Janet. It's your dad who decided

to call me Jenny.' She smiled at Andrew. 'New life, new name,' he had said.

Calum was asleep long before they reached Prior's Ford. As they came past the school towards the village green Jenny cried out, 'Oh, Andrew, look!'

While they were away the Christmas tree had been erected and dressed. It stood close by the war memorial, its coloured lights brightening the dark night with their promise of the festive season to come. Joe Fisher, in obedience to the village tradition, had set up decorations outside the Neurotic Cuckoo, but not lit them until the tree was established. Now, coloured lights sparkled along the edge of the pub's roof, Christmas trees stood in the lit windows of the bar and the dining-room, and a flashing Santa Claus flanked one side of the entrance, while a glowing snowman guarded the other.

'Calum – look, darling! Christmas is coming.' He stirred slightly and murmured something round the thumb he had stuffed into his mouth before falling headlong back into sleep.

'Leave him, Jen, he'd be too tired to appreciate it. And he'll probably be grumpy when we disturb him. I think I'll just carry him upstairs and get him into bed.'

'It's like a promise for the future,' Jenny said softly as the car passed the tree and slowed to make the turn into River Lane. 'It's telling us that everything's going to be all right. We'll have a lovely Christmas, the three of us, and next Christmas there'll be four of us. We'll be a complete family.'

Andrew took one hand from the wheel for a moment so that he could reach out and touch her cheek. 'Yes, we will,' he said.

But deep inside, so deep that he couldn't think just where it was hidden, a part of him still felt uneasy.

* * *

95

Christmas came and went, then 2004 gave way to 2005. The village pantomime was always held in January so that there was something to look forward to after the Christmas and New Year's Eve celebrations.

'And that's how it should be,' Fliss said as she bought her tickets at the village store on the first Saturday of the New Year. 'January and February are such dreary, difficult months to get through. March isn't so bad — at least we know then that the nights are getting lighter and spring's on the way.'

'And it gives us more time to rehearse,' said Steph, who was serving her.

'So how's the show going? Is it a good one this year? Not that it's ever bad.'

'I think you're really going to enjoy it, Mrs Ralston-Kerr. We're all having a lovely time. Meredith Whitelaw's been helping Mr Pearce and I think' — Steph lowered her voice and glanced around to make sure that neither Kevin nor Elinor Pearce was in the store — 'that she's made quite a lot of difference. And she's giving me drama lessons on Saturday afternoons, isn't that wild? Imagine me, getting drama lessons from a famous television actress! She says I could get a place in a drama college when I leave school!'

'I'm sure you could, dear. You're always a joy to watch on the stage.'

'Thanks, Mrs Ralston-Kerr.' Steph's pretty face flushed with pleasure. 'You enjoy the show, now.'

'Oh, we will,' Fliss assured her. It was a dull and rainy day, but as she passed the lit Christmas tree on her way across the green, she smiled up at it, warmed by its sparkling colours. She had dreaded every single winter since marrying Hector and coming to live in Linn Hall, but this year it was so different. This year, they had Calor gas heaters in the rooms they used, and on Wednesday Andrew Forsyth, who had spent several hours studying every part of the entire house, was coming to talk to the family about the best way to make use of the money they had been given.

They had even had a decent-sized turkey for Christmas instead of the usual chicken, and a proper traditional steak pie from the local butcher on New Year's Day.

As Fliss walked past the Neurotic Cuckoo and started up the hill towards home, a large, wet and very cold raindrop fell from an overhanging tree branch and managed to land between her spectacle lens and her eye, so that she had to stop, put down her basket, and take her glasses off so that she could wipe the moisture away. When she put her glasses on again the lens was smeary, but it didn't matter. She knew the way home well enough, and nowadays, it took a lot more than a raindrop to spoil her new-found happiness and optimism.

Normally Jess McNair took the farm eggs to the village store each week, but she was happy to agree when Ewan offered to go in her place.

'If you're sure, son. I've got a load of baking to do and I'd like to keep it going while the oven's hot.'

'It's a cold day, Mam – you stay indoors,' her younger son said, and set off in the old four wheeler with more enthusiasm than he would normally feel for a trip to the village.

Once the eggs were delivered he hurried across to the Neurotic Cuckoo, his heart leaping when he saw that Alison Greenlees was behind the bar. The place was quiet, and a book lay open before her. Her elbows were propped on either side of it, and her pointed chin rested on her hands. When Ewan went in she looked up, startled, pushing her long fair hair back from her thin face in a strangely defensive movement.

'Hello. Any chance of a half pint of lager?'

'Yes, of course.' She hurried to get the drink while he turned the book around with the tip of a finger and saw, to his surprise, that it was a detective novel.

'I like his books too,' Ewan said when Alison set the glass before him.

'I didn't know you read,' she said, and then, her pale face flushing, 'I mean – I didn't mean—'

'You mean, when does a farmer find the time to read books?' he said, grinning. 'When and where I can find a quiet minute, and it's not easy. But I've always liked reading. We'd a good English teacher at the school and he used to lend me books. Will you have something to drink yourself?'

For a moment he thought that she was going to refuse then she said, 'An apple juice, if that's all right.'

'Aye, of course it is.' Ewan's heart began to race as he fished a note from his pocket and laid it on the bar. The place was empty and he wouldn't get a better chance. 'Quiet today.'

'It's always quiet in the afternoons. My parents have taken Jamie into Kirkcudbright to do some shopping.'

'Oh aye?' His mouth had gone dry; he took a good swallow of his drink in an attempt to lubricate his tongue, which suddenly felt clumsy. Unfortunately, it was too large a swallow, and he almost choked. He came very close to spluttering the drink all over the bar, Alison and her book, but only just managed to swallow it down instead. Then he had to whoop for breath.

'Are you all right?' Alison's brown eyes were concerned. He fished a handkerchief from his pocket and scrubbed at his mouth, furious with himself.

'I'm fine,' he wheezed. 'The drink just went down the wrong way.' At any minute now the door could open to admit another customer. If he didn't grab his chance it could be lost for ever. He stuffed the handkerchief back into his pocket. 'Alison, it's the pantomime next week.'

'I know.' She nodded to the poster displayed behind the bar.

'I've got three tickets for the Wednesday night and I was wond'rin', like, if you and wee Jamie would like to go with me.'

'To see the pantomime?'

'Aye. It'll be good,' he hastened to assure her. 'It always is.'

'I don't know. Is Jamie not too wee for that sort of thing?'

'He'd enjoy it. So would you. What d'ye think?'

For a terrible moment he thought that she was going to refuse, then she gave him a shy smile and said, 'It's very kind of you, Ewan. Yes, we'd both like that.'

'That's . . . that's great!' Ewan said with a huge sigh of relief.

When Steph McDonald stepped onto a stage she had the ability to change completely. The only way that she herself could explain it was that it was easier to be someone else than to be ordinary Steph. As the audience flocked to the village hall on the first night of the pantomime's four-night run, she watched in the dressing-room mirror as Meredith's skilled fingers applied stage make-up, obliterating Steph and replacing her with Prince Charming.

'I wouldn't have thought that you could do make-up, Ms Whitelaw. Don't you always have special people to do that sort of thing for you?'

'Of course, dear, but take my advice – learn how to apply your own make-up. That way you aren't totally dependent on others, and you know when they're getting it wrong. There.' Meredith stepped back, wiping her fingers on a towel. 'I think that that will do.'

'It looks wonderful. Thank you!' Steph vacated the chair in favour of Freya MacKenzie.

Although it was now January, the village hall was still decorated and carols were being played through the sound system as the audience flocked in from the cold dark night outside.

'This looks so pretty!' Alison Greenlees said as Ewan ushered his guests to seats in the front row. 'Look, Jamie, up in that corner, Santa's come to see the pantomime too.'

The little boy's clear brown eyes, so like his mother's, sparkled as he saw the familiar red-garbed figure. 'Presents?' he said hopefully.

'Not tonight. Santa's given out all the presents for this Christmas. He's come to see the pantomime, just like you.' Alison lifted her son on to a chair, looking around the hall. 'This looks so welcoming on a dark January night.'

'That's why the show's always held after the Christmas and New Year events are over.' It made sense to have wee Jamie seated between the two adults, but Ewan wished that he could be closer to Alison. 'Another reason is that there's always the school concert before Christmas, and other pantomimes in the area. And some local folk go away over Christmas to visit family. This way, they're not missing out on seeing the local pantomime. What are you smiling at?'

'Just thinking about the excitement that'll be going on backstage,' Alison said. 'I used to belong to a drama club, before Jamie was born. I know what it's like.'

'You like drama clubs?' Ewan's face lit up. 'I'm in this one.'

'Really?' Onstage or backstage?'

'Both, depending on where I'm needed, but usually backstage work, helping with the scenery. But with all the problems farming's had in the past few years, and my dad having to lay off the farm workers we had, I've been too busy to do much with the club.'

'Hello.' Ingrid MacKenzie slid into the seat next to Alison's with her husband and younger daughter following. 'Nice to see you. Are you looking forward to the show, Jamie? Our Freya's playing Princess Rosebud – the principal girl,' she went on as Jamie nodded solemnly.

'I thought you would have been in the pantomime too,' Alison said to Ella, who wrinkled her snub nose and shook her head firmly.

'Catch me going on the stage! I prefer football,' she said as the lights went out, the curtain rose and the chorus launched into their opening song.

Jamie managed to stay awake for the entire show, but by the time the curtain calls were over and the hall lights went up again, he was drooping against his mother, heavy-eyed. Ewan scooped the little boy into his arms and Jamie settled his head on the young farmer's broad shoulder with a contented sigh.

It was cold outside, and very dark; as the audience left the lit hall they had to get used to the sudden change. 'Take my arm,' Ewan suggested as he and Alison made their way down the steps, and to his secret delight, she did so, keeping her hand tucked into the crook of his elbow during the short walk back to the Neurotic Cuckoo.

'Would you like to come in for a cup of tea?' she suggested diffidently as they reached the side door.

'Aye, that would be nice.' He followed her into the warm kitchen, where they were welcomed by Gracie.

'I thought you'd be home round about now. I made some sandwiches, and there's a bit of baking.'

'Is Dad managing in the bar or should I go through?'

'He's fine; Alastair's helping. You take the bairn up to his bed, Alison, while I make fresh tea. Give me your coat, Ewan, and sit yourself down by the table. Did you have a good time?'

'Aye, we did. The pantomime's always a favourite in the village. The wee chap managed to stay awake till the end.'

'It was kind of you to take him – and Alison.'

He felt himself blush. 'It was my pleasure, Mrs Fisher.'

'It's nice to see Alison with some colour in her cheeks,' Gracie confided, flashing a glance at the door to make sure she wasn't overheard. 'You'll know about . . . about her, I suppose?'

'I heard. It was a terrible thing.' Alison's husband Robbie had worked in his in-laws' public house in Glasgow until the night a group of young men were barred for bad behaviour. They had gone round to the back yard and when Robbie took a crate of empties out they gave him such a savage beating that he died. Three of them were now serving time in prison for his manslaughter.

'She's not over it – mebbe she never will be. But we're hoping—' Gracie began, and then, as her sharp ears caught a sound from beyond the closed door, she swung round to the stove, where the kettle was simmering, saying brightly, 'I used to love going to the pantomime when I was a wee lassie. That was our Christmas treat, every year. There you are, Alison. Is Jamie settled?'

'He didn't even wake when I put his pyjamas on.' Alison slipped into a chair opposite Ewan's, smiling at him. 'He had a lovely evening – we both did.'

Later, walking homeward through the now-quiet village,

Ewan held on to the memory of Jamie's solid little body nestled in the crook of his arm, the toddler's silky hair against his face. He recalled a moment during the pantomime when Alison turned to laugh up at him, her normally sad face alight.

The walk from hall to public house, carrying Jamie, and with Alison holding his arm, had been all too short. That must be what it was like to be a husband and father, he thought as he turned off the road and onto the lane, heading towards the lights of the farm.

It was something that he would like to experience again.

13

At the end of January, a week before John Cameron was due to be released from hospital, Jenny and Andrew drove back to Dundee to collect Maggie – or, as Jenny called it, 'to fetch her home'.

'Darling, you're going to have to watch what you say,' Andrew cautioned her as the car headed north. 'As far as Maggie's concerned she's at home now, waiting to be uprooted and carried off to a place she doesn't know. Prior's Ford won't be home to her for quite a while.'

'You're right, of course,' Jenny agreed, adding almost at once, 'but I think she'll be calling our house home sooner than you think.'

'I really hope so. But let's just take things slowly, shall we?'

'You're such a worrier, Andrew,' his wife said, and then, anxiously, 'D'you think she'll like her room?'

'Of course she will. It's perfect.'

'Perhaps it won't be to her taste.'

'Then we'll change it – later.'

It had been agreed that Calum would attend school as usual that day, and then go to Helen's afterwards. For one thing, Andrew wasn't happy about taking his son away from his school routine, and for another, they needed room in the car for Maggie's clothes and her personal possessions.

They arrived in time for a late lunch, to find two cases waiting in the hall. Maggie was very quiet, and although Anne made an effort to be cheerful, she looked as though she had scarcely slept the night before. Looking at the two closed faces, Jenny was suddenly conscience-stricken. For the first time she began to realise what they must both be going through.

'You're not going to lose Maggie,' she said to the older woman when the two of them were dishing up lunch in the kitchen. 'We're not all that far away, and you can phone each other whenever you like. You know that we're going to do everything we can to make her happy, don't you?'

'Of course I do, and I'd not want to see her go to anyone but you, for you're still family and always will be, to John and me,' Anne gave her a bright smile, and then, her face crumpling slightly, 'but we're going to miss her so much!'

'I know.' Jenny hugged her former mother-in-law. 'Oh, I know!'

Maggie and her grandmother clung to each other for a long moment when it was time to go. 'Tell Gramps . . . tell him to behave himself and do what you tell him,' Maggie said when she finally disentangled herself. Then, turning to Jenny and Andrew, she drew a deep breath. 'Let's go!' she said, picking up her rucksack and heading for the door.

As they drove back to Prior's Ford Jenny talked about the village, and Freya and Ella MacKenzie, and the McDonald girls, all looking forward to meeting Maggie. She told Maggie about the committee that Freya had organised to help to set up a children's playground in the disused quarry not far from the village.

'You're going to fit in so well,' she said enthusiastically. 'You're going to enjoy living in our village.'

Maggie didn't say much, even when they stopped for a break. While Andrew and Jenny made small talk she sipped at the milk shake she had asked for and answered their questions about her favourite school subjects and her favourite singers politely. By the time they arrived home Jenny, too, had fallen silent, unable to think of anything else to say.

As soon as they got into the house Andrew took Maggie's cases up to her room, while Jenny phoned Helen to let her know that she could send Calum home.

'How was today?' her friend asked.

'A bit difficult.'

'That's not surprising. Give her time – all the time she needs,' Helen advised.

Maggie was in her room when Jenny went upstairs, standing at the window, looking out.

'I can see a river.'

'That's the Dee. It runs past the end of our garden. I hope the room's OK.'

Maggie's dark eyes surveyed the freshly papered walls, the curtains with their tiny bunches of bluebells, the two comfortable chairs and the desk in the corner. 'It's very nice.'

'If you'd prefer to choose your own colour scheme and your own furniture, we can do that.'

'It's fine, really.'

Jenny picked up one of the soft toys piled on the cushions at the head of the bed and fidgeted with it. 'My friend Ingrid and I made these specially for you – Ingrid's daughter Freya's got lots of them in her room. You'll meet Freya tomorrow, and Ella, her younger sister. Freya's round about your age and you're going to be in her class at the academy. I think you're going to become really good friends.'

'Cool,' Maggie said as the front door opened and then banged shut.

'Calum's home. He's so excited about having a big sister! Come and say hello.'

'Is it all right if I use the bathroom first?'

'Of course. This is your home now,' Jenny said, and went downstairs to greet her son.

'Mum!' Calum launched himself at her as she reached the bottom of the stairs. 'We've started to make a Viking village at school, it's our new project and today we were working on a Viking hut—'

He followed her into the kitchen, the words pouring out of him, then as Maggie came into the room his voice faded and he ducked his head down so that he was staring at his shoes.

'You remember Maggie, Calum. She's come to stay with us and be your sister.'

'Yes,' Calum said in a gruff voice, peeping up at Maggie from beneath an untidy fringe of light brown hair. 'Hi.'

'Hello.' Maggie gave him a warm smile. 'Tell me about this Viking village, then. We did that in school two years ago. I might be able to give you some ideas, OK?'

Maggie went to bed at the same time as Calum that evening, which was a bit of a relief to Jenny and Andrew. Once the dinner dishes were washed they settled in the living room with a glass of wine each. Andrew slumped on the couch while Jenny kicked off her shoes and curled up on the carpet, her head resting on his knee.

107

'It's been quite a day! I didn't realise that it would be so . . . difficult.'

'I told you, you've been so keen to make everything work smoothly that you talked yourself into thinking that it would. We all need time, especially Maggie, poor kid.'

'I so want her to be happy with us, Andrew! I want to give her the best life she could ever have!'

'Me too – and I want the same for Calum. But let's concentrate on taking everything one step at a time,' he was saying when the door opened and Maggie came in, wrapped in a fleecy blue dressing gown.

'I just wanted to say thank you.' She came across the room and knelt by Jenny's side. 'Thank you for everything.' Her lips were cool and soft against Jenny's cheek, and her skin smelled of soap.

'Thank you, love, for coming to stay with us,' Jenny said round the sudden lump that had formed in her throat.

Maggie rose gracefully and bent to drop a kiss on Andrew's cheek, then she stepped back and surveyed them both. 'It's going to be all right,' she said. 'Really it is. Good night.'

Then she was gone, and Jenny was scrubbing tears away with the back of one hand. 'Oh, Andrew, she's right. It's going to work,' she choked. 'Maggie's come home to me at last!'

Maggie went slowly up the stairs, step by step, the blue dressing gown floating about her legs, one hand trailing along the banister, and into her bedroom, closing the door quietly behind her.

She looked round the pretty room, and for a moment, a lump seemed to clog her throat. She swallowed it down hard, blinking her eyes fast to keep tears from filling them. She didn't want any of this fresh, clean prettiness, she just

108

wanted the familiar, shabby room she had known for most of her life. But she couldn't have it because Gramps had taken ill and Gran wanted to concentrate on him from now on. So goodbye, Maggie; it was fun but time to move on and let the oldies get on with their lives.

The lump had been swallowed down as far as her heart, where it lodged, hurting. She picked up one of the soft toys from the bed – a golden-haired girl dressed in jeans and a T-shirt – and punched the pretty, smiling face as hard as she could before throwing it across the room. It hit the wall with a soft thwack then fell to the floor. Maggie picked up the rest of the toys and drop-kicked them one by one into a corner before throwing herself across the bed.

She had been banished to Prior's Ford and like it or not, she was going to have to put up with her new life. She was on her own now, but no matter what the cost, she was going to be all right.

She would make sure of that.

She would!

On the following day, a surprisingly pleasant day for January, the McNairs' old car drove slowly into the Tarbethill farm-yard, avoiding the worst of the ruts and the puddles from the previous day, and came to a stop outside the kitchen door. Ewan jumped out and hurried round to the passenger seat to help Alison Greenlees to alight, then reached into the back seat to unfasten Jamie from his child seat. As he lifted the little boy out, Jess, wearing her best dress beneath a clean apron, opened the door. It wasn't often that the McNairs had visitors these days, and she had been as excited as her younger son when she heard that Alison Greenlees from the Neurotic Cuckoo had agreed to come for after-noon tea.

Now, standing unnoticed for the moment in the doorway, she was struck by the group before her. Ewan had just straightened, settling Jamie comfortably against one broad shoulder, while Alison reached out to touch her son's cheek. They looked for all the world like a family – and a perfect family at that, Jess thought as her son turned and caught sight of her.

'Here we are, Ma. Hope the kettle's on,' Ewan said with careful cheerfulness. It was the first time he had ever brought a girl home to tea and he felt very self-conscious about it.

'It is that. Come away in, lassie, it's cold to stand outside.' Jess ushered them all into the kitchen, fragrant with the smell of the rock cakes she had baked for the occasion. 'It's lovely to meet you, my dear.' She enfolded the girl's hand within her own large, work-roughened fingers, then turned to the little boy. 'And this is your Jamie. He's a bonny lad.'

Jamie had spotted Old Saul, who had been wakened by the noise and was blinking sleepily at the newcomers. 'Doggie!' he said in delight, then, 'Down!'

'Be careful, Jamie, don't bother the doggie,' his mother said anxiously.

'Old Saul doesnae mind bairns as long as they don't hurt him.' Ewan lowered the little boy to the ground, sorry to be rid of his burden, and Jamie promptly hurried over to Saul.

'Gently now, Jamie,' his mother cautioned, and he squatted down, one hand very carefully patting the old dog's head. Saul's tail fluttered against the rug.

'We've got kittens too, in the parlour. D'you want to come and see them?' Ewan held out his hand and Jamie bounced back to his feet and took it.

'Ewan's good with Jamie,' Alison said as the two of them disappeared.

'He's always had a gentle way with the young animals on the farm,' Jess said proudly. 'Take your coat off, m'dear and sit by the fire while I see to the tea.'

'Our Ewan's in love,' Jess said to her husband that night when Victor had gone off to visit his fiancée and Ewan had hurried down to the pub. 'Wi' that lassie that's moved intae the Neurotic Cuckoo with her parents.'

'Ye're haverin', woman. That lass has a wee bairn.'

'Aye, but she doesnae have a man. D'ye not mind me tellin' you that he was murdered in Glasgow? That's why they came here, to get her away from the memories. She's an awful nice girl, Bert, and the wee one's well behaved. You should see Ewan's face when he looks at the two of them – he worships them both.'

'He cannae afford tae fall in love wi' a woman who's already got a bairn,' Bert reached for his newspaper. 'The way things are goin' this farm'll not be able to support him and Victor, let alone wives and bairns.'

'Och Bert, you'd not wish the lad to be a bachelor all his life, surely!' Jess had enjoyed motherhood, and was reaching the age where becoming a grandmother appealed. She was keenly aware that Victor's lass, a town girl to her nail-polished fingertips, didn't have much for his family or his background, and sensed that she wouldn't see much of any children born to Janette. Their daughter Alice had two children, but she and her husband were busy with their own farm, and rarely free to visit Tarbethill. Now Jess's hopes tended to be pinned on Ewan.

'I'm bein' practical, Jess, an' so should you be. Tarbethill can scarce support the four of us, let alone anyone else,' Bert said bleakly before snapping the newspaper open and disappearing behind it.

111

14

The snow arrived on the first Friday in February, big white flakes falling slowly at first, like unexpected visitors unsure of their welcome, then gathering confidence and falling faster and faster. Soon a layer of white blanketed the ground, and by the time the school day was over and the children, who had been quite unable to concentrate on lessons all afternoon, burst into the playground, squealing with excitement, the snow was deep enough for them to enjoy snowball fights on their way home.

On Saturday morning snowmen began to appear in most back gardens and on the village green, and in the afternoon the McNairs' hilly field became a white canvas dotted with colourful warmly clad figures, adult as well as children, dragging sleds up to the top and then hurtling downhill on them before starting the whole business all over again.

The snow fell steadily for several days and when it finally stopped, the cold crisp air preserved it for two weeks. Bert McNair and his sons were kept busy making sure that sufficient food was taken out to the beasts still in the fields, and searching out pregnant ewes that had taken shelter by the stone walls and been buried by drifting snow.

By the time the thaw came most of the adults in the village were more than ready for it, though the children mourned when over the space of one single night the snowmen they had created began to change. Round heads softened to become part of the bodies, carrot noses tilted downwards, pipes slipped from melting mouths and battered old hats fell to the ground to lie in slushy puddles.

The white snow turned to a watery yellowing slush and cars had to drive carefully down the village street to avoid soaking pedestrians on the pavement.

Once the open countryside was passable the Reverend Naomi Hennessey topped several layers of warm clothes with an old waterproof coat, wrapped a bright red scarf about her neck, pulled a jade green knitted cap down over her ears and pushed her feet into knee-high Wellington boots before setting off for Alastair Marshall's cottage.

Alastair had been happily hibernating for two weeks in the knowledge that the weather would deter folk from seeking him out. Startled when someone knocked unexpectedly at his door, he hurriedly turned the painting he was working on to face the corner before answering the summons.

Naomi was in the small lean-to porch, brushing herself down. 'Fell trying to climb over the stile,' she said as Alastair appeared. 'I've got so many clothes on that I can't bend properly in the middle or at the knees and elbows. I feel like a penguin. Thank goodness you're in, I didn't fancy having to walk back without a break.' She waddled into the cottage and began to peel off the top layer of slush-soaked clothing.

'Hang your outer things by the side of the fire.' Alastair unfolded an elderly wooden clothes horse. 'Coffee?' Although he had enjoyed his solitude, he was delighted to see Naomi, one of his favourite people.

'Instant, please.'

'You're in luck, for that's all I've got – and it'll come in a mug.'

'Good!' She gave him a wide smile, her teeth gleaming white against her brown skin, and held her hands out towards the fire, sighing with pleasure.

'What brings you here on a day like this?' Alastair wanted to know when he returned to find the minister settled into the only armchair in the room. He handed a mug over and perched on a stool.

'Boredom – and Easter. I know that it's some time away yet, but I've been thinking of doing a special Easter Story family service and I wondered if you could do some pictures for me. Storyboarding, I think it might be called.' Naomi drank some coffee and released a second contented sigh. 'Just right – nice and strong. I've jotted down some ideas, and marked the places I thought you could illustrate. About half a dozen in all.'

She dug into her shoulder bag and produced some folded papers. Alastair glanced through them before putting them aside.

'I'll work out some sketches for you. OK?'

'That's grand. So what have you been doing during the big snow?'

'Working, mainly.'

'Any news from Clarissa?'

'The last I heard she was sunning herself in Honolulu and planning to head for Samoa next.'

'Good for her. She's a strong woman, is Clarissa Ramsay,'

Naomi said warmly, 'I admire her. The first time I visited her after she was widowed she was so fragile that I wasn't sure if she could get her life back on track, but she certainly has.' Then, fixing her dark eyes on him, 'I suspect that you had something to do with that.'

Alastair's long face coloured slightly. 'Not really. I taught her how to drive, that's all.'

'That alone helped her to have faith in herself. We need to have faith in ourselves. It's not fair to leave it all on the Lord's shoulders, in my opinion. And you also showed her that she had a good friend in you – don't deny it. Folk need friends, especially when they've been traumatised. You helped her to heal herself, Alastair, so much so that less than a year later, she's off to see the world. I'm glad she's decided to settle here in Prior's Ford when she returns from her travels.'

'Mmm.' Alastair went to the big wooden log box he kept by the fire and laid two logs on top of the flames. Naomi watched him thoughtfully, then finished her coffee and heaved her sturdy body out of the chair.

'Time to head back.'

'Stay for a while – have another coffee.'

'I'd love to, but I've a sermon to write, and Ethan will be home from school soon, looking for food. He's always looking for food. And when I've fed him, he just starts looking for food again. Now I know what mother birds feel like with fledglings in the nest. I've only got one, with his beak permanently open – I don't know how the parent birds can cope with several youngsters.' With Alastair's help, Naomi began to haul on the clothes she had taken off when she came in, then she stumped to the door, pausing before opening it.

'I can't leave without making a confession. I'm a nosy

115

woman and while you were making that very welcome mug of coffee I took a peek at that sketchbook. The one with all the drawings of Clarissa Ramsay.' She nodded to where the book lay open on the table, and again, Alastair's thin face flushed.

'She put a photograph of herself into one of her letters, and I liked the colours,' he said gruffly. 'Her dress, and the flowers in the background – I don't usually do portraits, so I thought I'd try my hand at a few sketches. It's just an exercise; I'm going to throw them away.'

'Don't do that – you've got Clarissa down to a T; not just her likeness, but her warmth and that gentle sense of humour she has. You should give them to her as a welcome-home gift.'

'She wouldn't want those daft wee drawings!'

'I think you're wrong. She values your friendship – why else would she write to you?'

'That's just because she wants to keep in contact with the village. I'm supposed to write to her once a month to keep her up to date with the news, but I'm not much of a letter writer. It ought to be someone like you who writes to her,' Alastair said hopefully.

'I write sermons and she wouldn't want that. In any case, she asked you to keep in touch, not me.'

'But I don't know what to say! It's different for you – and Clarissa. You've both got more education than me, and you're both used to words. I'm not.'

'I hadn't thought of that. Teachers and ministers use words, artists like you speak through pictures, while dancers,' Naomi said, warming to her theme, 'speak with their feet and their bodies and singers use their voices. I do believe that I'm beginning to get an idea for my next sermon. Thank you, Alastair, for the coffee and the company. And the idea for a sermon.'

Trudging through the melting snow on her way home, she could still see, in her mind's eye, the sketches she had found in Alastair's book. She had been struck at once by what they said about the subject – and the artist. Clarissa Ramsay was in her late fifties while Alastair Marshall, in his early thirties, was young enough to be her son. But despite the differences in their ages they had formed a close friendship – a friendship that Naomi suspected was more than that, on Alastair's side at least.

She struggled over the stile, this time managing it without falling into the slush, and leaned back against the wet wood for a moment to catch her breath.

'Is it so wrong?' she asked the lowering grey sky, as she often did. 'Isn't loving someone more important than being of a suitable age? Well, I think it is. Lord, I don't like to see good people hurt and I don't think you do either. Be good to them both when the time comes, whichever way things turn out.'

Helen's interview with Meredith Whitelaw appeared as a double spread in the *Dumfries News* soon after the New Year, complete with three photographs; one of Meredith sitting in Willow Cottage's living room, one of her supposedly cooking in the kitchen, wooden spoon in manicured hand, and the third a publicity photograph of her in her role of Imogen Goldberg, the late matriarch of that well-known television soap opera, *Bridlington Close*.

The newspaper photographer sent to Prior's Ford had asked Bob Green, the chief reporter, not to send him on any more jobs involving glamorous television stars.

'Talk about being particular,' he said, still shell-shocked by the memory. 'Give me an agricultural fair any day! At least the cows don't keep going on about their best

117

side, and rushing off to change their clothes every two minutes!'

Helen couldn't even wait to go home before opening her copy of the *News* when it arrived in the village store. She opened it with trembling fingers, fumbling through the pages until she got to her article. *Celebrity in Prior's Ford* the headline read, with a subheading of *Meredith Whitelaw of Bridlington Close fame chooses Prior's Ford for a long holiday.* And then came the magic words – *By Helen Campbell.*

'Oh, my goodness! Here, take it!' She thrust the paper at Ingrid, who was with her, and reached out to a shelf to steady herself. 'Oh, look at that!'

'It's very nice, and your name looks good in print. Do you want me to read it out to you?'

'No, not here, it's too long. I'll look at it at home. I hope Miss Whitelaw likes it.'

'Of course she will – it's publicity and all public figures love publicity, even bad publicity unless it's very bad – and this isn't,' Ingrid added swiftly. 'Buy several copies while it's here. You'll want to send it to your family, and friends.'

'Good idea,' Helen said, and left the shop with half a dozen copies of the newspaper. At home she read it slowly several times; it seemed to be all right, but her hand trembled as she dialled the number for Willow Cottage.

'Do you know, she's not at all bad for a beginner,' Meredith was saying at that moment. She and Ginny were each reading a copy of the newspaper.

'She's not a beginner, she's written quite a lot of things for the paper.'

'You know what I mean, darling – she's not a professional, is she?'

'She could be. This is good. Shall I get that?' Ginny asked as the phone shrilled.

118

'I will, while you pour me a glass of wine.' Meredith picked up the phone. 'This is Meredith Whitelaw speaking . . . Oh, Helen, my dear . . . yes, I've just read it, as a matter of fact . . .very nice, dear, not bad at all for a local newspaper . . .'

Ginny, on her way to the kitchen to fetch the wine, rolled her eyes to the heavens.

15

The committee first set up by Glen Mason, then landlord of the Neurotic Cuckoo, to fight the proposed quarry reopening, had been known as the Prior's Ford Protest Committee. Now, with Robert Kavanagh in the chair, it was known as the Prior's Ford Progress Committee. Its main concern for the moment was the installation of a small playground at the quarry.

The committee met in the village hall in February, gathering round the table in a back room used only weeks earlier as the dressing room for the pantomime.

'Young Freya's given me a list of items for the playground agreed on by the children's committee, with each one costed.' Robert passed copies round the table to the other committee members. 'All very well laid out, as you'll see. And she's provided the list of websites they used.'

'I'm impressed – we have some efficient young people in this village.' Naomi Hennessey's peacock green sweater, scarlet woollen skirt and sparkling white smile brought a welcome splash of colour to the rather drab appearance of her fellow committee members. She looked, Robert thought with a rare flash of imagination, like a bird of paradise among a flock of wood pigeons.

'That it, then?' Lachie Wilkins asked hopefully. He'd promised to join some of the lads at the Neurotic Cuckoo that evening to get in some darts practice.

'Almost. Our next step is to find someone to do the work for us, and to find out what they'll charge for it.'

'I might be able to help you there, Bob.' Doug Borland, a large, cheerful man, was the village butcher and a recent addition to the committee. 'My lad Derek plays golf with a man who's got a small construction firm. I remember Derek telling his mum about some school playground this lad worked on. He might be worth speaking to.'

'We'd appreciate it if you could find out.'

'I'll arrange for him to see the site and then meet with the committee as soon as he can. We won't get the playground up and running for Easter, but it should be ready for the summer holidays, all going well.'

'Ah.' Robert cleared his throat, then said carefully, 'I think we should aim for the autumn. No sense in rushing it, is there?'

'Surely we can do it sooner than that.'

Robert clasped his hands together on the table. 'Helen, minute the meeting as closed, will you? What I'm about to say can't be recorded, or go any further than this room for the time being.' He let his gaze travel round the table, looking into every face for a few seconds before moving on. 'I mean it – not a word even to your families. I need your solemn promise on that.'

Eyes widened, and everyone leaned forward, huddling together and changing without realising it from a committee to a group of conspirators.

'What on earth is it, Robert?' Naomi asked.

'I need your solemn promises.'

'You've got them – hasn't he?' Naomi appealed to her fellow committee members. 'We surely don't have to mingle our blood or roll up our trouser legs, do we?'

'I'm serious! It's about the quarry.'

'It's haunted?' guessed Pete McDermott, then his grin faded as Robert snapped, 'Look, if you're going to treat what I'm about to tell you as a joke, I might as well shut up!'

'Sorry – go on, tell us. We'll all keep our mouths shut.'

Robert drew a deep breath, then said, 'It's peregrine falcons.'

'What is?' Naomi asked blankly.

'It's the quarry's secret. A pair of peregrine falcons nest there.'

'You're kidding!' Pete said incredulously, then as Robert shook his head, 'But that's bl— Sorry, Naomi. That's marvellous!'

'It is?'

'They're rare,' Pete explained. 'Well, not as rare as they used to be, but it's still great to have them in the area. When did you find this out, Robert?'

'It was Marcy Copleton who found out, not me. Young Jimmy McDonald that delivers papers for the village store saw a picture of a peregrine falcon on the cover of a magazine that Sam orders for me, and he told Marcy that he'd seen birds like that at the quarry. Marcy came to me and I contacted Scottish Natural Heritage. They checked it out, and it looks as though we've had a pair nesting there for a year or two at least, but nobody knew but the kids. And they weren't that bothered – to them, it was just a couple of big birds they saw from time to time.'

'But they play in the quarry. Wouldn't that bother the falcons?' Helen asked.

'Not necessarily. They like to nest somewhere high, and the sheer cliffs in the quarry are ideal, but they don't seem to mind noise providing it was there when they chose the site. Apparently peregrines have been known to nest on the sides of steeples in the middle of towns, and I've been told that a pair actually nest every year in a working quarry in this area, though their eyrie's far enough away from the worst of the noise. I'd a casual word with young Jimmy, and from what he said, our falcons,' Robert spoke the words with pride, 'are at the opposite side of the quarry from where the youngsters play, in a sort of a niche nobody ever visits.'

'So putting the playground equipment in the area where the kids play won't bother the birds?' Lachie Wilkins asked.

'Apparently not, Lachie. As long as we don't try to do any installation work while they're in residence. They're due to arrive early in March; that's the start of their breeding season. We could never get the work done by then, so,' Robert emphasised, looking round the table, 'we're going to have to wait until their young become independent, in September. We need to take our time when it comes to buying the equipment, and getting the quote for installation. Fortunately, the money doesn't have a spending time limit on it, and we don't want to rush at the job in any case. If something's worth doing, it's worth doing well. And I don't think that the youngsters will object to having the quarry as it is for one more summer.'

'These birds'll be a tourist attraction, won't they?' Pete asked, and Robert nodded.

'That's another piece of good news. The Scottish Natural Heritage people are looking at the possibility of setting up a hide, and even a web cam, but again, that can't happen before the autumn. And until we know that the birds won't be disturbed in any way, we can't let anyone know that they're here. We don't want greedy idiots harming themselves in an effort to climb the quarry walls to steal eggs. Or, even worse, fledglings. There are a lot of nutters about.'

'Lucky the quarry didn't start up again,' the butcher commented. 'That'd have driven the birds away for sure.'

'That's the reason the quarry folk changed their minds – when they were told about the falcons. Mind you,' Robert said, 'they gave in so easily that I reckon they were having second thoughts in any case. Right, then, that's it. But mind now,' he added as they began to push chairs back, 'Not a word to anyone until the SNH give us the all clear.'

As Robert Kavanagh divulged the quarry secret to his committee, Kevin Pearce was perched on the edge of a fireside chair in Willow Cottage, his eyes glued on Meredith Whitelaw, who lounged gracefully opposite.

Kevin could also have lounged comfortably, for the chair was certainly large enough to accommodate his skinny shanks, but his instinct was to get as near to the object of his adoration as possible; hence his rather uncomfortable perching, with his feet planted firmly on the carpet for balance.

'Good choice, Kevin,' Meredith was saying, gesturing at the three booklets on her lap. 'You have a really good sense of theatre.'

Kevin's happy blush spread from beneath his shirt collar to the very top of his balding head. 'Oh – it wasn't just me. The committee were involved as well.'

'But as di-rect-or' – as always, Meredith's rich voice gave the word its three syllables, weighting it with responsibility, and causing Kevin to squirm with pleasure – 'you would of course have the final word. And I think that those three plays will complement each other very well.'

'We usually do a full-length play in June, but this year we thought that we'd ring the changes, so to speak, with those three one-acts.'

'More work for you, though I sense that you give of yourself unstintingly,' Meredith purred. 'Even the amateur theatre can have its dedicated thespians, thin on the ground though they are. You, Kevin, are one of that very small but select group.'

'You're too kind, Meredith. But I was wondering' – Kevin's Adam's apple bounced up and down as he swallowed nervously – 'if you would honour us by agreeing to direct one of the plays.'

'Me?' Meredith's rings flashed fire at him as she spread one hand across her most attractive bosom. 'Oh, my goodness, this is a surprise!'

'I just thought – we just thought – that since we have such an illustrious visitor in our little village, getting you to work with the drama group would be a real feather in our caps.'

'But my dear man, I came here to rest from the rigours of starring for such a long time in a television programme. You have no idea how exhausting these soap operas can be. All I wanted when I rented this quaint little house was to be treated as an ordinary person for once in my life.'

'Oh.' Kevin's shoulders slumped. 'Yes, I quite understand. The last thing we want is to deny you your well-earned rest. I'll explain to the—'

'But on the other hand, you have all been so sweet to me, and so considerate, that I should put my own needs aside and show my appreciation in the only way that I, as a professional and experienced actress, can. Kevin, I will direct one of your plays, with pleasure.'

'Really?' In his excitement his voice shot up into a squeak, and he hurriedly got it back under control. 'But that's wonderful! So kind! Are you quite sure?'

'Quite sure. For you, and for Prior's Ford.' Meredith leaned forward and rested a hand briefly on his knee. 'Now then, which play shall I choose?'

'I thought—'

'This one, I think. *Reunion.* The one about the former school sweethearts who find each other again after years of hardship. Quite a good little piece. When are you holding auditions?'

'Oh, the three plays were cast before the pantomime was staged, to save time.'

Meredith raised an eyebrow. 'And who do I work with?'

'Cynthia and Gilbert MacBain – they've both been in amateur drama for years and they're our two stalwarts. Gilbert played the wicked uncle in the pantomime, and Cynthia was the duchess.'

Meredith's beautifully plucked eyebrows shot up. 'Aren't they both rather . . . mature for the roles in *Reunion*?'

'A little, perhaps, but Cynthia's amazingly good at playing any age onstage. And we thought that we would tinker with the lines just a little bit, to add several years on to the gap between leaving school and meeting up again.'

'Mmm. Quite a few years would have to be added, don't you think? Well, we'll see, won't we? Now, about *Visiting Vanessa*,' Meredith tapped a finger against another of the books on her lap, 'I like that play – I like it very much. So much so that I have a very special surprise for you, Kevin. I would like to play the part of Vanessa. I know what you're thinking,' she swept on as he stared at her, his mouth falling open. 'I am a professional actress, and professionals do not appear in amateur productions. But after years of television I have a fancy for treading the boards again, and it would be such fun for us to work together, you as di-rec-tor, and Meredith Whitelaw as your star. If you're worrying about the responsibility, you needn't. I promise to give you your place and do just as you tell me.'

'But – I – we would be delighted, of course. It's just that – the play is already cast. Cynthia has been given the part of Vanessa.'

'Oh, but she's going to be much too busy with my play,' Meredith said crisply. 'As you have said, the part is rather young for her, and she'll have to work hard to satisfy me. I'm sure you'll be able to explain that to her in a way that she will accept.' Meredith dropped her voice and added, huskily, 'Together, Kevin, you and I will set the stage on fire! We will give the good folk of Prior's Ford the best entertainment they have ever seen in their own village hall. We will— Ah, here comes Genevieve at last,' she added as her daughter arrived, unbuttoning her coat. 'There you are, dear. I was just about to offer Kevin some coffee.'

'Isn't it lucky that I came in at just the right time?' Ginny said blandly, smiling at them both. 'Black or white, Mr Pearce?'

'Not for me, thank you.' Kevin was scrambling to his feet. 'I really must be getting home.'

'What have you done now, Mother?' Ginny wanted to know when she came back from showing him out. 'He looked as though he had been kicked in the stomach.'

'Nonsense, he was just taken by surprise. He asked me to direct one of the three little plays his drama group are performing in June.'

'You didn't accept, did you? Surely that sort of thing's far below Meredith Whitelaw!'

'I did accept, as it happens. And' – Meredith handed one of the plays to her daughter – 'I'm going to star in that one.'

'*Visiting Vanessa.*' Ginny ran her eyes over the brief resume on the back of the book. 'You're going to play the part of an old lady being visited in her nursing home by the family she hates? You must be desperate!'

'No, just a little bit bored. I need some fun in my life, and if this is the only way to get it, then so be it. You smell of alcohol,' Meredith added as she took the book from her daughter.

'One pint of lager, nothing more than that, in the Neurotic Cuckoo with Lewis Ralston-Kerr and some of his friends.'

'Drinking in public houses is common.'

'Drinking alone on one's own at home is dangerous,' Ginny returned sweetly, collecting a used glass from the sideboard as she made for the door. 'Coffee, did you say? Black?'

'I don't know what Cynthia's going to say,' Kevin fretted to his wife when he got home.

'Yes you do, and so do I. She's going to be furious. And I can't say that I blame her,' Elinor said calmly. The book she had been reading when her husband arrived lay on her lap, with one finger marking her place. 'Why on earth did you agree to this idea of Meredith Whitelaw's?'

'Because she's *Meredith Whitelaw*! Think of the publicity I'll . . . we'll get,' Kevin corrected himself hastily as Elinor raised an eyebrow, 'with a famous actress appearing in our local show. How could I say no to *Meredith Whitelaw*?'

'Well, let's just hope that Cynthia understands that it is

a far, far better thing she has been asked to do etc.,' Elinor finished as her husband glared at her.

'You wouldn't?'

'No, dear, I wouldn't. You're the president, and the director. It's your place to explain things to Cynthia. And to the others. Cynthia has her following in the club, you know. They might not like what's happened either.'

Poor Kevin, she thought, as he nodded gloomily. He had backed himself into a corner, and now he was going to have to talk himself out of it again. And knowing Kevin, she reckoned that the more he talked, the bigger the hole he would dig for himself.

16

In his isolated cottage, Alastair was struggling to write a letter to Clarissa Ramsay. She wrote to him every fortnight, keeping him informed of her travels and giving him an address, each time, where she could collect his next letter. Hers were pages of vivid description, written in such an easy style that the words seemed to rise effortlessly from the paper. It was as though she was speaking to him. He read them over and over again, never tiring of them.

It was all right for her, he thought gloomily, eyeing the half page that had taken him the best part of an hour. She was well educated, and she had been a teacher. Words were part of her life, as natural to her as breathing.

He stared into the log fire, tapping the end of his biro against his front teeth. There wasn't even much to write about. The pantomime, the snow – both seemed so trite compared to the places Clarissa was visiting. If only he had more skill with words!

'Teachers and ministers use words,' he recalled Naomi saying. 'Artists speak through pictures . . .'

Perhaps if he sketched some scenes from the pantomime it would help him to find the words. He reached for the sketchbook that was never far from his hand, turned to a fresh page, and began to draw.

Some time later, aware of feeling cold, he blinked around the room to discover that the fire had dulled down to a blanket of glowing ash. Glancing at his watch, he was astonished to discover that it was almost midnight.

'Flippin' heck!' he said, and his empty stomach rumbled a grumpy agreement. Hurrying to the kitchen, he put the kettle on and started to slice bread.

In the morning, still tousled from sleep, he glanced over the three pages he had been working on the night before. They were covered with tiny coloured sketches, one page depicting scenes from the village pantomime, another showing a snow-covered hill dotted with tiny colourful figures, trudging uphill, dragging sledges behind them, others sweeping joyfully downhill on board their vehicles, having snowball fights, and building snowmen.

The third page held miniature scenes in the village itself – tiny people heading for the church on a Sunday morning, children playing on the green, a figure that was meant to be Alastair himself, surrounded by children in a school classroom during an art lesson, women chatting outside the village store – and one little sketch of Willow Cottage.

'Flippin' heck,' he said again. His half-page letter was still on the table; he took up his biro, read what he had written so far – which wasn't much – and then glanced back at the sketches. Then he scribbled on the letter, *Sorry, I'm rotten at letters. Naomi said I speak through pictures, so hope these will do. Cheers, Alastair.*

Swiftly, before he could change his mind, he folded the

three pages, added the letter, found an envelope and stuffed the lot into it.

Once in the village he hesitated before going into the store, wondering if he should go home and have another shot at writing a proper letter, then he shrugged and marched into the store and up to the Post Office counter.

For once, he was glad that Marcy Copleton no longer lived in the village; if Marcy, an outgoing, friendly woman, had been behind the glass she would probably have glanced at the name on the envelope and asked how Clarissa was getting on. But Sam Brennan, never a particularly talkative man, had retreated even further into his shell since Marcy walked out on him. He merely took the envelope, weighed it and collected Alastair's money without comment, which suited Alastair very well.

Neither fully realised it, and neither would have admitted it, but they shared a bond – both were missing a woman who had come into their lives, changed them for ever, and then left. And both were lost and confused.

On the way out of the store, Alastair literally bumped into Jenny Forsyth, who dropped her umbrella.

'Sorry.' He picked it up and handed it to her.

'It was my fault – I wasn't watching where I was going.'

'Are you all right?' Alastair asked.

'Fine – just busy, you know how it is,' Jenny said vaguely, and hurried off before he could ask any questions. She had been due at Helen's for coffee twenty minutes ago, but this morning her mind was all over the place.

'What's wrong?' Helen asked as soon as she opened the door.

'Nothing. Just a busy morning, that's all.' Jenny followed her into the living room. Ingrid had already arrived.

'Jenny, don't mess about,' she said crisply. 'You're worried about something – or coming down with something.'

132

'It's Maggie.' Jenny sank into a chair; as she sipped at the cup of coffee Helen thrust into her hand her friends exchanged glances over her bent head.

'She seemed all right when she was in our house yesterday,' Ingrid said. 'A nice girl — a bit quiet, but she's still settling in. Is she having problems at school?'

'No, she seems to be settling into her new school very well. It's just . . .' Jenny took another sip of coffee. 'She said from the start that she would look after her own bedroom, to save me extra work. She even changes her bed, and puts her washing in the laundry basket. When it's ironed, I put it on the little table on the upstairs landing. Andrew and I respect her need for privacy.'

'Quite right,' Ingrid approved.

'It's just that — this morning I was putting the ironing away, and without thinking I took Maggie's into her room. And . . .' She gulped, then said, 'All those nice soft toys we made for her were gone.'

'Gone where?' Helen wanted to know.

'I found them in her wardrobe, crammed any old how into a corner. And a picture Andrew took not long after she arrived, of her and me and Calum, was pushed in there as well. The only photographs she has on show are of her and her father, and her grandparents. It's as if she's swept us under the carpet.'

'No, into the wardrobe,' Ingrid said in her matter-of-fact way. 'And it probably means that she's got a tidy nature.'

'Perhaps she doesn't like to have too many things lying about her room,' Helen offered.

'But why didn't she tell me? I would have taken the toys out.'

'She wouldn't want to seem ungrateful. If I were you,' Ingrid said, 'I would forget what you saw and tell nobody,

133

especially Maggie. I hope you took the ironing back out and put it on the table as usual?'

'Yes, I did.'

'Good. I'm sure you have nothing to worry about.'

'Well, if you really think so. I expect it's just being unused to having a daughter around that's making me jumpy. I mean I put those soft toys in her room because I know that Freya loves having them.'

'But Ella, on the other hand, would be furious if I tried to put any in her room,' Ingrid pointed out. 'She used to throw her teddy bear out of her pram when she was a baby. No two children are alike.'

'Amen to that,' Helen agreed fervently.

Jenny drank her coffee, feeling comforted; but even as they reassured her, Ingrid and Helen exchanged meaningful glances above her head.

Even though Kevin tried to break the news as gently as he could, Cynthia MacBain did not react well to being told that she was no longer playing the part of Vanessa in *Visiting Vanessa*.

'But I auditioned for the part, and you and the other people on the auditions committee gave it to me because nobody else is as good as I am.' Cynthia was small and slender, with short curly brown hair. She looked younger than her forty years, which made it possible for her, with clever use of make-up, to play a wide range of ages. 'You can't just suddenly turn up here and tell me that I'm not wanted!'

'Of course you're wanted, Cynthia; you're our leading actress, and you have been for as long as I've been in Prior's Ford Drama Group—'

'Longer than that, actually, Cynthia's a founder member

134

of the group,' Gilbert MacBain pointed out. 'She was born here.'

'And Meredith Whitelaw's only been here for a matter of weeks, so why take the part from me and give it to her?'

'It's not a matter of taking it from you,' Kevin floundered, wishing that he hadn't chosen to sit on the sofa. It was very soft and his knees were almost on a level with his chin, giving him the feeling of being trapped. 'As you know, Meredith's taken an interest in our little group from the start, and she asked to read the three play scripts. Now she's kindly agreed to direct *Reunion* for us, and so I thought— She thought . . .' Kevin's voice tailed away under the pressure of two stony gazes, then he took a deep breath and plunged on. 'The thing is, she expressed a wish to tread the boards again, so to speak, and she thought— She was really keen on the part of Vanessa.'

'And you told her,' Gilbert said icily, 'that the play had already been cast, and my wife given the part. Which, I may add, she has studied so thoroughly that she is already almost word perfect.'

'I did say that all three plays had been cast, but we thought that perhaps you might be gracious enough to step back and allow Meredith to take the part, Cynthia. It would be quite a coup for our little drama group to have a television star appear in one of our performances. And she is only here for a year.'

'Would I be correct in assuming that you have already agreed to this preposterous situation?' Cynthia was a secondary school teacher, and rumour had it that when roused to anger in the classroom she could set burly teenage boys quaking. For the first time, Kevin began to realise that the rumour was true. Her grey eyes had turned to ice, as had her voice, and one slim hand was toying with the gold

135

chain about her throat as though she longed to tear it off and use it to strangle Kevin. He gulped noisily before saying, 'Well, I suppose I have.'

'I see.' She sounded like a judge passing sentence.

'Now look here, Kevin, you can't just come in here and expect my wife to—'

'Leave it, Gilbert!' Cynthia's voice had a sudden whip-like crack to it that made both men jump, or, in Kevin's case, bounce on the sofa cushions. 'Kevin's mind has been made up and there seems little point in the three of us wasting any more time in this conversation. I expect that Kevin's in a hurry to get back home.'

'Oh. Yes.' He started to scramble from the sofa. 'I'm sure that you'll enjoy being directed by Meredith in *Reunion*,' he offered breathlessly when he had managed to get to his feet.

'I won't be appearing in *Reunion*, Kevin. Nor will Gilbert.'

'But who else—?'

'That,' Cynthia said, sweeping to the door, 'is not our problem. Gilbert and I are going to take a leaf from Ms Whitelaw's book and *rest* for a season. No doubt she can find other dismissed actors to fill our roles. Goodnight, Kevin.'

Meredith had chosen to stay away from the drama club rehearsal immediately following her decision to take over the lead part in *Visiting Vanessa*, possibly realising that the news might receive a mixed reaction – as indeed it did.

As soon as Kevin entered the village hall he knew that everyone was aware of what had happened. There was an air of excited tension about the place, and the MacBains' closest allies were gathered together in one corner, murmuring and casting dark looks at him.

He stripped off his coat and scarf and clapped his hands to summon everyone's attention. 'Gather round, people. As you may have already heard,' he said briskly, trying not to shy away as they surged towards him, 'there have been some changes to our programme. The first is that Meredith Whitelaw, stage and television actress, is going to tread our boards. She is playing the part of Vanessa in *Visiting Vanessa*.'

The subdued murmur of interest and pleasure was drowned out by one of Cynthia's admirers, who wanted to know, 'And what about Cynthia MacBain? She auditioned for the part – and she got it.'

'Cynthia has very kindly agreed to step down on this occasion to make way for Meredith. After all,' Kevin said loudly against a buzz of voices, 'Meredith is only here for one year, and it's a feather in our cap to have her in one of our plays. She plans to invite some of her famous friends to the show, which could help us a lot as far as publicity's concerned.'

'There's no denying that,' someone agreed.

'But it's not fair on Cynthia!'

'She's agreed to step down, hasn't she? What's done is done. We should just get on with it. We don't have much time as it is.'

'There's another announcement,' Kevin broke in. 'Meredith is going to direct *Reunion*.'

'With Cynthia and Gilbert in it?'

'Well, no – they've decided to take some time off from the drama club.'

'I don't blame them,' one of Cynthia's closest friends, and the woman Kevin planned to cast in *Reunion* in Cynthia's place, said loudly, 'I hope you're not expecting me to help you out, Kevin, because I won't.'

137

Kevin hurriedly announced that they would concentrate on the third play that evening, and during the tea break he canvassed the more experienced club members in the hope of finding replacements for *Reunion*, but without success. They were either too busy learning the parts they already had in the other two plays, or they didn't want to offend Cynthia and Gilbert.

'I can't go with just two plays – they won't fill the evening,' he agonised to Elinor, 'and we haven't time to find another play.'

'What about young Ewan McNair?'

'He's only played small parts – he's not got enough experience.'

'That's because you haven't given him the chance. He was good in last year's pantomime, and he learned his lines very quickly, as you may remember. And he's the right age group for that play, not to mention being quite easy on the eye. Ask him,' Elinor urged as Kevin hesitated. 'Beggars can't be choosers.'

As he reluctantly made his way over to Ewan, who had a small part in the third play, *Curses, Foiled Again!*, she sighed, wishing that Kevin had the sense to see that Meredith Whitelaw's meddling with the drama group had begun to have a knock-on effect, like a row of dominoes set up to be toppled. She had a nasty feeling that in this case, her husband might find himself standing at the end of the long row, and that all the dominoes might fall on him.

Ewan McNair had got into the habit of making his mother's egg delivery to the village store whenever he could be spared from his normal farm work. Each time, after the delivery was made, he called in at the pub for a half pint of lager and a chat with Alison, who was often on duty in the bar in the mornings.

On the morning following the rehearsal he made the usual egg delivery and then hurried across the green to the Neurotic Cuckoo, where he laid a small book on the bar. 'I thought you might like to look at this.'

'What is it?' Alison opened it, then glanced at him, eyebrows raised. 'A play?'

'It's a one-act play the drama group's rehearsing, and Meredith Whitelaw's going to direct it.'

Her brown eyes widened. 'Meredith Whitelaw? That's fantastic!'

'Yes. The thing is,' Ewan forged on after taking a fortifying gulp from the drink she had served him, 'this play's about two folk who meet up at a class reunion. The people who were cast for the play wo— can't be in it now, so Kevin Pearce asked me last night to step into the breach.'

'But that's wonderful, Ewan – having the chance to be directed by a professional like Meredith Whitelaw! I hope you agreed.'

'I don't have much choice, really. Kevin was very insistent but I'm scared witless. I've not done much acting—'

'I'm sure you'll be fine! I look forward to seeing you on the stage.'

The drink didn't seem to be helping to ease Ewan's dry throat. He swallowed, then said, 'You said once that you had been in a drama club too.'

'That's right – before Jamie was born. D'you want help with your lines?' Alison offered. 'It's no bother.'

Ewan took another drink then wiped his mouth with the back of his hand. 'What I'd really like is for you to play Elspeth, opposite me.'

139

Alison stared at him. 'Me?' she said, then shook her head, dropping the book to the counter and pushing it towards him. 'No. No, I couldn't possibly.'

'Your mum said you were one of the leading lights in your club.'

'But that was ages ago, before— No, I couldn't get back up on a stage.'

'Please, Alison,' he was so desperate that he reached across the bar and took her hand in his without realising what he was doing. 'I've only played small parts before, apart from the pantomime before last, but that was different. There's only the two folk in this play and I'm that nervous about doing it, but Kevin says he hasn't got anyone else to ask. I'm the bottom of the barrel as you might say, but I think I might be able to do it if you were there with me. We could help each other. We could rehearse on our own between rehearsal nights if you like.'

'Ewan, I really don't think—'

'Will you just take the play and read it? Don't say no until you've read it – please!' He was openly begging now.

She hesitated, teeth nibbling at her lower lip, then reluctantly, she took the play back. 'I'll read it, but I'm not promising anything,' she said.

17

Jenny was busy making a cheese sauce when the doorbell rang.

'That'll be the milk boy looking for the week's money. Could you pay him, Maggie? I daren't leave this sauce or it'll go lumpy. You know where the money is – in that glass dish on the shelf beneath the telephone.'

Maggie, sitting at the kitchen table reading a magazine, got to her feet and trotted out of the kitchen, only to return almost at once. 'The money's not there.'

'Yes it is. I put it there this morning same as I always do on a Friday. The exact amount.'

'It's not there – honest!'

'Are you sure you looked in the right place?'

'That glass ashtray sort of thing with the blue rim, right?' Maggie's voice had a slight edge of irritation to it. 'I'm not stupid.'

'I didn't say you were – stir this for me, will you? And keep stirring or it'll go lumpy.' Jenny handed the pot and ladle over and hurried to the hall, where the milkman waited on the front doorstep.

'Afternoon – it's a bit parky out here,' he greeted her.

'Sorry, I won't be a minute.' She glanced into the glass dish, which was indeed empty, then went to the living room to fetch her bag. She distinctly remembered counting out the exact change that morning, and the memory was reinforced when she glanced into her purse and saw that all it held now was a twenty-pound note and a few coins. She had had quite a struggle to get together enough change to pay for the week's milk delivery.

The milkman sighed when the note was offered. 'Haven't you got anything smaller, love?'

'No. I'm really sorry,' she apologised as he began to scrabble in his worn leather bag.

'I don't understand it,' Jenny said when the man had gone and she was free to return to the kitchen. 'I distinctly remember putting the money out this morning – it was almost all the change I had. What could have happened to it?'

'Don't look at me – I didn't take it,' Maggie instantly went on the defensive.

'Oh, Maggie, I didn't think that for a minute!' Jenny said, horrified, and then, in a clumsy attempt to balance things up, 'Calum, you didn't take it, did you?'

Calum, who had come thundering down the stairs while his mother was talking to the milkman, set down the bottle of orange juice he had been carefully pouring out. 'Take what?'

'The money I left out for the milkman.'

'Course not!' He, too, looked hurt.

'Of course you didn't – neither of you. Perhaps I only thought I'd put it out earlier. Sometimes when you're used to doing something, you think you've done it when you haven't done it at all,' Jenny said, and felt terrible when Maggie gave her a hurt glance before leaving the kitchen. Only seconds later, Calum did the same.

And when she looked into the saucepan she saw that the cheese sauce had gone lumpy beyond all hope of recovery.

Gracie Fisher poured out second cups of tea for herself and her daughter. 'You go for it, Alison.'

'I don't know, Mum. It's years since I've done any acting.'

'But you were good at it – you enjoyed it, you can't deny that. And you need to get out and meet folk, and have some interests. You can't spend the rest of your life in here with us.'

'I'm not exactly a free agent,' Alison pointed out swiftly. 'I've got Jamie now.'

'And you've got us to help you to look out for him. It'll be good for him to have a mother who mixes with folk. It's not healthy for a woman to devote every minute of her life to her kids. You said you liked the play, didn't you?'

'Yes, but—'

'And Ewan's desperate for you to be in it with him.'

'There are other girls who could do it.'

'That's not what he told me when he was in the bar last night. They're doing three plays and everyone in the drama club's needed. The poor lad said he'd only agreed to take that part in the hope that you'd come into the play as well. He's scared stiff about working with Meredith Whitelaw.'

'You think I wouldn't be scared stiff about that myself?'

'But you could give each other support, Alison. Anyway, you're a grand actress; you'll be all right. If you won't do it for Ewan, or for yourself, do it for me,' Gracie coaxed. 'Think of the pleasure it'll give me to be able to write to your Auntie Beryl and tell her that you're working with Meredith Whitelaw from *Bridlington Close*!'

'But what if Ms Whitelaw doesn't think that I'm good enough for the part.'

'She will,' Gracie said confidently. 'Oh, she will!'

On the following evening Ewan, scrubbed, shaved and dressed in his best suit called at the pub for Alison, and the two of them, clutching their scripts, walked the short distance to Willow Cottage.

'I'm terrified,' she said as he opened the gate.

'Me too, but I'd be a sight worse if it was someone else instead of you auditioning with me. I stayed up half the night trying to learn the lines.'

'So did I,' she admitted with a nervous giggle. Then, pulling her shoulders back, 'Listen, Ewan, we have to believe in ourselves. We have to tell ourselves that we can do this. And we will!' Then she gave a startled squeak as the door was thrown open.

'Welcome, my dear young people, welcome! Alison, and Ewan, do come in!' Meredith, in a silky floral patterned two-piece suit, swept the two of them into the sitting room, where Kevin waited, glass in hand. 'Would you like a drink before we begin the reading?'

Ewan opened his mouth to say that he would, and then closed it when Alison said firmly, 'Best not.'

'Well then, let us begin. Take a deep breath, my dears, and then allow yourself to relax, and move forward into the play. Let it settle around your shoulders like a much-loved coat. *Become* Elspeth and Tony.' Meredith scooped Gielgud, who had just strolled into the room, into her arms, and settled back into her chair, stroking the cat and looking, as Ewan and Alison agreed later, like the villain in a James Bond film.

The play was well written, and to their surprise, both of them found that her advice to 'relax and move forward into the play' actually worked. The next thirty minutes flowed past, and they were both startled when the last line was spoken and Meredith began to applaud.

'Excellent!' she said as Gielgud, irritated at having his sleep interrupted, leapt from her knee and stalked out of the room. 'I do believe that we have cast our play. Don't you think so, Kevin?'

'It seems so.' Kevin, who had tended to look down on the quiet young farmer, was secretly jealous. There was no doubt, after listening to the read–through, that Ewan had a certain raw talent. And there was no doubt that the girl, shy though she looked, was a natural actress. Trust Meredith to have those two in the play she had decided to direct!

'We three,' she announced to her cast, 'are going to work well together. I have much to teach you, and you will look so good together on the stage. So *right* together!'

Alison and Ewan blushed, and glanced away from each other.

March arrived, and all at once changes were afoot in Prior's Ford. Snowdrops, crocuses and golden daffodils burgeoned in gardens and along roadsides, and the trees began to produce tight fat buds.

At Linn Hall, workmen began to cover the three-storey building with scaffolding in preparation for the first, and most important stage of its renovation – a watertight roof. Acting on advice from their bank manager and from Andrew Forsyth, who was advising them on the renovations to the Hall, Lewis and his parents had decided that fifty thousand pounds of their unexpected windfall money could be spared for the outdoor work.

Lewis, Duncan Campbell and Ginny Whitelaw spent hours at the kitchen table, deciding how to make the best use of every penny. Ginny had never been happier. Put in sole charge of the neglected kitchen garden while Lewis and Duncan concentrated on the rest of the estate, she had started off by mapping every inch of it. Jimmy McDonald, a lanky red-headed teenager brought in by Lewis to help her, turned out to be the perfect assistant.

'It's great, this, in'it?' he enthused as the two of them worked their way through brambles, couch grass, and ivy to find out what lay beneath. 'It's like bein' an old-fashioned explorer findin' uncharted territory for the first time!'

Ginny, pausing to stretch her aching back muscles, grinned at him. 'Great!' she agreed, and knew that she and Jimmy were going to be the perfect team.

'The garden's been well designed,' she reported to the Ralston-Kerrs later. 'The original raised beds are still there beneath the weeds, separated by really nice old red brick paths. It's just a case of clearing all the rubbish away. I reckon that you've still got some usable plants there as well, once they've been pruned back and given some tender loving care. There's a fantastic herb garden too, the best I've ever seen.'

'We've only ever used that little bit near the gate to grow herbs, and that long bed down one wall where Duncan's always planted potatoes and vegetables,' Fliss admitted. 'There's never been time to do anything more. I don't remember ever seeing the kitchen garden the way it should be, do you, Hector?'

'In my grandparents' time, I think, but I was just a child then. You think that it's worth restoring?' Hector asked Ginny, who nodded vigorously.

'Once the entire area's up and running the way it should

be, I reckon that you could be entirely self-sufficient as far as vegetables and herbs are concerned, and some fruits, too – and still have enough surplus to sell in that shop Lewis plans to set up.'

'That's just what I wanted to hear. Think of the money we could make selling direct from here, Dad.'

Ginny looked round the table at the Ralston-Kerrs, the nicest family she had ever met in her life, and thanked her lucky stars that her mother had decided to spend her 'resting period' in Prior's Ford.

Lucinda Keen, or rather the male journalist masquerading as the agony aunt who ran a popular letters page in the weekly *Dumfries News*, cashed in all his premium bonds and went off to France to live with a woman he had met in an Internet chat room, much to the relief of his wife and family, although they were peeved about the bonds.

'That's us right up the Swannee without a paddle,' the editor moaned. 'One of you'll have to take it on. Bob?'

'No way, I've got enough to do. You'll have to scrap it.'

'I can't do that, it sells papers. So –' Gerry Crandall looked at his three reporters, but they all kept their heads down, refusing to meet his gaze – 'who's it going to be?'

'That lassie that sends in the news for Prior's Ford – Helen Campbell – she's quite good,' Bob said thoughtfully. 'She might be willing to take it on. It wouldn't be a bad idea to give the job to a woman – most of the letters come from women.'

'How much would we have to pay her?'

'I don't think she'd be looking for a lot. You could invite her in for a chat – negotiate an initial amount and promise an increase if it works out.'

'Aye, go on then – give her a ring and ask her to come

147

and see me,' Gerry said, and as he mooched back to his office there was a general sigh of relief from the other reporters.

'Nice one, Bob,' someone muttered. 'It's not a job I'd fancy.'

'I'll bet Helen will, though,' said Bob, picking up the phone. 'She's a keen lass, always looking for experience.'

'Our section needs to be beside that hut over there,' Freya explained, pointing. 'That's ours. And the playground for the little ones can go over there, so that we each have our own territory. We'll need some benches at the wee ones' play area, for the mothers.'

'It's a bit of a dump, isn't it, love?' George Griffin eyed the old workman's hut doubtfully. 'Wouldn't you rather have a nice new hut as well?'

'Thank you but no, we would not. Am I right?' Freya asked her committee. Heather McDonald, Gregor Campbell, Calum Forsyth and Ethan Baptiste, Naomi Hennessey's godson, all nodded agreement.

'It's our gang hut,' Ethan explained to George, and to the Progress Committee. 'We like it and we want to keep it the way it is.'

'Though if there's enough money, we wouldn't mind if you repaired the roof,' Gregor added. 'It lets in the rain.'

'Uh-huh, if you're sure.' George, the man recommended by the butcher's son, took a good long look at the plans, then suggested, 'Now then, let's all of us just take a good slow walk round the area, and you can show me exactly where you want things to go, so's I can get it right in my mind.'

As he set off with the children, the adult committee hung back.

'Does he know that there's no hurry, Bob?' Pete McDermott wanted to know.

'Aye, but not why. It suits him because he's already got enough work to keep him going into August. I've had a word with the youngsters too, and as I thought, they're quite pleased to have one last summer of the place as it's always been.'

'What about the birds?' Naomi asked.

'See where the cliff sticks out?' Robert pointed to the far side of the quarry. 'If you go round there, past the bushes, you'll see that there's a sort of an alcove, and that's where the eyrie is, right at the top. Nobody ever goes there because there's a bit of a pond – a dip that collects rainwater, and the undergrowth round it's quite thick. They'll be safe, and the only time they'll be seen is when they're in flight, high up. Come on, we'd best find out what these kids are trying to get George to agree to. Sharp as tacks, this lot,' Robert said, and led his committee to where the builder and the children were gathered in a huddle, talking earnestly.

Helen trailed behind the others, only half her attention on playgrounds and peregrine falcons. Ever since the phone call asking if she was interested in becoming an agony aunt she had not been able to think of anything else.

'The big question is – can I do it?' she had asked Duncan, who came back with, 'How would I know?'

'You might be a bit more helpful. I'm having to make a big decision here.'

'Sorry – but what does a man know about being an agony aunt?'

'The last one was a man.'

'Better him than me. Look Helen, if you want to do it, that's fine with me. As long as it doesn't take up too much

149

of your time,' he added hastily, alarmed in case her new job entailed him giving her more help with the kids and the house. Duncan was an outdoor-indoor man – he was outdoors when he worked as the gardener at Linn Hall, and for him, indoors meant enjoying a pint and a game of darts at the Neurotic Cuckoo or relaxing by the fire with a newspaper – and perhaps a pint.

'It'll mean a bit more money coming in, and we could always do with that.'

'In that case, tell them you'll have a shot at it,' Duncan said. 'You can always chuck it if you find it's too much for you.'

So Helen, not at all cheered by her husband's somewhat lukewarm encouragement, had agreed to have a talk with the editor about becoming his new agony aunt. The meeting was tomorrow morning, and she had been feeling sick with nerves all day.

18

The *Dumfries News* was situated on two floors of a narrow building, the ground floor mainly given over to the printing side of the paper, with a very small reception at the front. The reporters' room took up most of the first floor. Once, the room had been loud with the tapping of typewriter keys but now that computers had been installed the tapping was muted.

When the receptionist phoned upstairs to announce Helen's arrival, Bob Green, the reporter she had first met during the controversy over the reopening of the quarry, came down to fetch her.

'Another step forward for you, Helen,' he said jovially as she followed him up the narrow staircase. 'Gerry Crandall's chuffed to bits at getting a proper agony aunt; the fellow who did it before was pretty awful.'

'I don't know if I'm going to be much better.'

'You'll be great – you have to be,' he added as they reached the top of the stairs and arrived in the large editorial room where several men and woman worked at desks. Nobody bothered to look up. 'It was me who suggested that Gerry should give you this interview,' Bob went on as she followed him between desks to a corner of the room where two walls, one with a door and the other with a window over-looking the reporters' room, had been installed to create a small office. 'He's in here – the editor gets a hutch of his own.' He opened the door, said, 'Gerry? Helen's here,' then propelled her inside and returned to his own desk.

Gerry was a thin, balding man who looked permanently anxious. There was a precarious pile of papers clinging to his desk, and his clothes smelled of cigarette smoke, while his fingers were nicotine-stained.

'It's all fairly straightforward, dear. Folk need help and sometimes they can't turn to anyone who knows them, so there's a great need for agony aunts – you might say it's a social service you'll be doing. You help them to solve their problems, you get paid for it, they're grateful and so am I because it fills a page every second week. See?'

'I'm not sure I'll be good at it.'

'The last Lucinda did all right, and what does a man know about women's worries? Most of the letter writers are women, y'see. We'll be keeping on the name of Lucinda Keen – you don't mind that, do you?'

'No not at all,' Helen assured him. It was good to know that nobody in the village, other than Duncan, Ingrid and Jenny would know who Lucinda Keen really was.

'D'you read our agony aunt page, dear?'

'Oh yes, every time. You get a lot of letters in, don't you?'

Gerry coughed and shifted restlessly in his swivel chair. It creaked, and a waft of smoke-laden air swept past Helen's nose. 'To tell the truth, we don't always get that many letters. When that happens, you could mebbe write one or two yourself.'

'Make them up, you mean?'

'Aye, and then answer them yourself. That's what the last Lucinda did. And Bob says you're writing a novel, so you'll be good at making things up.' His phone rang and he snatched the receiver up. 'Hello? Oh aye – I'm in conference right now, I'll call you back in a few minutes, OK?' Then, replacing the receiver, he produced a plastic bag that must have been on the floor at his side. 'That's the letters waiting to be read and answered. Can you let us have your replies for a week on Monday?'

'Er – about payment,' Helen said.

Bob winked at her as she went back through the editorial office, but she didn't even notice him. Moving in a daze, she found her way down the stairs, out into the street, and along to a bus stop.

When her bus arrived she clambered aboard and sat staring out of the window throughout the journey, seeing nothing, and aware of nothing but the weight on her lap of letters filled with problems, all the writers eager for her to put things right for them. All looking to Helen Campbell, housewife, mother, very ordinary person, to make a difference to their lives.

She began to wonder if she had just made a terrible mistake.

'It's from Molly,' Lewis said, scanning the letter that had arrived in the morning's post. 'She wants to come here on a visit.'

'What – here?' Fliss asked nervously. 'You mean, to Linn Hall?'

'Yes, of course to Linn Hall.' Lewis was grinning broadly.

'When is she thinking of coming?'

'She says tomorrow by train but I'm going to phone to say that I'll drive there tomorrow and stay overnight, then

153

bring her here on Wednesday. She shouldn't be climbing off and on trains when the baby's due in about six weeks.'

'But the place is covered with scaffolding – and workmen. And Jinty and I haven't even begun to air the bedding for the gatehouses – we were going to get started on that next week.'

'Mother, Molly won't be sleeping down in the gate-house,' her son pointed out gently. 'She's not coming as a backpacker this year; she's a guest. She'll be sleeping in my room, with me.'

'Will she? Are you sure that that's – acceptable?' Fliss, normally good at coping with whatever life threw at her, clattered used coffee mugs busily around on the table, unable to meet her son's eye. She glanced at Hector, but he was already making for the security and safety of the butler's pantry, gripping his refilled coffee mug.

'My dear mother, Molly is about to have my child, and I hope that eventually she'll agree to marry me and move in here permanently, as one of the family. It's only natural that she should share my room. I do have a double bed,' Lewis pointed out, amused by his mother's panic, 'and in any case, we don't have a spare room fit for habitation at the moment.'

'I suppose not. Of course, you're quite right.' Fliss began to pull herself together. 'We'll look forward to seeing her.'

'I certainly will.' Lewis returned to work, whistling a cheerful tune.

Fliss walked down to the village that afternoon, and was fortunate enough to find Jinty McDonald, her helper, friend and confidante, baking in her kitchen.

'Sit down and I'll get the kettle on as soon as I've got this lot in the oven. You know what dough can be like – it doesn't like to be neglected.'

154

'I'll see to the kettle, and the tea if you tell me where the caddy is.'

'If you're sure, Mrs Ralston-Kerr. It's over on the dresser, under that newspaper.'

'Jinty, when are you ever going to start calling me Fliss? We've known each other for I don't know how long.'

'It doesn't seem right, with me in a council house and you in the laird's house, and me working for you.'

'You mean you in a snug warm place and me in a leaking sieve that lets the wind in — and the two of us working together.' Fliss held the dented kettle under the cold tap, gave the tap a good hard twist, then leapt back as a jet of water shot into the kettle before rebounding out again, soaking her and everything around her. 'Oh, sorry! I'm so used to working with our old stiff taps.'

'There's a cloth on the windowsill. Mop yourself first, then see to the rest,' Jinty said calmly. 'Won't be long now before you have nice modern taps, will it?'

'I can't wait — though I'll probably soak myself every time I use them for the first year. But what a pleasure that will be!' It had been decided that, after the roof, the bulk of the small fortune the Ralston-Kerrs had fallen heir to would go towards Linn Hall's, re-wiring and installing a new central heating system. With any luck, the money left over after that might just stretch to updating things like taps. 'Anyway,' Fliss went on as she mopped herself, then the sink area, the windowsill and the floor, 'don't evade the issue.'

'The what?'

'I mean, call me Fliss.'

'I can't!'

'Of course you can!'

'No, I can't!' In her embarrassment, Jinty worked the roller too hard. 'Look at that now, I've turned this pastry

155

into tissue paper!' She began to fold it in readiness to start again, and then, as she picked up the roller, 'I could call you Mrs F instead of Mrs Ralston-Kerr.'

'It would be a start.' Fliss turned the tap on again, this time carefully, and managed to fill the kettle and put it on the stove without further mishap. 'Where do you keep your matches? I need to light the gas ring.'

'You don't need matches. Turn the first knob and then press the button at the front of the stove.'

Fliss did as she was told and gave a little gasp of pleasure as the gas ring popped into life. 'That is so clever! I wonder if we'll have enough money left over to get one of those?'

'You'll be wanting me up at the Hall soon,' Jinty said when the baking was in the oven and the two of them had taken their tea and a box of biscuits into the small, cluttered living room. 'There's bedding to air and the gate-houses to be cleaned out ready for the young folk who come for the summer work.' Then, as Fliss said nothing, 'But that's not what you're here to talk about, is it?'

'Lewis got a letter today from Molly – that girl who worked in our kitchen last summer.'

'The bonny wee redhead he fell for? The one that's expecting his bairn?'

'So she says.'

'And so he believes, from what you've told me.'

'Mmm. The dates could fit, but I just wonder,' Fliss confessed. 'But that's probably just me being silly. She wants to come to the Hall for a visit. Lewis is driving to Inverness tomorrow to fetch her. He says she'll share his room. Is that . . .' Fliss paused, blushing, then tried again. 'Is that acceptable, d'you think?'

'It is nowadays, with young folk. Our mothers would have leathered us if we'd even thought about that sort of thing, wouldn't they? But there's no shame to it now,' Jinty assured her comfortably. 'In any case, where else would she sleep? The other rooms in the Hall haven't been used for years; they'll be freezing cold – and damp. Once you get that central heating installed we'll get them aired out and put to rights. More tea?'

Fliss pushed her cup forward, soothed and cheered by her friend's calm acceptance of Lewis's plans.

Ginny knew nothing of the coming visitor until she turned up for work on the following day to discover that Lewis wasn't on the estate.

'He's gone off to fetch Molly – she's comin' to stay for a few days,' Duncan Campbell said.

'Molly?'

'Aye, his girlfriend. A bonny lassie that was one of the backpackers last year. Lewis took a right shine to her. He went to visit her round about Christmas and now she's comin' here. He's tickled to bits about seein' her again.'

'Yes, he will be,' Ginny agreed, and headed for the kitchen garden, where she viciously attacked a bramble-covered corner that she had been avoiding until then. Today, she suddenly felt in the mood for a battle royal.

She and Jimmy had planned to spend Sunday in the kitchen garden, weather permitting. When Ginny arrived at Linn Hall, Fliss Ralston-Kerr was mixing something in a large baking bowl while a red-headed girl washed dishes at the big old sink.

'Hello, Ginny,' Lewis's mother greeted her. 'Isn't it freezing cold? We were just about to make some hot chocolate – Lewis and Duncan are down in the spinney and they said they'd be back by now. Oh – you haven't met Molly, have you?'

157

'Hi,' the girl picked up a towel and swung round from the sink, drying her hands. She wore a green knitted jersey beneath a pair of overalls, and her bright red hair fell to her shoulders in two plaits. 'Lewis told me what a help you've been, Ginny.' She held a hand out, and Ginny, realising that she was still staring in shock at the pregnancy bulging out the front of the overalls, pulled herself together and shook hands, stammering out a greeting.

'I'll have to come out later to see what you've done in the kitchen garden,' Molly chattered on. 'I was on kitchen duty last year and I used to go there to fetch herbs. Here you are!' she broke off as Lewis and Duncan came in, bringing a waft of icy air with them. 'I was just saying to Ginny here that the kitchen garden was a real mess last year. I'll need to see what she's done with it.'

'She's worked wonders already. I see you've managed to get that old bramble out, Ginny – I think it was older than I am. Well rooted in.'

'Just like you, at Linn Hall,' Molly teased, hugging him and lifting her pretty face for his kiss. 'Kettle's on,' she added, turning, still within the circle of his arms, to smile at Ginny. 'You'll have a drink before you start work, won't you?'

'I had something before I left home. I think I'll just get on with the work now,' Ginny said, and fled to the refuge of the walled garden, where she snatched up a fork and attacked the iron-hard ground vigorously. Why had nobody told her about Lewis's girlfriend, the pretty redhead who was clearly about to give birth quite soon to Lewis's baby?

On the other hand, why should anyone think of telling her? What had it to do with her? Nothing at all. 'Absolutely nothing at all,' Ginny muttered, lunging again and again until the fork finally began to make an impression on ground that had not been cultivated for years.

19

'I wish,' Alison said as she and Ewan walked together from the Neurotic Cuckoo to the village hall for their first official rehearsal, 'that I hadn't said I'd do it.'

'Because you're playing opposite me?'

'Of course not, it's because— Imagine being directed by Meredith Whitelaw!'

'I know. But she liked the read-through and we're almost word perfect now.' The two of them had been working hard on their lines in the hope of making a good impression when they had to rehearse before the rest of the drama group. 'You'll be all right,' Ewan said. 'You're good.'

'Good and scared.' Alison's laugh was distinctly wobbly, and he reached out into the darkness to take her hand in his. 'We'll be all right,' he said with a confidence he didn't really feel. 'We'll both be all right – you'll see!'

They were horrified when they reached the hall to find that *Reunion* was going to have full use of the stage for the entire evening. Nerves meant that they both got off to a wobbly start, but then the private rehearsals they had done together kicked in, and much to their surprise, Meredith let them run through the entire play without stopping them. Then she mounted the stairs to the stage and beckoned them to her.

'A very brave attempt, my dears, and I am pleased to see that you have worked hard on your lines,' she said. 'And now, we get down to work.'

The rest of the evening was like a masterclass in acting. The other actors, supposed to be working on their own plays in the hall itself, stopped what they were doing to watch Meredith bring the characters of the two shy people, former schoolmates meeting years later at a class reunion, to life. She halted the play again and again to demonstrate moves, glances and speeches, and Ewan and Alison, both under her spell, found themselves becoming the characters.

'I've never felt like that at a rehearsal,' Alison said in wonder when they were allowed a brief break.

'Nor me. I just stopped being me, and became Tony. And you – well, you were Elspeth, not Alison.'

'You were both terrific,' said Steph McDonald. 'Aren't you lucky to be directed by Miss Whitelaw? She's tutoring me too, but don't tell Mr Pearce,' she added with a swift sidelong look at Kevin, who was talking to Meredith. 'He's a good director, but he doesn't have Miss Whitelaw's expertise, does he?' Then, as Meredith clapped her hands to show that the break was over, she scuttled off.

The second half of the evening went well, with only one problem. As the final lines were spoken and the two of them turned to look at Meredith, seeking approval, her voice rang out from the darkened hall. 'What do you think you are doing?'

'It's the end of the play,' Ewan said.

'Not until Tony kisses Elspeth!'

'We usually leave that sort of thing to nearer the dress rehearsal,' he explained, his face flaming.

'Oh, for goodness' sake!' Meredith stamped a stylishly booted foot. 'How amateurish can you get?' She swept up the stairs and across the stage to stand before them, one hand gripping Ewan's wrist, the other gripping Alison's. 'Listen to me! Tony is a man who has never achieved anything in his life, while Elspeth is a woman who is trying to gather herself together after a morale-shattering divorce. Once, these two people shared a lovely, innocent childhood friendship in the school playground. Now, years later, they meet – two lonely people, wounded by the arrows of life, and in thirty wonderful minutes they both rediscover that first innocent friendship. They both begin to sense again the happiness and confidence that adulthood has cruelly stripped from them. In here' – she laid a hand against her left breast – 'They feel the slow, warming growth of hope, of belief that together, they can put the past and its mistakes behind them and rebuild their lives, properly this time.'

She turned and moved to the front of the stage, holding out one hand towards the hall, where the others had gathered together, fascinated.

'They are elated,' Meredith's voice rang through the hall, drawing the caretaker from her little office to lean against a wall, enraptured, 'caught up in emotions that they had believed dead for ever – that they never thought they would experience again.'

She paused for a long moment. Nobody moved or spoke or even breathed. The hall was lit by ordinary light bulbs hanging from the ceiling, but it seemed to Steph that Meredith Whitelaw, motionless on the stage, was spot lit.

'And then' – Meredith said at last, in a throaty whisper

161

– 'they move together, to become one. And they kiss.' She lowered her arm very slowly, letting the final word linger before turning to the two people on the stage.

'But you didn't kiss – because in amateur circles, it's not done until the dress rehearsal!'

'It's . . . difficult,' Alison almost whispered. 'People . . . laugh at kissing during rehearsals.'

'Idiots laugh!' Meredith announced, and then, glaring down into the hall, 'but fortunately, there are no idiots in this particular group. If there were, I would not be wasting my time in this hall.' Then, with a sweet smile. 'I think that we have done enough for this evening. Next week, my dears, we will rehearse the play again, and this time, it will end with the kiss – and nobody will laugh!'

'She was . . . magnificent,' Alison said in awe as she and Ewan left the hall. 'What a wonderful voice! Aren't we lucky to be directed by her?'

'Mmm.'

'What's wrong?'

'Nothing.'

'I'm beginning to get to know you better, Ewan McNair. Is it having to do the kiss in front of everyone?'

He was glad that it was too dark for her to see the colour that suddenly, burned into his face. 'I'm – I'm not used to that sort of thing,' he mumbled.

'Kissing on the stage in front of other folk, you mean?'

'I'm not used to kissing at all, if you must know,' he blurted out, embarrassment making him angry. 'I've never had what you could call a proper girlfriend before, except when I was at school. I've never had the time – you don't, when you're trying to keep a farm from going under.'

'You don't need to let that worry you. Not with me.'

'But you've been married!'

'Ewan—' they had almost reached the Neurotic Cuckoo; Alison halted, caught at his arm and pulled him round to face her. Then she reached up to cup his hot face in her two cold hands, drew his head down to hers, and kissed him.

'There,' she said when they drew apart. 'That's what kissing feels like. It wasn't too difficult, was it?'

'No.' The word came out in a gruff voice that seemed to be stuck at the back of his throat.

'And it was absolutely fine, take my word for it. If it helps, remember at rehearsals that it's not you and me kissing, it's Tony and Elspeth. And keep thinking about what Miss Whitelaw said about them because it was beautiful. Then you'll be able to do it no trouble at all, and nobody will laugh. They won't dare to, after what she said about idiots laughing. Are you coming in for a cup of tea?'

'I'd best get back.'

Ewan floated home, scarcely noticing the ruts and puddles in the farm lane. Tonight, he had been in the company of the two most incredible women any man could meet – Meredith Whitelaw, and Alison Greenlees.

And in the space of an evening, he reckoned that they had changed his life for ever. He felt as though he had left the farm a boy, and was returning to it a man.

'Kevin, you're a genius,' Meredith said as she waited for Kevin to switch off all the lights before leaving the village hall. 'Those young people are perfect together. The chemistry is quite amazing. You couldn't have found two people more suited for *Reunion*.'

'They're very good, aren't they?' Kevin still couldn't understand why he had not recognised Ewan McNair's talent before this.

'Much better, I'm sure you'll agree, than the couple originally chosen.'

'I don't know about that—'

'I am. I prophesy great things for this show, Kevin. In fact, I am going to invite some of my theatrical friends to come to see it.'

'That would be wonderful!'

'It means that we must work hard, the two of us, and work together,' Meredith said as they made for the door. 'But we will do it. There's a strong bond between us – you must have felt it!'

'Yes, yes I did. I do!' If only, Kevin thought, the world could see him now, the friend and confidant of a famous household name!

She waited until he had locked the door, then took his arm as they set off. 'I've been thinking, since I met you – wouldn't it be wonderful if you could come up with a really believable way of slotting me back into *Bridlington Close*? Nothing silly, like someone going into the shower then coming out to find that they'd just dreamed about my character's death. My idea about the twin sister, for instance – you could do that, couldn't you?'

'Well, I . . . er . . . I'm . . . I've always dealt with factual articles, Meredith; I've never tried fiction.'

'But words are words, it's just a case of where you put them, isn't it? You may have been a journalist, but I know that you have a creative soul – why else would you be devoting so much time to this drama group? A talented wordsmith like you wouldn't have any bother coming up with a good storyline. We could work on the general idea together. You would only need to write a treatment – ten or twenty pages, say – giving my new character some really interesting storylines, and perhaps two or three half

hour episodes as well. Then I could send them to the
director. I'm sure that he'd be delighted to see them. The
show has definitely become a bit jaded since I left it –
they need new blood, and you, Kevin, are the very person
to provide it.'

'But I've never written a screenplay.'

'You'll learn. All you need to do at the moment is to
think up a really good storyline. You do watch *Bridlington
Close*, don't you?'

'When I have time,' lied Kevin, who considered himself
above watching anything other than documentaries and
sport. Then, having a sudden brainwave, he added, 'Actually
I think it's gone downhill a bit since your character was
written out.'

'That is so sweet of you, Kevin, and so perceptive. What
the programme needs is a strong character – someone to
get in there and take charge. Someone with a professional
background, possibly. That was the problem with my character – she was rather too domesticated. I was never able,'
Meredith said thoughtfully, 'to really open up and demonstrate my true ability. There's no reason why the twin
shouldn't be something in the City – a banker, or the head
of a strong organisation. But why would she come to a
backwater like Bridlington Close, you ask.'

Kevin, who had not thought to ask that at all, nodded,
and hoped that Meredith would come up with an answer.

'Perhaps she's recuperating from an illness, or surgery.
Or taking a step back from her career, asking herself whether
she's worthy of better, higher things. Yes, I quite like that.'
Meredith put a hand on Kevin's arm, bringing him to a
sudden stop and swinging him round to face her. 'She
comes to Bridlington Close in order to find herself – much
as I have come to Prior's Ford – only to discover that her

165

sister, the twin she has not seen in years, is dead. She feels guilt – such guilt! – because there was unfinished business between them. Some feud that only they knew about – we can decide on that later – and so she decides to atone for their past estrangement by staying on and putting her late sister's family to rights. What do you think of it so far?'

'It sounds wonderful!'

Meredith released Kevin and started to walk on. 'Then, perhaps, she starts up a new business in the area, but that too can be worked out later. There – don't we work well together, Kevin? You already have your outline, and all you have to do now is to flesh it out.'

'Yes, of course.' Kevin felt elated, excited, but also as though he had been hit by a load of bricks. When they reached Willow Cottage and Meredith invited him in for a nightcap he declined, anxious to hurry home and record as much as he could remember of her plot before it vanished from his mind.

'I'll make a hot drink, shall I?' Elinor suggested when he arrived home.

'Give me five minutes – I have to note some things down first.' Kevin raced upstairs to his small study, switched on his computer, and started to type furiously. When he had finished he read it over and realised that what he needed to flesh Meredith's ideas out, as she herself would no doubt put it, was a knowledge of the soap itself, and the characters in it.

He returned downstairs, following Elinor into the kitchen. 'Good rehearsal?' she asked.

'It went well.'

'I managed to get some sewing done while I was watching

television.' She poured milk into a pan, put it on the stove and fetched mugs from a cupboard.

'Was *Bridlington Close* on this evening?'

'Yes it was. Why do you want to know?'

'What are the people in it like?'

'Oh, just ordinary people, really. That's what soaps are like. Could you pass me the Horlicks, dear?'

'Why do people watch soaps if they're about ordinary people?'

'I don't know. Perhaps it's more legal than crouching in your neighbours' gardens, peering through their windows. Or it might be something to do with good writing. Why?' Elinor asked again.

'Meredith has asked me to work on a treatment that would get her back into *Bridlington Close*. As her character's twin sister,' Kevin added as his wife stared at him over the top of her spectacles.

'But you're not a proper writer – I mean,' she added hastily as he began to bridle, 'you're not a fiction writer or a drama writer.'

'She has faith in me, which appears to be more than some people have.'

'Oh, Kevin, be realist – oh heck!' Elinor rescued the pan just as the milk began to boil ominously up its sides. 'Some people are better in one area of writing than in others. You were good at journalism.'

'That doesn't mean I can't have a shot at a screenplay.'

'I suppose not.'

'So.' Kevin, still offended, picked up his mug – the one with his name on it – and marched from the kitchen. When Elinor followed him to the living room, he was flicking through the television magazine.

'When's this *Bridlington Close* on next?'

'Monday evening.'

'I have a rehearsal on Monday evening. Will you record it for me?'

'Of course. And I really do wish you good luck with the screenplay, Kevin. I'm sure you can do it.'

Privately, Elinor felt that it was all going to end in tears, as happened so often with Kevin.

20

'I don't *want* a birthday party!'

'But sweetheart, it's your fifteenth birthday, and it's the first time we'll be able to celebrate it with you.'

'Will Gran and Gramps come to it? And Uncle Malcolm and Aunt Lizbeth?'

'Well − no, they can't travel all the way here,' Jenny said. 'Your granddad's not well enough to travel, and neither is Aunt Lizbeth. But I know that they've already bought presents to send here for you, and you're going to stay with them during the summer holidays,' she added swiftly as Maggie's mouth began to tighten. She was already beginning to recognise indications of trouble ahead.

'If they're not going to be here I'm not bothered about having a proper birthday.'

'But we want you to have one − me and Andrew and Calum, and all your friends. Freya, and Ethan, and Merle and Heather McDonald. It's our first chance to share your birthday with you. And then there are the people you've come to know in your class at school. In fact,' Jenny was struck by a sudden thought, 'we could hire the village hall if you want.'

'Really?' Maggie began to show some interest.

'I don't see why not. Perhaps we could do an Easter theme. Last year we had an Easter Egg hunt in one of Mr McNair's fields, with games and a fancy Easter Bonnet competition. It was lovely!'

'That's babyish,' Maggie said scornfully. 'If I'm going to have a proper birthday party in the village hall I'd want a disco we could dance to.'

'I can arrange that. And you could get something nice to wear. I tell you what,' Jenny said, inspired, 'I'll buy you a new outfit to wear at your party, as my gift. We'll go shopping for it together on Saturday.'

'But I have to choose it myself. You're not going to get me kitted out like some stupid Easter Bunny or Little Miss Muffet!'

'Of course not! It'll be something you choose yourself. I'll just pay for it,' Jenny promised, happy to see the girl smiling again. 'So I can go ahead and book the village hall for the party then?'

'Yes, all right.'

'What party?' Calum asked from the doorway.

'Maggie's. She's going to be fifteen at the end of this month and we're going to have a party for her.'

'Great! Can I come?'

'No!' Maggie said swiftly, and then, as both Calum and Jenny stared, taken aback, 'I mean – it's for teenagers, in the village hall with a disco. It's not for kids.'

'I'm not a kid!'

'Of course not,' Jenny said swiftly, 'but Maggie's right, it's not your sort of party, love.' Then, as his mouth began to turn down at the corners, 'but you can have a sort-of party of your own instead.'

170

'Promise?'

'I promise. Is that the time – I'll have to get on with the dinner,' Jenny said, and hurried to the kitchen.

'I'm going to have my own party,' Calum told Maggie, who gave him the look that she only gave him when there was nobody else there to see it.

'That's right,' she said. 'Your very own little kid party!' And she swept past him and went up the stairs, sniggering.

Calum stared after her, gulping back tears. At first Maggie had been a great big sister, but only at first. Now she kept sneering and laughing at him, calling him 'stupid' and 'dumbo'. She was careful never to do it when his parents were around, and he felt too ashamed to tell them. Perhaps, he thought as he went into the garden to kick a ball around, she was behaving the way all big sisters behaved. Perhaps it wasn't his fault. He wished he knew.

'I thought you might fancy a cup of tea.'

Ginny, down on her knees in order to do close-quarter battle with some determined weeds, glanced up to see Molly Ewing standing over her.

'Oh, thanks, I would.' She sat back on her haunches and accepted the mug, uncomfortably aware that her face must be as red from exertion as Molly's hair. The other girl moved to a wooden bench by the kitchen wall and lowered herself into it, grunting slightly, then took a mouthful of tea from her own mug.

'I'll be glad when this little so-and-so finally arrives.' She gave her swollen belly a light slap with her free hand. 'I feel like an elephant, and it's horrible not being able to go dancing or have any sort of fun.'

'When's it due?' Ginny knew nothing about babies; to her unpractised eye it looked as though Molly could give birth at any moment, and she felt slightly worried at being alone with her.

'May – I've got ages to go yet. You've done wonders with this garden.'

'We're hoping that by the autumn it'll be starting to produce enough to keep the household going, and sell to more shops.'

'Lewis's mum says that your mum's Meredith Whitelaw – is that true?' Molly asked, and when Ginny nodded, 'That's fantastic! I wish my mum was famous and glamorous like yours.'

'A mum's a mum,' Ginny said. She had grown up in her mother's shadow, and all she wanted now was to be known for herself, not as Meredith Whitelaw's daughter.

'That's all right for you to say. My mother's OK, but it would have been magic if she'd been famous. You must have met a lot of well-known people, like Ross Kemp, or Jason Donovan, even.'

'I've met some actors, but never them.'

'What are you doing working in a garden in Prior's Ford?' Molly wanted to know. 'Didn't you want to go on television too?'

'No, and even if I had wanted to, I can't act. I prefer gardening.'

'I'd love to go onto one of those shows where they discover new talent. I auditioned once when I was in London and they were looking for people to be in the chorus of a musical, but I didn't get far. It was fun, though,' Molly said wistfully. 'D'you live in London?'

'Quite near. Hertfordshire.'

'London's exciting, isn't it? I'd like to live there. I like to travel in the summer – sometimes abroad, sometimes in the UK, earning my keep here and there. I'm going to be really fed up, having to stay home this summer.' Molly looked up at the Hall roof, where men were working. 'This place is going to be terrific when all the work's done.'

'Yes, it is. When are you and Lewis getting married?'

'If he'd his way we'd be married by now; it'll happen some time, of course, but I'm not in any hurry to settle down.'

'But surely once you have a baby to look after—'

'That's not going to make a lot of difference. My mum's tickled pink at the thought of a baby in the house again; she can't wait to babysit. Finished?'

'Yes, thanks.'

Molly levered herself up from the bench and took Ginny's empty mug. 'I'd best go – Lewis is taking me out for lunch.' She turned and looked up at the house again. 'Imagine me being the mistress of this place one day! Aren't I lucky?'

'Yes, you are,' Ginny murmured to the other girl's retreating back as she waddled down the path, her hair shining in a sudden ray of sunshine. So lucky to have a baby, and Lewis.

She sighed, and went back to her work. Some people were meant to be lucky, and some just weren't.

'I inherited this place from my father and he inherited it from his! It was paid for generations ago and takin' out a mortgage is as good as handin' the place over to the buildin' society or the bank,' Bert McNair thundered.

'Only if you don't keep up with the mortgage payments.' Ewan had only been trying to help his parents, but now he wished that he had kept his mouth shut. 'If you borrow enough to cover the monthly payments as well as keeping us going for the rest of this year, it gives us time to find a way of making more money.'

173

'And what if we don't find a way? I've never been in debt in my life, boy, and I won't let it happen to me now – not at my time of life!'

'But if it's the only way, Bert,' Jess said helplessly. 'Ye cannae stand by and let the beasts starve, they've done nothin' wrong.'

'Of course they'll no' starve, woman, d'ye think I could be that heartless? But they're goin' tae have tae go eventually – tae the market, or the abattoir, for I've had enough of this worryin'!' Bert stormed.

His wife and his younger son exchanged appalled looks.

'Then,' Bert went on, 'we can rent out the rest of our fields tae those still lucky enough tae have beasts.'

'Victor was on about the money you could make if you sold the big field to a developer,' his wife mentioned tentatively.

'An' have boxy wee houses built all over it? Have ye lost the wits ye were born with? Tarbethill's got some o' the best grazin' land in the district. Land that's built on's lost for ever. I'll rent it out but I'll no' see it sold for buildin'!'

'What about the old cottage? We could mebbe do it up and rent it out for holidays,' Ewan suggested. The cottage had housed a farm hand and his family when Bert was young, but it had lain empty for years now, used as a store for all sorts of bits and pieces.

'It'd cost a fortune to get it put right,' Jess said doubtfully.

'P'raps Victor and me could see to it between us. I'll take a look at it when I've got time. Mebbe I could be the one to take on a loan instead of you, Dad.'

'And how would ye pay it back since you don't get much more than yer keep and a wee bittie spendin' money as it is?'

'I could get work at one of the big farms in the area,

or mebbe work for two or three of the smaller places – if you could manage without me.'

'That would mean Victor pullin' his weight more,' Bert muttered. 'Ever since he met that town girl he's spent more time with her than here. Where is he right now, eh? With her and her fam'ly when he should be here, tryin' tae help us tae work out what's best tae do.'

'Ye cannae fault the laddie for courtin', Bert,' Jess argued. 'It's only natural.'

'I wish he'd found someone o' his own sort tae court,' her husband said grumpily. There was a short pause, then, winking to his surprised wife, he went on, 'Now *there's* a way you might save us single-handed, Ewan . . .'

'Aye?' Ewan perked up.

'It just came tae me that if the daughter of one o' the big farms were tae catch yer eye we could mebbe bring the two farms together . . .'

'Me? Don't be daft – I'd as soon get a bank loan and work all the hours tae pay it than marry some lassie I don't care for!' Ewan, pink with embarrassment, scrambled to his feet. 'I'm away – there's a rehearsal on in the village hall tonight.'

'I thought you said you hadnae to be there until later this evening?' Jess asked.

'Aye, but the play Miss Whitelaw's in gets started tonight and I'd like to see her on the stage.' Ewan grabbed his coat. 'See you later.'

'You shouldnae tease the boy like that, Bert,' Jess admonished when their younger son had gone.

'Who said I was teasin' him? If we could get him married intae one of these big farms he'd have somethin' tae take over when we're gone. As it is, there's goin' tae be nothin'.' Bert's shoulders slumped again. 'Certainly not enough tae

175

keep him and Victor goin', with or without families of their own.'

'I've a feeling that Victor's more likely to move to the town if he marries Janette. I don't see her as a farmer's wife. And Ewan's got a fondness for the publican's daughter.'

'Aye well,' Bert grunted, reaching for his pipe and his tobacco pouch, 'We should mebbe be grateful that publicans do better than farmers these days, eh, Saul?'

The old dog, hearing his name mentioned, lifted his head slightly from the rug while his tail gave a few thumps, and then subsided.

'At least Ewan tries to come up with ways to help us to keep Tarbethill going,' Jess pointed out. 'That's more than Victor does.' Then, as her husband said nothing, 'Bert, how long do we have before we have to give serious thought to a bank loan?'

'Six months, mebbe – if we're careful. But we cannae go on like this for another year, that's for sure.' Bert lit his pipe and then blew out a cloud of blue smoke, peering through it as it swirled about his balding head, looking into the past, when he had worked Tarbethill Farm with his father, courted and married Jess, and raised two sons to work the place he loved with him.

In all those years he had done his best, so where and why, he wondered, had it all gone so wrong?

21

'In a *handbaaaag*?'

Meredith's rich voice rang to the very rafters, and the little knots of people gathered here and there in the hall itself all stopped what they were doing to gape at the stage, where she reclined gracefully on a sagging armchair. The actors sharing the stage stared at her, then at their scripts, and finally turned as one to look down at Kevin Pearce, who stood in the middle of the hall, script in hand.

Nobody gaped more than Kevin. He gulped so hard that Alison Greenlees, quietly rehearsing lines with Ewan McNair, saw his Adam's apple shoot up his scrawny throat and then fall down again just as she had become convinced that it was going to leap into his mouth.

'Er – er – Meredith?' he squeaked. 'That line – it's not in the script.'

'I know that, dear, but it just occurred to me, when this very nice woman playing the part of my daughter brought on that *fascinatingly* large bag, that it was such an *apt* line,' Meredith explained sweetly.

'Actually,' the woman playing the part of her daughter explained, 'I didn't mean to bring it onstage, Kevin. It's my knitting bag. I was knitting in the wings when I suddenly heard my cue and I just pushed the knitting into it and brought it on without thinking.'

'But it's such a good idea,' Meredith protested. 'Kevin, she absolutely *must* bring it on with her every time, then I can say, "in a *haandbaag*?" D'you see?'

'Not really, Meredith.' Kevin cast an imploring look at his wife, but Elinor, stitching busily in a corner of the hall, kept her head bent over her work, partly because she didn't want to get involved in an argument with their distinguished guest player, and partly because she didn't want Kevin to see how amused she was.

'Meredith —' Kevin trotted to the stage, where he peered up at the actors — 'the thing is, that line from *The Importance of Being Earnest* isn't actually in this play. *Visiting Vanessa* is about an ordinary family visiting their ordinary old grandmother in a nursing home.'

'Yes, but the moment I saw that bag it occurred to me that the play would be so much more interesting if we made Vanessa a professional actress in a home for retired thespians, reliving past memories the way old people sometimes do.'

'I don't think we're allowed to do that with a published play.'

'I'm sure we're not,' a friend of Cynthia MacBain's said in a loud whisper to the man standing beside her. 'It'll ruin the rhythm of the play.'

'Oh, tosh,' Meredith said sweepingly. 'Who's to know? Is the author going to come to this little village hall to see the play being performed? Are the publishers going to send an inspector along to make sure that we dot the I's and cross the T's? I doubt it. It's all supposed to be fun, isn't it?' she asked the others on the stage.

'I suppose it is, really,' the woman with the knitting bag looked at the others, who nodded.

'We've never interfered with a play before and I don't think we should start now,' Cynthia's friend said loudly, stepping forward to be counted.

'Oh, come along, darling – can you honestly say hand on heart that you've never interfered with anything?' Meredith rose from the chair with all the grace of a Venus rising from the waves and moved to the front of the stage so that she could speak to her rapt audience. 'It's such fun – so *liberating*! Be bold, Kevin – let us interfere just a little!'

'But—'

'A touch here and there. For instance, when they give Vanessa the pen to sign her will, she could look at it like this' – she clasped her two hands and held them above and slightly in front of her – '*Is this a dagger I see before me?* And so on.'

'I'm not sure that—'

'Kevin's right, we can't do it!'

'I don't know if there's any harm in it,' one of the actors on the stage said. 'I think it's quite an interesting idea, It would brighten up a rather dull play.'

'My sentiments exactly. Let's take a vote on it,' Meredith said, 'Ayes to this side of the hall, Nays to that side.'

There was a thundering of feet as the Ayes moved to one side of the hall and a pattering of feet as the Nays huddled together in a hostile, frustrated little group. Kevin was left standing in the middle, clipboard in hand and his authority, for the moment, in shreds.

'Poor Mr Pearce,' Alison said as Meredith returned to her chair and triumphantly boomed out the handbag line again. 'Ms Whitelaw's quite overpowering, isn't she?'

'It won't do Kevin any harm,' Ewan assured her. 'He tends to be a bit bossy and I think most of the group are enjoying watching him lose, for once. Anyway, he's thrilled to have her in one of the plays, and it's sure to help when it comes to selling tickets. Now – d'you want one more run through, or do you want to leave it at that for this evening?'

'Let's run through the play once more. I'm beginning to enjoy myself,' Alison admitted, beaming at him. 'I'm so glad you asked me to do this play with you.'

'I wouldn't have wanted to do it with anyone else,' he said.

As soon as she had seen the children off to school, Helen Campbell hurried back to her council home on Slaemuir Estate where she took a mug of coffee upstairs to her bedroom and switched on the old computer. Then she opened a shoebox containing the letters she had been given at the newspaper office, took one out and read it once, twice, then for a third time.

'Oh, heck!' she said. The writer suspected that her boyfriend was seeing other girls behind her back, and didn't know whether to confront him with her suspicions or hold her tongue. Apparently he was the best boyfriend she had ever had, and she didn't want to lose him.

She put the letter back and picked up the next one. It was much the same, and so were the third and the fourth. She replaced them all in the box and walked over to the Gift Horse, where she knew she would find Jenny and Ingrid.

'It's such a responsibility,' she said in despair. 'What if I give the wrong advice and they act on it and it spoils their lives?'

180

'Then it serves them right for not having the courage to make their own decisions,' announced Ingrid, never one to suffer fools gladly. 'If one of us has a problem we cannot work out by ourselves we talk to the other two, don't we? Why can't these people do the same?'

'Some of them don't have friends like us,' Helen told her, 'and sometimes the secrets are about the very people they know, so they can't talk to them. One poor woman—'

'Stop right there, Helen,' Jenny jumped in. 'These people trust you because they've got nobody else to trust. You can't go talking about them to anyone, even us.'

'But I'm not qualified to take on the responsibility for their problems! I don't think I can do this. I'm not a Lucinda Keen person! I'll have to take the letters back and tell them to find someone else.'

'Of course you can do it,' Ingrid said in that brisk way she had. 'It's a question of using common sense and you've got lots of that. If people used their own common sense they wouldn't need to write to magazines and newspapers, and bare their souls on these silly television programmes.' She screwed her nose up in disgust.

'Perhaps I should watch some of those programmes as research – if I could find the time.'

'I wouldn't bother,' Jenny advised. 'The people who go on them are more in need of psychiatric help than the sort of people who write to an agony aunt page. Go for it, Helen. Who says you can't be Lucinda Keen? You're a mature woman, a daughter, sister, friend, wife and mother; you know as much about everyday life as anyone else. It's up to them whether or not they take your advice. All most of them want is to put it all down on paper and send it to a complete stranger who doesn't know them – like sending letters up the chimney to

181

Santa at Christmas. Just doing that probably makes them feel better.'

'Jenny's right,' Ingrid agreed.

'But they'll still buy the paper to find out if their letters are in it, and what Lucinda Keen thinks they can do about it!'

'I suspect that in most cases they'll have solved their own problem before the newspaper comes out,' Ingrid said. 'In any case, why should you let the editor pay someone else for something that you can do?'

'And you might even find material for that novel you're going to write one of these days.'

'I can't do that, Jenny! I can't put real people's problems in a novel.'

'You'd need to change things about a bit, of course, but it's all human life, isn't it? Look,' Jenny said, 'All you need to do each time you read one of those letters is to imagine that it's come from a friend who needs your help. Then do the best you can for them.'

When Helen got back home she made another cup of coffee and then, on an impulse, she added a good dollop from the bottle of whisky Duncan kept in a cupboard for special occasions. Back in the bedroom, she gulped down some enhanced coffee and picked up the first letter again. '*Imagine that you're the letter-writer's friend,*' Jenny had advised.

All at once Helen remembered Carrie Wilson, a girl she had gone through school with. On their very first day in the infant class Helen had found Carrie, a skinny, carroty-mopped child, weeping in the girls' toilets during playtime because she hadn't had the courage to ask permission to go there earlier, and had wet her knickers. The girl had been in such a state about it, refusing to be taken to the teacher to explain what had happened, that eventually Helen had come up with the idea of exchanging her dry knickers for Carrie's wet pair and facing the teacher on her own. She had been given a gentle scolding about the need to put her hand up as soon as she knew that she had to go, then had been given a dry pair of knickers kept in the classroom for emergencies. At the end of the school day she and Carrie had swapped underwear again and Carrie had taken possession of the bag containing her damp panties.

Ever since then Carrie had relied on Helen for advice and help, and Helen had never failed her. Now, making herself read the letter as though it had come from Carrie, she found an answer.

Bringing up a fresh document on the screen, she began to type. *Before you walk down the aisle with your boyfriend, wouldn't it be wise to face him with what you know? You need to find out now if he respects you and will continue to respect you. If you have to drop him, remember that there is at least one other man even better than he is, waiting to meet you and make you happy. Perhaps it's time for you to go and look for him.*

She read it through several times before printing it out, then moved to the next letter. Before she knew it, the coffee mug was empty and half the letters – every one of them written for Carrie – had been dealt with. Rushing downstairs to prepare lunch for the children, she discovered that she was beginning to enjoy her new job.

22

From the beginning of March Robert Kavanagh had enjoyed a good brisk walk twice a week – good exercise after a winter mainly spent indoors, he told anyone who remarked on it. He also pointed out that a solitary walk gave a man the chance to do a bit more thinking, thus keeping his brain in good condition as well as his body.

His solitary walks always took him from the village to the riverbank, past the old priory ruins and the quarry. After another two hundred yards or so he would pause, make sure that nobody was watching, and then double back to the part of the quarry rarely visited by the locals. There, he made himself as comfortable as he could among the bushes and used his binoculars to scan the man-made cliff rising high above.

His patience was rewarded on the day he saw a huge bird circling high overhead, level with the top of the cliff. Soon it was joined by another, slightly larger bird. The peregrine falcons were back in Prior's Ford.

Robert kept up his walks, and to his great excitement,

managed to be at the quarry on the morning of their aerial courtship ritual, the male showing off to his mate by circling and diving about her, and offering her food which she took from his talons by rolling onto her back while in mid-flight.

'Honestly, Robert, I think you're more excited about those birds courting than you were when you were trying to catch me,' Cissie said that afternoon, 'you haven't stopped talking about it since you got back from your walk – well, only for long enough to phone that man in the Scottish Natural Heritage office to tell him all about it.'

'But it's such good news, Cissie. This is going to put Prior's Ford on the map, once everything's organised. What we need to do now is to find some way of setting up a hide in the autumn, so that bird watchers can see our birds next year. We might even be able to set up a web cam. There'll be eggs in the nest soon, you mark my words. You should have seen their mating ritual, Cissie—'

'You've already told me all about it and I don't know that I approve of you watching such things. You're beginning to sound like a Peeping Tom.' Cissie buttoned her coat and picked up her bag. 'I'm off, I don't want to be late for the Institute meeting.'

'You won't let a word slip out about the falcons, will you? You know that it has to be a secret until we've made sure that visitors can't disturb them.'

'Why would anyone at the Institute want to hear about birds? We're going to have a lady showing us how to do floral decorations and I'm hoping to come up with an idea for something to put into the flower show when it comes round. There won't be any time to chatter about birds,' Cissie assured him. 'Make yourself some fresh tea – that might calm you down.'

* * *

The village hall had been booked for Maggie's birthday party, and invitations sent out. Jenny, Ingrid, Helen and Jinty McDonald had baked, soft drinks had been ordered, and on the day itself the hall was decorated.

'I'm a bit nervous about Maggie's outfit,' Jenny said as she clambered up a ladder, carrying one end of a paper streamer. 'I promised her that she could choose it herself, as my birthday present, and it's a bit – adult.'

Helen was holding the ladder steady. 'I'm sure it'll be all right. After all, she's on the threshold of womanhood now. Careful!'

'I'm fine.' Jenny managed after a struggle to get the streamer secured, and swarmed back down the ladder. 'I'm not sure what Andrew's going to say.'

'Oh, you know what men are like, they always think that children should be children for ever,' Helen said as the two of them carried the ladder further down the hall. 'My turn now. You go and fetch the other end of the streamer.' She began to mount the ladder.

'He's insisting on coming to the party,' Jenny said as she handed the streamer up to her friend. 'He's muttering about alcohol smuggling and underage drinking.'

'Well, you never know these days. Better safe than sorry. Oh, darn this thing, it's not going to go in,' Helen was saying when the two older McDonald boys, Grant and Jimmy, arrived.

'Hi, Mum said to come over and make ourselves useful,' Grant said. 'What are you doing up there, Mrs Campbell?'

'She's coming down, that's what she's doing. Come on, Helen,' Jenny chirped, 'the cavalry have arrived!'

'Don't make a fuss when you see what Maggie's wearing for her party.'

'What do you mean — don't make a fuss? It's something horrendous, isn't it?'

'Of course it's not horrendous! It's just — what teenagers wear to parties nowadays, that's all. And you're not used to seeing teenagers dressed up, so I don't want you to say anything. Just promise me that you'll be casual about it. Tell her she looks nice and leave it at that,' Jenny instructed her husband.

But even she was taken aback when Maggie came downstairs to announce that she was ready to go to the village hall. She had already known about the black satin hipsters and the electric blue satin blouse, low cut and tied in a knot to expose the girl's bare midriff. She knew about the black high heeled sandals with the silver sequins scattered over them, for she had bought the entire outfit, handicapped by her promise to let Maggie choose whatever she wanted as her birthday gift. But she had not known about the eyebrow pencil, the dark blue eye shadow, plum-coloured lipstick and the gel that turned Maggie's black curls into spikes sticking up all over her head.

The girl posed, hands — with fingernails painted the same colour as her lips — on her hips. 'Well? What do you think?'

'Very nice,' Jenny said valiantly, aware that Andrew was frozen in horror by her side. 'You look very grown-up, dear.'

'Andrew?' It wasn't just the make-up and the clothes and the hair gel that had changed Maggie into a different person, Jenny realised. Her entire attitude was different; she could tell that by the way her stepdaughter's heavily mascara-ed lashes rose and fell as her dark eyes swept appraisingly over Andrew.

'Very — yes, very grown-up,' he said, and when Jenny went upstairs to fetch her coat he hurried after her, closing the bedroom door behind them.

187

'What the hell did you think you were doing, letting her buy those awful clothes?'

'I couldn't stop her. I'd promised to let her choose them herself. I didn't know that she was going to buy that sort of thing. And I didn't know about the make-up and what she was going to do with her hair. But it's only for the one evening, Andrew. She's at an experimental age.'

'I'd worked that one out for myself. Thank God Calum's not here, I'd hate him to see his new sister looking like a – a strumpet!'

'Oh, Andrew, that's not fair – she is not a strumpet!'

'No? What's that sparkly thing in her navel? You didn't let her get it pierced, did you?'

'Of course not, it must be stuck on.' Jenny fastened her coat hurriedly. 'Come on, we'd better go – and don't make a fuss, please!'

In place of the party Jenny had promised Calum, Peter MacKenzie, Ingrid's husband, had offered to take Calum, his own younger daughter Ella and Helen's oldest, Gregor to a cinema for the evening, while Helen's younger children were spending the evening at Jinty McDonald's house so that Helen and Ingrid were free to help with the party.

To their credit, neither of them reacted to Maggie's appearance, other than to tell her how nice she looked. Jenny looked enviously at Freya MacKenzie, who wore a loose white embroidered blouse over black velvet trousers, with her long fair hair held back by a black velvet band.

'She looks so smart – I wish Maggie had opted for something like that,' she whispered to Helen as they organised the food in the kitchen.

'She's learning to express herself – it's still your Maggie under all that party stuff.'

Once the other guests arrived Maggie began to look

quite normal. Andrew's eyes bulged as the classmates she had invited tossed their coats aside. Many of them had heads of gelled spikes, and some of the girls seemed to be wearing very little.

'Is that – yes it is, it's a tattoo!' he hissed into his wife's ear. 'And there's another. And that girl talking to Maggie – that's not a skirt she's wearing, it's a scarf!'

'It's the fashion, and it's only for one evening. Don't make a fuss, Andrew!'

'Have you seen that blonde girl? She looks as if someone tried to lasso her with that dress when she was passing below their window – and almost missed. I'm just glad that I decided to come; I wouldn't put it past some of those lads to try to smuggle alcohol in,' he muttered. Then as Naomi's godson Ethan arrived, conventionally dressed, 'Good for him – nice to know that some people know how to dress in public. Look at the poor lad, he doesn't know what's hit him.'

'I think he's rather enjoying himself,' Jenny said as Ethan, beaming, made a beeline for the group of scantily dressed girls gathered around Maggie. Then the disc jockey got to work and it was no longer possible to have a proper conversation without screaming at each other.

Jenny noticed halfway through the evening that the youngsters seemed to have split into two groups; the smaller section was made up of Freya, Ethan, and the more conventionally dressed boys and girls, while the larger group were the spiky-haired youngsters in what to adult eyes could almost be called outlandish outfits. Maggie was in their midst, whispering and giggling and squealing louder than anyone else.

When the disc jockey took a break and the refreshments were brought out, Jenny noticed that some of the guests tasted the soft drinks, then made faces at each other and put their glasses down without drinking any more. Now and again a few partygoers drifted from the hall, in twos, threes or fours, and each time Andrew, as watchful as a sheep dog, shot out after them and rounded them up.

'The little beggars were going out for a smoke, and God knows what else,' he reported when they were finally back home. 'I caught two of the lads with hip flasks. They weren't pleased when I poured the contents out onto the ground.'

'At least Maggie didn't sneak out.' Maggie had been more interested in giggling with her girlfriends than anything else.

Later that night Andrew got into bed and collapsed against the pillows with a sigh of relief. 'God, Jenny, that was one of the worst evenings of my life! What does Maggie see in that bunch of young layabouts?'

'That's not fair. They were enjoying themselves at a party; letting their hair down. They're probably really nice kids in their normal lives.'

'You wouldn't say that if you'd heard the language some of them used when I took their drink from them or made them stub out their cigarettes – and interrupted whatever one or two of them were up to with the girls. It was all I could do to hold back from giving them a clip on the ear.'

'Then they could have reported you to the police and you'd have ended up in court.'

'That's the trouble with this country nowadays; far too much kid-worship.'

'You're beginning to sound like a grumpy old man.'

'That's because I feel like one, and what's wrong with that? Maggie's allowed to have her hair gel and her glittery belly-button, why can't I be allowed my grumpiness?'

'Yes, but Maggie will grow out of being a teenager, while you just keep getting grumpier,' Jenny snapped, suddenly tired of his carping. If the truth were known, she too was concerned over the way Maggie had dressed and behaved. As soon as they returned home she had announced that she was tired, and gone upstairs without a word of thanks for the evening.

'Your girls looked so nice,' Jenny sighed the next day as Ingrid and Jinty helped her to put the village hall in order, 'but I couldn't say the same about Maggie.'

'She's a nice girl, and you can't blame her for wanting to be different for her birthday party.'

'Jinty's right. Maggie's at a restless age, too. She'll settle down,' Ingrid comforted.

Jenny thought about the missing milk money, and the five-pound note that she could have sworn had been in her purse the week before, then suddenly wasn't. She wished that she could talk to someone about her suspicions but couldn't bring herself to betray Maggie by saying them aloud. Instead, she asked, 'How does Freya get on with her? I'd hoped that they'd become good friends, but Maggie spent most of the evening with youngsters I didn't even know.'

'It was natural for her to mix with the friends she only sees at school.' Did you see Ethan?' Ingrid asked, amused, 'He's got a crush on my Freya, but his eyes almost came out on stalks when he saw Maggie last night.'

'So did Andrew's, but for an entirely different reason.'

'Men can be very conservative. If it had been left to them we would probably still be wearing bustles, and pantaloons down to our ankles.'

As she and Jenny walked home, Ingrid reached into her

bag and took out an envelope. 'This came yesterday, from Marcy.'

'She doesn't give away much, does she?' Jenny commented when she had scanned the single page. 'Just that she's fine and the job's OK.'

'I think she says a lot more than she means to. If she were enjoying her life she would tell us. If you ask me, she's unhappy, and she's missing Prior's Ford, and her friends.'

'And Sam?'

'Oh yes – Sam most of all. Marcy Copleton's a very courageous woman, Jenny; she doesn't cry on shoulders, and yet to me,' Ingrid took the letter back, 'this paper is wet with her tears.'

'So why does she have to be so stubborn?' Jenny burst out impatiently. 'Why not come back where she knows she belongs?'

'Perhaps I should have said that she is proud rather than courageous – though she's both. I have a suspicion that deep down, Marcy doesn't believe that she deserves to be loved. Think about what we've learned from the few words she's said over the years; parents who didn't show affection, then living with a husband who gambled away every penny she earned and pushed her into debt.'

'And then she came here, and found Sam and love.'

'Yes, but by then poor Marcy had become so suspicious of the world, and so used to being let down by people she thought she could trust, that she couldn't allow herself to feel safe. Why do you think she and Sam were always having disagreements? It was because Marcy had to keep testing him, wanting him to prove his love for her. And that silly quarry business was the final straw for her – Sam was for it, she was against it, and he wouldn't budge. So she left him.'

'It wasn't all one-sided, though. He was just as pig-headed as she was.'

'Indeed, and that is why I suspect that our Sam, also, has a difficult background. We know nothing about his past, do we? Perhaps two wounded souls found each other, but they couldn't heal each other.'

'Ingrid, you're beginning to sound like a cross between a romantic poet and an armchair psychiatrist. I wish she hadn't sworn us to secrecy – it's not fair on poor Sam! He's missing her so much, and he's turning into a recluse. Can't you tell her that?'

'I do, but as you see from her letters, she never mentions him.'

'I think we're going to have to find some way of getting them together,' Jenny announced as they reached her gate and parted company.

23

As always, every pew was filled for the Easter Sunday family service. The weather was kind, and sunshine pouring through the stained-glass windows filled the small church with colour. Huge vases of daffodils and narcissi at either side of the altar wafted a faint scent of spring to those sitting near to them.

Naomi Hennessey, with the assistance of story boards painted by Alastair Marshall, told the Easter story in vivid word-pictures and then the older children from the village school acted out their own version, with songs written by one of their teachers.

'Very nicely done, too,' Jinty McDonald said to Jenny as the congregation spilled out of the church afterwards. 'I always feel that the Easter story's a bit difficult for children, with the crucifixion and Christ being entombed when he turns out to be alive. But Naomi managed to avoid the nastiness and just concentrate on the good side of things.' Then, lowering her voice to a confidential murmur, 'Talk about getting dressed up for church – that outfit would upstage the Queen at a royal garden party.' She nodded towards Meredith Whitelaw, stunning in a peacock blue suit with a wide-brimmed matching hat.

'It's great to have a real celebrity living in the village, isn't it?'

'I'll not deny that. And she's a kind woman — she's promised to give Steph a reference when she applies to a drama college. Ah well,' Jinty said as the two of them turned down River Lane, 'time to think about feeding my brood.'

As Jinty went homewards to exchange her good Sunday clothes for a pinny and a kitchen stove, Ewan found Alison among the crowd.

'My mum wondered if you and Jamie would like to come to the farm this afternoon.'

'You go, love, Jamie really enjoyed visiting the farm last time. He's still talking about it,' Gracie told Ewan.

'Mum enjoyed it too. She's planning an Easter egg hunt for him.'

'That's kind of her. Yes, we'd love to come.'

'Great. I'll come for you at two o'clock, and get you back home before five.'

'And stay on for your dinner, Ewan,' Gracie urged.

'You're being a bit of a matchmaker, aren't you?' her husband said when she told him about their dinner guest.

'He's a nice lad — and he's fairly got our Alison taking an interest in life again. I can never thank him enough for that,' she said with a catch in her throat. 'There was a time after Robbie was killed when I thought we were going to lose our lass as well, Joe. You mind the way she was? Not eating, not speaking, wasting away in front of our eyes.'

'Aye, I mind it well enough.'

'If she hadn't had Jamie to think of I don't know if she'd be alive today. It was a good move, coming here, and young

Ewan McNair's managed to bring the life back to her eyes
– bless him!'

After her guests had eaten their fill of her home-baking
that afternoon, Jess McNair handed a small basket to Jamie.
'Now then, my wee lad, everyone on a farm has to earn
their keep, so I'd be glad if you'd come with me to the
henhouse to collect eggs.'

'I've never been on a farm before,' Alison said when her
son had gone off, clutching Jess's hand. 'I was raised in the
city but I really like the country now that I'm living here.
It's better for Jamie – safer, and there's good fresh air too.'
She started to gather the used plates together.

'Leave them, I'll do them later.'

'Did you not hear your mother, Ewan? Everyone has to
pull their weight on a farm.' She smiled at him and then
turned to the sink, the movement swinging her long fair
hair about her shoulders. 'Did you never want to do anything
else but farming?' she asked over the splash of water from
the tap.

'Never – I was born to farm.' Ewan put the unused bread
into the bread bin and the scones into their tin. 'Tarbethill's
been in the family for a long time and I'll be happy to go
on livin' here for the rest of my life, God willin'.'

'Do you ever go on holiday?'

'Oh yes, I've been here and there, and I did a bit of
travellin' abroad for three months after I finished school
– that was my mother's idea; she said that Victor and I
should both take a break, to make sure that we didn't feel
trapped here – but the way I see it, holidays are for folk
that need to get away from what they do all year. I don't
need that.'

'Where's the washing-up liquid? Thanks,' Alison said as

he pointed to the bottle on the windowsill. 'Does your brother feel the same as you do?'

'You know that old song about how are you goin' to keep him down on the farm, after he's seen Paree? Victor's a bit like that. He enjoyed travellin', and he's courtin' a Kirkcudbright lass who's not got much time for Tarbethill. So I don't know if he'll want to stay on here. Not that the farm's big enough to support the two of us anyway, nowadays.'

He picked up a dishcloth and began to dry the dishes she had stacked on the draining board. 'Farmin' doesnae pay the way it used to. We lost all our beasts in the foot and mouth outbreak a few years back and it cost a fortune to replace them. They'd all been born and raised on the farm. It was a terrible time! We've had to cut back on the milk herd and my dad's talkin' now about gettin' rid of the rest. It'll be a wrench if we have to do that. There's still the sheep, but our two best fields are rented out to larger farms now to make money. I'm goin' to try to do up the old farm cottage – I thought we could mebbe let it to holidaymakers.' He stared down at the cup he had been drying for the past minute. 'I couldnae bear the thought of the McNairs and Tarbethill partin' company,' he said. 'I'm not like Victor – I'm a right stay-at-home. I never want to leave here.' Then, looking at her with something close to despair in his blue eyes, he said, 'I have to think of some way to keep us goin'!'

'Mummy, mummy!' Jamie came charging in through the door, the little basket clutched tightly against his chest and his eyes wide with delight. 'The hens laid real Easter eggs – and I found them in a nest and Mrs McNair says that I can take them home!'

'I was thinking,' Alison said as Ewan drove her home later, 'about an article I saw in a magazine recently. It was about wormeries.'

'Wormeries?'

Jamie, in the back seat, was giggling over the way his Easter eggs jumped in their basket as the car bounced over the ruts in the lane, and Ewan was trying to make the journey smoother.

'Wormeries — apparently people use worms to make compost to sell, and they can sell the worms too, to fishermen. And I was wondering if your father would be interested in setting up something like that to make money for the farm. I think we might still have the article — but it's probably a daft idea,' Alison added apologetically.

'I've heard about these wormeries but I never thought of it for us. I'd like to see that article if you can find it.'

Helen's voice spilled through the receiver into Jenny's ear, bubbling with happiness. 'I just got a phone call from the editor and he likes my replies to those letters he gave me to answer. Isn't that wonderful?'

'It's only what I expected. I knew you could do it.'

'That's more than I did,' Helen admitted. 'I almost took them all back to ask if he could find someone else to do it. But then I remembered what you said about pretending that I was advising a friend, and *then* I remembered a girl I used to know in school that always needed help and advice. So I just pretended that every letter came from her — and it worked! So I'm going to go on with it. It means less time to spare for my novel, but it's great to get paid every month, even if it's only a small amount. I like having my own money instead of always having to ask Duncan when I need extra. And I'm still being paid for writing, even if it isn't the novel.'

'Well done, Helen, I knew that you'd make a terrific agony aunt,' Jenny said warmly.

'Thanks again for having faith in me. Calum says can he

stay for another half hour? He and Gregor are in the middle of creating Jurassic Park out of Plasticine.'

'Yes, as long as he makes it half an hour and no longer. Better Jurassic Park in Plasticine than those horrendous computer games.'

'I count myself quite lucky that we can't afford computer games for our children – I'm sure it restricts their imaginations. Then I wonder if they're being deprived. It's difficult being a parent,' Helen said cheerfully. 'Always worrying about their emotional growth while you're trying to cope with them physically growing out of expensive things like shoes and coats.'

'Mmm. Helen, have you noticed anything different about Calum?'

'I can't say I have. What sort of different?'

'He's been a bit quiet recently, as if there's something on his mind.'

'He's been as bright as a button all morning.'

'Good – I'm just being too mumsy,' Jenny said, and hung up. Then she jumped as Maggie asked from where she sat halfway up the stairs,' What's an agony aunt?'

'I didn't see you there.'

'I was waiting until you came off the phone to ask if you know where my blue jacket is. I can't find it anywhere.' Maggie came down the stairs two at a time. The gel and the spiky hairstyle and the weird clothes of the party were gone and she was back to being her usual pretty self in jeans and a long-sleeved sweatshirt, with her favourite Scooby Doo slippers on her feet.

'Two of the buttons were coming loose so I sewed them on last night.' Jenny led the way into the living room where she collected the jacket and handed it over. 'I thought you were going to spend the morning at Freya's.'

Maggie wrinkled her nose and crossed her eyes. 'I was, but she's all wrapped up in planning this new playground they're going to build at the old quarry, so I came home again.'

'Don't you want to help with the playground? Freya's done a great job of bringing the village children together to decide what sort of playground they want. They've even worked out the cost of everything.'

'Well, terrific for them, but playgrounds are for kids! What's an agony aunt?' Maggie asked again, trailing into the kitchen behind Jenny.

'Someone who answers letters people send in to a magazine or a newspaper, asking for advice.'

'Is that all? I thought it was more interesting than that.'

'It *is* interesting. Helen started writing a column about what was going on in Prior's Ford recently for the *Dumfries News* – things that the school's doing, and the Women's Institute and so on – and then the editor asked her if she would like to try her hand at doing the agony aunt page. She's just finished her first lot and the editor likes it.'

Jenny got out the chopping board and delved into the vegetable rack, while Maggie leaned back against a worktop. 'Why would people be daft enough to write to a stranger about their problems? Can't they work things out for themselves?'

'Sometimes you can be too close to a problem to be able to think it through clearly. And sometimes when you need to talk to someone about your worries, there isn't anyone you can trust. That's when you might write to a stranger who doesn't know you and can't go blabbing to your friends about your private business.'

'It still sounds a bit weird.' Maggie scratched her head, yawned, then said, 'I'm bored.'

'Want to help me with lunch?'

'I'm not that bored!'

'Calum'll be home soon, and Andrew.' Andrew had taken the car to have a new exhaust fitted. 'Have you written those thank you letters to your grandparents and Aunt Lizbeth and Uncle Malcolm yet?'

'Nope.'

'You could get started on them if you haven't got anything else to do.'

'I don't see why I should go to all that bother. I said thanks when I phoned Gran last week.'

'She phoned you, to wish you a happy birthday.'

Maggie shrugged. 'Whatever – anyway, I said thanks.'

'A letter would be nice. They sent you lovely presents.'

'Guilt gifts.'

'What are you talking about?'

The girl heaved a sigh, crossing her arms across her chest. 'They sent decent gifts to make up for not bothering to visit me and in any case, they have to do that because I'm their granddaughter and their niece. It's their duty.'

'And it's your duty to thank them properly.'

'Why should I have to be dutiful? I didn't ask to be born.'

'Maggie!'

'Well, it's true. I didn't ask to be born and if you want to know the truth, I wish I hadn't been.'

'Oh, love, don't say that!' Jenny reached out to the girl, but Maggie swiftly sidestepped so that Jenny's hand closed on empty air. 'It's not true.'

'It is. They gave me nice presents because they feel guilty about not wanting me. You made me come here because you feel guilty about abandoning me when I was little. You'd all be happier without me but you haven't got the guts to admit it.'

201

Jenny began to get angry. 'Don't be so melodramatic! You're fifteen now, old enough to understand what it's like for other people. Your grandfather couldn't help falling ill, and I know that Lizbeth would have loved to take you, but how could she look after you when she's so ill herself?'

'I could have looked after her,' Maggie snapped 'I'd rather be there, looking after her than stuck here!' She flounced into the hall and Jenny heard her running upstairs.

Bewildered, she hovered at the foot of the stairs, wishing that Andrew was home to help her deal with the situation and unsure as to whether to follow Maggie, or leave the girl on her own for a while.

Then the bedroom door opened and Maggie came down the stairs, her shoes and coat on.

'I'm going out,' she said as she walked past Jenny.

'Out where?'

'I don't know – to Kirkcudbright, probably.'

'But lunch will be ready soon.'

'I'll get a hamburger.' Maggie opened the front door.

'Maggie, wait!' But the door had crashed shut and other than running after the girl and risking a shouting match in public, there was nothing Jenny could do.

Much as she wanted to talk to Andrew about Maggie's sudden outburst, Jenny decided against it. Andrew had warned her when she was set on bringing the girl to Prior's Ford that Maggie was no longer the loving, trusting toddler she had last seen. He would only point out what Jenny already knew – that Maggie was at a difficult age, and she should have given more serious thought to her plans.

In other words, she had made her bed, and she would have to lie in it. Difficult though she might be, Maggie was still a child and Jenny the responsible adult who had no option but to put the scene they had just gone through behind her, and say nothing about it, even to Jinty and Ingrid.

When Andrew and Calum asked where Maggie was, she told them casually that she had decided to go into Kirkcudbright to meet a friend from school. To her relief, the girl arrived home in the middle of the afternoon, relaxed and cheerful, behaving as though their row had never happened.

It had been a storm in a teacup, Jenny told herself; a normal teenage-daughter-and-mother argument.

24

April brought milder weather, and the lambing season. Alison saw little of Ewan, other than at rehearsals, where he looked tired and preoccupied. He rarely had time to visit the Neurotic Cuckoo and she was surprised at how much she missed seeing him.

The first of the year's tourists began to appear in the village, and the Gift Horse opened for business, its two bay windows and its shelves bright with ornaments, toys made by Jenny, Alastair Marshall's paintings and Ingrid's greetings cards.

The shoebox Alastair kept Clarissa Ramsay's letters and photographs in was more than half full; he would soon have to find another box as her year away was only now heading for its halfway mark. Almost every day he read through her letters, each one so filled with the excitement of visiting places she had only dreamed of before that he could hear her voice as he read.

Hello, Alastair, I've just arrived in San Francisco – can't quite believe I'm actually here! The flight was fine. I had a window seat and got the most terrific views of icebergs and snow as we flew over Greenland and Hudson's Bay. Not a part of the world to crash! The hotel is downtown and I'm on the twelfth floor. Three days and nights here to do San Fran before the cruise. Longing to get my head down. I'll write again before leaving dry land.

Love, C

There were photographs too – Clarissa alone or posing with other travellers on board the ship taking her from San Francisco to New Zealand via Hawaii, Samoa, and Fiji; Clarissa admiring masses of tropical blossoms in Hawaii, and standing outside Robert Louis Stevenson's house in Western Samoa. Alastair never tired of looking at them and marvelling over how young and happy she looked.

I have just experienced the Day That Never Was. We crossed the International Date Line, which means that an entire day was missed out – to think that for the rest of my life I will be one day short. I wonder what I would have done with it? We will never know.

There were photographs of the fire-walkers in Fiji; The people in these islands are Polynesian, big, golden-skinned and very warm and friendly. The women often have great manes of black hair hanging down their backs. All the islands have the most glorious vegetation, with flowering shrubs and every shade of green . . . Fiji bade us farewell with a quite spectacular thunderstorm. It was very hot and very humid as February is their wet season. Yours happily but damply . . . New Zealand is so cool and fresh after Fiji . . . and we had a wonderful day in Auckland . . . we went in a catamaran to the Bay of Islands, where cannibals used to eat missionaries, poor souls. The missionaries, I mean. Taking lots of photographs because I know that

205

when I get home to Prior's Ford I'll find it hard to believe that I have actually been to all those wonderful places . . .

Alastair, who had wondered if her travels had made Prior's Ford an uninteresting place to return to, felt cheered every time he read that casual phrase, *when I get home to Prior's Ford.*

She loved the tiny pictures he had drawn for her, and asked him to keep sending them, *so that I can remember Prior's Ford clearly and keep my feet on the ground. I do miss the place – and I miss you*, she had written.

He put the letters and photographs back in their envelopes and turned to his sketchbook. Before he went to bed that night, one page was filled with pictures of a ewe in one of the Tarbethill Farm fields with her tiny twin lambs, colourful groups of worshippers mingling outside the church after the Easter service, the blossom beginning to appear on the cherry trees and children playing on the village green and on the stepping stones by the old priory. After some thought, he filled in the final empty space with a sketch of Willow Cottage waiting, like Alastair, for her return.

Linn Hall's roof was almost watertight now, and the next part of the plan was to install central heating. The two gatehouses had been prepared as dormitories for the young backpackers who roamed the country during the summer months, taking work wherever they could find it. Most of those employed by the Ralston-Kerrs would help Alastair and Duncan in the grounds while one, or perhaps two, helped Jinty and Fliss in the kitchen.

Fliss had taken to making lists, something she had never felt the need for before, and coming up with ideas such as selling off the impressive collection of antique chamber pots, used in the days when Hector's grandparents had held house parties.

'They've been so handy for catching the drips when it rained, but now the roof's being fixed we don't need them, do we? Some are quite pretty, and Jinty thinks that they could be worth quite a lot. So what do you say, Hector? Shall we send them to an auction house? We can always do with more money.'

'Why would anyone want to buy a china chamber pot nowadays?' her husband asked, puzzled. 'Everyone's got bathrooms now − it seems to me that most of 'em have more bathrooms than we have. Nobody uses chamber pots any more.'

'Not for their original purpose, but they're used nowadays as ornaments and for putting things in − like pot plants.'

'Good Lord!' Hector found it hard to understand why anyone would possibly want to put something made to cope with a basic bodily function on show in their living rooms, let alone plant flowers in them. 'Extraordinary. I can't think what my grandmother would have to say about that.'

'I imagine that she would have said we should get rid of them, and if we make money at the same time, good luck to us. I'm going to collect them all together, then ask one of the local auctioneers to have a look. Is that all right with you, dear?'

'Do whatever you like; I've certainly not got any plans for them − and that includes growing flowers in 'em!' her husband said firmly.

Lewis was in his element. He and Duncan, with help from Ginny, had started clearing out the old stables in preparation for turning them into a shop selling vegetables, herbs, flowers, and seeds. To his surprise they unearthed a treasure trove of implements, some reaching back to the days when the stables were used to house the family horses and carriages. There were also items from the days of the first cars as well as unwanted pieces from the house and some old gardening implements.

'There's such a lot of history here!' Ginny said, awed.

'A lot of rubbish to be got rid of, too,' Duncan grunted.

'I'm not so sure about that. Look – this is an old jelly pan, isn't it? And there's a box of pots and pans there – they must have been thrown out when new stuff was brought in.'

'That wasn't in my time,' Lewis said. 'My mother's still using the pots and pans and plates my grandmother used.'

'And there's an old harness that might be all right if it was oiled and polished up.'

'What for? You're not planning to get yourself a pony and trap, are you, Lewis?' Duncan guffawed at the thought.

'Even if he was, this stuff would be too old, but it would be great for atmosphere,' Ginny pointed out. 'The stables are roomy enough for things to be hung on the walls, or displayed here and there. Once they've been cleaned up they could look really impressive. Let me sort through them and pick out what should be kept. The rest could be sold to collectors.'

'You think someone would buy this tat?'

'It's not tat, Lewis, it's antiques, and yes, people would buy just about everything here. There's a craze on just now for items from the past.'

'The house is full of stuff that's been locked away for as long as I remember. My mother and Jinty were talking the other day about getting an auctioneer in.'

'Tell your mother not to hurry, Lewis,' Ginny advised. 'The first thing to do is to find someone reliable to take an inventory of everything you don't need – here in the stables as well as in the house. Then you can talk things over with a good auctioneer.'

Ginny had never enjoyed herself as much in her life as she did in Prior's Ford. Especially now that Molly Ewing and her bump had returned to Inverness. For her, the year was going by too fast.

Little did she know it, but even as she and Duncan and Lewis started picking through the items in the stables, the phone was ringing in Willow Cottage, about to put an end to Meredith's 'resting' year.

A mere five minutes after the telephone rang in Willow Cottage the instrument across the village green in Daisy Cottage burst into life. Elinor, who happened to be passing through the hall at the time, took the call.

'Just a moment,' she said sweetly, and laid the receiver down gently on the hall table, sticking her tongue out at it as she did so. Then she went to the bottom of the stairs to call, 'Kevin? Telephone for you.'

'I can't be interrupted just now – tell whoever it is that I'll call them back.' Kevin was working industriously on the treatment for Meredith, and at last, after many false starts, he felt that he was beginning to get something worth showing to her.

'It's Ms Whitelaw, dear. Are you sure you're too busy to—'

But Kevin was already thundering down the stairs, frantically signalling to his wife to keep quiet. He brushed past her and snatched up the receiver. 'Meredith? Glad you called; I was just working on that treatment and I think I might have come up with . . .'

But Meredith wasn't listening. 'Kevin – wonderful news. I wanted you to be the first to know!'

'Oh? You've arranged for some of your colleagues to come to the show in June?'

'No, much better than that! I've been offered a part in a costume drama in eight parts. I'm going to be in most of the episodes, my agent says. Isn't it exciting? I've never done a costume drama before.'

'When's this happening?'

'They start filming in three weeks' time and it'll take up most of the summer. By then I expect more work will have come in. Usually one thing leads to another in my profession.'

'Three weeks?' Kevin's voice rose to a squeak and Elinor, realising that things were not going his way, went quietly to the kitchen.

'My dear, I *know*! They've scarcely given me time to turn around, let alone get packed and find somewhere to stay during the filming. It's in Dover, did I say? With some of the interior shots done in London. And I didn't even have to audition – the director said, "I want Meredith Whitelaw." So flattering!'

'But Meredith, what about our three one-act plays?'

'Kevin, darling, you surely can't expect me to put a little amateur village show before my proper work as a professional actress! Ewan and Alison will be fine, you just need to keep an eye on them and make sure that they keep working.'

'But *Visiting Vanessa* . . .'

'I know, it was coming along so well, wasn't it? But the woman who was going to take the part before you offered it to me can do it, surely? Not as well as I would, of course, but I'm sure it will all work out.'

'I've been working on that treatment you wanted,' Kevin offered feebly, 'I think I've just come up with a good storyline.'

'That's wonderful, darling. Send it to me – you never know, I might need it one day. Must go and pass on the good news. Bye,' said Meredith and put the phone down.

Kevin stood for a moment, staring at the receiver, then laid it back in its cradle and went slowly to the kitchen.

'Bad news, dear?' Elinor asked gently as he slumped into a chair at the kitchen table, head in his hands. He didn't seem to have the energy to raise his head, but she caught a few words as he murmured into the sleeves of his thick jersey. 'Meredith . . . part in a television series . . . leaving in three weeks . . .'

'Is she coming back?'

His head swung slowly to and fro.

'Oh dear.' She put a steaming cup of coffee before him and laid a plate beside it. 'Have a chocolate biscuit, dear, it'll help you to feel better.'

'The worst of it is, Elinor,' Kevin said, after a few reviving sips of coffee and a mouthful of chocolate biscuit, 'that I'm going to have to ask Cynthia MacBain to take the role again.'

'So you will. Oh dear.'

'It won't be easy.'

'No, it won't. Poor Kevin.' She reached across the table and patted his hand. It was what wives did – and in all the years of her marriage to Kevin, Elinor had had to do it more than most.

Ginny went round to the back door, as she always did on her return to Willow Cottage after working at Linn Hall, so that she could sit on the step and haul her boots off.

As soon as she went in she realised that Meredith, as was so often the case, was on the telephone. Ginny placed her boots neatly on the sheet of newspaper kept just inside the door and went for a shower.

211

'So much to do, darling, and in such a short time,' Meredith was saying into the receiver. She flapped a hand at her daughter, but since Ginny had no idea whether the gesture meant 'Wait here, I want to speak to you,' or 'Get upstairs and change out of those disgusting clothes,' she continued on her way.

She took her time in the bathroom, shampooing her hair and singing loudly, tunelessly and happily as the hot water eased slightly sore muscles and sloughed away the dust of a good day's work. After towelling her head vigorously she ran a comb through it, put on a sweater and comfortable old trousers, then headed back to the kitchen, still singing.

'Is that you, Ginny?' her mother called from her bedroom.

'No, it's a burglar imitating my voice.'

'Come in here, I have something to tell you.'

'I'm starving; I'll make a sandwich first, and a cup of coffee. Want one?'

'You can get something to eat after I've told you!'

Ginny sighed and went in to find Meredith going through her wardrobe. Several items of clothing were folded and lying on the bed.

'There you are at last! Why didn't you wait in the hall when I told you to?'

'You didn't tell me, you waved at me and I didn't know what it meant.'

'It meant, wait here! And I banged on the bathroom door, but between the water running and that terrible noise you were making you obviously didn't hear me.'

'Obviously not. What are you doing?' Ginny asked as Meredith took a skirt from its hanger and began to fold it.

'Packing. We're going back to London, isn't it exciting?'

'Going back to London? We've only just got here!'

'Don't be silly, darling, we've been here for ages. My agent

212

phoned.' Meredith beamed. 'I've been offered a part in a costume drama – eight episodes and filming begins almost right away. They want me there by the middle of next week. So there's no time to waste.'

Ginny's sense of contentment and wellbeing suddenly vanished. 'What sort of part?'

'I don't know much about it – they don't even need an audition,' Meredith said proudly. 'It's a Lady something and I'm in most of the episodes, I know that much. Costume drama, Genevieve – I've not done that for years. I can't wait to get at those lovely long skirts and petticoats and wide-brimmed hats. They make one feel so feminine! No, Gielgud,' she chided, lifting the cat from the bed, where he was clearly thinking that a pale pink angora sweater would make a very comfortable mattress. She scooped him into her arms, kissed the top of his head, and deposited him on the landing, closing the door behind her as she returned to the room.

'When are you leaving?'

'The day after tomorrow. I've checked the trains and arranged for the hired car to be collected from the station and phoned Mrs Norris and asked her to get the flat aired.' Mrs Norris was their housekeeper.

'But you took this house for a year, you can't just change your mind halfway through. And what about my job, and you helping out with the drama club?'

'That was just a bit of fun; they managed without me before and they can all manage perfectly well without me again. This is much more important than a piffling little amateur club. I've told Kevin and he understands completely. I don't suppose that it'll take you long to pack since you didn't bring much. Still, best get started.' Meredith made shooing motions at her daughter.

'I'm going to make a sandwich and some coffee first. I'm starving.'

'Close the door behind, you, I don't want Gielgud in here.'

As Ginny opened the bedroom door, Gielgud, who had been sulking on the landing, gave her a hard blue stare. She opened the door a little wider, jerking her head slightly towards the room. He blinked and then slid past her ankles.

She closed the door and went downstairs slowly. It had been such a good day, and she and Lewis and Duncan had made so many plans. Next week the poly tunnel was arriving; it had been her idea to set it up in the kitchen garden. She had drawn up a list of new plants for the area and now, with her work only half done, she was going to have to leave. She probably wouldn't have much trouble getting her old job back but it wouldn't be the same as being part of a team working to bring the Linn Hall gardens back to their former glory.

She hadn't even had time to find the waterfall that had given Linn Hall its name, and had fed the dried up lake.

Why, she wondered despondently, did life have to be so bloody unfair?

25

Ginny slept badly and woke at half six the next morning. By seven she had showered and dressed and was in the garden, tearing the compost heap apart and reorganising it. When she had finished, she made herself some breakfast and carried it out to the garden, where she soaked up the morning sunshine while she ate.

Meredith was never seen by anyone, even her daughter, before ten in the morning. She claimed that she slept late, a habit instilled in the days when most of her work had been on the stage. 'Late to bed, late to rise,' she would explain sweetly to everyone, but Ginny suspected that her mother rose much earlier than she claimed in order to put on her make-up and work on her hair. Even at home, Meredith was immaculate when she appeared in the mornings.

It was almost half past ten when she appeared at the back door, coffee cup in hand.

'There you are, darling. I thought you'd gone to that job of yours.'

Ginny, weeding one of the borders, got to her feet. 'I phoned and told them I'd be late.'

'You should just have handed in your notice. There are things to do here before we go.'

'Before *you* go. I've decided to stay here.'

Meredith blinked her false eyelashes. 'But you can't!'

'Yes I can. You've taken this place until November, so I can stay on until the let's up. I like Prior's Ford and I like my work at the Hall. I want to see the gardens through the summer – then I might come back. Or might not. Is there some coffee left?'

'But how am I going to get back to London, with all my luggage, not to mention Gielgud?'

'I'll drive you to the railway station and see you settled on the train, then hand the car over to the hire company you got it from. They might have something more suited for me – something a lot less expensive, too. When you get to London, there'll be porters and taxis. You'll be fine,' Ginny said, and went to fetch her coffee.

Wearing her agony aunt hat, Helen had dealt with a dozen letters from the current batch quickly and competently. She was beginning to build up confidence in herself, though she did wonder if the whisky-adulterated coffee she made before tackling the letters also played its part.

Because Duncan was sure to notice if the level in his whisky bottle went down so much, she had had to invest some of her earnings in the smallest bottle of the cheapest whisky on the village store shelves. The day was coming, she knew, when she must face the letters without spiritual aid, so to speak. But not yet.

Checking her watch, she saw that she still had the best part of an hour to herself before the children arrived home from school. She withdrew the next letter from its envelope and read it. Then, puzzled, she read it a second time before carrying it downstairs.

Jenny, who hated ironing, welcomed the interruption. 'Yes, of course I'll come over if it's important. Nothing wrong, is there?'

'No – well, maybe. I don't know,' Helen said. 'Just come, will you?'

When Jenny arrived five minutes later, Helen started talking as soon as she had ushered her visitor into the kitchen. 'I was working on the agony aunt letters, and then I opened this one.' She held the single sheet out but instead of taking it, Jenny took a step back.

'I don't think I should read it – at least, not until it appears in the paper.'

'You have to read it, Jenny!'

Puzzled, Jenny took the page, covered in careful, rounded handwriting.

Dear Lucinda Keen,

My mother died when I was born and my dad married again so that I would have a mother. But when I was still very young she deserted us both and we had to go and live with my Gran and Granddad so that they could look after me when my dad was working. I was very happy with them but my dad died in an accident two years ago and then my Granddad fell ill. Now I've been sent away to live with my stepmother, and you know what they say in the stories about wicked stepmothers. She doesn't even try to understand how hard it is for me to have to live with people I don't know. She puts her real son before me every time and I feel like an outsider. I have been told that I must stay with this family until I am old enough to be on my own, but I hate it. I miss my Gran and Granddad, and my school and my friends. Is there someone I can turn to for help?

It was signed, *Unhappy Teenager.*

Watching her friend's face, Helen saw distaste at reading someone else's letter swiftly replaced by surprise, then dawning astonishment.

'I thought you might recognise the handwriting,' she said.

'I certainly recognise the tone of the letter, but it's not her handwriting. She must have got someone else to write it for her.'

'So it *is* Maggie. She sounds really unhappy, Jenny.'

'You don't think that this nonsense is true, do you? She's putting it on!'

'But she doesn't know that I'm Lucinda Keen.'

'She does, she overheard me talking to you about it on the phone one day. She's taking a rise out of you – out of both of us. Look at the information she gives – her mother died when she was born, and her father two years ago. And her grandfather falling ill, and me having a son of my own. She hoped that you would pick up these clues and show the letter to me.'

'Why would she do that? She's such a nice, well-behaved girl. And she seems happy to me.'

'I haven't said anything to anyone, but there have been problems.' Jenny told her friend about the money going missing, and Calum becoming quiet and reserved. 'She's sulky and bad-tempered and not nearly as easy to get on with as I thought she would be. Andrew tried to warn me but I was so set on getting Maggie back that I wouldn't listen. I haven't told him anything about the missing money or the temper tantrum she had the other week when she walked out of the house,' Jenny admitted. 'It's beginning to look as though he was right, and I should have thought things through properly.

But there wasn't time – and if I show this letter to him, he might decide that we'll have to make other arrangements for her. That would mean a children's home or a foster family, and I couldn't bear to let that happen!'

'Perhaps you should have a word with her grandmother.'

'Absolutely not! She's got enough to worry about. That's another thing,' Jenny said, 'Anne and I phone each other every week, but Maggie refuses to phone them, or even talk to them sometimes. I have to pretend she's out, or in the bath.'

'I'll tear the letter up.'

'Thanks,' Jenny said, then almost at once, 'No, let me have it. I've been hoping that she'd settle down, but perhaps the time's come to confront her and bring things out into the open.'

Meredith Whitelaw left Prior's Ford as she had entered it – sitting in the front passenger seat and waving an elegant hand at anyone they passed on the way through the village. The boot was packed with luggage and Gielgud, who hated travelling, wailed his farewells and good riddances from his basket on the back seat.

'I have to say that a bit of colour's gone out of the place with her leaving,' Jinty said to her daughter Steph as they waved back from the doorway of the village store. 'It was nice, having a celebrity in our wee village. It gave us something to talk about.'

'I'll miss her. She was very kind to me.' Meredith had given Steph her card, and told her to get in touch when she left school. 'But first, my dear,' she had added as the card changed hands, 'you must complete your education. Acting is a precarious career, and you never know when you'll have to fall back on other means of earning your living.' And then, fixing Steph with a firm gaze, 'And don't think that you can always rely on a man to pay your bills. Men tend to think that they should be the only person in a woman's life, and actresses need to be free and independent if they want to get on in their careers.'

Steph repeated this advice to her mother as the two of them turned towards home, each carrying two bags of shopping.

'She's right, you know. It can be the most wonderful thing to have the right man in your life,' said Jinty, who adored her husband, Tom, 'but a woman has to be able to earn her own keep. Love's grand, but independence is good too.'

'I don't think I want to get married anyway.' Steph swung the shopping bags as she walked, 'I like the idea of being independent.'

'But you'll surely want children.' Jinty adored children and now that her own childbearing days seemed to have come to a close she was already looking forward to being a grandparent.

'I can have children without having to get married. People do.'

'Not McDonalds, my girl, so you can just forget that footloose idea,' her mother said grimly.

Ginny had had a busy but satisfactory day. Once her mother and Gielgud were seen off on the train she returned the sleek, expensive car to the hire company and then wandered round several used car companies. Her father, a man she rarely saw as he now lived with his current family in Australia, had not forgotten her entirely. When he and Meredith parted company he had set up a trust fund for his young daughter.

By the time she reached her twenty-first birthday the trust represented a tidy sum, but having no immediate need for the money, Ginny had put it into a high-interest savings account and forgotten about it, turning a deaf ear to Meredith's urging to invest in a new wardrobe, visit a really good hairdresser and take lessons in deportment. She had even, to Ginny's disgust, dropped hints about plastic surgery.

'How are you going to find your soul mate if you don't make the most of yourself?' Meredith had screeched at her stubborn daughter.

'If he's my soul mate *he'll* find *me* no matter what I look like. I'm quite happy with this nose, and the sort of bust you'd like me to have would only get in the way when I'm trying to weed,' Ginny had retorted, and the money was left to gather interest.

Today, for the first time in the two years since getting access to the money, Ginny finally spent a chunk of it on a nice little grey Mini, perfect for her needs.

She arrived in the village by bus, having arranged to collect the car in a week's time, and closed Willow Cottage's front door behind her.

'Hello, house,' she called softly, and then said it again, louder. 'Hello house, I'm home!'

Then she raced up the stairs and into her room, where she bounced on the bed, giggling like a teenager, before racing back downstairs, taking the steps two at a time.

'Home, home, home alone!' she sang, dancing along the hall. 'And it's no more Genevieve – hello Ginny!'

The rest of the year was going to be great!

Kevin Pearce didn't feel in the least like dancing; he felt like getting into bed and pulling the duvet over his head and staying there until someone solved all his problems.

Since Meredith had dropped her bombshell, Elinor had tried more than once to get Kevin to ask Cynthia MacBain to return to the drama group.

'You're going to have to speak to her before the next rehearsal.'

'I know – I will!' he snapped back every time, then found one excuse after another for putting the moment off. Part of him kept hoping against hope that Meredith would change her mind, or that the job offered to her would fall through, but the day came when he watched from behind the living-room curtains as Ginny loaded up the car and then drove her mother to the railway station in Dumfries.

Elinor was shopping; peering round the fall of the curtains Kevin saw her come along Adam Crescent, a bag in each hand. The car passed her and he glimpsed the movement within as Ginny waved to his wife. Elinor, her hands full, nodded in return. By the time she came into the house Kevin was in an armchair, reading the *Radio Times*.

'That's Meredith Whitelaw away.'

'Is it?'

'I just saw her go by, giving that royal wave of hers.' She went into the kitchen and he followed.

'You really will have to speak to Cynthia now, Kevin – either that or cancel that play.' Elinor took off her coat and then began unpacking the bags and putting everything away neatly. 'She knows, of course. I met her in the butcher's just now and she remarked on Meredith Whitelaw's sudden departure. What was it she said? Oh yes, something about sinking ships.'

Kevin winced. 'You could have mentioned how nice it would be to see her – and Gilbert, of course – back in the drama group.'

'It's not my job, dear. I only do costumes – you're the

director, the one in charge. In any case, for all I know you might have someone else in mind for the part of Vanessa.'

'You know perfectly well that there's nobody else I can ask!'

'Then the sooner you talk to Cynthia the better.' Elinor opened a packet of spaghetti and began to ease handfuls of the long thin stalks into the spaghetti jar. 'I'm going to have to alter the costumes and time's moving on. Cynthia's more – cushiony – than Meredith. To be honest, I imagine that their measurements are similar, but Meredith has a very good corset-maker. It must have been uncomfortable for her, but I suppose that's all part of being a professional. Measuring her was like hugging an armadillo. Did you notice?'

'Notice what?' A strand of spaghetti had escaped during the transfer; Kevin, who had slumped into a chair, picked it up and began idly to snap it into tiny bits.

'How well corseted Meredith Whitelaw is.'

'How would I notice that?'

'You would have if you'd hugged her.' Elinor folded her shopping bags and put them away.

'Hugged Meredith Whitelaw? You didn't think that I—'

'Of course not, dear. Don't do that, Kevin, it'll go all over the floor.' She swept the tiny bits of spaghetti into the palm of one hand and deposited them in the swing bin. 'Why don't you give Cynthia a ring and arrange to go over to see her? You can't put it off any longer.'

26

'Kevin, how nice to see you – it's been so long,' Gilbert MacBain said when he opened the door. 'Please come in. Cynthia is awaiting you in the lounge.'

His voice, like his glare, was icy, and Kevin went up the snowy white steps and into the pot-pourri-scented hall feeling like a doomed man ascending the gallows steps and knowing that he would never walk back down them.

The thought made him run a finger absent-mindedly beneath his shirt collar to ease it as he followed Gilbert into the lounge, where Cynthia sat enthroned on a basket chair with a high fan-shaped back. Her expression, like her husband's, was glacial.

'Kevin – what a pleasure,' she said flatly, extending a hand. Kevin hesitated, not sure whether he was supposed to shake it or to kiss it, but decided on a limp shake. Remembering the way the sofa had almost sucked him in on his last visit, he scurried to perch on the edge of an upright chair.

'Sherry? Gilbert and I usually have a glass at this time of day.'

Kevin began to shake his head, but clearly, the sherry had been poured as soon as they spotted him coming along the road. Gilbert was already at his wife's side, a silver salver bearing three glasses of pale sherry balanced elegantly on the upraised fingers of one hand.

'I heard,' Cynthia said casually, taking her glass, 'that Meredith Whitelaw has left the village earlier than expected.'

'Yes.' Kevin's voice came out in a strange croak, and he had to clear his throat and try again. 'Yes, she had to return to London. Something to do with a part in a new period drama.' He took a glass from the salver and sipped at its contents. The sherry was so dry that his tongue cringed and his lips almost contracted into a rosebud.

'Really? How nice for her.'

'The thing is, Cynthia − Gilbert − Meredith having to rush off like that has left the drama club in a difficult situation. The hall's booked for the first week in June and the programmes and tickets have to be with the printers within the next two weeks.'

'And your leading lady has let you down. How very difficult for you, Kevin,' Cynthia sympathised throatily. 'It's a bit late for you to back out now, isn't it? I must say that walking out on you at this late stage sounds to me like an amateurish thing to do. Don't you agree, Gilbert?'

Gilbert had been relishing his sherry. 'I'm not sure that I would agree with you, my dear, when you say "amateurish". You and I and Kevin here are amateur thespians, and we would never let people down at the last minute, would we?'

'Now I come to think of it, you're right. We would never do that. Haven't I always said that amateur actors are often more dedicated than professionals? We put our hearts and souls into anything we undertake because we're passionate about the stage and the written word. Professionals,' Cynthia said, her voice clearly holding the word between finger and thumb as though it were unclean, 'do it for the money and for no other reason.'

Kevin saw his chance, and seized it. 'You could well be right, both of you. You've never let the drama group down and I know that you never would!' Then, as they both nodded assent, 'so I know that you won't let us down now, in our hour of need.'

The MacBains glanced at each other, puzzled, then Gilbert said, 'You mean that you've come here today to ask us to do front of house for the show? I'm not sure that we'd—'

'No, not at all. I'm speaking about Cynthia being in the play – *Visiting Vanessa.*'

Again, Cynthia and Gilbert glanced at each other in surprise, then Cynthia leaned forward to say gently, 'But I'm not in that play any more, Kevin. Don't you remember?'

'What I mean is, we want you to be in it. To play Vanessa.'

'Me?' Cynthia leaned back against the chair cushions, letting the tips of her fingers rest on her breast. 'But I'm resting, as the professionals say. I'm taking time out, since I'm not wanted for this show.'

'You *are* wanted!'

'You mean – now that Meredith Whitelaw has let you down? I'm not sure that I care to step into her shoes, Kevin. I'm rather enjoying having a rest.'

It took Kevin another half hour of coaxing, then pleading, and another glass of mouth-shrinking sherry, but when he finally emerged, blinking and exhausted, into the daylight, he had managed to persuade Cynthia to take back the part of Vanessa.

He felt elated during the walk from the MacBains' front door to their gate, but on the way home to tell Elinor the news, he began to get the distinct impression that he had just been coerced into playing his part in a skilfully handled scene. A scene that had been planned and possibly rehearsed by Cynthia and Gilbert before he rang their doorbell.

'Well?' Elinor asked when he got home.

'She's going to play Vanessa.'

'I'll alter the dress,' Elinor said. 'I have her measurements on record. You were away for quite a while. Was she difficult to persuade?'

'Not at all, she was actually quite pleased to get the chance to be back in the play. We just started chatting about this and that, you know how it goes. There's just one thing – she and Gilbert are away on holiday at the beginning of June so we've agreed to move the performance to the beginning of July.'

'Might be bad for ticket sales, July.'

'Can't be helped,' Kevin said, thinking of the celebrities who, Meredith had assured him, would attend the show. No chance of that now. 'We were all very friendly, over a glass of sherry,' he said. 'Any Irn Bru in the house? My mouth's dry.'

On rehearsal night Cynthia swept into the village hall, head high and the ends of the chiffon scarf looped about her throat fluttering in her wake.

'The perfect entrance,' Jinty murmured to Elinor as the newcomer graciously acknowledged the smattering of applause led by her stalwart friends. 'Prior's Ford's answer to Meredith Whitelaw!'

Gilbert, beaming, strode behind his wife carrying a briefcase which, when opened, proved to have nothing in it other than the script of *Visiting Vanessa*. He took it out and offered it to his wife, who waved it away.

'We should all be word-perfect by now, shouldn't we,

Kevin? Enough time has been lost as it is.' She smiled sweetly round the gathering. 'Would anyone mind if we started tonight with a run-through of my play? It's been a while, as you all know, and I'm probably rather rusty.' And to cries of, 'Never!' she mounted the steps to the stage and took her place.

She was word perfect, but there were one or two awkward moments, such as the entry of Vanessa's daughter, clutching her large knitting bag. She paused, staring at Cynthia, who prompted her in a stage whisper.

'Mother, it's Wednesday and here I am again.'

'I know the line – I just wondered if you were going to say, "In a handbag."'

'Why on earth would I want to say that?'

'Miss Whitelaw said it,' the woman faltered.

'But it's not in my script, dear – is it in yours?'

'No, she just thought – since I had this big bag . . . Kevin?'

Kevin hurried forward to explain.

'I think that just sounds silly,' Cynthia said when he had finished.

'Me too,' a voice rang from the wings. 'But nobody listened to me!'

'I mean, why start talking about handbags?'

'Shall we just get on with the rehearsal?' Kevin begged through set teeth.

On Friday, Jenny left the *Dumfries News* on the kitchen table, and watched as Maggie, on her return from school, started flicking through it. When she found the Lucinda Keen page she ran a finger swiftly along the letters. Then she pushed the paper away and was on her way out of the kitchen when Jenny said, 'Is this what you were looking for?'

Maggie took the letter from her hand and glanced at it, her face colouring. 'Where did you get that from? It was Mrs Campbell, wasn't it? She'd no right to go showing it to you! It's private!'

'A private letter meant for publication in a newspaper? And she had every right to ask me about it. She guessed where it came from and she was worried about you.'

'I don't know what you mean. It's got nothing to do with me.'

'It's a bit late to claim that, Maggie, not after telling me that it was private.'

'That's not my handwriting.'

'You got someone else to write it for you. Just what do you think you're playing at?'

'It was just a joke,' the girl muttered sulkily. 'I told some of the girls at school about Mrs Campbell being Lucinda Keen in the papers, and we did this as a laugh.'

'Mrs Campbell didn't think that it was funny, and neither do I. Maggie, we've done our best to make you feel at home. If we can do more, you only need to tell us.'

'You can let me go back to Gran and Gramps.'

'You know that he needs looking after all the time. Your gran's not as young as she used to be.'

'At least they love me!'

'I love you! I loved you the first minute I saw you, and I've loved you ever since.'

'But you went away!' Maggie yelled. 'You left me and you left my dad and you didn't care. I cried and cried – Gran told me. She said it broke her heart to see me.'

'And it broke mine to leave you.' Jenny's eyes were brimming with tears. 'Maggie, I was so pleased when your Uncle Malcolm asked me to take you. I thought I finally had the chance to make up for what happened before.'

'Don't be so stupid, how can you ever make up for what you did to me? I was only little!' Maggie screeched. 'You can't turn the clock back, can you?' Jenny took a step forward, reaching out for the girl, who jumped back.

'Don't touch me!' One arm flailed out to fend Jenny off, but caught the china bowl of fruit that was always kept on the kitchen dresser. The bowl hit the floor and smashed; bananas skidded across the floor while oranges and apples rolled everywhere.

'What's going on?' Andrew asked from the doorway, and they both stared at him, shocked by his sudden appearance.

'It's — it's all right,' Jenny said swiftly, rubbing tears away with the back of one hand. 'An accident. Maggie and I were—'

'It's not all right!' Maggie shouted her down. 'It's never going to be all right again so stop lying! You're always *lying* to me, saying you want me and you love me when you don't. You hate me being here and I hate it too and I wish we were all dead!'

She barrelled past Andrew, who was thrown back against the door frame, and they heard her running up the stairs; then her bedroom door slammed hard.

'What the hell was all that about?' Andrew asked into the sudden shocked silence.

'It was — nothing,' Jenny tried to say brightly, and then spoiled it all by bursting into tears.

'Why didn't you tell me you were having problems?' Andrew wanted to know after his wife had been hugged, comforted and soothed with the aid of a glass of sherry.

'You'd warned me that things might be difficult, and you were right. I should have listened, but I just kept hoping that she would settle in. But now — well, you heard what

230

she said.' Jenny drained her glass and reached for her bag, rummaging through it for her make-up. 'She hates us — hates me, for leaving her when she was little. And I can't blame her, Andrew. I hate myself for it as well. I always have.'

'Don't go down that road, Jen, the past can't be changed. And you can't prove that she took money, can you?'

'No.' She opened a tube of foundation cream and began to apply it to the reddened skin around her eyes.

'This letter' — he waved it at her — 'could be a silly prank that she and her school chums thought up, as she says.'

'D'you think I'm making too much fuss about all this?' She half-hoped that he would say yes, but he shook his head.

'Not entirely — I saw her and heard her when I came in just now. I just think that we need to give her more time. D'you want me to talk to her?'

'No! That's what she'll be expecting and it'll only make things worse. You're right, let's just behave as though nothing's happened. There — do I look all right? Calum'll be coming back from Helen's soon and I don't want him to see that I've been crying.' Then, glancing at the clock, 'What are you doing home so early?'

'I felt a bit off colour.' He rubbed at his stomach. 'Something I ate, probably. Or just overwork. Perhaps you should talk to Ingrid, or Helen. They've both got daughters, they might be able to advise you.'

'Mmm.' Jenny got to her feet and picked up the empty sherry glass. 'I'd better go and get the kitchen cleaned up.'

Maggie stayed in her room, and when Calum was sent up to tell her that dinner was ready he came back down to report that she wasn't hungry.

Jenny kept the girl's food hot, and when they had had

231

their meal she took a tray upstairs and tapped on Maggie's door.

'I've brought your dinner.'

'Don't want it!'

'I think you do.' Jenny opened the door and Maggie, sitting at the computer they had bought for her, spun round angrily.

'I said I don't.'

'No sense in starving yourself just because you're angry with me.' Jenny put the tray down. 'Maggie, I can understand the way you feel. I've never forgiven myself for leaving you, but you weren't my daughter and if I'd taken you with me your father would only have fetched you back.'

'You could have stayed.' Maggie had turned back to the computer and was sitting with her head tucked down and the fingers of one hand fiddling with her hair.

'I couldn't. I can't explain why – perhaps one day I will, but not now. But I never stopped loving you and I never stopped missing you, and you coming to live with us was just what I wanted. I was so happy about it.'

'Nobody ever asked me what I wanted!' Maggie's voice was almost indistinct.

'I know, that's the rotten thing about being your age – not being in control of your own life. Illness and death – they happen, and they change things, and we can't do anything but try to cope with them.'

Jenny waited, then as Maggie said nothing, she finished with, 'Your dinner's getting cold. I'll leave you to eat it. And now that the air's cleared, perhaps we can all start again, and do better this time round.'

27

Ginny drew up outside Willow Cottage, got out, and eyed the grey Mini with satisfaction.

'There now' – she patted the bonnet – 'you're home, and we're going to get along just fine, aren't we? We're suited, you and me.'

Sam Brennan had come out of Rowan Cottage, walking as he usually did these days, with his eyes fixed on the ground, not even noticing the car's arrival. He had just put his hand on the gate's latch when he heard someone say, 'We're suited, you and me.'

'Sorry?' Startled, Sam looked up and saw the girl who had moved into Willow Cottage with her mother. She stared back at him, just as startled, then grinned.

'I didn't see you there; I was actually talking to the car. My mother's had to go back to London and I've finally got rid of that big car she insisted on hiring. I got this instead.' She patted the bonnet again.

'Oh – right. It's – it looks like a nice wee car.'

'I think so. Much more me. Ginny Whitelaw, by the

way.' She thrust out a hand, and he looked at it in surprise, and then shook it.

'Sam Brennan.'

'I know – I've been in and out of your shop for the past five months or so, but it just occurred to me that we've never met properly, even though we're neighbours. Are you a Prior's Fordian, then?'

'No, but we've – I've lived here for years.'

'I like it.' Ginny opened the Mini's boot and began to take out polythene trays filled, to Sam's surprise, with small plants. 'It's a bonny wee place. I like that word, "bonny". It's descriptive. And "wee", come to think of it. D'you think you could hold these trays for me?'

Since Marcy left him, Sam had done all he could to avoid social contact with his fellow villagers, but short of being rude, there was nothing for it but to take the trays.

'Thanks.' Ginny delved into the boot again and began to haul out a large and heavy plastic sack.

'Wait a minute – you take these and I'll see to that.'

'I can manage; I'm used to it.'

'Take them,' Sam said, and she did as she was told.

'It's heavy,' she said apologetically as he began to lift the sack. 'It's fertiliser that I need for the garden.'

She was right – it was heavy, but Sam was used to heavy work. 'Where do you want it?'.

'Round the back. Just outside the back door would be fine,' she called after him as he began to stagger up the path.

It was getting dark, and by the time he got to the rear of the house a light was on in the kitchen. Ginny Whitelaw opened the back door as he was lowering the bag to the ground.

'Thanks, that's kind of you. Come in and have a drink.'

'Actually, I was just going to the Neurotic Cuckoo.'

'Oh – meeting someone?'

'No.'

'So nobody's expecting you? I have beer,' Ginny offered hopefully.

'Well – thanks,' he said, cursing himself for not thinking up a better excuse, 'but I can't stay long.'

An hour later he left Willow Cottage, having had a surprisingly enjoyable time with Ginny Whitelaw. Unlike almost every other woman in Prior's Ford she didn't show any interest in his private life, and his silence, which he knew was beginning to isolate him from former friends, didn't bother her at all. He had been free to enjoy his drink, and a second, before the fire in the Willow Cottage's comfortable living room while Ginny talked about her work at Linn Hall.

'I'm sorry,' she said when he rose to go, 'I've been a dreadful hostess, going on about myself all the time and not giving you a chance to say anything.'

'That's all right, I'm not much of talker at the best of times.'

'That's understandable, given that you spend your working life dealing with customers. Me – I'm so used to living in my mother's shadow that it's lovely just to be able to talk to someone about the things I enjoy most. Thanks for listening,' she said as she opened the front door.

'My pleasure – and I hope you enjoy your new car.'

'Oh, I will!' Ginny said.

As Sam closed Willow Cottage's gate a couple that had come from the Neurotic Cuckoo passed by. 'Evenin' Sam,' the man called cheerfully. 'Weather's gettin' better, eh?'

'Aye, it is.'

'He was coming out of Willow Cottage there,' the man's wife muttered as they went on their way.

'Was he?'

'Course he was! Men never notice anything. He must have been visiting that girl Ginny. She's on her own now that her mum's gone off to do another television series. I wonder . . .' the woman said thoughtfully.

Sam paused at his own gate, looking over at the Neurotic Cuckoo's lit windows. He had planned to go to the pub and to drink enough to ensure that he would sleep that night, in the double bed he had once shared with Marcy. But for some reason, the hour spent in Ginny's company had left him feeling refreshed and, ridiculous though it may sound, cleansed in some way.

So he went home and to bed, where he fell asleep swiftly, clutching the pillow that had been Marcy's tightly in his arms.

Sam Brennan, Ginny thought as she closed the front door and went into the kitchen to make some supper, was a very sad man, for some reason. She had seen him smile for the first time that evening, and had been struck by how much it suited him. She wondered if she should have invited him to stay and eat with her, but it was too late now.

In any case, she could do it another time. She could invite anyone she wanted into Willow Cottage now that she was on her own.

On her own! A week after her mother had left, the thought still made her feel as though she had just downed a glass of sparkling champagne.

In the morning, word was all round the village that Sam Brennan and Ginny Whitelaw were getting to be very friendly.

'And why not?' Jinty McDonald said when the gossip reached her ears. 'She's a nice lass, and he's a decent enough man – and they're both fancy-free now that Marcy's not in the village any more.'

'P'raps that's why she left – because he's got a wandering eye,' her informant suggested.

'Rubbish – Marcy's been gone a good while now and poor Sam's been as miserable as sin without her.' In the winter months, when she wasn't needed at the Hall, Jinty helped out in the village store. 'He's become a right hermit since she left. There's no way he was looking at other women!'

'Well, he is now. He looked as pleased as Punch when we saw him coming out of her gate last night. And he sounded chirpy when Bob spoke to him, instead of just grunting the way he usually does.'

'Well, if he has found someone else, then good for him,' Jinty said firmly. 'It's time he got a bit of cheer back into his life. And that Ginny's a nice lass.' Though, she thought to herself, if Ginny fancied anyone, it was young Lewis. Jinty had seen the way she'd looked at him and Molly when she thought nobody else noticed.

Helen heard the latest gossip at the school gates, and rushed over to the Gift Horse where her friends were preparing for the new season, as soon as she could. As she arrived, Jenny appeared from the back shop with two mugs of coffee.

'Hi, Helen, you're just in time. Take mine and I'll fetch another mug.'

'I haven't got time – I've just heard that Sam Brennan and Ginny Whitelaw are seeing each other.'

'Really?' Ingrid raised her eyebrows. 'I didn't know that.'

'Well, it's all over the village. Don't you think that Marcy should know?'

The other two looked at each other, then Ingrid shook her head. 'It's not our business, and it might not be true. In any case, she might not care.'

'We don't know that, and we're the only people who know where she is. We want her to come back, don't we? This might do the trick.'

'And it might not.'

'That would be up to Marcy, wouldn't it?' Jenny said, and Helen nodded vigorously.

'That's what I think. If she does nothing about it then we have to assume that she doesn't care for him any more. But if she still does care, it might just give her the push she's needing.'

'We don't even know if it's true, though,' Ingrid protested. 'You know what this village is like – stories spread like ripples in a pond.'

'Who cares whether it's true or not? Now's our chance to try to get her back where she belongs – in Prior's Ford, with her friends, and with Sam. Promise you'll write to her, Ingrid. And you don't need to say that you're not sure if it's true.'

'You want me to tell my friend a lie?'

'Of course not. But there are ways.' Helen wished that Ingrid's view of right and wrong wasn't quite so definite. 'You could say that their friendship's the talk of the village; it wouldn't be a lie because it is, this morning at any rate.'

'Jenny?'

'It would certainly give us the chance to test Marcy's reaction. If she does nothing, then we have to accept that she and Sam have no future together. And if that's the way it is, then I'm all for Ginny Whitelaw becoming part of his life because I can't bear to see the poor man so unhappy.'

'Since you put it like that, and since you are both agreed,' Ingrid said, 'I will write to Marcy this evening.'

It had been a long period of hard work for the family at Tarbethill Farm, but now that the lambing season was over and the dairy herd moved from the big barn where they spent the winter, life was getting a little easier. To save money on animal feed the previous year's calves, which would normally have been fattened up in order to fetch a good price at the market, had been sold to more prosperous farmers.

'It sticks in my gullet, so it does,' Bert grunted to his sons as they watched the animals being driven off in a large truck. 'We'd have made good money if we'd been able to afford tae keep them longer. Instead o' that, here I am gettin' rid of them for a pittance, knowin' that someone else'll make a good profit on our stock!'

'If we can't afford tae fatten 'em, Dad, we wouldn't have made much on 'em anyway. Best tae have somethin' in the bank now than less later.'

'If you ask me you'd be as well sellin' off the entire herd for all the size of it,' Victor said. 'Farmin's only workin' these days if it's done on a grand scale. We don't have enough cattle or sheep tae make proper money.'

'Nobody's askin' you,' his father barked at him, and stumped off.

Ewan sighed. He had been hoping to bring up the subject of a wormery, but thanks to Victor putting his foot in it, as usual, the chance to have a word with the old man had gone for the moment.

It took several more days before his father seemed calm enough to listen to the proposal.

'A what? Who'd want to farm earthworms, for pity's sake! Ye cannae milk 'em or shear 'em or eat 'em, can ye?'

'I'm not talkin' about earthworms, Dad, and wormeries do well, seemingly. You have to get special worms, tiger worms they're called, and you put them into bedding – that's the right mixture of organic materials,' Ewan added, glaring at his brother, who had started to snigger. 'And they turn it into compost that you can sell. You can sell the worms, too, as they multiply, for bait for fishing, or tae folk who want tae start their own wormeries. They can be all sizes, wormeries. Ours would be large scale. I was thinkin' about the wee field across the other side of the river. We've not used it for a couple of years now.'

'Worms,' Victor pointed out, 'don't take kindly to bein' fenced in. They wander. Ye'd need tae train up a worm dog tae herd them an' bring them back.'

'Will you just give me a chance tae explain? I'd have tae dig big ditches and line 'em with plastic to keep them in.'

'Is it cruel to keep them penned up like that?' Jess wanted to know. She didn't care for worms, but at the same time she couldn't bear the thought of any live creature being ill-treated.

'They like it, Mam. They've got plenty of food, and plenty of room. It's like a sort of worm nursery, and it's a grand way of recycling organic waste,' Ewan said earnestly.

'Recycling hot air, more like!' Victor gave another snort of laughter and picked up his coat. 'I'm off out – I feel as if I've hardly been down the lane for months!'

At the door, he turned and looked at his brother. 'Worms!' he said. 'I've never heard the like! Where did ye get a daft idea like that from?'

'It was Alison mentioned it first . . .'

'I might've known,' Victor sneered. 'If Alison Greenlees told ye tae shave yer head and then paint it yellow wi' purple dots, ye'd do it.'

'Shut up, Victor!' Ewan yelled, doubling his fists. 'I've read about wormeries, and they work. And ye can just keep yer tongue off Alison!'

'Gladly,' Victor said, and slammed the door.

June arrived and the village gardens became rainbows of summer colours. Climbing roses covered walls and fences and doorways in every shade of red, pink, white and yellow, and the air was filled with the fresh clean smell of cut grass as lawnmowers whirred. Shears clicked around hedges and bushes, while borders trimmed paths like colourful ribbons. The villagers joyfully cast off warm clothing to replace it with light, summery garb and the first holiday makers arrived to refresh themselves at the tables set outside the Neurotic Cuckoo and buy mementos in the Gift Horse.

After hours spent in the quarry, his binoculars sweeping up and down granite walls glittering in the sunshine, Robert Kavanagh was finally able to contact Scottish Natural Heritage to report increased activity around the peregrine falcon's nest, indicating that the eggs had begun to hatch out.

This year's young backpackers had started work in the gardens at Linn Hall, where Lewis fretted over the non-appearance of Molly's baby.

'It was supposed to arrive in May and now we're into June. D'you think everything's all right?' he appealed to his mother and Jinty.

'Of course it's all right. Molly's a healthy young lass, and bairns aren't born with watches and calendars,' Jinty said briskly. 'They take their own time. It'll come out when it's good and ready, and not before.'

'What does Molly say?' Fliss asked her son, who phoned Inverness every day in the hope of hearing good news.

'She's getting a bit fed up with the waiting too,' he said, and left it at that. Molly actually said a lot more than that. She was extremely bad-tempered each time he phoned, wishing she had never set eyes on him, and complaining bitterly about her sister sunbathing in the back garden in a swimsuit, deliberately flaunting herself in order to provoke poor Molly, who wallowed like a beached whale in the house, fat and ugly and not fit to be seen.

He wasn't sure if either of them could bear to wait much longer for this baby to be born.

At last, Bert McNair agreed to let Ewan have the use of Tarbethill's smallest field for his wormery.

Once he realised that Ewan was getting the field, Victor insisted on being given the same rights.

'I'm the oldest and I don't see why he should get some land of his own when I don't have any.'

'It's more a strip than a field,' Bert pointed out. 'It's never been used much in all my lifetime, let alone yours. He might as well have the use of it.'

'It's still not fair, Dad. If he gets something, then so should I. The cash value of his field, mebbe.'

'You what? That field's no' worth a hundred pound, and you ken fine that I don't even have that tae give tae ye!'

'Then let me have land of my own too. That field on the main road, across from the lane. I'll take that one.'

'An' what would ye dae with it? It's no use for ploughin', and not much good for stock either. That's why I let the village use it for things like that Easter egg business last year.'

'If it was mine, I could charge a fee if anyone wanted tae use it. Or, I could turn it intae a wee caravan park.'

'If ye're thinkin' what I think ye're thinkin',' his father

snapped, 'ye can just forget it. There'll be no buildin' boxy houses on McNair land – I told ye that before and I'll go on tellin' ye so long as there's breath in my body!'

'I know you won't have any buildin' on our land,' Victor said irritably. 'But where's the harm in rentin' it out tae folk wi' holiday caravans? That wouldnae damage the field. The flat area nearest the road could hold a good twenty vans, and the hilly bit with the trees and bushes could maybe take some smaller vans.'

'I'll think about it,' Bert said.

28

Sam Brennan was not a great fan of birds, particularly those who managed all too often to foul one of the village store's windows as they swooped overhead.

He went out into a wet afternoon armed with a bucket of water and a mop to clean up the latest mess, then froze in the act of putting the bucket down as he noticed the woman staring at his cottage.

Her back was towards him, and she was quite tall – about the same height as Marcy Copleton – and dressed in a long black coat with the hood pulled over her head as protection against the fine but steady drizzle. A large holdall stood beside her.

Sam's mouth was suddenly dry, and his heart had begun to thump. Marcy had a coat like that, with a hood. Marcy . . .

He walked swiftly across the road and onto the green and, by the time he got to the figure, he was running, terrified that she would hurry away before he reached her, or perhaps fade from view and turn out to be a figment of his imagination.

'Marcy!' The word burst from him as he reached out to touch her shoulder. Startled by the urgency in his voice the woman spun round, taking a quick step away from his outstretched fingers, her own gloved hands clutching protectively at the bag slung across her body and her blue eyes widening with apprehension.

It wasn't Marcy.

Sam stopped short. 'S – sorry, I'm sorry. I thought you were someone else.' Then, as she said nothing, but continued to eye him suspiciously, 'I live here – in Rowan Cottage. I thought when I saw you that you were – a friend, looking for me.'

'I was looking at Willow Cottage,' she said coolly.

'It belongs to Mrs Ramsay – she's not in the village at the moment. The cottage has been let for the year.'

'I know. I thought that the people who've rented it might be able to help me, but there's nobody at home. Do you know a man called Alastair? An artist who lives around here?'

'Alastair Marshall, that'd be. He rents one of the farm cottages.'

'Can you direct me to it?'

'D'you have a car?' When she shook her head, he indicated the main street. 'You go in that direction, past the old priory and then take the first turn to the right. It leads to a footpath. You go over the stile and then you'll see the cottage on your right. You can't miss it, it's on its own, in front of a clump of trees. It isn't far.' He glanced at her feet and saw that they were well shod in knee-high boots that looked expensive, but practical enough. 'You could leave your bag with me if you want – Sam Brennan, I own the village store,' he added hurriedly as she continued to eye him suspiciously.

245

'I'll manage.' She lifted the bag and turned away, tossing a crisp, dismissive, 'Thank you,' over her shoulder.

He stood looking after her, the sudden rush of adrenaline he had experienced at the first sight of her ebbing away. He must have looked and sounded like a right idiot! Not that it mattered, he thought as he began to walk slowly back across the green, because she wasn't Marcy. He squeezed his eyes tight shut, trying in the darkness behind the lids to see where Marcy was at that moment, as in a fortune-teller's crystal ball. But it was no good.

An engine roared, and he opened his eyes just in time to avoid stepping into the road in front of a motorbike.

'Are you daft, Sam Brennan?' an angry woman wanted to know as he crossed to the store. 'Leaving a bucket full of water unattended on the pavement like that. Look at his sleeves – I'm going to have to wash that jacket now!' One hand gripped a small child by the back of his jacket collar; the little boy, his sleeves soaked in soapy water from elbow to wrist, grinned up at Sam, delighted by the result of his moment of freedom.

Alastair, returning from helping out at a nearby farm, experienced a sense of déjà vu as he approached the stile leading to his cottage. It couldn't possibly be happening again! But it was.

The sky overhead was grey with clouds so low that they almost rested on the tops of the trees, the grass was wet around his ankles – it was almost exactly as before, except that the rain had eased to a fine wetting mist and the figure on the stile was warmly wrapped and hooded against the inclement weather, whereas Clarissa, in an open coat and flimsy dress, had been soaked by the downpour the first time he laid eyes on her.

The woman on the stile had been staring down at her

hands, but when she heard his feet swishing through the grass she looked up, pushing the hood back from her face.

'Alastair Marshall? I don't know if you remember me,' said Clarissa's stepdaughter. 'I've been to your cottage, but it was empty, so I thought I would wait for you here.' She climbed down from the stile. 'Could we have a word?'

On the one and only occasion Alastair had met Alexandra Ramsay and her brother Steven in Willow Cottage, he had thought her the most beautiful woman he had ever seen, and on their second encounter he had no reason to change his opinion.

Even with shadows smudged below her sky–blue eyes and her hair, as richly coloured and glossy as the chestnuts the local boys loved to harvest in the autumn, slightly mussed from the hood, with long tendrils loosened and wisping around her face, she was still breathtakingly lovely.

As she unbuttoned her coat she looked around his low-ceilinged living room, cluttered as always with canvases stacked against one wall and the easel by one of the two windows with his palette close by. The stairs to the upper floor led directly from the living room and Alastair realised to his horror that a pair of trousers had been thrown over the banister, and the mug he had been drinking from that morning sat unwashed on the mantelshelf, cheek by jowl with a pile of papers awaiting his attention.

He glanced at the holdall he had carried for her, and prayed that she wasn't expecting to stay here. Apart from the fact that the only spare bedroom was cold, with patches of damp sketching quite interesting shapes on the low ceiling, he tended to use it as a storeroom for items that couldn't find permanent sites elsewhere in the cottage.

'Let me . . .' He took her coat, hung it over the newel post at the bottom of the stairs, and cleared a chair of its magazines. 'Sit down.' Because of the weather he had lit the fire before going out; now he knelt by the dusty hearth and stirred up the glowing embers before adding some logs from the basket. 'Rotten weather for May. Can I get you some coffee?'

'You wouldn't have any brandy, would you?'

'Em – no, but I do have wine – plonk from the village store.'

She hesitated, glancing at the clock above the fireplace. Its hands stood at four. 'That would do.' She was wearing a long dark-red knitted jacket over an ivory coloured blouse and a calf-length flared black skirt.

'You know that Clarissa's still abroad?' Alastair ventured when he had brought the wine and apologised for the lack of proper glasses.

'Yes, of course.' Alexandra sipped from her tumbler, then said, 'She keeps in touch with us.'

'With me, too. I got a letter just the other day, posted in Australia. She was about to embark on a sail to Shanghai.'

'I would never have thought that Clarissa could manage a round-the-world trip – she always seemed so timid.'

'She's anything but,' Alastair said sharply.

She brushed the comment aside. 'I expect you're wondering why I'm here.'

'I was a bit surprised to see you, since Willow Cottage's been let for the year.'

'No, I expect you're wondering why I'm here in your cottage when we scarcely know each other.'

'Well – yes. Though it's good to see you again,' he hastened to assure her, then wished he could grab himself by the scruff of the neck, haul himself into the kitchen, and give himself a good kicking for sounding like a complete cretin. He wasn't good at social skills; he never had been good at them. That was why he liked to live on his own, away from the need to know how to speak to beautiful, sophisticated strangers. He could almost hear Humphrey Bogart's gritty voice in his head – '*Of all the stiles in all the villages in all the world she had to sit on mine . . .*'

'I needed a break – a few days away,' Alexandra's cool voice banished Bogart, 'and I'm here because I want to ask your advice about the public house – the Homing Pigeon?'

'The Neurotic Cuckoo.'

'I knew that it was something to do with a bird. My brother and I had a decent meal there the first time we visited Clarissa so I thought I might stay there; then I recalled that she had said something in one of her letters about a change of landlord. So as you're the only other person I know in the village, I decided to ask your advice before booking a room there.'

'Oh, I can recommend it,' Alastair said at once, relieved to know that he wouldn't be expected to invite her to stay at the cottage. 'The Fishers are very nice people and Gracie's a good cook. In fact – why don't I take you there for dinner, so that you can meet them and book your room? I'd invite you to eat here, but I haven't got much in.'

'Oh – thank you.' She lifted a lock of hair that had been curling against her cheek and tucked it behind her ear. She was wearing neat little gold earrings in the shape of seashells.

'More wine?'

'Thanks.' She held out the tumbler and asked as he tipped the bottle over it, 'Is Willow Cottage being looked after?'

'Oh yes, Clarissa doesn't need to worry about that. The woman who rented it, Meredith Whitelaw, has had to return to London, but her daughter's staying on for the rest of the let.'

'Meredith Whitelaw,' Alexandra repeated slowly. 'I know that name from somewhere.'

'She's an actress – she was in that soap opera *Bridlington Close*, until a few months ago.'

'I don't watch soap operas.'

'Nor do I – well, I don't watch anything as I don't have a television set. If I want to see football or snooker I go to the pub. But a lot of the women in the village are fans of the programme. Meredith's arrival caused quite a stir.'

Telling her about Meredith, and about Ginny getting work at Linn Hall and deciding to stay on when her mother left the village helped to fill in some more time. Alastair fed the fire as he talked, mainly because his visitor seemed to be huddling into her chair, as though chilled. When the basket was empty, he took it out to the back yard to be refilled from the supply of logs in the shed.

When he returned, it was to find that Alexandra had fallen asleep in the old chair, her head tipped back against its curled headrest. He put the basket down very gently, then stood looking down at her for a moment. She hadn't just come to the village on a whim, there was more to it than that. Clarissa had told him that her stepdaughter was very good at her job. Alexandra, she had said, was like her father – ambitious and dedicated, putting her career before everything else. But it was term time, and what was a dedicated, career-driven teacher doing in Prior's Ford when she should be in her classroom?

She stirred slightly and murmured something, but didn't wake. Suddenly realising that when she did, she would probably want to use his bathroom, Alastair sped silently upstairs to tidy it up, polish the mirror, and find a fresh towel.

When he returned she was on her feet, studying the painting on the easel.

'Clarissa has a painting like that, hasn't she?'

'That's right, one of the lanes in summer. She liked the light and shadows and the way the trees met over the lane. I've sold quite a few of those in the Gift Horse.' He glanced at his watch and saw to his relief that the afternoon was drawing to a close. 'They'll soon start serving dinner at the pub – if you don't mind eating early.'

'That's fine; I decided to come up by train and it was a tiring journey. I'd like an early night. Can I use your bathroom?'

'Of course,' Alastair said.

29

'Oh – you've got Clarissa's car,' Alexandra said when Alastair led her round the back of the cottage.

'She asked me to look after it for her – and said that I should use it in order to keep it running. You should have it while you're here. After all, you're more entitled to it than I am.' He ushered her into the passenger seat, noting that she accepted the offer of the car as her right, with no argument, then got in behind the wheel. 'There's a road to the left further along the main road, past the priory, that leads to this cottage.'

They had reached the Neurotic Cuckoo and were getting out of the car when Ginny Whitelaw came along from Willow Cottage. 'Hello, Alastair, going in for a drink?' She eyed Alexandra, who had managed to sweep her hair back into its usual chignon and apply make-up in Alastair's very basic bathroom, with open interest and not a little envy.

'Going for dinner, actually.'

'Me too. I feel in need of cheering up and pampering.'

Alastair beamed at her, delighted at the prospect of having

an ally to help him entertain Alexandra. 'Why don't you join us?'

'Thanks, but I don't want to play gooseberry.'

'You're not!' He was shocked to think that anyone could even consider a romance between him and the lovely and successful Alexandra. 'This is Alexandra Ramsay – her stepmother owns Willow Cottage. Alexandra, this is Ginny Whitelaw, who's going to have dinner with us.'

'Why take a room here when your stepmother owns the house I'm in?' Ginny wanted to know when she heard of Alexandra's plans. 'You should be staying there.'

'I couldn't intrude.'

'To tell the truth, I wouldn't mind some company. And I assure you that I don't go in for girly chats,' Ginny added after quick glance at the other girl's expression. 'Having been raised by my mother, I treasure silence.'

'Well, in that case . . .' Alexandra said doubtfully. 'It will only be for a few days.'

'Stay as long as you like,' Ginny said as Joe Fisher arrived at their table with menus.

'Anyone want a drink?'

'I,' Ginny announced, 'will have a large gin with a little tonic in it.'

'Had a bad day?'

'You could say that.'

'Someone was telling us that young Lewis has become a father. A wee lad, isn't it? An heir for the Hall!'

'A girl, actually, last night. He's gone off to Inverness to see her – and her mother, of course.'

'Well now, that's something to celebrate right enough,' Joe said cheerfully.

★   ★   ★

To Helen's and Jenny's disappointment, Marcy had not yet replied to Ingrid's letter about Sam's apparent friendship with Ginny.

'Are you sure that you made it clear that they were getting to know each other?' Helen asked.

'That would not have been the truth, would it?' Ingrid was rearranging a shelf of little dolls bought from whole-salers and dressed by Jenny. 'Sam and Ginny are neighbours and as far as I can tell, that's all they are.'

Sometimes Ingrid's passion for the truth and lack of interest in embroidering it irritated the writer in Helen. 'But you did tell her that he was seen leaving Willow Cottage one evening, and people are talking?'

'Yes, I told her that, though I think that the villagers, including,' Ingrid paused in her work to turn and impale Helen on her cool blue gaze, 'people who should know better, are taking off on flights of fancy.'

'This is Sam we're talking about – Sam, who's spurned every invitation to dinner and every friendly approach since Marcy left. The very fact that he went into Willow Cottage of his own accord speaks volumes to me.'

'Perhaps Ginny needed a fuse mending. Whatever the reason, I did tell Marcy, as I promised, but she hasn't replied so there's no more we can do. There now,' Ingrid stepped back to survey the shelf. 'How does that look?'

'Mmm. Can I try something?' Helen deftly moved the little figures into groups. 'There – they look more natural that way, like mothers taking their children to school, or home again. You should ask Alastair to draw a background for them and put it on the wall behind the shelf.'

Ingrid clapped her hands. 'What a wonderful idea! Your imagination comes in useful sometimes, Helen.'

*   *   *

The roofers and the young people working in the grounds of Linn Hall had finished their mid-day meal and returned to work, and only his parents, Jinty and Ginny were at the table when Lewis arrived home from a week in Inverness.

He breezed into the kitchen, a spring in his step and a sparkle in his eyes, and immediately produced a pack of photographs from his jacket pocket.

'Here she is. Eight pounds three ounces and hardly ever cries,' he said proudly.

'How's Molly?'

'She's great, Mum. The two of them came home from the hospital the very next day.'

'They do that now – nothing to it. You'll be wanting something to eat.' Jinty looked up and down the length of the big kitchen table. 'You'd not believe that this board was piled with food thirty minutes ago – that lot are like locusts. I've got some home-made soup in the fridge, though, and Ewan brought eggs from the farm this morning.'

'Sounds great, Jinty, but have a look at these first.' Lewis began to spread the photographs across the table, saying, as Ginny got up, 'Hang on, Ginny, this won't take long. There's me holding her, and this is me and Molly with her, and that' – a forefinger pushed a picture towards Fliss, who gazed down at the bored-looking teenager holding a shawled bundle as though not quite sure what to do with it – 'is Molly's sister Stella. And these are her parents, Val and Tony.'

Val, a plump woman, smiled down at the baby cuddled to her ample breast, while her husband, a protective arm about his wife and grandchild, grinned into the camera. 'The baby's lovely, Lewis. And Molly's parents look like very nice people.'

'They are. You'll like them when you meet them. So who d'you think the baby looks like, Mum?' he wanted to know as the photographs were passed from Fliss to Jinty, Ginny, then Hector.

'Well – I don't really know,' Fliss had to admit.

'Don't ask me,' Hector said hurriedly, 'babies all look the same to me.'

'Molly says she's got my nose, and my chin. And her hair's dark.'

Ginny, who privately agreed with Hector, kept quiet.

'But she's got pale skin, so I reckon she's going to be a wee redhead like her mother,' Jinty said. 'Most babies are born with dark hair, and then it changes. Have you decided on a name yet, Lewis?'

'Molly likes Rowena Chloe.'

Hector had been looking through the photographs, at a loss as to what to say. Now he suddenly boomed, 'Ah! Pretty names – well done, Lewis. Children get some strange names nowadays. I heard a mother shouting to her son when I was in town the other day – what was it? Micawber?'

'I don't think so, dear. Surely not,' Fliss protested.

'It was something like that. Dashed weird, whatever it was,' Hector said, and then, 'Well, must get on.'

'So what's been happening here?' Lewis asked as his father disappeared into the pantry.

'They're more or less finished with the roof. Watertight at last,' Fliss crowed. 'For the first time since I came to the Hall I'm looking forward to some rain so that I can enjoy not having to worry about drips. The next thing will be the central heating.'

'And you need to organise an inventory of all the furniture and ornaments and paintings,' Jinty reminded her, 'so that you can decide what to keep and what to sell.

'Yes, I know. I'm not quite sure how we're going to set about it. Hector's not keen on taking it on. Lewis?'

'No point in looking at me; I've got my hands full with the outdoor work. Anything new happened while I've been away, Ginny?'

'The new poly tunnel's up – it looks good. And Duncan and I spent an afternoon at a garden centre and got most of the plants on our list.'

'Great.' Lewis headed for the door leading to the hall. 'I'll change into my work clothes then have something to eat before I go and find Duncan.'

'I have to get back to work,' Ginny said when he had gone. She glanced at the photographs and confessed, 'I've never thought that new babies looked much like anyone. They're just babies at that age.'

'I agree with Ginny,' Fliss said when she and Jinty were alone. 'I absolutely hate it when people ask me who they take after. I didn't even see Lewis as resembling his father or me when he was born. He was just – another baby.' She began to gather up the photographs.

'I'm quite good at recognising features – I've had more practice at it than you have.' Jinty picked up a picture that showed Rowena Chloe on her own, her hazel eyes wide open and her rosebud mouth pursed. She studied it for a long moment, then said, 'To be honest, I don't agree with Molly. This wee one's got a nose and a chin all right, but they're not your Lewis's. Has he thought of having a DNA test?'

'You mean – you don't think she's his daughter?' Fliss had been stacking the photographs neatly on the table; now she let go and they flopped into an untidy heap.

'I mean that I don't know. Some men can't deny their own children from the start, but others – well, I just don't see anything of Lewis in this wee face, not yet at least.' Jinty gathered the pictures together, neatened the edges, and

257

tucked them into their packet. 'But given that she could be heir to this place, I don't think that Lewis should just take Molly's word for it.'

When Ginny returned to Willow Cottage at the end of the day, a delicious aroma met her at the front door. She sniffed the air, and then went to the kitchen, where Alexandra Ramsay, her hair caught back in a ponytail and her slim figure enveloped in one of Clarissa's aprons, was stirring a casserole.

'I thought you might like a beef stew,' she said when her hostess arrived, 'as a thank you for letting me stay here. It's almost ready.'

'It's lovely to come home to the smell of cooking – not something I've ever been used to.'

'Nor me – my parents were both career people.' Alexandra tasted the gravy cautiously, and then picked up an opened bottle of wine. 'More of this, I think.' As she added a generous dollop and gave the dish another stir before covering it and returning to the oven, she added, 'I went into town to replenish the larder and the wine rack. Fancy a glass before dinner?'

'I'll just get washed and changed first. Won't be long,' Ginny said, and hurried upstairs. Splashing about in the bathroom, the smell of the rich stew still haunting her, she began to feel better about her unexpected houseguest. She had made the offer of a room without thinking – after all, Alexandra had more right to stay at Willow Cottage than Ginny herself. And she had assured Alexandra that silence was preferable to girly chat, but in the few days since her lodger moved in the silence had been far from comfortable. Alexandra was so tense that the very air around her vibrated, and although Ginny slept like a top after spending all day outdoors she had been awakened once or

258

twice by the sound of the other girl going downstairs in the night.

The casserole, and the offer of a glass of wine, was a breakthrough. So was the discovery that Alexandra, like Ginny herself, had not had what Ginny thought of as a cosy-Mum upbringing. Padding from the bathroom to her bedroom on bare feet, Ginny recalled the aching envy of her schooldays when fellow pupils spoke about mothers who were interested in how their day had gone, went shopping with them, helped them to choose clothes, and, best of all, had hot dinners on the table when their daughters returned from school.

Not that she had been neglected – a series of housekeepers kept the flat clean, and made the meals, but having occasionally been invited to more ordinary households Ginny soon discovered that food created out of duty never tasted as good as that made with love.

Meredith taught her how to put on stage make-up rather than the everyday kind, and the few occasions when mother and daughter went shopping for clothes turned into battles, with Meredith trying to force her into pretty-girl garments while Ginny, from an early age, clung to racks of T-shirts and jeans.

It was a warm evening, so they had a glass of wine in the back garden before dinner, and finished the bottle during the meal. Then Alexandra produced some excellent brandy to enjoy with their coffee.

'What sort of work are you doing at Linn Hall?' she asked as they settled in the living room with coffee cups and brandy glasses.

'Gardening – I love it. I've been put in charge of renovating the kitchen garden and I'm having a wonderful time. What do you do?' Ginny ventured to ask.

'Head of Business Studies in a girls' school.'

'Do you enjoy it?'

'Sometimes. I was wondering,' Alexandra said after a long pause, 'if you would mind me staying on for a few more days – another week, perhaps?'

'Not at all, stay as long as you like,' Ginny said idly, and took another sip of brandy. Alexandra had put classical music on the music centre, and Ginny settled back in her chair, letting the violins lull her into a semi-doze. Then two phrases – 'Head of Business Studies' and 'perhaps another week' swam into her head and began circling round each other. When they finally came together she sat upright.

'Would you like something to do while you're here?'

'What sort of something?'

'I've just had an idea,' Ginny said. 'They need someone to make an inventory of all the furniture and pictures and ornaments in Linn Hall, but nobody knows how to go about it. It seems to me that you would be the perfect person for the job.'

'It's a long drive, Lewis, and you've only been back for about ten days. Do you really have to return to Inverness so soon?'

'I have to register Rowena's birth, Mum.'

'Can't Molly's father do that?'

'Yes, but I want to do it because I'm Rowena's father. In any case, I want to see her again. I'll only stay for two nights this time; there's a lot to do here.'

He dropped a kiss on her cheek, and went out to his car, whistling. From the kitchen window, Fliss watched him drive off, wondering if she should have steeled herself to ask if he was really sure that he was the father of Molly Ewing's baby.

★   ★   ★

260

To her surprise, Alexandra was enjoying her work at Linn Hall more than she had enjoyed anything for a long time. Some of the pictures and ornaments had been there since the Hall's early days, and recording everything she found was a slow but fascinating job. It suited her to be on her own, and she loved the excitement of opening drawers and cupboards, not knowing what treasure she might find within. She was working her way through the rooms on the second floor and she tended to stay upstairs during lunch and tea breaks, preferring to eat with Fliss and Jinty after the others had returned to work.

The people she saw most often – the Ralston-Kerrs, Jinty and Ginny – showed no interest in why she had come to Prior's Ford or how long she planned to stay, and one day slipped easily into the next. In the evenings, she recorded the day's findings on the computer at Willow Cottage and went out for solitary walks that usually ended up at Alastair's cottage.

'You don't mind me dropping in, do you?' she asked him.

'Not at all, though I don't know why you'd want to come to a tip like this.'

Strangely, for someone who until now had always preferred neat, clean surroundings, she found the cottage soothing. But she didn't like to say so. 'I like to watch you at work, but say if you'd rather I didn't interrupt you.'

'I don't mind you being here.' He hesitated, wondering if he dared to suggest what was in his mind. Alexandra, in the sweater and trousers she now wore most of the time, her hair caught back with a twist of ribbon instead of in its formal chignon, was more approachable than she had been before, so he took the plunge. 'I was wondering if you'd let me paint you.'

'Me?' Her voice and her beautifully arched eyebrows shot up in astonishment. 'Why, for goodness' sake?'

'Because you're – interesting to look at.' He had been going to say 'beautiful', but for some reason his tongue refused to get round the word. 'I'm not looking for elaborate poses – just a few quick sketches would do.'

'Well – if you want to, why not?' Alexandra said.

30

'Hell-ooo?'

'Hello, dear, is your mummy there?'

'Yes she is, she's watching the television but my daddy's gone to the pub because his throat's dried up again and he doesn't like juice.'

'Could you ask your mummy to come to the phone?'

'Yes I could.' There was a brief pause, filled by what could only be described as heavy breathing, before the voice asked, 'Do you want me to?'

'Yes, please,' Fliss said, then almost dropped the receiver as the child on the other end of the line yelled 'MUMMY – the PHONE!' into her ear.

There was another pause, filled only by the sound of heavy breathing, then came Jinty's voice, 'Faith, how often have I told you? Give it to me.' Then, after a brief, muttered altercation, 'Hello?'

'Jinty, it's Fliss. Lewis has just phoned – he's coming home tomorrow and bringing Molly and the baby back with him for a few days so that we can see her – the baby,

I mean. But we haven't got any of the things that babies need!'

'Well now, I expect they'll be bringing her clothes and so on, and food – or is she being breastfed?' Jinty asked briskly.

'I don't know. It's not the sort of question one asks one's son at short notice.'

'Whichever way, they'll have it organised. They'll all be in Lewis's room, I suppose? We've still got our old cot in the attic, I could get the boys to fetch it down this evening.'

'Lewis said that Molly has a sort of carrycot for the baby to sleep in, something that goes on wheels and turns into a pram. They're bringing that with them.'

'There you are, then – all sorted. I wonder if they're bringing extra bedding for the wee one, just in case? Our Faith's got a lovely life-size baby doll and a big pram for her, too, I'll wash through the doll's bedding now and bring it with me tomorrow, just in case it's needed. Don't fret, Faith,' Jinty said in an aside as the voice that had answered the phone began to protest in the background. 'Pearlanne won't catch her death, I've got a nice fleecy blanket that'll keep her cosy, and the little baby'll write her a nice thank-you letter, won't she, Mrs F?'

'Oh yes, and send her a box of chocolates too.'

'Just the letter will do. When are they arriving?'

'Late afternoon.'

'I'll come in good and early tomorrow morning so that we can change Lewis's bed and give his room a good going over. Don't you worry, Mrs F, by the time they arrive tomorrow we'll have everything shipshape.'

'Oh, thank you, Jinty!'

Why, Fliss wondered as she hung up, couldn't she have been blessed with Jinty's common sense, instead of flapping through life like a hen that had just had its head cut off?

★   ★   ★

264

At just that moment, the phone rang in Willow Cottage. Ginny, on her way into the garden, turned back to answer it.

'Is that Mrs Ramsay?' a deep, confident voice wanted to know.

'Mrs Ramsay's away at the moment. I'm her tenant.'

'Oh. I'm actually trying to get in touch with her step-daughter. Do you have a contact number for Alexandra?'

Ginny hesitated for only a second before saying, 'I'm sorry, I don't.'

'You haven't heard from her at all recently?'

'No.'

'Very well,' the voice had taken on an irritated edge. 'I'm sorry to have troubled you.' There was a click and the purr of an open line. Ginny put the phone down and turned to see Alexandra, who had gone upstairs for a bath as soon as they got back from their day's work at the Hall, halfway down the stairs.

'You look puzzled – is there something wrong?'

'No, just someone looking for Mrs Ramsay – I think it was one of those ghastly people wanting to install a kitchen or a bathroom. They lost interest when they discovered that I'm only the tenant.'

'The bathroom's free now.' Alexandra had changed into a cream silk shirt and clean blue jeans. Her hair was still damp from shampooing, and she looked fresh and cool.

'I'm going to do a spot of work in the back garden first, then I thought we might eat at the pub to save cooking.'

'That sounds like a good idea. I'll dry my hair outside.' In the kitchen, Alexandra slipped her long, slender feet into sandals then settled on the bench in the garden.

'I can't see any work needing done – that lad Jimmy does a good job, doesn't he?'

'He does, but I like to potter a bit now and again.' As

she worked, Ginny glanced over at Alexandra, brushing her hair with long smooth strokes, and wondered why she had lied about the phone call. It had been an instinctive re-action; although Alexandra had given no reason for her sudden appearance, Ginny suspected that she was running away from something – or someone. And that someone was probably the man who had phoned, looking for her or news of her whereabouts.

Finally, she stuck the garden fork she was using into the soil and stood up, dusting flecks of earth from her trousers as she walked over to the other girl.

'I've got a confession to make. That phone call – it wasn't for Mrs Ramsay. Well, it was, but not about a new kitchen. It was a man, wanting to know how to get in touch with you.'

The brush strokes slowed, then stopped. 'Did he give his name?'

'No, and I didn't ask. I should have called you to the phone but I don't think you want anyone to know where you are at the moment. You can dial one four seven one if you want to call him back.'

'No, I don't, and thank you for covering for me.' Alexandra glanced at her watch, then said, 'I don't know about you, but I'm getting hungry. Off you go and have your bath, then we'll eat.'

As Lewis drove Molly and the baby into Prior's Ford, the double doors of the primary school opened like two cupped hands to release a flock of excited, noisy children. They spilled through the doors, down the steps and into the play-ground like a cluster of balloons suddenly released from their strings. Some of them, indeed, fizzed around the playground like balloons that had been blown up and then released without being tied.

'Goodness,' Molly said as the chattering, laughing, pushing, bouncing, chasing mass flowed untidily towards and through the school gates, some excitedly colliding with the mothers waiting for them outside, while others old enough to go home on their own trickled in an uneven snaking line along the pavements, 'would you look at that lot!'

'It's the first day of the summer holidays.' There was a lollipop man on the pavement, but Lewis slowed the car down just in case. 'A great moment, I remember it well.'

'You never went to that school, did you?'

'Of course I did.'

'But your folks have the big house; surely you went to a posh school.'

'My folks didn't have the money to pay for a posh school. In any case, I liked being in the local primary.'

'Oh,' Molly said as the car turned into Adam Crescent. She had already made up her mind that Rowena Chloe, slumbering in the back seat, was going to go to a posh school, but perhaps this wasn't the time to say so.

Thanks mainly to Jinty, all was ready by the time Lewis's car drew up outside the kitchen door. Jinty, eager to see the baby, hurried out to meet them while Fliss winkled Hector from the pantry.

As he emerged, Molly came in, followed by Lewis, a carrycot dangling from one hand and a large bag from the other. Jinty, carrying another two bags, took up the rear.

'Hello! Thank you for saying we could come. Lewis was desperate to let you see Weena. She's slept all the way, hasn't she, Lewis, apart from a stop to feed and change her.'

'She's a good baby,' Lewis said proudly, setting the carrycot on the kitchen table. 'Come and see.' He drew the top cover

267

back to reveal a white knitted cap topped by a huge pink tassel. The hat moved and a protesting squeak emerged from the blankets.

'Oh good, she's awake.' Molly drew the covers back and scooped the baby into her arms. 'Here she is – this is Rowena Chloe!'

Fliss and Hector edged forward to see a tiny face consisting of a large pink dummy above two screwed-up eyes. Gradually the eyes opened, then a kitten-like sneeze dislodged the dummy to reveal a moist pink mouth and snub nose, and all at once the little face turned into a real person.

'Oh, she's lovely! Can I hold her?' Jinty reached with hungry arms, then drew back, suddenly aware of her manners. 'Sorry, Mrs F, you should have first shot.'

'No, that's all right, Jinty,' Fliss said hurriedly. 'You take her and I'll make some tea. I'll hold her in a minute.'

'I'll help you – I've not forgotten where everything is.' Motherhood hadn't changed Molly a bit. Her red hair still swung about her shoulders in two plaits, and she rattled on as she and Fliss set out the tea things, passing on best wishes from her family.

'My folks think the world of Lewis and they're thrilled with Weena as well. Lewis is a super dad; we even had him changing her nappies yesterday. It was a laugh, but he soon got the hang of it. Have you any biscuits or anything? I'm starving – it must be the breastfeeding. My dad says I'm still eating for two.'

There was no denying that Rowena was a lovely baby. When Fliss's turn to hold her could be put off no longer, she sat down and held her arms out nervously, certain that she would drop the poor little mite. But as soon as the warm, solid bundle settled into her embrace she was transported back to the first time, twenty-seven years before, when she had held Lewis. Her pent-up breath escaped in a soft sigh as Rowena eyed her solemnly, then cooed approval.

'Yes, that's your other nana, isn't it?' Molly cooed in reply, stroking her daughter's petal-soft cheek. 'We thought she might call my mum and dad Nana and Papa, and you and Mr Ralston-Kerr Gran and Granddad, if that's all right?' Then, to the baby, 'Where's this, then, Weena? It's Linn Hall, isn't it? This is where Daddy lives and one day we're going to live here too, aren't we? And one day a long time away, when you're a big grown up lady, it'll all belong to you, yes it will!'

She put a finger in Rowena's open palm, and as the baby gripped it, Molly looked up at Hector and Lewis, and said, 'That's right, isn't it? A girl can inherit this estate just like a boy, can't she?'

During the week Molly and her daughter stayed at Linn Hall, Prior's Ford Drama Group took to the village hall stage to perform their three one-act plays.

The three-night run attracted large and appreciative audiences; although most villagers enjoyed the pantomimes more than the plays, the drama group, like all the other village activities, was well supported. This time the furore caused by Meredith Whitelaw's sudden disappearance made the event more attractive.

On each of the evenings Cynthia MacBain's first appearance onstage was greeted by a round of applause from her supporters, who bought tickets for every performance and sat in the middle of the hall so that they could encourage all around them to join in the acclaim for Prior's Ford's very own leading actress. Kevin Pearce, who had dreamed of Meredith's famous friends occupying those very seats and later gathering in his home for after-show drinks, bared his teeth in a smile that was more of a grimace, and joined in the applause.

'I thought the character was unable to walk,' Ginny murmured to Alastair on the first night, as the curtains rustled open and Cynthia rose gracefully from her armchair to curtsey to the applauding audience.

'That's right. This is what you call poetic justice,' he whispered back. When the play ended the storm of clapping, cheering, whistling and stamping made the rafters ring, and as the curtain opened again and Cynthia, on her feet once more, led the other actors forward to take their bows, her husband scurried through the hall and up the steps to the stage to present her with a huge bouquet.

'A different bouquet each evening,' Jinty said as she cleared used lunch dishes from the kitchen table at the Hall the day after the third and final performance. 'Huge, they were, Steph said. They must have cost Gilbert a fortune.'

'And made one for the florist too, lucky so and so,' Lewis remarked. 'Next year he'll be buying his bouquets from our shop – right, Duncan?'

'Aye, if we can get those youngsters to move their arses a bit quicker.'

'But what about last night, eh?' Jinty's eyes danced. 'Didn't young Ewan and Alison steal the show?'

'Ewan made a right fool of himself!'

'Away with you, Duncan, it was lovely to see the two of them together like that.'

'What happened?' Molly wanted to know. She and Lewis had gone to the first evening's performance.

'You know how the play about the two folk that had been school sweethearts ended with them kissing?'

Molly nodded. 'I thought they were never going to get to that kiss – talk about shy!'

'It turned out that they werenae so shy after all,' Duncan

270

sniggered. 'When the curtain opened to let them take their bows the two of them were still at it. I thought I was goin' to have to throw a bucket of cold water over them.'

'It was lovely,' Jinty said again. 'Wasn't it, Mrs F?'

'It'll take months for Ewan to live that down.' Duncan drained his mug of tea and got to his feet. 'I'd best get back to work.'

'Me too,' Lewis said. 'We'll definitely have the shop up and running properly by next summer, won't we, Ginny?'

'I hope so.'

'Hoping won't do it – we're going to make it happen.' Molly was holding her daughter, and as Lewis passed them, he touched the baby's cheek with one finger. 'Fancy making yourself useful, Molly? I could so do with an extra pair of hands.'

'If someone looks after Weena for me.'

'I'll do it,' Jinty said at once, and Molly shot to her feet and thrust her daughter into Jinty's arms before scurrying after Lewis.

'I must say,' Jinty settled Rowena into the crook of her arm, 'that Cynthia MacBain did very well in that play, though I'd've liked to have seen your mum playing the part, Ginny. It's not often that we get a professional actress in our village hall.'

'I think Mrs MacBain was better than my mother would have been. Amateurs put more welly into what they do,' Ginny said before she too returned to work.

31

Ewan hadn't dared to put his nose through the door of the Neurotic Cuckoo since the drama club's show. His face still burned like a furnace every time he recalled that evening. The play had gone well – so well, indeed, that he had stopped being Ewan McNair and had actually become the character in the play. The final kiss, so carefully choreographed by Meredith Whitelaw, had gone well, and he clearly remembered crossing the stage to Alison and taking her into his arms.

But after that, came a blank. For some reason he didn't remember hearing the curtain closing to applause, or opening again. It was only when he heard the sudden roar from the audience, then the laughter and whistles and stamping feet that he came to his senses. He and Alison had sprung apart swiftly, but it had been too late – the damage was done.

Unfortunately, his mother, Victor, and Janette, who now wore Victor's engagement ring, had all been in the audience on the final evening and Victor had teased him so unmercifully the next day that the two of them had ended up rolling about the farmyard, locked in battle with the dogs barking and their father flailing at them with his stick.

Jess, drawn to the kitchen door by the uproar, had had to bring out the first aid box and administer stinging iodine to both sons while her husband administered a lecture that stung even more, ending with, 'And ye'll both go tae yer beds tonight without any supper!'

'Don't be daft, man, they're adults,' his wife snapped at him. 'You cannae treat them like bairns any more!'

'Then tell 'em tae stop behavin' like bairns,' Bert roared back at her, and stumped off, the dogs cringing at his heels.

For a whole week afterwards Ewan, denied the luxury of a pint with his pals, and meetings with Alison, threw himself into work, the harder the better. In order to fill every minute of the day from dawn to dusk he hired himself out to other farmers as well as doing his regular work at Tarbethill.

He had been finding out more about creating a wormery, and while half of the money he earned from the extra work went to his mother, the other half paid for the hire of a digger, enabling him to start gouging out long troughs in the field his father had given to him. Once completed, the troughs would be lined with plastic and then filled with a carefully balanced compost mixture. Once that was done and the worms installed, his new project would be up and running.

He had just finished working on the field one evening and was on his way back to the farm when he found Alison Greenlees waiting for him.

'How are things coming along?' She nodded at the trenches in the field behind him.

'OK.' He rubbed a hand over his hot sweaty face, then

ran his fingers through his hair. He must look like a right sight!

'Have you ordered the worms yet?'

'I've got a while to go before I can do that.'

'Oh. I'm looking forward to seeing them. You've not been to the pub for a while. Have you lost your taste for our beer?'

'I've been busy.' Ewan latched the gate and started along the road towards the lane leading to home. Alison fell into step beside him, her hands thrust into the pockets of her long woollen jacket.

'Ewan, I know fine why we've not seen you for the past two weeks – it's what happened after the play, isn't it?'

'Of course not! Well – mebbe. I feel as if I made a right fool of myself!'

'We both did,' said Alison. 'But d'you not see that it happened because the play went so well? That kiss – it wasn't you and me that kissed each other, it was Tony and Elspeth, the folk we were pretending to be in the play.'

'D'ye think so?'

'I know so. It's the sort of thing that can happen when folk are working hard on a play. Look at all the famous actors and film stars who play opposite each other and then get married – and quite often they get divorced because the one they really wanted to marry was the character and not the person. If you see what I mean.'

Ewan didn't quite grasp what she meant, but at least she was providing some sort of reasonable excuse for his daft behaviour, and he snatched at it like a drowning man grabbing a passing branch. 'I never thought about it that way, but I suppose you're right.'

'I definitely am,' said Alison, who had been just as confused as Ewan by the strength of the emotion she had felt on that night. She had wanted to stay in his arms for ever, and she still didn't quite know whether it was because he was the character in the play, or whether it was because he was quiet, dependable, lovely Ewan McNair. 'I spend half my life hoping that Johnny Depp'll come into the pub one day and ask me to marry him, even though I know I might not like him in real life.'

They had reached the entrance to the farm lane. 'D'you want tae come tae the farm for a cup of tea?'

'I have to get back to the pub. I just came out for a wee stroll and a bit of fresh air.' She didn't tell him that someone in the pub had mentioned seeing Ewan McNair working in that particular field. 'But why don't you come and have a pint? You must be as dry as a — something or other.'

'By the time I go home and get myself cleaned up it'll be near closing.'

'I'll take you in the side door so's you can have a wash in our kitchen. Come on, Ewan,' she said as he hesitated. 'You've got to get back into village life some time, and everyone's forgotten about what happened. If they mention it, just give them a glare. That's what I've been doing. So — are you coming?'

'Aye,' Ewan said, as a heavy weight he had been carrying around for the past two weeks began to roll off his broad shoulders. 'Aye, why not?'

It was good to be back in the pub with his friends again, and with Alison. He managed to shrug off the inevitable teasing, and it wasn't until later that night, when he was in bed and almost asleep, that he realised that although Alison's explanation for that kiss going out of control sounded reasonable, and probably was for her, it was wrong.

He hadn't been Tony, kissing Elspeth. He had been plain

275

Ewan McNair, kissing Alison Greenlees, and it had been so wonderful that he had completely forgotten that the two of them were in a play.

In order to keep the Gift Horse open, Ingrid and Jenny had to holiday at different times. This year, Ingrid and Peter MacKenzie took Freya and Ella off to Norway to visit Ingrid's family, while Jenny ran the gift shop with the help of Steph McDonald. When Ingrid returned home, the Forsyths went to spend the first two weeks in August in Elgin, where Andrew's parents lived. They were booked into a caravan park on the town's outskirts.

'Andrew's parents are quite nice, but their house isn't large and Mrs Forsyth's so house proud that I worry all the time in case Calum drops crumbs, or leaves fingerprints on one of her beloved ornaments,' Jenny told Helen. 'Staying in a caravan also means that we'll have time together, just the three of us. I think Calum needs a breather, after all that's been happening.'

'You all need a breather.'

'You're right. Andrew's been working too hard, and it'll be good to get away and recharge our batteries. I just hope that Maggie doesn't decide that she wants to stay on with her grandparents afterwards. That would be – well, it would be terrible. I know she can be difficult, but I don't want to lose her. And her grandfather's no stronger, so they couldn't cope with her full time.'

It had been arranged that on their way to Elgin, the Forsyths would drop Maggie off at her grandparents' home so that she could spend time with them, and with her uncle and aunt. She had hoped to spend Easter with them, but John Cameron had had another spell in hospital and to Maggie's disappointment the visit was cancelled.

'I think you're doing the right thing. She needs to see them, and you three need time on your own. As for what happens next – why don't you wait and see?'

'Good advice. Aren't you going on holiday this year?'

Helen tucked a strand of hair behind one ear. 'Can't afford it.'

'Not even now that you're doing regular work for the newspaper?'

'Not this year, at any rate. You know what kids are like – you spend a fortune buying new shoes, and by the time you're got them home their feet have grown and before you know it, you're back in the shop, buying a larger size. But I'm putting a bit of my earnings aside every month. Luckily, Duncan doesn't know how much I get. Next year,' Helen said firmly, 'we'll go on holiday. I'm determined!'

When Jenny had last seen her former father-in-law, days before she fled from her marriage to his son, he had been a healthy man who looked younger than his years. Now he seemed to be half the size he once was, huddled into a large armchair, a blanket tucked about his knees. His smile, though, was as warm and loving as ever.

'Here's my wee lass, back again!' He held out a frail, veined hand to Maggie. During the drive north Jenny had tried to prepare the girl for the change she would see in her grandfather, but even she was shocked. For a moment, feeling her stepdaughter shrink back against her, she wondered if Maggie would be able to cope with the new situation. Then, to her credit, Maggie ran forward and bent to kiss his cheek, taking his hand in both of hers.

'Gramps! Oh, it's so lovely to see you – and you too, Gran!'

'Would you look at her, Anne?' There were tears in the old man's eyes, 'You're a young lady now, and such a bonny one too. We've missed you, pet. And Janet – you're a sight for sore eyes, right enough! Where's your man, and the lad?'

'In the hall. We didn't all want to crowd in on you at the one time.'

'Ach, away, I'm not half as bad as I look. Bring them in, and let me meet them!'

As Andrew drove off an hour later, his wife by his side and their son in the back seat, he said, 'They're nice people, your in-laws.'

'Ex in-laws. And they're lovely folk; they were always so kind to me. But I hope Maggie'll be all right. It must be hard for her to see her grandfather so frail.'

'She'll be fine. You can see that the two of them dote on her, and she dotes on them. Let's just concentrate on ourselves for the next two weeks, eh? Let's just relax,' Andrew said.

'Yes, let's!' Calum said loudly from the back seat.

'Mmm, that would be nice.'

Jenny tried to relax as the car covered mile after mile. She hadn't told Andrew about the parents' night she had attended two weeks before the holidays. He had been working late and she had gone on her own, which turned out to be just as well.

In general, Maggie's teachers were pleased with her academic ability, and somewhat to Jenny's surprise, she was told that her stepdaughter, sulky and difficult at home, was well-behaved and biddable at school. She had been able to pass these reports to Andrew, who was relieved to hear them, but had said nothing about the final meeting of the evening, with the assistant head teacher.

'Maggie's an obedient student, and her class work's adequate, but we're concerned about her, Mrs Forsyth,' the woman said. 'She can be quite withdrawn at times, and she seems to have

278

difficulty in making friends. As a result, she tends to mix with one or two of our more disruptive students. I don't think that they're good for her.'

'She's had a difficult time.'

'I know that she hasn't been in the school for long – it might help us both if you told me about her situation,' the woman suggested, and then, when Jenny had finished, 'Ah – now I understand what her English teacher meant. It seems that a lot of Maggie's free expression work tends to revolve around children being held prisoner by evil adults – sometimes wicked stepmothers. Does that surprise you?'

'Not entirely. A friend of mine writes an agony aunt column and Maggie sent her a letter about her cruel step-mother. Fortunately, my friend realised who had sent it. But I really do love Maggie, and we're not at all cruel to her!'

'I believe you, Mrs Forsyth, but I think you'll agree with me that at the moment, Maggie appears to be quite a confused and unhappy child. We have a psychologist we can call on – would you be willing to speak to her, and let her meet Maggie?'

'Yes, if it would help. But could we leave it for the moment? Maggie's going to spend two weeks during the summer with her father's family. She's been missing them, and I'm hopeful that spending time with them might help her.'

If it didn't, she thought as she and Andrew and Calum headed towards two Maggie-free weeks, she would have to talk to Andrew about the school psychologist.

Calum was singing tunelessly in the back seat and when she glanced at Andrew she saw that he was smiling to himself. The two of them were visibly relaxing now that Maggie had been left behind. If only she had listened when her husband and her friends advised her to think carefully before agreeing to take responsibility for a teenager she no longer knew. She had thought – had assumed – that everything would work out for the best if she wanted it to hard enough. But it hadn't.

What had she done to Maggie, and to her family?

'My adventurous stepmama has whizzed through Hong Kong and India, and now she's in America,' Alexandra said, the day before she herself was due to go home. 'She got there in time to attend her cousin's daughter's wedding, and now that that's over, the two of them are off on a drive round the USA and Canada.'

Alastair was at his easel. 'The three of them,' he corrected her. 'The cousin's partner's there as well.' He laid down a brush and selected another.

'I forgot. She keeps in close touch with you, doesn't she?'

'We're friends.'

'You haven't mentioned——?'

'Of course not.' For some reason, Alexandra was determined that Clarissa shouldn't know that she was in the village. A friend keeping an eye on her flat sent the mail to her every week and her brief letters to her stepmother were posted from England.

'When she first came up with this mad idea of travelling the world,' Alexandra said, 'I was certain that she'd scurry back before the first month was out, but she hasn't. I always thought of Clarissa as a little grey mouse, scurrying here and scurrying there, usually after my father.'

Alastair shot her a swift, exasperated sidelong glance. 'You shouldn't jump to conclusions. Your stepmother's not a mouse, she's an eagle, soaring free. She's got a lot more courage than you realise.'

'You're very fond of her, aren't you?'

'I like her. I like a lot of people. And I don't try to analyse them. Fancy a coffee?'

'Yes please. I brought some decent stuff.' She dipped into her shoulder bag and flourished a jar at him.

'I don't want to leave this at the moment. You know where the kitchen is. And I want my usual village store brand.'

'Philistine,' Alexandra said amiably, and went into the kitchen while Alastair, recalling how much she had intimidated him when they first met, marvelled at how comfortable he now felt with her. She had changed since her sudden and unexpected arrival in Prior's Ford; in the space of a few weeks she had become much more relaxed. He felt as though he was now beginning to see the real Alexandra, and he quite liked her, though he was still slightly awed by her beauty and her intelligence. He was sure that Ginny should take a lot of the credit for the change.

'How are things going at the Hall?' he asked when Alexandra returned with the coffee.

'Quite well; the Ralston-Kerrs are nice people, aren't they? So – gentle. The inventory was more fun than I first thought.' She took her coffee to the window and perched on the broad sill. 'They have some amazingly beautiful pieces of china and crystal, all packed away in dusty cupboards. Mrs Ralston-Kerr kept saying, "My goodness, I didn't know we had that!" They're going to sell most of the things I've found. They should make a small fortune.'

'Good; they can always do with more money.' Alastair, caught by the way she was silhouetted against the small, bright window, deserted his easel and picked up a sketch pad.

'Not again,' she protested, laughing.

'You are incredibly sketchable. If someone left *me* a lot of money I'd pay you to be my model.'

'No thank you.' Five minutes passed, during which he

worked and she stared out of the window. Then she said, 'Have you ever made a fool of yourself? I mean, a completely appalling fool of yourself?'

'Often. It's part of the great tapestry of life, isn't it? We all do it.'

'I don't – I didn't, I should say. I was always so careful not to. But now I've just made the most awful fool of myself. I didn't realise that it could hurt so much.'

'Only if you let it.'

'I fell in love for the first time in my life,' she said abruptly, then gave a short, hard laugh. 'At least, I thought it was love. Then I discovered that he was happily married. Just making use of me!'

'I take it that it's over and done with?'

'Of course.'

'Then chalk it up to experience and try to forget about it.'

'Do you believe that we should honour our parents no matter what they do?'

'You're being very serious today, aren't you?'

'I need to know and you're the only person I can ask.'

'I love my parents,' Alastair said thoughtfully. 'I don't know if I could claim to honour them. I respect them – would that do?'

'In our house, love wasn't really an option but I'd say that Steven and I were brought up to honour our parents, especially our father. I admired him tremendously because he was strong, and successful. He brought us up to be like him, and I really did want to be like him, though looking back now, as an adult, I don't think I ever liked him very much. I was a teenager, still at the school where he was headmaster, when I happened to see him in his car with a woman – one of the teaching staff. It was – horrible. After that I watched and listened and didn't miss a thing. When

282

he and my mother split up he told everyone that it was because she was more of a career woman than a wife, but by then I knew that it was his infidelity that drove her away.'

'Ah.'

'I never told my mother that I knew, and I never told Steven about it. It's strange,' Alexandra said thoughtfully, 'but for some reason, although I felt contempt for my father's weakness I still admired him in every other way. I set out to be just as ambitious and just as successful as he was, but at the same time I swore that I would never make a fool of myself the way he had, in my eyes. Then I met David and let him charm me into thinking that I'd found someone worth loving. What a fool I've been! I'm just as worthless as my father was after all – and I'm so disgusted with myself!'

'Hold on there – you're only human. Human beings make mistakes. That's what helps us to learn.'

'It's certainly helped me to learn never to trust my heart again!'

'That's a pity, because having a heart is another of the burdens that we human beings have to suffer.'

'Your parents should have called you Goody Two Shoes,' she snapped.

'They did, but I had it changed by deed poll as soon as I was old enough.'

Despite herself Alexandra laughed, then said, 'When I was a child I used to put my head under the bedclothes when I wanted to hide from everyone. This time, I ran away to Prior's Ford. And I'm glad I did, because I finally found someone I could talk to without fear of being judged or my secrets being repeated.'

When she had gone Alastair set aside his sketchbook and

went out, choosing fields and woods where there was little danger of meeting anyone other than a farmer working his land. Clarissa had never told him why, on the day he first met her, she had been sitting on a stile in the rain, soaked through and disorientated. Now he wondered if she, like Alexandra, had discovered that Keith Ramsay had not been the upright citizen everyone thought he was.

If so, Clarissa, unlike Alexandra, hadn't run away. She had faced the truth, and the world, head on, and created herself anew.

Now, he admired her even more than he had before. And, strangely enough, he also felt more protective towards her.

'Come home, Clarissa,' he said to the trees and the blue sky and a white cloud formation shaped like a huge bird with its wings stretched in flight. 'Come back to where you belong.'

32

The Alexandra who opened the door of Willow Cottage to Alastair was the Alexandra he had first met. Her hair was drawn tightly back into a chignon, her make-up immaculate, her nails varnished. She wore the flared black skirt, ivory blouse and dark red knitted jacket she had arrived in.

'Come in,' she said, and then, when he hesitated, 'what's the matter? Has something happened?'

'No – sorry. It was just that – I was thinking about something else. Sorry.'

'I brought the car out, as you'd see. Come on in. I'll just fetch my coat, won't be a minute.' She turned from him and went up the stairs, her flared skirt moving gracefully about her knee-length leather boots.

The living room was more or less back to the way Clarissa had left it, the photographs of Meredith Whitelaw gone. A book about gardening lay on the table, bristling with scribbled bits of paper in place of bookmarks. Alastair, who loved views, went to the window and looked out on the village green to the left and the main street to the right.

'Ready,' Alexandra said, appearing in the doorway, her black hooded coat over one arm. Then, as he moved forward. 'Oh, wait – there was just one more thing to do before I go.'

She dropped the coat over the arm of a fireside chair and moved towards him. 'Kiss me,' she said.

'What?'

'Kiss me – properly.' Before he could say another word her arms were around him and her soft mouth opening against his. He made a muffled sound of astonishment – possibly protest. Whichever it was, he would never know, for all at once he was holding her tight, his tongue flickering into her mouth.

It seemed to him, looking back on it afterwards, that the kiss lasted for a long time, and yet it was over too quickly. 'Thank you,' Alexandra said as she freed herself from his embrace and stepped back.

'For – what was that all about?' His voice seemed to have got itself twisted around his tonsils.

'I wanted to know what it felt like to be kissed by a decent, honest man. And now I do. Thank you,' she said again, then picked up her coat and held it out to him. He took it and she turned and slid her arms into the sleeves.

'Shall we go? My bag's in the hall.'

'I'm not sure that I'm safe to drive now,' Alastair protested as he picked up her bag and followed her outside.

'Don't be silly.' Her voice was crisp and businesslike, the voice she probably used for her students at work. 'It was only a kiss. Here are the car keys. I'm going to miss this place,' she said as they drove along the main street.

'You'll come back to visit Clarissa.'

'Of course, but it won't be the same as this time. It'll never be the same.'

'It's called moving on.'

'I suppose it is. Remember what we agreed.'

'I'll remember.' They had realised that sometime, someone was bound to mention Alexandra's visit to Clarissa, and had agreed that she had come to Prior's Ford to recuperate after catching a virus.

'I doubt if she'll swallow that,' Alastair said as Prior's Ford fell behind and the car picked up speed. 'Clarissa's not a fool.'

'But she's discreet — she would never dream of asking for further details and if you don't say any more about it, that will be that. Just don't let her see those sketches you made of me.'

'I'll send the best of them to you.'

'Don't trouble yourself. They belong to your world, not mine. I'll tell Steven all about my visit when I get back, though not why. And when Clarissa calls in on her way home I'll casually mention being here and doing the Linn Hall inventory.'

'Don't stay,' she said as he carried her bag into the railway station. 'I'm in good time for my train, and I hate goodbyes.' She took the bag from him, put it down, and held out her hand. 'Goodbye for now, Alastair. And thank you,' she said.

He watched her walk away without a backward glance, and when she was swallowed up in the crowds he went back to the car, wondering what the hell was wrong with him.

He had been kissed, passionately, by the most beautiful woman he had ever known, and yet it hadn't meant a thing to him. Which, given that she was way out of his league, was just as well.

Maggie Cameron stood at the bedroom window, watching the road outside.

What if they didn't come back for her? What if they decided that she was better off staying with her grandparents? What if – it was the most frightening 'what if' of all, but she had to face it – what if they just decided, while enjoying their holiday without her, that they didn't want her to live with them any more?

She couldn't entirely blame them if they never wanted to set eyes on her again. She knew that she had been difficult, but Jenny had tried so hard to make everything perfect and to turn Maggie into a sweet, loving daughter that it had turned Maggie's stomach.

She squeezed her eyes tightly shut against a sudden rush of self-pitying tears, so tightly that red lines flashed against the darkness, then opened them wide until her cheeks ached from the strain. The tears had been successfully vanquished, but the road was still empty. Surely they should have been here by now?

She had longed to return to her grandparents and had secretly planned to persuade them to let her stay. She had even brought the false diary in which she had recorded unkind acts inflicted upon her by Jenny and Andrew, but on the previous night she had torn the pages out and shredded them into confetti, and then dumped them in the wheelie bin. Nothing was the same in her grandparents' house and she no longer wanted to stay there.

Her granddad's frailty scared and even repelled her, and she couldn't bear the way the worry over his health had aged her gran. It was just as bad at Uncle Malcolm's house – Aunt Lizbeth was as cheerful and funny and loving as ever, but her health, too, had deteriorated in the months since Maggie had last seen her.

Why did everyone have to get ill like that? It wasn't fair! Sometimes, lying in bed at night, she wondered if it was her fault. Her mother had died when she was born, her father had been killed at work, and now Gramps and Auntie Lizbeth were fading away before her very eyes.

A car came into view, and she retreated swiftly into the shelter of the curtain. But it wasn't Andrew's car. Perhaps if she made an effort to be nicer to people – but that wouldn't work. She had always been quite good, and it hadn't stopped Auntie Lizbeth and Gramps from getting ill, or saved her dad.

She wished with all her heart that she had someone to talk to, someone who would understand how confused and downright miserable she felt all the time. It had been great, meeting with her old friends again, but knowing that nobody wants to listen to a Moaning Minnie, she had immediately started to brag to them about the great life she had in Prior's Ford, and how cool it was to have a trendy young mum and a wee brother who adored her. She had even invented a boyfriend called Eric, who was so gorgeous that her friends were all green with envy.

She was so caught up in dreaming about Eric's dark hair and blue eyes that when the car she had been waiting for appeared, she almost forgot to hide behind the curtain. They had come back for her!

Car doors opened and shut. The doorbell rang and she heard her grandmother greeting the newcomers and then calling up the stairs, 'Maggie? They're here, pet!'

'OK,' Maggie yelled back, taking one last look round the room that was no longer home. An hour later, she said her farewells to her grandparents, making a big show of hugging and kissing them and finding it quite easy to bring tears to her eyes as she clung to her gran.

'You can come back any time you want, you know that, love,' Jenny whispered, taking her arm as they went down the path.

Maggie pulled free. Once in the car, she turned to the window, watching her gran until the car went round the corner. Then she heaved a sigh and slumped back in her seat, letting her face fall into sullen lines and gathering resentment around her shoulders like a comforting cloak.

It was easier that way.

Alastair, who had always kept the best until the last, even as a little boy, looked at the photographs before reading the letter. Clarissa appeared in most of them, looking tanned and fit. When she left Prior's Ford she had long brown hair caught into a loose bun at the nape of her neck, but now it was cut short, taking about ten years off her age. In some of the photographs she was with her tall, burly cousin Howard, in others, his blonde partner, Lily, posed with her. And in some, she was with both of them.

As ever, Clarissa had scribbled her thoughts on the back of each picture.

This is me with Lily on the steps of the very impressive Lincoln Memorial. To walk up those steps and between the pillars to see the statue of the great man himself is really awe-inspiring! You almost feel like kneeling at his feet . . . me with Howard at the Vietnam Veterans' Memorial. It really catches your breath, and the sense of peace and at the same time, great sorrow is so strong. People leave flowers here, and letters, but there are so many names! When you realise that every single one of them represents a young life cruelly cut short, it's a wonder that we still allow our politicians to play at war games. We are so, so shamefully stupid! . . . Me with Lily and Howard, with the White House in the background. Isn't it splendid? I'm just glad that we had this photograph taken before we visited the Vietnam Memorial, otherwise you might be looking at a picture of me trying to hurl a stone at the place, followed by a picture of me being hauled off to prison . . . To think that I have had to wait for so long to see Niagara Falls! This is me with Lily on the Canadian side, which is the best side — we have just spent the night in a hotel overlooking the falls. They are floodlit in the dark, and if I hadn't been so tired I could have stayed out on my balcony all night just looking at them, and listening to them. It's strangely reassuring to look at those millions of gallons of water pouring over the lip, and know that it's been happening for unimaginable centuries and, God willing, will go on happening for ever. I so envy the first people to lay eyes on those falls!

Alastair laid the pictures aside, and turned to the letter, hearing her voice as he hungrily gobbled up the written words.

Although Howard was born in England, he has become so American in every way. It's lovely to see him again — I remember playing with him when we were little — but oddly enough I identify more with Lily, who comes from Newfoundland and speaks with a lovely soft accent that makes her sound like someone from — I'm not sure where, it might be Bristol. She calls me 'Moy dearr' and it's lovely. So now it's goodbye to America, which has been another wonderful experience, and the Intrepid Trio are off to explore Canada. Our first stop is Toronto, and then we're visiting friends of Howard's and Lily's in Calgary. I met them at Howard's daughter's wedding. For some reason I can never decide whether Calgary reminds me of cowboys and horses, or religion. Soon, I hope, I will find out which.

So how are things in Prior's Ford? I love your thumbnail sketches. Even though I've had a truly wonderful time over the past eight or nine months they always make me feel homesick. So much so that I've decided against having a look at Europe next. That can wait till another day. Howard and Lily are going to deliver me to a Canadian airport, probably Toronto, on their way back to the US. From there I plan to fly back to London and spend a week there with friends, then I'll look in on Steven and Alexandra on the way home.

I'll probably arrive back in Prior's Ford round about mid-September.

I know that the house has been let until the end of November, but I can stay at the pub until the let's up. Looking forward so much to seeing you again, C.

Mid-September! That meant that he would see her in about three weeks' time. He couldn't believe it.

'Can I have a word?' Sam Brennan asked when he had given Jenny her change and helped her to pack the shopping into her basket.

'Yes, of course.'

To her surprise, he came round the counter and led her to a spot where he could keep an eye on the door. Nobody else was in the store.

'This is awkward, but I need to let you know about it. Your stepdaughter was in here the other day, and I caught her pinching something.'

Jenny's heart seemed to stop in mid-beat. Giant fingers squeezed her chest tightly and her lips fluttered as she tried to catch a breath, then with a bang that hurt the ribs imprisoning it, her heart started up again.

'Maggie? She stole something from you?'

'I wouldnae say stole — don't get upset about it, I just felt I should tell you. Kids lift things now and again out of bravado or for a dare,' Sam said.

'Wh—What was it?'

'A bar of chocolate. It's all right,' he said swiftly as she began to fumble for her purse. 'I saw it happening and I took it from her and sent her off with a flea in her ear. But I'd be grateful if you'd have a word with her. Make sure it doesn't happen again.'

'I will.' Jenny's lips felt strangely stiff, as though they didn't belong to her. 'I'm very sorry, Sam. Thank you for being so nice about it.'

He put a surprisingly gentle hand beneath her arm and began to walk with her towards the door. 'Och, I was a kid myself once, I know all about tempt—'

The door opened while they were a few yards away from it. Jenny, who was staring at the ground as she walked, was aware of Sam's hand jerking against her arm, then falling away as Marcy Copleton said from the doorway, 'Hello, Sam.'

The familiar voice brought Jenny's head up. 'Marcy?'

'Hi, Jenny.' Marcy smiled at her, and then her smile faded. 'Is something wrong?'

'No, nothing. I was just surprised to see you, that's all. But delighted – are you back to stay?'

Marcy gave a slight shrug of the shoulders. 'I don't know yet,' she said, her eyes moving to Sam. 'It depends.'

Suddenly Jenny realised that she was playing gooseberry. 'I was just going,' she said and hurried to the door.

Marcy stepped aside to let her through, her eyes on Sam, who moved towards her as soon as the door closed behind Jenny. She took another swift step to one side, but he went past her to lock the door and then turn the sign to 'Closed.'

'It's early afternoon. You'll lose custom.'

'To hell with that. Is this you back to stay?'

'I'm back to talk, that's all I know at the moment.'

'Cup of tea?'

'It's a start,' Marcy said, and followed him into the back shop.

33

Jenny's thinking was all over the place when she left the store. She turned towards home and then, seeing the church door open she went up the steps and into its cool, dim interior.

The silence and the peace immediately laid calming hands on her and she knew she had come to the right place. But as she walked down the aisle there was a flurry of movement from near the altar, and Naomi Hennessey's rich warm voice said, 'Oh, Jenny, it's you. What a relief! Mrs Ogilvie's so proud of the way she does the flowers, but for some reason this arrangement's been setting my teeth on edge so I thought I'd sneak in to indulge in a bit of tampering. For an awful moment when I heard you come in I thought it might be her.'

'I just wanted to sit down for a moment or two. Is that all right?'

'Of course it is. God adores company and so do I. There's nothing the two of us like more than a full church on a Sunday morning.' Naomi turned back to the two vases flanking the altar, moving a flower here, and a spray there. Then she stepped back. 'There. What do you think? Be honest.'

'It's very nice. Naomi, can I speak to you about something?'

'Of course. Come into the vestry. I'd invite you to the manse but Ethan's got some friends in, playing computer games.'

'You look well,' Sam said, as he handed Marcy a mug.

'Thanks.' She sat in the chair she had always used, the one he hadn't gone near since she left.

He took the other chair. 'What have you been doing with yourself?'

'This and that.'

'Classified information? Only given out on a need-to-know basis?'

'Something like that. I've come back because I wanted to, but I don't know if I'll be staying. So I'm keeping my other life to myself in case I decide to return to it. And if I do, this time it'll be for good.'

'I see. I'll start negotiations, shall I?' He leaned forward in his chair, elbows on knees, 'I want you back, Marcy. I've missed you.'

'I've missed you too. We can be good together — if we could just stop trying to needle each other.'

'I know. I've had a lot of time to think and I could cut my own throat over the fuss I made about that damned silly quarry business.'

'It wasn't all one sided. I'm not sure that we can live with each other, Sam.'

'I'm not sure we can live apart either. I haven't enjoyed being without you. I'm willing to try harder.'

'We both have to change. It won't be easy.'

'It depends on how badly we want it to work.'

'Yes. How have you managed in the shop?'

'Jinty's helped out and young Steph, bless 'em. I've got a woman in to do the summer, when Jinty's busy at Linn Hall.'

'D'you want me back behind the counter?'

'Of course. What about living arrangements?'

'I thought I'd move back into Rowan Cottage – separate rooms for the time being.'

He turned his hands palm up in a gesture of agreement. 'The spare room's ready and waiting for you.'

'No, for you. You know that I've never liked the wallpaper in that room. I don't suppose you've changed it while I was gone?'

'I'll take the spare room, then. You drive a hard bargain.' Then, when she shrugged, 'How long is this trial period going to last, then?'

'Until the right time – or until we find out that it's not going to work and there's no point in going on.'

Someone tried the shop door, and then knocked impatiently.

'I think you'd better open up again,' Marcy said. 'Think of the money you're losing.'

'I know, it's tearing me up inside,' said Sam. And for the first time, they smiled at each other.

'Lots of young people are finding life hard these days,' Naomi was saying in the vestry. 'They're moving out of childhood and into adulthood, and as if that's not frightening enough, they're also busy juggling with hormones. Life is going too fast for them. Think back to that stage in your own life.'

'I know what you mean, but I didn't feel the need to behave badly towards my parents, nor did my friends.'

'You've just put your finger on it, Jenny, when you

mentioned your parents. Maggie never knew her mother, she lost her father and was raised by her grandparents, and now she's with you.'

'We've tried, Andrew and I, to make her feel secure with us.'

'I've no doubt of that.' The minister's rich voice was like a comforting ointment spread over aching muscles. 'And I've no doubt that Maggie's loved by all the adults in her life; but right now she probably feels that she's got no control over the way her life's going, or who's responsible for her wellbeing. Is it safe for her to move her total trust from her grandparents to you? And are you going to be able to give her the stability that she desperately needs? She hasn't been with you for long enough to be sure, and that can be quite terrifying. Some youngsters get it into their heads that they need to earn love and respect, and some are so desperate for those things and so afraid of them being withheld, that they feel the need to challenge the adults in their lives. Prove that you care about me, no matter how horrible I am and how badly I behave. Ethan was like that when I brought him over from Jamaica two years ago.'

'Ethan? But he's a lovely boy!'

'Yes he is, and he always was. He was excited when his parents decided that I should bring him to Britain in order to give him the chance of a better education and a better future than he faced at home. He couldn't wait to come to Britain, but once he arrived and realised that he was far away from his own large family, living in a strange country with someone he didn't know well was traumatic. Added to that, he suddenly found himself in a world filled with white people – there aren't many Jamaicans in this part of the country. For the first six months or so he kicked against the traces and did everything he could to get me to send

297

him back home. But I just kept on loving him – though you should have seen the pillows I chewed to bits during the night! I did a lot of praying during that time, I can tell you, and a lot of whinging,' Naomi added with her rich chuckle. 'It's a wonder that God didn't get fed up with me, but He hung on in there, and so did I, and so did Ethan, bless him. And in time, life fell into place for both of us, as it always does. As it will for you. But the thing to remember right now is that Maggie has to know that you and Andrew love her no matter how obnoxious and difficult she is.'

Jenny brushed away sudden tears. 'The more she pushes against us, the harder it is to love her.'

'She knows that, Jenny, and she's just as miserable about it as you are. She's throwing every obstacle she can think of in your way, doing her best to break you. Believe me, being difficult is very hard work, especially for a child like Maggie, but she needs to convince herself that you and Andrew really care about her, and really want her in your home, and in your lives. It's a Catch-22 situation.'

'How far is it going to go? She's stolen money from me, and now she's tried to steal from the village store. And her teachers are beginning to realise that there's something wrong. We've been offered a meeting with the school psychologist.'

'What does Andrew think about that?'

'He doesn't know about it, or the stealing,' Jenny admitted. 'He's been working so hard on a project, and he looks tired all the time. I don't want to worry him. He warned me that Maggie wasn't the little girl I remembered, and he tried to make me think carefully about what we were doing, but I wouldn't listen. I just wanted to have her back in my life, and now I feel as though I'm the one who has to sort things out.'

'Don't shut Andrew out,' Naomi warned. 'He has the right to be involved. And it might be a good idea to get professional assistance – better for you and Andrew and Maggie, not to mention Calum.'

'I just wish I could find some way of getting through to her before it comes to that! Would you speak to her, Naomi?'

'Of course, if you really need me to, but I think that it would be best for you to deal with her yourself. That letter she wrote to Helen's newspaper page . . . from what you say, she wasn't telling the truth, but at the same time, the passion behind the writing was probably genuine. Perhaps she wanted you or Helen to understand how she feels, deep down. You could do that too. You could write down the way you feel about Maggie, the guilt of leaving her and the happiness at believing that you had a chance to make up for it. About how much you love her and how miserable you are to see her so unhappy. Write it all down in a letter and put it under her bedroom door.'

'Do you think that that might work?'

'I don't know, but it could be your last attempt before telling Andrew what's been going on, and perhaps taking up the school's offer of help. And it would probably help you to get it all down on paper, and to know that she'll read it. But you'd have to concentrate on writing about how important Maggie's happiness is rather than yours, or your family's. This letter is for her, remember.'

'It would be worth a try.'

'Take your time over it,' Naomi counselled. 'It might be the most important letter you'll ever write, so don't rush it. And don't expect swift results. In the meantime, just try not to let things get you down. If I were you, I would let Maggie know, quietly and calmly, that you know about her trying to take something from the store without paying for it. Hopefully, realising that you can handle it without making a fuss will deter her from doing it again.'

299

'Is child psychology part of your training?' Jenny asked as she gathered up her shopping and prepared to leave.

'Actually, it comes from my own stormy teens. I can remember detesting myself for the way I behaved; that's why I know that being nasty to adults is incredibly tiring, and incredibly boring too. It's like falling down a deep hole – you hate being there but you just can't seem to find a way out. And you're desperate for someone to reach down and grab your hand, but you can't ask, and nobody seems to understand that. Give the letter a try, and come back to me any time you want to talk, or let off steam.'

'Thanks. Oh, I nearly forgot – Marcy walked into the store just as I was leaving. She's back in the village!'

'Hallelujah!' said Naomi.

'That goes for me too. I'd better get over to the Gift Horse to tell Ingrid before I go home.'

The shop was empty when Jenny went in. 'Ingrid? Guess who I saw in the store!'

'I'm in here,' Ingrid said from the back shop. 'And guess who's with me?'

'Oh, I'm too late.'

'I thought you'd have come over here as soon as you left the store,' Marcy said. 'Where were you?'

'I had to go and have a word with Naomi about something.' Jenny hugged the new arrival. 'Marcy it's great to have you back in Prior's Ford.'

'Not necessarily for good, though. I was just telling Ingrid that Sam and I have a lot to work out and if we can't, then I'm leaving again, and this time for good.'

'So we've just got to hope that you settle your differences. A glass of wine, Jenny? We're celebrating. You know, Marcy,' Ingrid went on as she fetched another glass and poured wine, 'he's missed you so much. We've all tried to help him, but he didn't want anyone but you.'

'I've missed him, too, but there's something about me and Sam when we get together that makes it difficult for both of us.'

'Can't live with each other, can't live without each other,' Ingrid suggested, handing a glass to Jenny.

'Something like that. I suppose the whole place'll be buzzing about my return now.' Marcy sighed.

'It'll be a two-day wonder. Look on the bright side, the women will be flocking into the store to see you – and buying things. More money in the till.'

'I'll tell Sam you said that, Ingrid, he'll appreciate it.' Marcy emptied her glass and put it down. 'I'd best go and unpack and find out what state the house is in. And by the way, I came back because I thought it was time to come back, not because of that daft letter you sent about the girl living in Willow Cottage.'

'Of course not,' Ingrid said almost meekly, and then, as Marcy strode off across the village green, she winked at Jenny. 'What's wrong with a few white lies between good friends?'

'Absolutely. You don't need me just now, do you?'

'We're quiet, and this is supposed to be your day off.'

'I'll get home then – and I've just remembered that I'll have to go back to the store. I forgot something.'

After dinner was over Jenny said casually, 'I thought we could all do with a treat this evening.'

'Why?' Andrew wanted to know.

'No reason. Surprises are nice, that's all.' She produced a large paper bag. 'Calum – a bag of liquorice allsorts, and don't eat them all at once.'

'Goody!'

'Andrew – extra strong mints. Maggie, this is for you.'
She handed over a large bar of chocolate. 'Sam Brennan
told me that you like fruit and nut chocolate, so I thought
– why shouldn't she have some as a present? And I got one
for myself while I was at it.'

Colour rose into the girl's face. 'Thanks,' she muttered.

'It's my pleasure, sweetheart,' Jenny said. 'It really is.'

'I'm quite sure that Clarissa would be happy for you to
stay on in Willow Cottage,' Alastair had told Ginny when
he went to break the news about Clarissa's change of plan.
'After all, your mother took it until the end of November.'

'It's all right – there's a spare bed in the Linn Hall gate-
house, so I'm going to move in there. The other workers
will be leaving mid-September but the Ralston-Kerrs don't
mind me staying on for another six weeks after that.'

'There's a Calor gas heater in the gatehouse, so you
should be warm enough,' Fliss had told her, 'but won't it
be terribly quiet for you on your own at the end of the
drive, once the others are gone? I wish we could offer you
a room here, but they're not habitable yet.'

'I'll be absolutely fine, honestly,' Ginny assured her. Truth
to tell, she couldn't wait to be on her own in the gate-
house, surrounded by big old trees, and actually living on
the estate she had come to love. Being there until November
meant that she could get the kitchen garden settled for the
winter before she had to return to London.

Life kept throwing up surprises; she had had to force herself
to be a dutiful daughter and accompany her mother to Prior's
Ford, and now, she didn't want to leave the place that was
more of a home to her than anywhere she had ever been.

34

With love, always, Jenny.

Jenny put the pen down, gathered the three sheets of paper together, and began to read through them from the beginning. It had been hard work, and her admiration for Helen and her ambition to be a professional writer had grown by leaps and bounds during the struggle.

When she reached the end, she folded the pages carefully and slipped them into an envelope. For good or ill, she had done the best she could, and now it was up to Maggie, she told herself as she went upstairs. After sliding it beneath the girl's bedroom door so that she would see it as soon as she came home from school, she almost went back to retrieve it. She could improve on it, she thought, a hand on the doorknob. She hadn't explained things properly . . .

Then she turned swiftly away from the door and made herself go downstairs. It was over, the letter was written, and the die was cast.

★ ★ ★

'They've arrived!'

'When?'

'Ten minutes ago.'

'Oh, Ewan, that's great! Can I come to see them?'

'That's why I'm phoning you. After all, you're a partner in this business.'

'I can be there in half an hour.'

'I won't do a thing until you get here,' Ewan promised.

'Mum, they've arrived.' Alison put the phone down. 'Is it all right if I go over to the farm right away?'

'Aye, of course. Jamie'll be fine.'

'Thanks.' She dropped a kiss on her mother's cheek and hurried out, bumping into her father in the doorway.

'Where's she going in such a rush?'

'The worms have arrived at the farm and she's going to help Ewan to get them settled.'

'Is that all?'

It was going to take a good while, and quite a lot of money, for Ewan to get the ditches gouged out, lined, and filled with the correct composting mixture and worms. Alison had come up with the idea of setting up a small container wormery in the meantime, to get Ewan's new business venture under way, and she had put up half the cost.

'The way she looked when she came through that door, I thought it was something exciting,' her father said now, picking up his newspaper. 'But it's just worms.'

'It's not that at all, Joe. It's love, and you should be pleased for her. A cup of tea?'

'What d'you mean, love? For worms?'

Men, Gracie thought, could be quite slow sometimes, while women knew, and had known since Eve first spied an apple, that love could flourish in many places, including wormeries.

'A cup of tea,' she said, picking up the teapot.

Alastair let himself into Willow Cottage for one last check before leaving for Dumfries. Everything was in order; Jinty had kindly given the place a good going over, and her son Jimmy had the garden looking perfect. There were vases of fresh cut flowers in the hall and the living room, and the fridge, freezer and store cupboards were filled. Upstairs, the bed had been turned down invitingly, and as a final touch he laid the perfect pale pink rosebud he had just taken from the garden on the pillow where Clarissa would rest her head that night.

Then he went downstairs, locked the front door behind him, and set off for the railway station.

'I should have taken before and after pictures.'

'Oh, hello.'

Lewis was in shadow against the sun, and Ginny, kneeling by one of the herb beds, had to shade her eyes as she looked up.

'You've done wonders with this area. It's almost looking the way it was in the old photographs.'

'Apart from the poly tunnel, but that's going to be worth its weight in gold.' She got to her feet, dusting soil from her jeans. 'In another two weeks' time I'll start to move the more fragile plants in there to winter. I should have them all snugged down by the time I have to leave.'

On her advice, Lewis had installed another, larger poly tunnel elsewhere in the grounds so that he and Duncan could also save delicate plants from the winter frosts.

'I was wondering – would you be available next year? Perhaps from April until October? We could really do with your help and it would be a shame if you didn't get to see the results of your hard work.'

'Yes, I could be available,' Ginny had a struggle to sound casual. 'I'd like to come back.'

'That's great!' He threw his arms wide and for a mad moment she thought that he might be going to hug her. Then he flapped his arms once or twice, and said again, 'That's – great. I'll let Duncan know. He'll be pleased.'

When he had gone, she went over to a corner of the kitchen garden where she knew she would not be seen, and danced a brief jig. She was coming back! She would see Linn Hall again, and her beloved kitchen garden.

And Lewis.

Clarissa was almost the last passenger through the barriers, and Alastair was beginning to worry when the small figure appeared, steering a trolley with one hand and waving furiously with the other.

'Alastair!'

'Clarissa!' he roared in return and plunged forward through the crowds that had left the train before her. When they met, both grinning like idiots, they hugged each other hard.

'Shades of *Brief Encounter*,' Clarissa said with a slightly embarrassed chuckle as they released each other.

'You look great.'

'So do you.'

'You've had your hair cut.'

'You haven't. It was so hot in some of the places I visited.' She ran a hand through her stylish cut. 'And I feel much less frumpish now.'

He took charge of the trolley. 'D'you want some tea before we set off?'

'Lord no, I'm awash with the stuff. Alexandra told me she'd been north for a short visit while I was away,' she said as they headed for the station carpark.

'Yes, she was.'

'And you looked after her. I do believe she was impressed by you.'

'I doubt that,' Alastair said as they reached the car.

The bus from Kirkcudbright stopped outside the village store, flooding the pavement with the secondary school students.

Maggie Cameron walked down River Lane with Freya MacKenzie and the McDonald clan – Jimmy, Grant, Heather and Merle, in her first year at Kircudbright Academy. The McDonalds peeled off into Slaemuir council estate while she and Freya went into Mill Walk estate. There, they parted.

'Had a good day, love?' Jenny called from the kitchen, as she always did.

'OK,' Maggie said non-committally, as she always did, and went up to her room. A long white envelope was lying just inside the door. Puzzled, she dropped her schoolbag on the floor and picked up the envelope.

She withdrew the letter, and sat down on her bed to read it.

Robert Kavanagh, crouched in the bushes at one end of the quarry, scanned the skies through his binoculars, watching the birds circling high above.

He had seen both the adults this afternoon, and two of the young. They were fully-fledged now, and confident on the wing. Soon, the family would be gone, the eyrie empty. Then work could start on the playground, and the hide.

Next year, the adult falcons would return to Prior's Ford. There was no doubt of that in his mind. And he would be waiting to welcome them.

He walked back to the village briskly, thinking of the extra tourism the birds could bring to Prior's Ford. Reaching home, he put his key in the door as a car came along the main street.

Instead of passing Robert, it turned into Adam Crescent, and stopped outside Willow Cottage.

'Welcome home,' Alastair said, switching the engine off.

Clarissa leaned forward to study the neat front garden, the flower-edged path to the front door, the shining windows.

She had had a wonderful year, but it was good to be home, where she belonged. In Prior's Ford.

Look out for the next book in the Prior's Ford series, *Trouble in Prior's Ford*, published by Sphere in January 2010.

1

'I'm taking you to the pub for a drink,' Clarissa Ramsay said as she and Alastair Marshall left the village hall. 'You deserve it for courage above and beyond the call of duty.'

'I only saw to the slides. You were the one who had to give the talk.'

'I didn't mean just that, I meant you having to judge the rock cake competition as well. I didn't realise that we would be expected to judge things,' said Clarissa, who had had to deal with the homemade jams competition.

'The rock cakes were good . . . well, most of them. It was the dirty looks I got from the people who didn't win that unnerved me. You were great,' Alastair said admiringly as they turned into Adam Crescent and began to skirt the half-moon village green. 'As cool as a cucumber, even at question time.'

'Being a school teacher trained me for every eventuality, including dealing with parents. To be honest, I quite enjoyed myself, but I'm sure you were bored to tears, ploughing through all those letters I sent while I was away, then having to listen to it all over again while we sorted out the photographs for the talk . . . and again, this afternoon.'

'I've enjoyed every minute of it.' He had, more than she realised. Clarissa had been brought to Prior's Ford by her domineering husband when he retired, only to die suddenly a mere seven months later. Alastair, an artist, had come across her one wet day, sitting on a stile in the middle of a field, rain-soaked, wretched, and with no idea of what to do next with her life.

When he took her to his shabby farm cottage on the fringe of the village he hadn't realised at the time that it was to be one of the most important days of his life. Although Clarissa was in her fifties and Alastair in his mid-thirties, they had become firm friends. With Alastair's encouragement, Clarissa regained her confidence to the extent where she had rented out her cottage for a year and gone off to travel the world, an adventure that had resulted in being asked to give a talk about her experiences to the Prior's Ford Women's Institute.

It was mid-April. Easter was behind them but the schools were still on holiday. A group of teenagers loitered by the war memorial on the green, and as Clarissa and Alastair neared the pub a couple detached themselves from the group and came towards them.

'Hi,' Alastair said amiably as they passed. A dark-haired girl mumbled a 'hello' back, while the youth with her, his head covered with dyed blond spiky hair and with three hoops through the lobe of one ear, shot them a swift side-long glance that seemed to Clarissa to take in an incredible amount of detail in a single second.

'Who's that pretty girl?' she asked when the youngsters were out of earshot. 'I've seen her around the village a few times since I got back.'

312

'That's Maggie Cameron, Jenny Forsyth's stepdaughter. Apparently Jenny acquired her as part of a brief marriage before she and Andrew met. Her first husband died and Maggie was raised by his parents, but her grandfather's suffering from ill health, so she's come to stay with the Forsyths. The lad's not local but I've seen them together a few times. Must be her boyfriend.' Alastair, tall and lanky, reached out a long arm and pushed the pub door open, holding it in place while he eased back to let Clarissa pass. 'After you, ma'am.'

Jemima Puddleduck skimmed over the bridge and in no time at all was bowling into Prior's Ford. Ginny Whitelaw, at the wheel, heaved an enormous sigh of contentment and slowed Jemima down so that she could look her fill.

The village had not changed in the seven months or so since she had last seen it. The sunshine on this mid-April day gave the well-cared-for houses and shops a scrubbed-fresh look. The primary school, the community hall, the Village Store, butcher's shop and church were all as she had last seen them.

Ginny drove past the green before easing the steering wheel to the right. Jemima, obliging as ever, turned into Adam Crescent. The first house at this end of the crescent was Willow Cottage, where Ginny and her mother had stayed the year before. 'Hello, you,' she said affectionately to the house as she passed, neat and tidy behind its little front garden.

At the centre of the crescent a young woman was sweeping the pavement before the village pub, a long, freshly-whitewashed building. 'Hi, Alison,' Ginny called through the open passenger window as she stopped the pickup. 'Remember me?'

Alison Greenlees stooped to the window. 'Hello, Ginny – working at Linn Hall again this summer?'

'I am indeed; back to see how the kitchen garden's been getting on without me.' Ginny climbed out of the pickup and walked round the bonnet to lean against the passenger door, glancing up at the painted sign above the pub's open door. THE NEUROTIC CUCKOO it proclaimed, beneath a painting of a bird that might or might not be a cuckoo, but certainly seemed to be troubled. 'Good old Cuckoo,' she said affectionately, 'I'll be in for a pint tonight.'

'You're welcome to have one now,' Alison offered. 'Mum's gone to the Women's Institute meeting, Dad's taken Jamie fishing, and Alastair's having a drink in the bar with Mrs Ramsay – the lady who rented her cottage to your mother last year.'

'Are there many fish in the river?'

'Possibly, but I said fishing, not actually catching. Jamie's got his own wee net and he just likes splashing around with it. Coming inside?'

'Thanks, but I'd like to get settled in first.' Ginny studied the other girl, noting the healthy colour and sparkling eyes in a face that last year had been thin and pale. 'You look well. In fact I'd say, as a gardener, that you're positively blooming.'

Alison's parents, Joe and Gracie Fisher, had become the landlord and landlady of the Neurotic Cuckoo almost fifteen months earlier, following the death of Alison's husband. A barman in the Fishers' Glasgow pub, he was murdered by a group of drunken youths he had evicted earlier that night.

When Ginny first arrived in the village Alison had been thin and withdrawn, but over the winter she had gained much-needed weight, her brown hair, in a page-boy style

314

that almost reached her shoulders, was glossy, and the once down-turned mouth now smiled easily.

'I'm not a pale city girl any more. The country air suits me.'

'It certainly does. So . . . how's Ewan?' Ginny asked with a lift of the eyebrows.

'He's fine.' Alison's tone was carefully casual, but her colour heightened slightly. 'Working hard on the farm, as usual. His new wormery's doing well.'

'That's good. Still walking out together, are you?'

'I wouldn't call it that. He's busy there and I'm busy here.'

'So you don't see much of each other these days?'

'Well – Jamie likes being taken to the farm and Mrs McNair's very good to him,' Alison said evasively. 'Are you likely to be looking for a room? Our guest rooms are both vacant at the moment.'

'I'll probably bunk down in the gatehouse with the other summer workers at Linn Hall.'

'OK. It's good to see you back again, Ginny.'

'It's good to be back,' Ginny said warmly, walking round to the driver's side of the pickup. 'I'll be in tonight for that drink.' Then, as she settled into the driving seat and switched on the engine, 'You might have stopped blushing by then.'

'I used to be quite intimidated by Alexandra,' Clarissa was saying in the lounge bar. 'She was at university when I first met her, but even then she was so cool and confident, but when I called in on her last September, on my way back home from my travels, I felt that she was much more human.' Then, fixing Alastair with the sort of gaze she must once have used to wrest the truth from reluctant pupils, 'I can't help wondering if you had anything to do with that.'

'Me? Good Lord, no . . . how could I?' He tried hard to meet her eyes, but found it difficult. 'I scarcely know the woman.'

'She mentioned you quite frequently, as it happens. I don't know how you managed to break through her protective shell, but she likes you.'

'She scares me,' Alastair said firmly. It wasn't entirely a lie. The first time he encountered Clarissa's stepdaughter and stepson at the dinner party where Clarissa announced her intention to set off to see the world, Alexandra had terrified him. But while her stepmother was away she had paid an unexpected visit to the village and Alastair had found himself helping her, as he had helped Clarissa. It was a surprise to find that even a cold beauty like Alexandra Ramsay could fall in love with the wrong man – in this case, a married man – and get hurt. But he had given his word to keep her secret, and Alastair never broke his word, as Clarissa knew.

'It's so good to be back again,' she said, letting him off the hook. 'I can't believe that when Keith died I almost went back down south. Going off on my own to see the world made me realise where my home really is . . . right here, with genuine friends.'

'I'm glad to hear it,' Alastair said lightly, knowing that she had no idea how much he meant the words. During her absence he had hungered for her letters, tearing them open when they arrived, devouring the contents, looking again and again at the enclosed photographs showing the real Clarissa emerging from the dull-coloured chrysalis that had been her marriage to a man who, he suspected from comments made by Alexandra, had not been faithful to her. She had left Prior's Ford a quiet, middle-aged ex-teacher, dressed conventionally and with brown hair worn in a tidy knot at the nape of her neck, and returned looking at least ten years younger, her hair short and in a soft feathery style, skin glowing and eyes sparkling; a woman not afraid to wear bright colours and modern styles.

The problem facing Alastair Marshall now was that she had left the village as a good friend, and had returned as much more than that.

And, given the difference in their ages, he didn't feel that he could ever tell her of his feelings.

Jemima Puddleduck passed between identical gatehouses originally built for the head gardener and head groom and swept up the long driveway leading to Linn Hall.

Sunlight warmed the Hall's honey-coloured stone walls and made the three tiers of windows glitter. The leaking roof had been renewed over the winter and the great sweep of gravel before the front door was free of the weeds that had covered it the year before. Driving round to the rear of the house she saw that the flagged court-yard between the house, stables and kitchen garden was also weed-free.

A smart people-carrier was parked close to the kitchen door. Ginny raised her eyebrows at it; she couldn't see Lewis Ralston-Kerr wasting a penny of the money his impover-ished parents had been gifted on a big car. Then, as she brought Jemima to a standstill by the stables, she spotted his shabby little car lurking behind the strange one.

Once out of the pickup she couldn't resist taking a quick peek at the kitchen garden before announcing her arrival. The year before, she had rescued the large walled area from obscurity and gone some way to restoring it to its former glory; it had been her special project and she longed to see how well it had come through the winter.

She had almost reached the gate when she heard from behind her a strange mixture of heavy breathing and scratching. Before she could turn to investigate something banged against the backs of her thighs and then she was on the ground, slightly winded and being smothered in some sort of woolly blanket while her face was washed by a warm flannel.

'Muffin!' a voice yelled, 'Get off, you daft mutt!'

The blanket and the flannel suddenly retreated and Ginny was free to roll over on to her back and blink up at Lewis Ralston-Kerr.

'Sorry, Ginny, he's just . . . Muffin, stop it, I said! . . . too friendly. Here—' He hauled her to her feet.

'What is it?' Ginny asked of the large creature gambolling around the two of them. 'And what did you call it?'

'Muffin. Silly, I know, but Mrs Paterson – the old lady who owned him – apparently thought that he looked like a little toasted muffin when she got him as a puppy.'

'So it's a dog?' Ginny brushed herself down. 'He looks more like a Shetland pony having a bad hair day, or perhaps a great pile of unravelled double knitting wool that's taken on a life of its own.'

'Now that you mention it, Mrs Paterson was never seen without knitting in her hands, even in church. Perhaps she knitted him herself. She died, poor old soul, and nobody was willing to take Muffin in. So, as this is the perfect place for a large dog, we offered.' Then, 'I like the pickup,' Lewis said.

'Meet Jemima Puddleduck. She's more useful than the little car I bought when I was here last year. I've got room for plants now – and I've brought quite a few for the kitchen garden.'

'Good, I'm glad you're going to see it through another

year. Come on in and say hello. Molly's here,' Lewis said as he led her towards the back door, 'with her parents and her sister, and Rowena Chloe, of course.'

Ginny swallowed back the sudden rush of disappointment at the news that Lewis's red-headed girlfriend and mother of his daughter was at Linn Hall. 'That explains the people-carrier,' she said lightly.

'She, her parents and her sister are moving on in about an hour – they're all going on holiday and we're looking after the baby while they're away.' They had reached the open door and Lewis ushered her into the large old-fashioned kitchen, announcing, 'Ginny's arrived.'

Jinty McDonald, who lived in the village and helped out at Linn Hall, poured tea for the newcomer from a large battered metal teapot while, Fliss Ralston-Kerr, Lewis's mother, began to introduce her visitors to each other, before being interrupted by the plump red-haired woman sitting opposite Ginny.

'No need to be so elaborate about it, Fliss pet, we're all family here. I'm Val, dear,' she told Ginny, 'Molly's mum. And this,' she laid a possessive hand on the arm of the burly man by her side, 'is my husband Tony. You know Molly, don't you?'

'Hello, Ginny.' Molly Ewing still wore her glowing red hair in two long plaits, and still looked too young to be a mother. 'How are things?'

'OK. You?'

'Great!'

'And that's our other daughter Stella,' Val prattled on, indicating the bored-looking teenager reading a book at the end of the table.

'Hi,' Stella said briefly before returning to her book. She had none of her sister's or her mother's lush roundness, and her hair was more auburn than Molly's, though they had the same green eyes.

'And this,' Lewis said proudly, lifting the baby from Molly's lap, 'is Rowena Chloe. Isn't she gorgeous? Just like her mother.'

As he dropped a kiss on her soft red curls, the baby reached out to pat his face with a hand that held a half-chewed crust. It fell to the ground and a loud gulp told that Muffin had claimed it. Rowena's round little face puckered up and she let out a protesting wail as she reached down to the dog.

'Never mind, pet, I'll get you another,' Jinty cooed, setting a mug of tea before Ginny.

'Isn't this a grand place?' Val Ewing rattled on. 'I remember when our Molly worked here that summer, she said in her letters that it was the grandest place she had ever seen. Like a palace.'

'A tumbledown palace,' Fliss Ralston-Kerr said ruefully.

'But that's all behind you, isn't it, now that you've got all that money given to you to do it up? It's going to be lovely once it's finished. We can't believe that one day our Molly's going to live here, mistress of Linn Hall, can we, Tony? It's like a fairy tale!' Val beamed round the table.

Someone was missing, Ginny realised. Mr Ralston-Kerr was probably hiding in the large pantry used by the family as a living room, since the usual family rooms were too chilly, even in summer. A shy man, he must feel quite intimidated by the Ewings, who seemed – Molly and her parents at least – to have taken over the place.

'Oh, Molly said that you're Meredith Whitelaw's daughter. Is that right?' Val asked, and when Ginny nodded, 'That must be lovely. *Bridlington Close* on the telly hasn't been the same since she left. What's she doing now?'

'Filming a television series.' After her character in a television soap had been killed off the year before, Meredith Whitelaw, in search of somewhere to sulk, had rented Willow Cottage in Prior's Ford. Ginny had accompanied her, out of pity for her humiliated mother rather than affection. During her time in the village, Meredith had played havoc with the local drama group before being offered a part in a costume drama for television and departing as suddenly as she had arrived.

'When's her new show going to arrive on our sets?' Jinty held out a new crust to Rowena Chloe, who snatched at it. 'We're all desperate to see it.'

'Quite soon, I think. They've almost finished filming.'

'It was lovely having a celebrity living in the village,' Jinty told Val.

'Well, it must have been,' Val enthused, while Ginny watched Lewis, noticing how comfortable he seemed to be with the baby in his arms. She envied Molly for having found him.

Maggie Cameron took her new boyfriend's hand as they reached the bus stop. He pulled his fingers free at once, but as the bus taking him home to Kirkcudbright came into view he turned her to face him and gave her a long, lingering kiss, snaking his tongue into her mouth and holding her close by clamping both hands on her bottom. She didn't care for that sort of kiss, but pretended that she did. She still couldn't believe that Ryan, seventeen years old and in the year above her at school, and handsome too, with his fair hair and piercing blue eyes, had chosen her from all the girls who fancied him. She was so lucky, but at the same time terrified of letting him down and being dumped.

'See ya,' he said, breaking away as the bus arrived. He leapt up the steps, one shoulder nudging aside a woman who had just alighted.

'See ya,' Maggie called after him.

'They've got no manners these days, young people,' she heard the woman complain to her friend as they walked away. Maggie shrugged, and grinned. They could say what they liked – what did she care?

The past fifteen months hadn't been kind to her. An orphan raised by her grandparents until her grandfather's ill health made it impossible for her to stay, she had been moved from Dundee to Prior's Ford to live with her stepmother, Jenny Forsyth. Jenny's apparent desperation for a sweet, loving daughter had alienated Maggie, who retaliated by being as difficult as she could.

It was like living on a battlefield, and deep down she had been wretched until Ryan had come into her life. For the first time since arriving in Prior's Ford, Maggie Cameron was happy.

But she had a lot to learn. She quite liked Alastair Marshall, an artist who lived in an old farm cottage outside the village, and there was nothing wrong with Mrs Ramsay, even though she had been a teacher. She had said hello to them earlier without thinking, and had then had to endure merciless teasing from Ryan for behaving like 'a nice little girlie'.

Ryan was so cool, and she was so nerdy! As she headed down River Lane to the smart housing estate where she now lived, she vowed to herself that she would work hard to become the sort of girl Ryan wanted . . .

'Is that you, Maggie?' Jenny Forsyth called when she heard the front door open.

'Yeah.'

'Cup of tea? I was just thinking of putting the kettle on.'

'No.'

Jenny went to the kitchen door as Maggie began to climb the stairs. 'I'm making a risotto for tonight. OK?'

'Fine.'

'Had a nice afternoon?'

'OK. Ryan came over.'

'That's nice. You should have invited him for dinner. We'd like to meet him.'

Without answering, Maggie continued on up the stairs and went into her room, closing the door loudly behind her. This was her sanctum, and nobody else was allowed in. Here, in her own space, she could be herself.

'*You should have invited him for dinner, we'd like to meet him.*' She imitated her stepmother's anxious-to-please voice, and then shared a laugh with her reflection in the mirror.

Her Ryan, coming here for dinner and meeting that lot downstairs?

As if!

Secrets in Prior's Ford

Eve Houston

There is consternation among the villagers of pretty Scottish borders town, Prior's Ford, when a firm is interested in reopening an old granite quarry. Almost overnight neighbours and friends fall out, with some welcoming the work the quarry will bring while others are ready to fight to preserve the village's peace.

Publican Glen organises a protest group – but when the local newspaper takes an interest in him and the story, he starts to feel very nervous indeed. When Jenny Forsyth attends a protest meeting and sees the quarry surveyor she also discovers a problem. So does the surveyor, for they recognise each other from years back when they lived different lives, a past Jenny has tried very hard to forget.

Clarissa Ramsay is too preoccupied to care much about the new threat facing the village. She and her husband, Keith, moved to the village a year earlier but Clarissa is newly widowed. But when she discovers Keith had a secret life she resolves to make some radical changes in her own . . .

While up at Linn Hall, the impoverished Ralston-Kerrs, struggling to keep the estate that is their ancestral heritage from going under, find that the quarry reopening represents a test of loyalty to the village that regards them as its lairds.

987-0-7515-3961-5

Now you can order superb titles directly from Sphere

☐ Secrets in Prior's Ford   Eve Houston   £6.99

The prices shown above are correct at time of going to press. However, the publishers reserve the right to increase prices on covers from those previously advertised, without further notice.

———————————— sphere ————————————

Please allow for postage and packing: **Free UK delivery.**
Europe; add 25% of retail price; Rest of World; 45% of retail price.

To order any of the above or any other Sphere titles, please call our credit card orderline or fill in this coupon and send/fax it to:

Sphere, P.O. Box 121, Kettering, Northants NN14 4ZQ
Fax: 01832 733076   Tel: 01832 737526
Email: aspenhouse@FSBDial.co.uk

☐ I enclose a UK bank cheque made payable to Sphere for £ . . . .
☐ Please charge £ . . . . . . to my Visa, Delta, Maestro.

Expiry Date ☐☐☐☐   Maestro Issue No. ☐☐

NAME (BLOCK LETTERS please) . . . .

ADDRESS . . . .

. . . .

. . . .

Postcode . . . . Telephone . . . .

Signature . . . .

Please allow 28 days for delivery within the UK. Offer subject to price and availability.